Just One More...

By Sam Hendricks

Sam Hendricks

Extra Point Press, Austin Texas, United States
www.XPPress.com
Library of Congress Control Number: 2013952757
ISBN: 978-0-9824286-4-1
Copyright © 2013 by Sam Hendricks
All rights reserved
Edited by Trish Hendricks and Raechelle Wilson

This book is a work of fiction. Names, characters, places and incidents either are products of the author's imagination or are used fictitiously. Any resemblance to actual events, locales or persons, either living or dead, is entirely coincidental and not intended by the author. Any dialogue or behavior ascribed to the characters in this book, real or imaged, living or dead, is entirely fictitious.

Visit the author at www.FFGuidebook.com
Visit the publisher at www.ExtraPointPress.com
Printed in the United States of America by Lightning Source
Bulk purchases please contact info@ExtraPointPress.com

Version 1.05

Acknowledgements

A big hug and special thanks to my publicist, editor and communications specialist, Trish Hendricks. She is a world-class consultant and, more important, a world-class sister. Thanks for getting what this is all about and for continuing to help turn my literary dreams into reality. Without her support and help, none of my books would be as coherent as they have been these past few years.

My mother, Fannie, also gets my biggest thanks since she always encouraged me to reach for new heights and always has a smile and love that cheers me up even to this day.

To my father who passed away many years ago, but is still missed each and every day.

To my lovely wife Birgitte, I owe everything. She completes me. However, I fear our turf wars over the family computer have just started as she introduces the world to SewDanish, her Scandinavian Textile Art company that can be found at www.SewDanish.etsy.com and her website at www.BirgitteHendricks.com. Let the battle begin.

Thank you to Raechelle Wilson for her invaluable assistance with editing and her spot on comments about the content.

A special thanks to my reviewers: Tom "Duck" Donalds, John "Kuz" Kuczka, Dean "Smurf" Reed, Trish Reed, Charles "Boggy" Rouse, Ned "Neckless" Rudd and Charles "Tuna" Midthun who spent countless hours reading and critiquing this book for me. This book is much better thanks to the suggestions you all made.

Sam Hendricks

Fighter Acronyms

AAA-Anti Aircraft Artillery
AAI- Air-to Air Interrogation
AB-Afterburner
ADI-Attitude Director Indicator
AIB-Accident Investigation Board
AGM-Air-to-Surface Guided Missile
ATO-Air Tasking Order
Bx-Base Exchange
CAS-Close Air Support
CFT-Conformal Fuel Tank
CYA-Cover Your Ass
C2-Command and Control
DL-Data Link
DPI-Desired Point of Impact
Dumb Bomb-conventional bomb
ECM-Electronic Counter Measures
EOB-Electronic Order of Battle
EP-Emergency Procedures
FEBA-Forward Edge of Battle Area
FOV-Field of View
GLO-Ground Liaison Officer
GPS-Global Positioning System
HMD-Helmet Mounted Display
HOTAS-Hands On Stick And Throttle
HUD-Heads-Up Display
HUMINT-Human Intelligence
HVT-High Value Target
IAD-Integrated Air Defense
IFF-Identification Friend or Foe
ILS-Instrument Landing System
JDAM-Joint Direct Attack Munition
JFS-Jet Fuel Starter
JTACS-Joint Tactical Air Control System
LST-Laser Spot Tracker
LAWS-Low Altitude Warning System
LGB-Laser Guide Bomb

Lima Charlie-Loud and Clear
LJDAM-Laser JDAM
MCG-Mid Course Guidance
MPD-Multi-Purpose Display
MPCD-Multi-Purpose Color Display
NIM-Nose Index Marker
NVGs-Night Vision Goggles
SAM-Surface to Air Missile
SATCOM-Satellite Communications
SF/SP-Security Forces/Security Police
Shack-Direct Hit
SIB-Safety Investigation Board
Sierra Hotel (Also called Shit Hot)-Great
SIT-Situation Display
Tango Uniform (Also called Tits Up)-Broken
TCN-Tactical Air Navigation
TDC-Target Designator/Slew Control
TEWS-Tactical Electronic Warfare System
TFR (TF)-Terrain Following Radar
TL-Transition Line
TOT-Time on Target
TP-Targeting Pod
TTR-Target Tracking Radar
UAV-Unmanned Aerial Vehicle
USAFE-United States Air Forces in Europe
WAG-Wild Ass Guess
WSO-Weapon System Officer

PART I

The Accident

Sam Hendricks

Chapter 1

Isleham, England

"Jumpin Jack Flash" by the Rolling Stones played loudly as Kate's car twisted and turned down the narrow country lane, barely avoiding a suicidal pheasant. The drive was from her quiet Cambridge flat nearby. Normally a Laura Mvula fan, Kate listened to the old stuff on occasion. Her soft caramel-colored skin sparkled, a stark contrast to the dull gray clouds just above the roofline of the Isleham thatched cottages. Stepping lightly from her salt white Mini Cooper, she braced against the cold wind. Black racing stripes danced down the small hood, as if poured out by the fast speeds on lonely back roads to start the New Year. The smooth "Mini Coop" top contrasted with her curly black tangle of hair. Normally she kept it straight for work, but since this was a holiday she decided to go a little wild. The frizzy "birds nest," as she called it, kept a few snowflakes from descending to the ground.

The Accident Investigation Board (AIB) gathered for their final meeting before the scheduled release of their report. The bitterly cold, cruel fen wind of East Anglia howled outside the Merry Monk pub as five people met in secret for a late lunch. Old-timers recalled the cold as enough to freeze toothpaste. Kate had neither the desire nor the inclination to fact-check them. A light dusting of snow, remnants of last night's flirtation with winter, spun around the streets like children chasing an errant kite.

The rest of her party arrived fashionably early too, the last just five minutes before 2 P.M. Smiling broadly, the restaurant's owners ushered the group into the private room they had reserved for the afternoon. Menus already peppered the table, inviting the board members to enjoy a sumptuous feast.

No one grumbled about the fact they were called to work on January 1. They were all United States Air Force officers and all had worked every holiday imaginable during their careers. It went with the job of protecting the country they loved. Duty, honor, and sacrifice were the bedrocks of their service. Besides, everyone knew about the meeting well in advance and the reasonable (1400 hours) time set for the conference. That and the fact that the Merry Monk served some of the best food in this part of England helped smooth over any misgivings.

Sitting across from a well-mannered flight surgeon, Kate smoothed out the creases in her battleship-grey dress and scooted her deep, comfortable leather chair just close enough to the table to hide her rust-colored pumps. On her right sat the flight maintenance expert, and on her left, the only other woman on the six-person board, a judge advocate. The weapons specialist, another USAF Major, and the pilot, who served as board president, completed the panel.

The interior of the pub was bright. Their oval table filled the room, but its light color contrasted the wooden low-beamed ceiling. Kate's emotions teetered between unease and comfort. She knew the group well and felt comfortable with them, yet you never knew what the final outcome would be in these situations. They gathered to figure out why an aviator died and the U. S. Air Force lost a fifty million dollar aircraft on a combat mission in Libya.

***

Snow fell from moisture-laden clouds. The dull white spheres dropped evenly in rows yet never accumulated on the ground. Emile thought that strange from the rear cockpit as her F-15E Strike Eagle fighter jet flew dangerously into North Korean airspace.

Everything was strange. She was flying with the man she loved, although he did not know it. Unrequited love was a bitch. She was doing a job she loved. Yet she had a sense of dread in her stomach; like tires screeching on pavement.

The takeoff from Osan Air Base, South Korea, was uneventful. Both aircraft in her formation, Strike 01 and 02, received fuel from a waiting KC-10 air refueling tanker just east of the airfield. They held at 20,000 feet waiting for the go-ahead to proceed with their combat mission. Emile knew she had other things to think about and shook her head to get back her pacing.

Sean's cool voice over the intercom brought her mind back to task.

"How are we doing on our timing?" It was always "we" when they were good and "you" when something went wrong. Well, thought Emile, Sean was not like that. But others in the Strike Eagle community sure took all the praise and pushed away the blame when things went to hell in a hand basket.

Sean was asking now about their time on target, TOT. They only had a small window of opportunity. Their TOT was 20:16:00. They had one minute of slop on both sides and thus a two-minute window to drop their weapons in the target area.

Emile checked the clock. "We can push a minute late and make the back-end TOT, and three minutes late and still be in our TOT window if we fly as fast as possible. That will mean cutting some corners on the low level route and arriving back to Osan with very little gas."

"Copy." Sean's short, crisp reply acknowledged her facts. He followed the reply with a radio call.

"Strike flight, FENCE in."

Sean sent the directive to the crew members in each plane to prepare for combat.

Aircrew fenced in to set cockpit switches as appropriate when entering the combat arena. FENCE out was a directive call to reset those same switches after leaving the combat area.

The combat area is sometimes referred to as the FEBA (Forward Edge of Battle Area). In the big picture, fencing in meant you were ready to kill and fencing out protected those on your side from accidents or mistakes.

"Strike 01, from 02," Sean's wingman, Preston Floyd, chimed in from his plane.

"Strike 02 go," said Sean.

"Yeah." Preston paused. "Strike 01, we have a double generator failure over here. I think our electrics are tango uniform."

Tango Uniform (otherwise known as "tits up") was fighter code for the system that is dead, broken or inoperative. The term comes from WWII when attitude indicators of aircraft from that time would turn upside down when failed. The resulting inverted "W" looked like a pair of breasts and thus pilots referred to it as "tits up".

Emile held her breath. Tango uniform was never a good sign.

Without missing a beat, Sean replied. "Copy that. Standby 2: we will make a gentle left turn to stay in our holding pattern and roll out to look at the problem."

Sean frowned and glanced at the 80,000-pound flying machine accompanying him six thousand feet on his left.

Preston sounded too calm for both of his main generators to have failed, Emile thought. In that case, the emergency generator would take over and provide some rudimentary navigation and flying controls.

"Ok Em." Sean was suddenly in her ear. "Remember me saying…"

"With emergencies, slower is faster," Emile finished for him. Sean felt that with emergency procedures (EP) it was better to take your time and get it right, than rush it and mess something up catastrophically.

"Emile, keep a tight watch on the time and dig into the checklist for double generator failure if you can," Sean said. After eight months flying together, Emile easily picked up the hint of doubt in his voice.

"Push in four minutes with clearance," she said, trying to steady her voice. "You don't think they have a double gen failure?"

"We'll see," said Sean. "But I bet you five bucks it is something else."

Emile smiled as Sean keyed the radio again. Five bucks or no, Emile knew better than to play Sean's odds. He only bet when he knew he would win.

"No deal," she muttered, dropping her head to dig into the 200-page emergency procedures checklist.

"Strike 02," said Sean, "easy left and remember: aviate, navigate and communicate." It was the oldest saying in the fighter pilot business. It reminded aviators to fly first, figure where you need to go and finally, communicate the problem. There were too many accidents where the pilot did not heed rule number one, and ended up in a smoking hole somewhere. Unfortunately, blood paid for those sage words of wisdom.

Sean rolled out of the turn.

"Strike 02," he called, "what's your telelight panel showing"

Each cockpit in the dual seat F-15E had its own telelight panel that informed the crew when a system had a problem. Some malfunctions illuminated a telelight (light panel that told aviators the various conditions of aircraft systems); others created a word caution to show up on the right most TV screen for each aircrew.

"Lead, we have a Left Generator light, Emer BST On and Boost System Mal light," replied Preston.

It was as Sean suspected. Preston was messing up and misdiagnosing his condition.

"Understand you have a single main generator failure, and the emergency generator has failed too. But the right main generator is working fine and has picked up the electrical load from the failed left generator."

"Ummmm," Preston hesitated. "Standby."

Several seconds later he came back: "We have cycled the left generator and it is back on line. We are good to go."

"Roger that, 2. Just remember your emergency generator is failed and so it will not help you if anything else goes wrong."

"2" Preston acknowledged with more of an edge now that he had solved his problem and knew they might continue their mission into enemy territory.

Suddenly, an electronic female voice piped up and announced, "Message, message."

"I got it." Emile started to manipulate some of the twenty buttons surrounding each of her screens.

The F-15E had TV like displays in each cockpit. There are two types of displays. One is a color display called the MPCD (Multi-Purpose Color Display) and the other is a MPD or simply a multi-purpose display. The MPD is a black and white screen. The front seat had three displays: a MPCD in the center and a left and right MPD. The back seat had four displays. Starting with the left side and working right they were the Left MPCD, Left MPD, Right MPD and Right MPCD. Therefore, the backseaters had color displays on the outside and two mono displays side by side.

Emile went to the text page on one of her two MPDs and read the text message aloud so Sean could hear it.

Strike 01 flight cleared to proceed with Mission TBH0069
Enemy Mig 21/29 SU-27 on high alert at all airfields
SA-3 active BE 210/017
Target area WX 6000-8000 OVC, light snow, winds 270/016
Contact Advance 20 on 299.5 with inflight report

"Magic 51, Strike 01 flight is…" Sean searched his card for the code word to let all mission support aircraft know they were pushing out to begin their journey. "Diamond."

The controller onboard the AWACS surveillance plane acknowledged his call as it if were a chore. Sean wanted to reach out, shake him, to say, "Hey, your only job today is making sure we don't get ambushed." But he let the angry thought wash away as he concentrated on the task ahead: flying into North Korea undetected and dropping several thousand pounds of bombs on a military airfield.

The two jets eased out of their orbit, and turned south to disguise their real intentions and routing, while letting down through the weather using their terrain following (TF) radars.

Once under the cloud deck and able to see the ground, both pilots dove for low altitude. Being down at low level, in and among the valleys and hills, provided the best protection. The flight needed to prevent enemy radar sites from detecting them. They leveled off 300 feet above the ground and only then began their turn towards their target.

The radios emitted a gravelly static. Radio silence. That was the plan. Magic 51 gave them an electronic order of battle (EOB) update minutes before they started their push. The update confirmed where the SAMs were on a bullseye reference and their status. Bullseye is an established reference point from which the position of an object can be determined.

The jets flew along at 300 feet, weaving their way between ridgelines and deep valleys at 500 miles per hour. They knew that the best way to stay unseen was to put terrain (preferably ridges or mountains) between them and the enemy radar sites. The only problem, thought Sean as he kept an eye on the ridgeline, was that North Korea had so many damn radar sites. The entire country was dotted with them: early warning, height finders, acquisition, target tracking sites. Sean knew that once they were detected, there would be little delay: missles would be next.

Strike 02 flew 2-4 miles away and about 30 degrees behind, exactly where Sean had briefed him to be.

The day's flight briefing had lasted over an hour. The day before, all four crewmembers planned the attack after receiving their target coordinates, TOT, and mission support information from the ATO. The ATO is the playbook for all missions within a certain theatre (area) for a given day. It lets aviators know what call sign to use, what weapons they have on board the aircraft, what their TOT is, what and where their target is and what reference to use. Other important data such as radio frequencies and Identification Friend or Foe (IFF) codes are also found in the ATO.

"FEBA in ten miles," warned Emile. "It's about to go hot."

Both Sean and Emile glanced at the Situational Display (SIT). The FEBA typically has an extreme concentration of mobile threats, including shoulder-fired missiles (manpads), anti-aircraft artillery (AAA), and surface-to-air missile (SAM) systems. The idea was to get through as quickly as possible; Strike flight pushed up the throttles.

Just a few minutes before braving the enemy threats their cloak of snow disappeared.

"Fucking weather guesser." Sean's anger filled the cockpit.

So much for the snow cover they'd hoped for crossing the Demilitarized Zone (DMZ). Stormy, the weatherman, was wrong again thought Sean. Why was it the weather geeks always seemed to be wrong when they were needed the most?

Sean and Emile spent hours each year sitting in on mission specific weather briefs and quarterly briefings on upcoming weather forecasts from the weather shop. It was always the same old same old for England, their home location: cold, wet and windy with an occasional peek of sunlight. Most joked in England if you wanted to see different weather just wait five minutes. Often the forecasters hedged their bets by stating "periods of sun punctuated by periods of rain." What the heck did that mean?

They planned to penetrate the FEBA down the Sangnyong-ni valley. By staying low, tucked inside the valley with ridges on both sides, they had protection from the mobile strategic SAMs recently placed along the DMZ. Of course, it did not hurt that today two F-16CJ aircraft were airborne at medium altitude playing a dangerous game of tag with the SAMs while a pair of F-18s attempted to jam those radars on either side of the F-15Es. Those same friendly assets were in South Korea for an exercise and the missions flown today were similar to ones they did all week up and down the DMZ. Today, however, it was for real: they were about to open a breach in the Integrated Air Defense (IAD) network of North Korea.

There is no line on the ground that represents the FEBA. It is frequently moving, often crooked and always dangerous. It is simply the battlefront across which the good guys and the bad guys face each other.

Today, in this ongoing, undeclared war, both sides stood looking at each other across the DMZ, a narrow strip of no man's land between the two powers.

Why do we always think of the enemy as bad guys? Sean mused as they neared their target. *Are they no braver than we? Do they not fight as hard for their homeland or family?* Sean made a mental note to ask Emile her thoughts on the subject, if they survived this combat mission.

Suddenly, their Tactical Early Warning System (TEWS) beeped announcing a new threat was looking for them: an SA-6 began to search for them from the West.

Chapter 2

Bill "Horse" Johnson, an aging colonel from Seymour Johnson AFB NC, and a senior Strike Eagle driver was the board president. He liked to eat well.

Plates of Denham pork fillets, Suffolk chicken, partridge breasts, hake and the obligatory order of bangers and mash now filled the table along with hand cut chunky chips and smoked garlic buttered potatoes.

Kate was a member of an Accident Investigation Board (AIB). The AIB used factual information from the initial safety investigation and other privileged testimony taken under the promise of confidentiality to determine what caused the mishap. They met to finalize their report.

Kate looked at the corpulent man who sat at the head of the table in a prime position of authority. She glanced at her own half-eaten plate, unseeing as she mentally reviewed the facts of the case at hand.

Dog 51 Flight took off from Aviano Air Base in Italy bound for Libya loaded with bombs and 31,000 pounds of fuel on an Air-Ground mission. Halfway to the target, during a routine operations check, Dog 52 noticed he had made an error with his fuel switches after coming off the air refueling tanker. Instead of feeding out his external tanks first as briefed, he fed out his conformal tanks. Instead of telling Dog 51 flown by Sean Walters, he "modified" the truth (Kate thought lied was a better word) and said he was at the same fuel state as his lead.

Sean called for the ops check "Dog flight ops check, 1 is 13 over 23, CFTs feeding": meaning he had 13,000 pounds of internal fuel and 23,000 pounds of total fuel and his conformal fuel tanks (CFTs) were now feeding. Implied in that statement was the two 4,000 pound external fuel tanks each F-15E carried were empty and now the CFT fuel could be used.

"Dog 52 same" meant the other pilot was within 500 pounds of his leader and feeding fuel from the same place. Sean's wingman justified his lie because in his mind he was feeding the CFTs, although it was by mistake and he now selected his external fuel tank to wing tanks so the wing tanks would begin to feed. His backseater caught his error as soon as the radio call came out of his mouth. Kate and the board heard it numerous times during their black box review from the aircraft.

"Ok," said the backseater. "We are at five thousand pounds of internal gas. What is going on up there? Check your switches."

"I got it. I had the external switch in CFT."

"Yeah, I gathered."

"I messed up, okay?"

"We need to let Rider know."

"If I tell Walters we'll air abort this mission. This is my last chance at a combat sortie."

His backseater paused, seeming to contemplate the enormity of their next decision. If they kept quiet and nothing unexpected happened, no one would ever know.

"I got stuck in the command post for two months. This is my only shot at the action," pleaded his pilot.

"I don't like it. The hairs on the back of my neck are standing up. I don't have a warm fuzzy about this."

"Look, let's just keep quiet about it and feed them out now. We'll be good in no time."

And so it went, with them out of sync in their fuel feeding. Dog 51 had no way of knowing about their deception.

Approaching the Libyan coast near Derna, east of Benghazi, the flight received indications an SA-6 surface to air missile battery was tracking them. The Straight Flush radar from the SA-6 locked them as they approached.

The flight performed defensive maneuvers prior to dropping their bombs and egressed north back towards Italy. Unfortunately for Dog 52, those defensive maneuvers entailed jettisoning their external fuel tanks, which were supposed to be empty at this point. Instead, they had about 1,500 pounds each. The lost 3,000 pounds of fuel, plus the additional gas used during their defensive maneuvering resulted in the F-15E arriving 100 miles from Sigonella, their nearest divert base, with 5,000 pounds less fuel than planned. They ejected 10 miles from the east-west runway at Sigonella when both engines flamed out due to lack of fuel. They were miles east of the Sicilian coast. The backseater survived with minor injuries. The frontseater left behind a wife and two children.

Vancouver, Canada

Six young men and two brave women were all ready to die for their cause. Their first meeting had been in Stanley Park, eight long months ago. They met informally during the summer Festival of Lights, discussing details quietly as others enjoyed the fireworks over downtown Vancouver. Grace came to the meeting with Janus, her boyfriend and the cell leader. The two had met in Afghanistan a year before.

Janus assembled the group with nods and prods. His greasy, gel thick, black hairstyle might have scared people away; his poorly trimmed mustache and beard did little to help his case. But the charisma came the moment he opened his mouth: Janus was a silver-tongued devil who could talk a grandmother out of her grandchildren. His dark features almost gave away his evil intentions, but he had just enough modern Hollywood flair to dispel any preconceived notions of being a bad person. Janus gathered his fellow radicals around him so he could speak quietly, yet unnoticed. Anyone looking at Janus could easily have made the assumption he was Lucifer from the Bible.

"What is the target?" asked Jafer, a young curly haired man with a clean-shaven face.

Momentary sonic booms filled the sky as a succession of fireworks burst in a glittering red and blue ripple.

"My superiors have informed me, but I am not to tell you until the time is right," boasted Janus, loving the power he carried among these people and his superiors back in the Middle East and Africa.

"Inshallah," Grace added reflexively. *God willing.*

The men and the other woman looked at her with both admiration and suspicion.

Speaking when not directly spoken to was culturally not permitted for a woman in many parts of the Arab world. Things were different here in the West and Grace wanted to make sure everyone knew how different. So she created this first test for Janus. He handled the small conundrum with his usual flair.

Janus had his group in the back of the crowd away from the majority. The darkness the back provided highlighted the glow of the popping pyrotechnic light display ahead and above them.

"This is my number two," he said. "Her name is Azrael. She also goes by the more American name of Grace. She will be obeyed as if I gave the order myself. Is that understood?"

Janus paused to look each individual, both male and female, in the eyes. He knew it was all about the eyes. They believed and they would follow his instructions. And hers.

In the distance children ran with sparklers hissing-ignoring the glow and explosions of the fireworks above them-lost in their own world.

"We will observe and infiltrate where we need to. And," he glanced back, beaming at Grace, "we will bring this city to its knees, Inshallah."

***

"I'm hunkering down, Emile."

Instantly Emile knew what Sean would do next and she punched 180 feet into the aircraft's Low Altitude Warning System (LAWS). If the Strike Eagle went below 180 feet another voice would announce "Low Altitude, Low Altitude." The aircrew lovingly referred to the female voice warning as "Bitching Betty," but she had saved more than a few lives.

Sean pushed both throttles forward to mil power and dropped the aircraft to 200 feet. The SA-6 search radar lost them in the terrain. As soon as the threat disappeared from the TEWS, Emile called out, "We're naked."

Sean smiled behind his oxygen mask. He knew she was using the appropriate code word, but it excited him. He loved women. All women. That was his problem, but what a problem.

He thought back to the day he got his call sign "Rider." He and a few dozen of his squadron mates were in Las Vegas for a Red Flag deployment. It was the closest thing to combat that aircrews flew: a two-week, multi-aircraft exercise flying in a realistic combat scenario over the Nevada desert with live weapons. The theory behind Red Flag is that aviators can learn from their mistakes before actually having to go to war. The flying is exhilarating. The crews fly hard and play hard. The playing just happens to be in Sin City: Las Vegas.

Sean and his mates were on the outskirts of town in a dive bar, which employed rather well endowed waitresses. The motif was cowboys and cowgirls. The young cowgirl serving drinks to the boys as the evening progressed became friendlier and friendlier. At one point Sean, honoring a dare, pulled a "rodeo" on her.

As she waited at the bar to pick up her order, Sean bent over to admire her cowgirl boots. When she leaned to see what he was doing he scooped her up, throwing her over his shoulder. Hoisted over his right shoulder, with his arm wrapped around her flailing legs, she was trapped and began to beat him on his back to let her down. She let out a shrill scream that was soon followed by a cry of "rodeo" from his squadron mates. Sean flipped her cowgirl skirt up to expose her pink panties and bit the cheek lightly. As soon as his mouth hit her bottom the counting began in the room.

"1-2-3." Of course, his teeth on her rump also made her kicking and beating increase in intensity. The crowd roared with laughter and clapping as his buds counted on. "4-5-6." Now the waitress grabbed his head with her own hands and clapped him around the ears. "7-8-9" and he lowered her to the ground. 8 seconds was the magic number.

Just like bronco or bull riding, in a rodeo the aviator had to ride the girl's behind for 8 seconds in that pose. Sean rose up sheepishly and met a punch in the right eye from the pissed off waitress. Sean, still a little dizzy from the lifting and the alcohol, fell back and hit the floor. His head snapped back and clanged the wood floor a little too hard. Seeing him hit the floor from her well-placed right hook embarrassed and worried her. She then bent down to help him. Eventually, all was forgiven. The flyboys' promise to return with even more friends persuaded the owner not to throw them out. Sean eventually apologized to and took home the waitress that night. Her forgiveness came the next day when Sean escorted her and her younger brother on to the flight line and had them sit in his F-15E-not many knew that part of the story. Ever since then he had been known as "Rider."

Rider jettisoned the image of that night and the waitress and fixated on surviving the next 60 minutes in enemy territory.

Once the threat subsided they went back to lookout duties. In the brief, Sean had explained to Emile he could lookout from 9 o'clock to 3 o'clock, as long as they were 500 feet or higher, but once they stepped down below that, he would concentrate on the terrain ahead that the jet was hurtling towards. In these low altitude settings, her visual lookout would need to expand to cover their beam (or 3 o'clock and 9 o'clock). In the other aircraft, the same duties were tasked. Both rear cockpit Weapon System Officers (WSOs) would look outside the formation and then clear inside the formation by "checking six," or looking behind the other aircraft.

The WSOs also helped their pilots maintain the formation. If Emile saw the wingman was getting too far away, or too close, she would alert Sean. In the other aircraft, Chad, call sign "Tiny," provided the same commentary to Preston. Tiny was an experienced WSO, the squadron Operations Officer in fact, with more than eight years of F-15E flying and 2000 flight hours. He did not pull any punches. He had already dressed down Preston for misidentifying the earlier malfunction. Now he coached him into staying in position crossing the FEBA.

Emile saw the missile first. The SA-14 came from below the two airplanes and corkscrewed right towards Strike 02.

Chapter 3

Kate thought about the pilot in Dog 51, the flight lead. She knew Sean "Rider" Walters from his antics on the base, mainly at the Officers Club (O'club). He was a smooth-talking ladies man. He was also a good person, as far as Kate could tell. He would give you the shirt off his back if you needed it. Just make sure you lock up your wife and daughter before asking him for it. Kate smiled.

Sean was mature in many ways but a lovable louse all the same. She liked Sean. Kate noticed she had unconsciously kicked off her shoes and now ran her pantyhose clad toes along her ankles. Kate savored her bitter chocolate tart, chestnut ice cream and praline dessert as she thought about Sean and his bad boy image. She found her mind drifting off to other thoughts, like when she met Sean.

Kate saw Sean on her first Friday in country at the Lakenheath O'club, but they didn't meet. Later her sponsor took her to the "Big House" at Mildenhall. "Big House" referred to the larger Mildenhall O'club. Her sponsor was much older than Kate and filled her in on all the history of the two bases.

The Mildenhall Officers Club dated back to 1930, although much of the good stuff comes from World War II and RAF Bomber Command around the battle of Britain, when the club was exclusively a British Air Base. But in 1950 it transferred to a joint RAF-U.S base. U.S. Strategic Air Command (SAC) flew B-29s then B-50s and B-47s Stratojets from the lone runway. Finally in 1959 US. Air Forces in Europe (USAFE) took it over from SAC and Mildenhall became a USAF base for all intentions.

The transfer from UK, to joint, to U.S. did not deter young ladies from coming to have a good time. Every Friday night, busloads of British girls would make their way to the front gate and walk to the nearby Officers Club. About once a month the club had a live band, which always yielded a large crowd. And of course, anytime you mixed aviators, who risked their lives everyday just getting those flying machines into the air, and women you got... well, a good time. Mildenhall was no exception to that rule and in fact it was notorious as the best place to be in all of Europe on a Friday night. Known as the "Big House," it was the final destination of the night for the aviators at Lakenheath after they visited the "Little House" - their own modest officer's club.

RAF Lakenheath and nearby RAF Mildenhall were the two main U.S. operated Air Force bases in the United Kingdom and were only separated by five miles.

Sauntering to the rectangular mahogany bar, Kate casually ordered her drink.

"Hi," she said, pondering the selection. "I'll have a dark and stormy."

"Coming right up."

While she waited for her drink she noticed a young pilot staring at her intently. He was very good-looking. Around six feet, with short black hair and a trimmed mustache he reminded Kate of a young Russell Crowe in a fitted flight suit.

Leaning towards her he asked playfully, eyes full of wonder, "I have to ask: what is a dark and stormy? I heard you order it and have been hypnotized ever since."

She looked at his nametag, Rider. All aviators wore their call signs as nametags on Fridays. This was the one her friend had warned her about: the infamous Sean Walters.

Kate played along with the wolf. She knew his reputation well enough. Sponsors provide a newcomer to the base with valuable information, and not all of it has to do with housing, shipping goods and how to get to the air base from London.

"Hypnotized by the drink, or by me?" Kate leaned closer to him, flirting back with her dimpled smile and piercing eyes.

"Both," Sean quipped instantly. "But you haven't answered my question."

Kate's drink arrived. Sean handed the bartender a twenty, ordered another beer for himself, and told him to keep the change. Impressed at his gentlemanly manners, she turned back to him.

"Thanks for the drink." She clinked her new libation with his half empty bottle of Old Speckled Hen. Kate decided to divulge the recipe.

"One part Gosling Black Seal Rum, two parts ginger beer, mix and pour over shaved ice. It's delicious." Trying to act cool, she took a larger gulp than she intended, choking on the drink.

"I see," he laughed, and handed her a cocktail napkin. Extending his right hand he introduced himself humbly. "Rider Walters, aviator extraordinaire."

"Well, 'Rider' Walters," she said, taking his hand in hers. "I've heard you are also a ladies man. I'm Kate Healy, by the way."

"Kate, my dear, you have been misinformed. I am a teddy bear, not a lion on the prowl as some may say."

Kate looked from his black flying boots all the way up his well-fitted flight suit to his smiling green eyes. She set her drink on the bar. "Rider," she said coolly. "Let's just get one thing straight: I'm in the security police squadron. I own a gun. I hunt lions for a living. You had better be on your best behavior around me and my staff."

Now it was Sean's turn to be surprised.

"Yes, ma'am." Then he smiled and, leaning into her to whisper in her ear, gave her a little lion "rrroarrr" and walked away into the crowd.

Kate took several opportunities to watch Sean that night. Her occupational training as a security forces team member gave her lots of tricks and techniques for casual yet unobserved attention. Sean was fun, but not too boisterous. More like a cute kid in a huge candy store. And all the other women in the place adored him, even those who seemed to be just friends or old lovers.

Once, Kate thought a female aviator caught her reconnaissance on Sean. She was slightly older than Kate, probably mid 30s; the thin redhead turned away just as Kate caught her intense stare, but not before Kate sensed the redhead's eyes burning into her.

Later that night, Kate and Sean were again at the bar waiting on drinks, a little more intoxicated. It was about midnight and the band only had 30 minutes left to play. The waiter brought their drinks but refused to take any money from Kate.

He shrugged and pointed to the three gentlemen at the corner table. "They bought this round for you."

Turning to see who their benefactors were, Kate saw three men enjoying a lively and spirited conversation at the table – each with several beer bottles in front of them. One had a football build while another was tall and lanky. The third had both a mustache and beard and smiled at them rather amused.

Sean and Kate both asked simultaneously, "Who are they?"
The waiter leaned in to draw them closer before whispering. "They are not really locals, but I do see them in here once in a while for a

drink or three. Their call signs are Neckless, Tuna and Slam. I believe they are former pilots."

Sean remembered the famous pilot saying and repeated it absent -mindedly to himself.

"There are old pilots and there are bold pilots but there are no old, bold pilots."

Sean tipped his drink in a salute to the gentlemen. The one with the beard nodded appreciatively back.

He looks like a Slam.

Kate decided to ask Sean about the redhead, but before she could broach the subject, Sean snapped his fingers and pointed to Kate as if reminded of something.

"My little toe," he said.

Kate frowned. "What on earth are you talking about?"

"You remind me of my little toe," he said again.

Kate laughed. "What, because I'm small? And cute?"

Sean was no dummy. He had caught Kate staring at him earlier and used this knowledge to his advantage by teasing her.

He paused and, without looking back at Kate, said into the air, "No, because I'll probably bang you on the coffee table later when I'm drunk." And walked away happily.

Kate stood there in shock. Had he just said that to her? Did he mean it? Was it a joke? If he thought she was that easy he had another thing coming.

She ordered a drink for her friend and then rejoined her. Two songs later she went over and asked Sean to dance.

***

More delightfully naughty thoughts ran through her head but came to a halt when, with grace and efficiency, the two brunette staff girls cleared away the dishes and served coffee and tea.

Now, the business at hand could commence. The board president asked for any additional comments before launching into a detail of his personal thoughts on the accident. Kate watched his jowls flop as he pontificated on the merits of emergency procedures training on a monthly basis. He seemed oblivious to the earlier observations from numerous individuals stating the wing commander's intent to emphasize situational emergency procedure training (SEPT) in the simulator.

Kate thought about the wing commander of RAF Lakenheath. She had worked with Brigadier General Brad "Bull" Cardwell on many occasions. The one-star general impressed her with his athletic ability and his diplomacy. He was a people person, always smiling, always shaking hands and remembering almost everyone's name and background or history. *I guess that explains how he seems to be so smart. When you remember people and events that well things seem to fall into place.*

Kate never called him "Bull" though. That was for his aviators. No, she called him General Cardwell as their relationship was much more formal, although she did get a personal glimpse of him that same night at the Mildenhall O'Club when she'd overheard him telling a story to some of the flyers. He recounted how, as a young aviator flying the mighty F-4 Phantom, he'd visited Mildenhall on numerous occasions over the years. On one such visit his weapon systems officer found himself dancing with the daughter of a woman he had slept with ten years earlier. Kate never did figure out if General Cardwell had simply substituted his backseater for what happened to him.

Either version would not surprise Kate. She expected those wild aviators to be amorous, but maybe not "Bull" Cardwell, since he had married his sweetheart out of high school at age 21. She passed away from cancer twenty years later and he soon married his second wife, a much younger lady. He was in the middle of that divorce now.

Kate was the assistant Chief of Security. Basically, she ran the 100th Security Police (SP) Squadron at RAF Mildenhall. It was her job to provide the base security using her security police (SP) otherwise known as military police (MP). Her squadron's standing mission was to guard the aircraft and defend the people who fly and fight. She was quite proud of her men and woman and quite bored as this AIB drew to a close.

Finally, with much flourish, the Colonel rose to his feet and announced the board's findings via an executive summary. "The Accident Investigation Board (AIB) President found, by clear and convincing evidence..."

Kate wrinkled up her nose involuntarily at that. Every accident board said "clear and convincing evidence" so the public thought the Air Force knew what it was doing. She quickly scanned the other members to see if anyone noticed her frown. All were fixated on the board president speaking, though likely just as bored. Kate hated his type. All they wanted to be was in charge. The board president was no different. He had no time for other's opinions if they differed from his.

"That the cause of the mishap was the pilot's switch error leading to the improper feeding of fuel from the conformal fuel tanks instead of the external fuel tanks, leading to a low fuel state when the external fuel tanks were jettisoned due to a threat reaction. Further, the AIB President found, by a preponderance of evidence, that the following factors substantially contributed to the mishap: one, a lack of airmanship from both mishap aviators in not reporting their correct fuel state and two, insufficient knowledge in minimum fuel recovery procedures. An additional causal factor is the way the F-15E community trains. The board president found more than forty percent of sorties and simulators focused on air-to-air training missions versus the primary Strike Eagle mission, which is air-to-ground. The F-15E community is getting better at air-to-air but at the expense of our air-to-ground skill sets. We have become jack-of-all trades but are masters of none. The contributing factors were links which if broken, would have precluded aircraft loss."

Kate got along with everyone. She thought it might be because of her experience as a high school cheerleader or her attendance at multiple schools. But there was something about Colonel Johnson. Kate did not care for his cocky attitude. Sean, and perhaps all aviators, had that attitude too; however Sean at least showed a human side sometimes. Bill Johnson acted like he knew everything.

Kate and the others stood to leave after the board president presented the final verdict. She exhaled a little too loudly. Perhaps hinting at the tension in the room, building then released as the report finally came to an end. Now everyone seemed pleasant and ready to go home. Kate frowned at the cavalier attitude some displayed.

She contemplated the findings. Sean would be cleared and the other aviators hung out to dry. Such was the case in the military

when accidents happened. And Sean still had to deal with the
demons he himself put up as roadblocks to his recovery.

***

Kate felt relief that her friend Sean was cleared. Yes, they were
friends, good friends in fact. After Kate took the initiative and
asked Sean to dance, things changed between them. They danced
like wild animals that night even after the band stopped playing and
the lights came on. Kate looked around for the redhead but she was
gone.

Feeling a little cocky herself, Kate invited him back to her place,
which at the time was the officer's temporary quarters on base as
she had yet to find her flat in Cambridge.

They made passionate, unbridled love in the early morning
hours that remained. Sean crept away before dawn, leaving Kate to
wake up alone. Kate later found out it was Sean's MO. He never
stayed to wake up in the morning with his liaison. Kate did not care.
If she was honest with herself she knew she had used Sean. Kate
was bisexual and that did not go over well in the military, contrary
to what all the liberals said about the repeal of "Don't ask, don't
tell." So Kate kept her bisexuality hidden. She was more gay than
bisexual. Arriving at a new location, she slept with the biggest ladies
man on base and then feigned a broken heart for the rest of her
assignment. Often these one-night affairs were faked to make
people think she slept with them. Men were so easy to deceive
when they were drunk and horny.

After that initial physical contact, Sean and Kate settled into
friendship. It suited them both. Sean had plenty of girlfriends with
whom he slept; the list was long and distinguished. Kate accepted
him as a loyal friend. Once Kate moved into her flat in Cambridge,
Sean loved having a place to crash. He took her up on the offer to
crash on her couch more times then she cared to remember, but
never again as a lover.

They talked about the accident one night over a bottle of wine.
Sean needed a night away from things (mainly his girlfriends). Right
after the accident Sean told everyone he was fine. Said he had no
problems. He was in denial. But when they talked a month later he

was in the anger stage. That night he kept coming back to the same things repeatedly.

"Why me?"

"I don't deserve this shit."

"The accident was not my fault and it's not fair to heap all that on me."

It was clear to Kate the accident troubled Sean and, contrary to his statements, he was not over it. On the couch later that night, he woke her with the sounds of a nightmare. She stumbled out to shake him awake at 4 a.m. He claimed to have the same dream almost every night: he was taking a test but his time ran out, and when he went to turn in the paper, he was naked.

Kate liked to think about that image. In fact, it was one she had some familiarity with in real life, but no matter how much she enjoyed seeing Sean's muscle tight abs and slender thighs, she did not like seeing him fitful in sleep.

Granville Island Vancouver, Canada

Snow fell softly on the city, heedless of the one million visitors descending upon the area for the Winter Sports venues. A light crust, some would be generous enough to call it a layer, caked the sidewalks, lonely picnic tables and recycle bins throughout the bustling metropolis.

Grace had to laugh. The tourist information she researched over 12 months ago boasted of mild winters and blossoms coming out as early as February. There were no blossoms from her vantage point in the Public Market at Granville Island.

Granville Island is one of the premier Vancouver attractions. Imagine an island in the middle of a city. It rests under the Granville Street Bridge bordered by False Creek. What Grace liked the most was that it was accessible in so many ways. Today she had reached the island by one of the two ferries, though she could just as easily have taken the bus or walked onto the triangular island.

Granville was half eclectic, artsy hippy town and half urban restaurant mecca. Galleries, studios and restaurants competed with shops, cafes and an outstanding fresh food market.

The Public Market was the best of the island. Grace loved the market's feel with its vendors offering a mixture of Mexican, Chinese, curry, espresso, sweets, traditional fish and chips, deli foods, salads and a famous burger grill that always had a line at the door.

Her attire for the team's weekly reconnaissance was an oversized red down-filled jacket. The jacket covered her blue sweater and some tight leather pants she just managed to squeeze into. Black knee-high boots completed the ensemble. The large black leather handbag contained pepper spray among other tools of her trade. A girl never knew what might happen to her on a stroll. Large black glasses gave her eyes some protection from the river reflection and obscured her face just a bit to prevent easy recognition from passersby.

Lately, Grace had taken to wandering this little island paradise, thinking through the plan upon which she was about to embark. Today she sat in the Public Market eating area munching on a plate of cod and some fresh cut French fries. Phil Collins' "I Don't Care Anymore" on her iPhone did nothing to lighten her mood. The depressing chant and rhythmic drum dispelled any cheer, and she thought of Tim. Her brother had loved that song. He was a big Phil Collins and Genesis fan. He even included some of those CDs in his shipment to Afghanistan when he went there with his wife as a missionary. Now those lyrics haunted her.

Grace hated – no, hate was not a strong enough word – she loathed snow. Snow was fun to look at but a real pain in the ass to work in. Her trim body and naturally toned skin was more adept to summer climates and warm beaches than winter wonderlands. She only had one fond memory of snow and that harkened back to her college days that seemed so long ago.

She shivered unconsciously and stared at the growing crowd at Celine Fish and Chips. A family two tables down, a young couple in love nearby and an elderly woman enjoying a morning coffee-all smiling and happy. They were all oblivious to the danger lurking nearby. Grace blended in well. She looked natural here. Her team was almost in place.

Grace left Granville Island, her spot of serenity, and took the ferry across the river. Boarding the small boat with her were two middle-aged men. Just behind them, muffled music caught her attention as a teenager walked on with a music player and earphones. Despite the attempt at noise redirection, the music screamed and screeched loud enough for everyone to hear. Grace scowled at the unwanted disruption. She glared at him, insinuating what she might do to him if she got him alone. She crossed her arms and waited. He turned his back to her as he moved away and he never knew how close he came to angering her. Grace had a temper like an April day.

Grace reflected on the youth of today as the ferry began its trip to the other side of the river.

Why did so many young people today think that everyone else wanted to hear their music? And what was up with the volume so loud others could hear the music even with headphones? I blame it all on the instant gratification culture they grow up in. Instant Internet everywhere via Wi-Fi or 3G/4G. Need to be on the East Coast. No problem-get on a plane and four hours later you are there. Need cash-just hit an ATM or better yet send it through the Internet via your email account. No one was patient anymore. Now, now, now and me, me, me.

Grace smiled as she reflected on her "cranky old man tirade." She had seen enough in her twenty plus years to earn her some bitterness, but not that much.

Grace debated what she would do to the boy, if only she were not on a mission. She could not risk operational security just to get petty revenge. On the other hand, if she was not on a mission and needed to do something to keep her skills active…Grace might follow him to a dark alley or isolated stairwell. Corner and confront him for a wild fight to get her blood pumping. She found the trapped ones fought best. Perhaps lull him with her body…

Both middle-aged men seemed to enjoy taking long looks at her figure. Neither minded her attire or her attention.

I'm sexual. What's under my clothes isn't good or bad, just a tool. Grace laughed and looked out over the choppy winter waters. Rogers Arena stood out in the distance. Its large, irregular shaped roof a wagging finger to the commuters saying, "Look at me."

From her smart phone it looked like they may be in for more heavy snow. Grace hoped not. It might interfere with their escape plans.

"Suicide Blonde" by INXS started up in her ears, stoking her feelings. She would not be a suicide blond. She had worked too hard to be exactly where she was. In the right place, at the right time. She was not going to sacrifice her life until her mission was complete. This mission was a stepping-stone.

Janus, her lover and commander, was a dalliance of convenience. She did not love the man. In many ways she abhorred him. She feigned absolute obedience to further her objectives. And only she knew about them. He was a tool and she was using him. She suspected he felt the same about her. The key was to keep him happy long enough.

In one week they were to execute his plan. Grace had subtly altered the attack to suit her desires. A small change here. A hint there and a well voiced apprehension about something else all served to modify the original scheme. Grace knew police response times now after observing their exercise last week. She knew how many and where the guards were located due to some inside information. Some of that information came freely; some was extracted.

The time for action was drawing near. Next week they would bring their Jihad to North American shores.

***

"Strike 02 break left, missile left...." Emile could not make her brain think which clock position the missile was boring in from.

At the same instant, Tiny saw the missile and called for the same maneuver inside his cockpit. Preston realized his error in using the min AB to get back in position and regretted it instantly. Now he slammed the throttle to below mil power and pulled the jet into a 6 G turn into the threat.

"Flares, flares, flares!" Tiny yelled as he activated the slide switch on his left hand controller. Movement sent a combination of chaff and flares spilling out of the underbelly of the aircraft to decoy incoming enemy missiles. Emile saw bright flashes as the flares burst open against the dusk sky.

Preston confirmed his tally on the heat seeking missile and put it at 10 o'clock just before rolling; the seeker locked on to the strong heat of the decoy flares and sailed well behind the aircraft.

"Miss," exhaled Preston as he jinked back right to return to formation.

"Shit hot!" yelled Sean from his aircraft, paying Preston the ultimate compliment in fighter pilot lingo.

But there was no time to gloat. Anti-aircraft artillery tracked Strike 02 as he attempted to return to his formation position.

"Strike 02, triple A, right two o'clock," exclaimed Preston as he scanned the sky for the tracers that would indicate the bullets trajectory towards him and his fighter.

"Get the fuck down and we won't have to worry 'bout no damn triple-A," growled Tiny.

Preston glanced at his altitude in the HUD and grimaced at the reading. His maneuver to defeat the IR SAM had resulted in a fly up to above the ridgeline. Red and orange tracers began to arc up towards them.

"Jink left and get down behind that ridgeline up ahead," commanded Tiny. "Chaff, chaff, chaff."

Chaff is an old radar countermeasure begun in World War II where an aircraft releases a cloud of thin aluminum strips to distract enemy radars. Aircraft use these self-defense measures to confuse the radars that guide incoming missiles.

Sean pulled the stick back to give his machine a slight upward vector. This bought him a few seconds to scan his right side and observe Strike 02 roll into his flight path. Just as Sean was about to maneuver out of the way, Strike 02 bumped over a ridge and bullets followed, just missing above them.

"Two's defending triple A." Edginess invaded Preston's radio call.

Sean banked hard left to clear them from both the AAA threat and Strike 02's flight path.

"Two continue."

Both aircraft banked away from the fire hose of bullets coming up at them, arcing up and left towards a spot 750' above the ground. Pilots often described AAA as like a fire hose of bullets coming up at them. Sean saw no more tracers and decided to get back on course.

"Strike 01's naked."

Preston came back more assuredly.

"Strike 02's naked."

"Strike flight return to course."

After a few moments, Sean called to Emile. "Bambi, you're mighty quiet back there." Sean rarely used Emile's call sign in the jet with her. His adrenaline must be pulsing, she thought. Fair enough.

"Twenty seconds late for TOT. Push it up to five-fifty to make up the time," she replied, ignoring his jab.

"Yes, ma'am," he chuckled. That was the Sean she wanted to hear.

"Remind me to check my FSS when we land."

"And what, pray tell, is an FSS," asked a busy Emile as she ran the air-to-air radar, sweeping it out eighty miles for enemy planes on an interception course.

Sean scanned the front quadrants of the aircraft's flight path and calmly regaled her with his definition. "Why Em, everyone has one. It's the Fart-Shit Separator. And after that last ridge crossing...."

Laughter filled the intercom. "I am afraid my FSS may have failed me and I may need to change my boxers when we land." Emile tried not to laugh but she could not control herself and an audible giggle slipped out. This only encouraged Sean.

"And you know what that means?"

"No, I give. What does that mean?" she asked, glancing for AAA and keeping an eye on their wingman.

"I'll be going commando at the O'Club."

Emile could not help but laugh. "Might be dicey for sock check," she said, thinking of how being caught without the official boxers was just slightly less embarrassing than not wearing any at all. It eased the tension in the cockpit and the next 10 minutes went as planned, and gave her plenty of time to think of Sean with his flight suit around his ankles.

She loved him. She knew she shouldn't. He was a reclamation project at best and a heart breaker at worst. But from the moment she'd seen his grizzled face she was smitten. Of course, he had no idea.

Ah unrequited love.

Those thoughts had no place in the high-stress dynamic environment they were currently flying in. She shook them off.

Once past the FEBA, both jets crept back to 500' to ease the stress of low flying. Earlier, the crews had donned night vision goggles (NVGs) and turned on their terrain following radars.

"Approaching the target run and we're on time. Set speed at five-forty," commanded Emile. Sean thought she might have been behind the power curve earlier in the mission but she seemed to have caught up and maybe was thinking ahead of the jet now.

25 miles to their target: Sunchon airfield, home of North Korea's latest Surface-to-Air Missile - the SA-21 Growler. The SAM was not operational yet, but human intelligence sources reported that North Korea had figured out how to find and lock the US.'s new F-35 stealth fighter. The North Koreans kept the radar hidden deep inside a series of mountainside bunkers that the experts said were impenetrable to cruise missiles. Of course, that was even if the U.S. could launch a ballistic missile in time to hit the bunker where the radar hid. The U.S. could launch a hundred cruise missiles from the sea or air, which would surely destroy Sunchon airfield. But that would start an international incident no U.S. president wanted. No, a surgical strike with plausible deniability was needed.

Timing was critical to success here. The special radar came out for testing at irregular times and only stayed exposed for 30 minutes.

After the NK excursions onto and the shelling of the Yeonpyeong islands, it was decided a message was needed. The Joint Chiefs of Staff tasked the USAF to take out the radar, and the F-15E became the messenger. Four F-15E crews rotated eight-hour airborne alerts waiting for orders. Imagery arrived into the cockpit via satellite downlink before their push showing the runway, control tower, admin buildings, maintenance shops and the parking apron where the SA-21 radar rested for today's test. Cloud cover prevented satellites from seeing the radar (they only tested on overcast days). However, Synthetic Aperture Radar maps allowed certain airborne platforms to take satellite-like pictures using high-powered radars mapping from different angles and comparing multiple maps to create an image. These platforms could see the enemy radar once it set up in the parking ramp. By the time the text message came to the airborne alert crews to execute their mission they had 20 minutes before the radar would enter the caves again.

Emile checked the armament screen one last time to make sure she had selected the correct weapons.

Approaching the IP, Sean wiggled the F-15E wings slightly signaling Strike 02 to take spacing. Preston slipped his Eagle back into a three mile wedge position just aft and left of Strike 01.

Emile confirmed the JDAM program was set first; the GBU-24 would come next.

"Target area designated, cleared to release, GBU-31 programmed," she said.

"Copy, cleared to release, five hundred feet, five-forty knots."

"Remember lofting the JDAM then dropping the GBU-24."

"Got it."

Their hearts pounded harder as the seconds clicked down to the target area. Each fixated on his/her duties exclusively.

"10 miles to target."

"Pull!" Emile directed just as Sean pulled back on the stick and lifted the F-15E into a 20-degree climb.

750' and climbing.

1000'.

Sean felt madly exposed as the aircraft reached 1250' and sighed with relief upon hearing the clunk of the 2000-pound GBU-31 bomb leaving the airframe's right side. Sean quickly pushed a button to change the weapons program to enable release of the GBU-24 Paveway III Laser Guided Bomb (LGB).

"Strike 01 weapon away, 10 TREL GBU24."

"Strike 02 weapon away, Laser code 1731 set," came the reply as his wingman lofted their GBU-31 and confirmed the laser code set in Strike 02.

Meanwhile, Emile moved the targeting pod into the target area, searching for the parking ramp. Earlier she used the coordinates passed to her from the text message and the image to assign the GBU-31 to the suspected bunker entrance. Now she used the known coordinates for the parking ramp to cue her targeting pod. As they climbed, the picture became clear in the screen. Low altitude masked them from threats but also kept them from seeing the target.

She found the control tower east of the ramp, and used it as a reference to find the ramp and then she saw it. There was the radar site.

NATO called it the Grave Stone radar. Its name fit it like a glove. Its boxy coffin-like shape rose vertically to provide Emile with the target she wanted. The support vehicles surrounding the structure's back made the layout look like a semi-circle, like a sort of graveyard and she shivered unconsciously. Two launchers formed the outer front perimeter. The radar with its long coffin shape axis and tall back radar device stood out significantly in the center of her own radar picture.

Instantly she passed Sean the information he needed before releasing their second weapon: "Target captured, cleared to release GBU-24." Target captured told him that she saw in the targeting screen the object they were bombing and she had good laser ranging, i.e. their laser illuminated the radar.

"Strike 01 GBU-24 release."

"Strike 02 target captured, laser 1731."

"Laser is off," confirmed Emile and Sean banked hard away from the approaching airfield. Glancing down he saw them come within 4.0 NM of the target and a SA-8 illuminate their TEWS.

Strike 01 was the mule and the bait. They launched a GBU-24 but did not intend to illuminate the target with their own laser if avoidable. Strike 02, 4 miles behind them saw the target better and faced the target head on; they were guiding the bomb from Strike 01 into the radar, freeing Strike 01 to get away from the airfield and its SA-8 SAM.

Sean hated SA-8s. They were small, fast missiles and because of the radar sites' limited range, they only shot you when you were close. This was both good and bad. You could stiff-arm the actual launchers and stay away most of the time, but once you penetrated the threat radius there was very little time to react. Sean briefed two seconds as a rough "wag" (wild ass guess) as to how long it took a missile to travel a mile. If you were shot at 4 NM that meant about 8 seconds at best to out maneuver the missile even if you saw it.

Emile saw the launch first in her targeting pod. Her job was to stay on the radar with the laser spot in case Strike 02 had a problem like a laser failure. Out of the top right corner of the TV screen she saw the SA-8 vehicle launch.

"Missile launch!" she yelled.

"Where?" Sean demanded.

Before she could answer, the jet banked into a hard left turn towards Sunchon AF. Emile felt the Gs overwhelm her and pull her head towards the TP screen. Straining against the G forces she peeked over the canopy rail and saw the small, fast missile approaching straight at them. She could even make out the green cone of the missile. She caught her breath as it streaked closer just a second away from impact.

Sean whipped the aircraft into a last ditch maneuver. Objects flew throughout both cockpits as dust and material became dislodged when briefly exposed to the negative G environment.

Wham.

The missile flew dangerously close to the left side of her cockpit but did not blow up. Emile held her breath as she watched it explode harmlessly on a ridge top. The proximity fuse failed to work saving their aircraft from damage.

Tiny kept the laser spot on the radar base, the widest part of the target as Strike 02 checked away from the SA-8 ring ahead. The weapon followed the laser beam perfectly. Tiny guided the weapon directly into the new radar. A fiery explosion rocked the southern half of the airfield. Pieces of the radar flew from the blast, destroying the SA-8 and sending billows of black smoke over the site. Secondary explosions rocked the airfield sending the inhabitants into chaos.

Tiny reported proudly, "Strike 02 SHACK!"

Sean did not even skip a beat in commanding the flight to "Egress 150" and head home. The attack was a success. Strike 01 had lofted their GBU-31 in a BOC (Bomb On Coordinates) mode towards the suspected cavern and hit; they dropped their GBU-24 on the radar and Strike 02 had lofted their GBU-31 into the mountain towards the bunker.

Things went wrong one minute later.

***

"Rider, I think we have a fuel leak here."

Sean shook his head. So close. They were almost home. Another 8 minutes and they would fight their way back across the FEBA and it would be Miller time.

"We are losing fuel like a sieve," Emile said, jolting Sean back to reality.

"Do we have enough to get back home?"

"Standby." That was the answer no pilot wanted to hear from his WSO. It meant they didn't know.

"I'm getting into the checklist pages." Emile buried her head down in the checklist. They approached an SA-3 ring on egress and needed to use terrain masking to hide themselves or it would launch on them.

Sean checked his TSD routing and noticed they were one ridgeline off course. As they rocketed out of the valley into relatively clear terrain ahead, he realized his fatal navigation error. They were tracking towards the SA-3 site.

"Strike flight check sixty left."

It was too late. The jet emerged from behind the mountains, instantly exposed to the SA-3 Low Blow tracking radar. After the attack on Sunchon, the SA-3 stood on alert and concentrated their coverage away from Pyongyang. The North Koreans knew the attackers were not stupid enough to egress over Pyongyang. Thus they focused their efforts on the eastern part of the country.

The SA-3 missile targeted Strike 01. Emile saw it and called it out to Sean, but gave no directive. She should have called a break right into the missile or last ditch, but Emile thought Sean had seen the missile and would react.

The SA-3 missile hit Strike 01 behind the wing line, mid-fuselage penetrating the fuel tanks, exploding and igniting the remaining 3000 pounds of gas in the internal fuel tanks. Sean and Emile died instantly.

Chapter 4

Vancouver

He was easy to seduce.

Married with two kids. Mid 30s and a football jock from high school. He never got used to the idea that life did not revolve around football, or around him. Leaving school as an athletic star but with no future plans, Brad did not marry his high school sweetheart, the captain of the cheerleading squad. She had things lined up. She went on to the University of Texas and a lucrative career in business.

Brad Jackson did the honorable thing and married the banker's daughter when she ended up pregnant with his child. Unfortunately for Brad, the bank went bust and the young couple were forced to move on and northward looking for work. She had an education fund from her father's good planning and graduated from community college, but their second child ended any plans she had of a career. Instead she kept their home happy (or so she thought) and raised the two boys, both so much like their father.

Tonight he called after bowling with co-workers to say he was going straight back to work a double shift. Sometimes his security job at the arena required extra work. He would see her the following afternoon. He sounded happy. Too happy.

Grace started her seduction with a few simple moves. The hair flip when he was around, bending over or letting her skirt ride a little too high while cleaning around his station. It did not take long for him to respond. Lunch and a walk in the park. He was scared, yet cocky, but sloppy. He kissed her affectionately, but she sensed no passion, only lust. This would be easy.

She allowed him to take her to the boathouse that day. Looking back it came to symbolize their relationship. Dirty, isolated and quirky. The sex was average. His wife, after two children, had lost much interest in his slightly aging body and so he found new energy through liaisons with strangers. Grace's words, not his. His entry pass code was easy to cajole out of him. Checking it was trickier but she had two other teammates inside the arena by the time the operation went into test mode. Fatima worked with her at the janitorial firm. Both had signed on about six months prior; Grace was hired first and then recommended Fatima. They did not work full time at the venue that would be their target, but only once or twice a week. That was enough to get the information they needed. Once Grace figured out which company did the cleaning at the various venues, it was easy to start to plan.

Amazing how the North Americans thought so little of the people that cleaned up after them, Grace noted. The millions of cleaners, servers and dishwashers who were unreported and illegal did so much of the heavy lifting, got little credit and yet much blame for their nation's woes.

Grace laughed to herself as she thought of all the people at Granville Island now. How many were unemployed and yet would not bother to accept a job cleaning toilets and offices as Grace and her team did now. No, everyone wants the tasks done but no one wants to be the one to do the job.

That was why they had settled on the hockey events. Less security on non-game nights and an easy building layout.

Rogers Arena, formerly known as General Motors Place, only had three main entry points. The front entrance and a left and right side entrance. The rear, actually the long side of the rectangular building, had no exit.

***

Sean and Emile exclaimed "Shit!" simultaneously as the red light in their cockpit illuminated. The simulator mission was over. They had died at the hands of an SA-3. The displays froze and the screens now despairingly displayed "Simulation over." In the distance, they heard the radio calls of Strike 02 but they were helpless to respond.

Their Standardization and Evaluation Flight Examiner (SEFE) calmly told them to get ready to fly again; magically their screens lit up and they were airborne. Afterward, flying a successful second mission from their restart, both crews attended the debriefing in one of the debrief rooms deep in the heart of the simulator complex. The entire mission played back in slow motion or real time depending on what training needed emphasizing. The large 54-inch TV screens presented differing points of view: aircrews could see what the SAM operators saw or what displays they had up at any given time in their cockpits. The audio could include just their radio calls or include their own personal comments inside the cockpit. The playback gave Emile the creeps every time she sat in one of the debriefs. It was as if the simulator instructors could look inside her mind and see exactly what she was thinking and why.

Sitting behind the large desk in the debrief room was a cute, freckled, red-haired female in a perfectly fitted flight suit. Major epaulets dotted her shoulders indicating she out-ranked Sean and all of his crew except Tiny. Rank never mattered in a flight or simulator debrief. It was all about how they flew. This was true for the most part until the players were colonels or above; then things got a little more diplomatic.

Sean sat opposite the SEFE. Her fiery red hair was wrapped in a tight bun behind her head.

She glanced up from her notes and saw his boyish eyes staring at her chest. Her grin revealed none of the simmering contempt she felt.

Why is it the first thing guys do when they meet a woman is look at her rack or her ass? They know it's offensive and yet they do it like some Neanderthal reflex.

Sean noticed she was appreciating his attention, so he flashed her a cocky, "I have been here before" look that left the rest of his flight members a little more confident but still wondering what might happen with this check ride. It was not unheard of to bust when hit by an enemy missile.

Major Tambra "Tally" Jenkins knew the history with Sean's flight accident. She knew he was still getting over the loss of a squadron mate. The rest of the simulator evaluation was flawless; a rare feat in and of itself, even more so after having the wind kicked out of you by a missile impacting your jet. Tambra flew in the other F-15E squadron at Lakenheath, the 494th Fighter Squadron, known as the mighty Black Panthers.

Tally was known around base as a tough as nails, no nonsense evaluator. She did not usually give check rides to the 492nd Fighter Squadron but this was an exception since their SEFE was sick. Thus Sean and his flight got the dreaded "Tally" profile. They knew her and her tactics. Sean was surprisingly well prepared.

She debated the merits of giving Sean a downgrade but decided against it. His flying was good and his tactics were superb. His flight leadership still seemed a little shaky. But that, she reflected, might still be the result of losing his wingman in Libya a few months ago.

Tally started off their debrief with the announcement that they had passed. For all his cock and bull bravado, Sean had not known for sure he would pass until this moment. Of course, he never let anyone see that. The key to being a fighter pilot was to act as if you knew everything. Especially when you didn't. Tambra saw Sean's young WSO begin to breathe again. The young blond filled out her flight suit a little more than Tambra would have liked as a supervisor. She was not plump, maybe just big-boned. Definitely not skinny like Tambra.

Beautiful face. Take a deep breath, Emile. That's right, breathe for me.

The girl was borderline hyperventilating now that the results were announced and she realized they had passed.

Was I ever that young?

She must have some Scandinavian in her, thought Tambra. Fair-skinned, high cheekbones, pouty lips and bedroom eyes.

Tally knew much about Emile but had only met her a few times socially at the club. This was her first real chance to observe her up close. The formal evaluation setting was putting Emile on edge. Tally enjoyed the power play.

Emile hid those blue eyes with her large smile. Her lips pursed into a smile at almost every occasion. Rumor had it she never seemed mad at anyone, except perhaps, sometimes, herself. This was one of those times. Emile must know her lack of a directive call might have caused them to be hit by the SAM. She sat passively, quietly rubbing her hands absent-mindedly. Another thing Tambra noticed when she looked at the girl sitting beside Sean was that Emile had small hands.

Tambra smiled briefly when she caught some black pen writing on the back of Emile's left hand. It said MPF. Military Personnel Flight, a reminder that Emile had to do something with the shoe clerks in administration soon. Small diamond stud earrings glittered from Emile's ear lobes.

"Nice earrings Emile. Would you wear them in the aircraft on a combat mission?" asked a perplexed Tambra.

"No" stammered Emile. "On a combat mission I would be sanitized. No name tag or any indications of rank, squadron or status that might give away any information to the enemy should I be captured."

"Then why are you wearing a name tag and earrings? Why fly with them in the simulator if you would not fly with them in the jet?"

Tambra hated the idea of doing things in the simulator you would not do in an airplane. Another reason she knew Emile would not fly with earrings was if you ejected there was a chance they could get caught on something while leaving the aircraft.

Sean stepped in to offer Emile some help. He knew she did not like confrontation. Although he would have given up a month's paycheck to see Emile let her blond hair down from the bun currently keeping it at bay and get into a cat fight with Tambra. *Mental picture. Save for another time*, thought Sean, before diving into his role of defender of the meek.

"Maybe it's because we had to do this simulator on a holiday due to all the budget cuts to our flying hours and increased sim hours." He had a small point. The latest budget crisis in Congress sent huge reductions to the military. The funding cuts hit flying hours hard. The reduced hours did save gas, wear and tear on the airframes, and the tree huggers loved it for saving the environment. However, the reduction in funds led to a lower proficiency level for the aircrews. The reduction in flights led to an increase in simulator hours in order to try and maintain some proficiency.

Tambra quickly took back her debrief authority.

"That's a new one, Rider. Blaming Congress because your WSO forgot to sanitize before a combat mission? Notice Bambi is the only one who failed to do so." Sean knew Tambra's smirk enraged Emile. He saw it in her face and neck as the small muscles there twitched. That and the fact Tambra used Emile's call sign, which she loathed, all added up to an uncomfortable tension in the small windowless room.

Tambra's debrief was quick and to the point. The end result: no downgrades; Emile should have been directive then descriptive in her SAM communications, but all passed with flying colors. After the debriefing, Tambra asked Captain Walters to stay behind. The other crew hastily left, glad to be done with a check ride given by the infamous "Tally." Emile lingered and made eye contact with Sean, her big, blue puppy dog eyes asking him if he wanted her to stay for moral support. His smile and wink told her all she needed. He was a big boy and could handle himself. Disappointed, she gathered her flight pubs bag and walked out of the room, intentionally leaving the door open. No reason to leave Sean and Tambra in a closed room like caged tigers.

Sean turned and nudged the door with his flight boot, dislodging the door jam while slyly asking, "So Tally, what's up?"

As he turned back to face her he heard the zipper on her flight suit slowly rattling down and her sexy voice saying, "You know you owe me. Lock the door."

***

Brad Jackson was late for his security shift. He was not going to make it in today.

She sat astride his torso. Slowly she inched her way forward dragging her small perky breasts across his chest. His breathing was slow. Grace listened to Heart singing "Heartless" in her ear bud at low volume. How poetic. He was in the blissful sleep zone, when the endorphins of sex had worn off and the fatigue of physical contact began to announce completion. He nodded with closed eyes, smiling as both her strong long legs, bent at the knee, pinned his arms. His eyes remained closed. They had done this ritual before. It was her way of relaxing him even more after sex. She began to stroke his hair with one hand while leaning into him and whispering how great their lovemaking had been.

Had he seen the look in her eyes he would have known she was lying. A subtle tingling in her face and neck illustrated her deception.

Slowly her other hand reached for the knife hidden in the folds of the sheets. Brad, although ignorant in many ways, was not dumb. His eyes opened just as her left hand clamped over his mouth. He tried to use his arms to deflect her attack but they were pinned to his sides. The right hand blurred across his face, slashing his neck with a ferocity that surprised even Grace. He gasped and emitted a muffled scream as blood spurted from the wound. The last thing he saw was his own crimson fluid staining the front of her sexy peekaboo panties.

Grace enjoyed the act of killing Brad. He was a louse.

Murder. Such an ugly word. Assassination sounded much cleaner. More thoughtful. There are three reasons to commit murder: love, money, or to cover a crime. This was definitely not money or love.

Grace cleaned up quickly. Blood washes up easier when you really want someone dead. Brad's clothes, lying in a heap on the floor where they fell soon after they entered the hotel room, would go to another terrorist waiting nearby. Brad would not be coming into work but someone else would be wearing his security uniform. Hopefully that would be all they needed to get an advantage. His ID card and password would be the entry for the rest of her team. Assuming his identity would make all the difference.

***

Her other accomplice on the inside was Ahmed, who joined the maintenance staff at the target directly. He had moved to Vancouver five years ago, so he was a local. She had to admit the AQNA had long-term plans in play. Ahmed was a great mole. He had working knowledge - both electrical and videotape - of the security systems.

Their attack would be on the Rogers Arena, known as the Canadian Hockey Place during the Olympic Games when sponsorship was not allowed. The arena hosted both the men's and women's hockey events. This week was the qualifiers for the World Championships. Twelve teams, including the US, French, Canadian and Finnish, were playing.

The normal security staff at Rogers Arena consisted of nine guards who were inside at all times. On game nights, the staff would triple and those personnel would be professionals. Game nights meant a civilian crowd of thousands. The concessionaires called the security team for game nights the "A team." The best. That, of course, meant the other guards (the ones for practice days) were the defacto B team and not as professional. It was sad but true. The B team was mainly ex-police officers or wannabes not able to stay in the force for one reason or another. The fact was most had some police training but those skills had slipped considerably over the years. Janus, with Grace's guidance, chose to attack on a Wednesday morning, a non-game day.

On non-game days, the armed security team would have four two-man teams: one roving team, a team at each entrance, and a front entrance supervisor. Grace and her crew would face nine guards of decidedly less ability.

***

The attack began later that morning. The call was too quick for Almetta, today's supervisor, to question him further. Brad called and told the receptionist to "tell Almetta I'm running late and will be there in forty-five minutes."

Brad lay motionless on a bed in the cheap hotel seven miles from work, pools of blood soaking into the thin sheets. Yasir played the tape recording just as Grace instructed. Created from videos she had taken of Brad during their liaisons, some from homemade sex videos she had goaded him into. Others were from their walks in secluded places or time spent in the bedroom just "hanging out." She manipulated him into saying every word she needed.

To say Almetta was overweight was like saying Moby Dick was a small whale. Almetta liked Brad. He had charmed her 5 foot 4 inch Alabama body for everything he could. Thus, she did not call in another worker but instead kept the now reduced team on the left side door. This would prove to be her undoing.

Brad's partner for this particular shift was Jennifer Rodriguez. Jen, as her friends called her, was just finishing buttoning her white blouse when Grace entered the female locker room. The room, if it could be called that, was really a glorified broom closet. There were only three female guards (one of whom was Almetta, the supervisor, who had her own office with a bathroom).

"Oh, I am sorry. I have a message from Almetta for Mrs. Rodriguez," stammered a doe-like Grace. She chewed a small piece of gum and smacked it to the obvious annoyance of Jennifer. Jen could smell the cinnamon on her breath

Grace always chewed something cinnamon before acting. It increased her alertness. Sometimes it was gum. Other times she used a cinnamon stick. Still other times a quill or bark of raw cinnamon worked for her.

"That's Miss Rodriguez," announced a now-impatient Jen as she tucked the blouse into her black pants. Looking down to make sure her gig line was straight; she looked back up into the barrel of a silencer attached to a Browning 9 MM. Her eyes narrowed, then went wide when she noticed Grace's grip on the weapon and the lightness with which her finger rested on the trigger.

"Keep quiet and you might live through this" Grace commanded.

Debate stretched across Jen's face.

"You have the look of someone about to make a life altering...make that a life-ending decision. I wouldn't if I were you. I have no problem killing you because if you do scream I'll put a bullet in that pretty little face of yours." Grace pasted on an innocent smile. The smile sent shivers down Jennifer's back. "I'd rather not but...."

Grace whistled sharply twice. Jafer immediately entered carrying a sports bag.

"Now if you would be so kind dear, I need your uniform." Grace waved the gun casually up and down Jennifer's body.

Stuck between disbelief, numbness and fear, Jennifer did not move.

"NOW!" screamed Grace.

With trembling hands, Jennifer unbuttoned the first two buttons of her tight blouse.

"You'll never get away with this," she mumbled feebly as her hands popped open the last five buttons, her shame at exposing herself to strangers gone with the realization trouble was at hand. She pulled the blouse off her shoulders revealing a boring grey bra.

Grace wanted Jafer to see this American woman strip before them. She was the B Team's best and seeing this would help build his confidence. Grace commanded Jennifer to turn around and place her hands behind her back. Grace removed Jennifer's shirt and then cuffed her while Jafer balled up a pair of her panties and stuffed them into Jen's mouth, covering her luscious lips with blue duct tape from the sports bag he brought in.

A gleam appeared in Jafer's eyes as Grace told him to take off Jenifer's pants. He walked up to the proud Puerto Rican, staring into her green eyes, before fumbling for her belt. As Grace held her cuffed hands, Jafer undid Jen's belt and tucked both hands into her pant sides unceremoniously jerking her uniform down to expose a pair of lacy black thong panties. Grace pondered the interesting combo of bra and panties momentarily then refocused.

"On your knees!" Jafer exclaimed, catching both women off guard. This one is going to be a little Hitler if I don't watch him, thought Grace as she prodded Jennifer onto her knees in front of Jafer. Grace looked him in the eye and effectively communicated two things with her glare: one, she was in charge and, two; they just did not have time for this right now.

She slipped off Jen's boots and pants. Jafer bound Jen's ankles with zip ties and then lifted and led her hopping to the bathroom.

Grace quickly slipped out of her own janitorial uniform and shimmied into Jen's guard uniform. Not quite a perfect fit but it would do.

Grace heard a low cry of anguish and turned, but Jafer quickly stopped her from peaking into the bathroom by exiting and closing the door. Her glimpse revealed Jen bent at the waist, hands cuffed around the toilet's base, on her knees. Her black hair, once pinned up in a pony tail, had escaped its restraint and spilled down the right side of her bare back. Her panties were down around her knees now, and her ass shined a bright red from the two or three obvious spanks Jafer had delivered during his quick change into Brad's uniform. Pulling out his gun, Jafer turned to go back in the bathroom but Grace cut him off quickly with a command in Arabic. She used what Ahmed meant in Arabic as the precursor to her command.

"Highly praised one, come here NOW! Don't waste a bullet on her. Save them for the guards who will be shooting back at you in a few minutes!" Jafer reluctantly did as told.

Jafer is a dog. Sometimes he needs treating as such.

Grace watched him suspiciously as he passed.

Side door left, camera three, began to act up again about five minutes after Grace entered the female locker room. This particular camera covered the alley outside of the left entry door. Ahmed just happened to be on duty and took the call to investigate the malfunctioning camera. He knocked twice on the female security guard's locker room. The door opened instantly and Grace emerged dressed in a security uniform and behind her walked Jafer in Brad's uniform.

The three of them slowly strolled toward the left side entrance turning onto a main hallway connecting the areas. Grace paced the hallway with her hands folded behind her back. Hockey players, both male and female, roamed the halls occasionally. None took any notice of the trio pacing the tiles.

Grace listened to her ear bud as she strolled down the corridor. Her device relayed transmissions from the police frequency she monitored. The Bluetooth-capable device was hard to see, easy to control and very expensive. Voice-activated and programmed for her voice and words (currently programmed for Korean commands), it never left her unless she showered or slept. When not needed to listen in on the authorities Grace used the custom-made instrument as a phone and music player. Grace loved music. All kinds of music. Life was like a grand music video to her.

As they walked, Grace confirmed with Ahmed in a whisper, "Camera three is on a loop, yes?"

"All good," he replied.

"Excellent."

This meant the security team at the main entrance was seeing taped footage of the buildings left side entrance-not live coverage.

Grace nervously scanned the corridor as they approached the critical juncture leading to the entrance. She did not want to go near the main entrance if she could help it.

"Prepare weapons," she instructed, pulling her own personal Browning 1911 from the back of her waistband and slipping off the safety. The sidearm Jennifer was to wear still hung on Grace's waist, as did Brad's firearm. Jafer had a Berretta.

Ahmed had a knife in his work boots and a garrote in his toolbox. He would get the two closer to the team on the left entrance door. Their surprise was complete. Within seconds, both male guards lay dead in the nearby closet. The coast was clear. Grace signaled for the white van and bus down the street to approach the entry door. Quickly four other terrorists jumped out and entered the building, three male and one female. Gathering up her team of seven, they moved on to carry out their plan.

Their plan involved Grace, Jafer and Ahmed securing the buildings left entrance thus allowing the rest of the team to enter the building unopposed. Grace kept Ahmed and the female with her. Jafer and three others moved to create a diversion at the main entrance.

The key was speed and efficiency. There was no way they could kidnap many hockey players from the ice since they all wore ice skates and it would a logistical nightmare to round them up. Instead, Grace and her group went directly to the conference rooms. Here the teams met between practices to go over plays and tactics. Grace found the room she wanted. French Men's Hockey Team - Room C. She burst in with gun in hand firing several rounds into the ceiling. The heated discussion in progress quickly died down. Ten men, eight players and two coaches, sat dumbfounded.

"What the fuck is going on," yelled one large man close to the front, in a thick French accent. Grace took one look at him and knew he would be trouble; his face registered utter shock as she cold-cocked him with her pistol. So fast were her actions that by the time he hit the floor, knocked out, the rest of the team just looked at each other with no time to react.

"Listen carefully and everyone lives," she yelled to get their attention. "You all are now the hostages of Al Qaeda North Africa. Long live the revolution. Obey us or we start shooting instead of hitting." She pointed at the loudmouth unconscious on the floor. Blood trickled from a cut on his head.

Glancing at the hostages she spotted a familiar face.

Success!

Grace's ear bud scanned the police channels. One anxious call to the Vancouver police department got her attention. Things were starting to heat up. The security team from the right entry door came to reinforce the main entrance and caught Jafer and his team in a crossfire. They were in trouble and falling back.

"Now move!" They all quickly stood. Many hunched over, attempting to make their large frames small. It was a sign of submission. Grace found it comical seeing large, burly men bend over like old women.

A block away Janus observed from a tall building with a clear view of the hockey arena front. He confirmed via her Bluetooth ear bud the approach of several police cars. As expected the two local police cars responding went to the main entrance and could not cover both side doors.

"LEO is at the front door." His commentary, short and to the point, amused her.

She taught him to use LEO, which stood for Law Enforcement Officer, lingo Grace picked up when she worked part time in Cambridge, England, during her first and second years in college. To earn some money for food and such, she did a little escorting on the side. She was a high-class escort with an American accent and a college girl form. She was popular and expensive, independent and wild.

Looking back it seemed so easy to get going. A friend asked her to join up for a threesome. After some initial trepidation Grace found out it was "just" for money. It would not be the first time she used her body and sex as a tool. Nor did it prove to be the last. She volunteered and enjoyed the experience. Later she started as an "Independent," advertising on just one premier website and accepting only emails from potential suitors. She had a few regulars but they were monthly events. Ultimately, it led to her dismissal. But because of who was involved, it did not make it onto her official records. She was able to transfer to the University of Virginia and finish her studies. She was a long way, now, from Mr. Jefferson's University.

She goaded the French hostages out of the room, into the hall and towards the exit. Gunfire erupted from the front entrance. Soft sporadic pistol shots and then louder, more frequent, automatic fire. Two of her accomplices ran around the corner, out of breath.

"Grace, they overwhelmed us. Muhamed and Yasir are holding them off but they say we must go now."

Grace shook her head in disgust. As parts of Janus' plan began to fall apart, she felt her epinephrine hormone kick in. Some called it adrenaline. Her body quivered at the neurotransmitter release. It kicked in her body's fight-or-flight response of the sympathetic nervous system. She knew her body well enough after 29 years. She went into fight mode, not flight. Not yet.

"Must I do everything?" she grumbled as she began to move towards the front.

"Take these men to the bus. I will join you soon. If I am not there in five minutes, leave to the rendezvous, understand?"

They all nodded, but Ahmed reached out his hand to stop her as the others moved toward the exit.

"Is it wise to rush to the front? You lead very well from behind and we must have a leader." Ahmed knew Janus was the figurehead but Grace had proven over the past few months to be the tactical master of their cell. Her plans and suggestions were the only things that allowed them to make it as far as they had today.

"You speak the truth." Grace swept the corridor behind them for the inevitable pursuit. "No. Go. I must do what I can to pull this goat fuck off." And with that she took off in the opposite direction, toward the main entrance and a firefight.

The French hostages were cooperative. Especially after Ahmed shot one in the leg to make his point that they needed to hurry. They left the injured man behind sobbing uncontrollably. By now their path was clear; no one dared poke their heads into the hall after hearing the gun shots.

As Ahmed herded the hostages onto a waiting bus, Jafer left the group to search the nearby offices. Two terrified secretaries huddled together in the nearest room under a large conference table. Jafer's footsteps echoed on the hallway floor as he approached their hiding place. Weeks later these ladies would relive nightmares involving the haunting sound of Jafer's footsteps as he came closer.

Betty was having problems breathing. The stress of the ordeal was putting a tremendous strain on her fifty-year-old body. Just bending down to get under the inadequate table concealment was complex. She made it thanks to the help of Gemma, her twenty-something co-worker.

Betty could not take it much longer. Gemma begged her to be quiet, but the woman's sobs began to leak out like a sand castle fighting the rising tide. Jafer heard the soft moans and peaked underneath the table. He did not say anything at first. He just waived the loaded gun in their direction and motioned them to stand up. They did so reluctantly, but froze when he told them to come to him. This made him angry. When he became angry, he mixed his languages. Balling his free hand into a fist he yelled at them in rapid-fire broken English.

"Come to me now or I will blow your heads off."

Moments later Grace and Yasir returned, rounding the last corner to find Jafer in the doorway and screaming into an adjacent office. Betty and Gemma both screamed from the office as Jafer entered. A quick look out the side entrance showed the bus running, loaded with the French hostages and Bashir at the wheel. The white van held the female terrorist Fatima and Ahmed. Ahmed was supposed to be on the bus, but Grace had no time to sort out the gaffe.

Grace covered her and Yasir's escape route with a quick check to make sure the authorities had not organized yet; she crouched and peaked into the office where the screams were coming from. One of the secretaries, Gemma, thinking Grace, in her uniform, was a rescuer, looked at Grace with expectant eyes. Jafer, thinking it was a real security guard, turned and shot waist high. Two shots zipped above Grace.

"It's me you idiot," she screamed. "Cease fire!"

Jafer obeyed sheepishly, but quickly recovered by sweeping his hand at the sobbing secretaries. "Look, more hostages."

Grace frowned at him with a look of disgust and exhaustion.

"Jafer, we do not have time for this."

"Nonsense, Allah has granted us ample time to secure many infidels."

"OK, you win. Get them to the van. I will check the last office."

"Ladies, move or else," A heavily accented Jafer roughly pushed Gemma, the closest, out the door and into the entrance hallway. Grace circled behind the hysterical women and cautiously checked the other office. Grace ignored the two distinct sobs coming from under the far desks and came up behind Jafer as he crossed the door threshold.

As Jafer entered the hallway, several different sounding shots rang out. Jafer spun and fell to the ground, a look of shock on his face. Gemma and Betty scurried to the side, crouching as best they could. Grace turned and fired rapidly down the hallway, ducking and weaving and pulling Jafer out of the building.

Taking aim, she fired two more quick bursts with her Browning and knelt down to check Jafer for a pulse. Her shaking head spoke volumes. She ignored the secretaries huddled off to the side of the hallway and rushed out the side entrance. A quick glance into the bus confirmed the hostages were in place.

Grace leapt into the waiting van and both vehicles roared off. Grabbing the walkie-talkie from Fatima, Grace contacted the trailing bus.

"Bashir is everything alright?" she asked.

Bashir scanned the arena from the back of the receding bus. He reported no police cars chasing. They had escaped with no pursuit so far. Just as if he jinxed himself, a single squad car appeared, rushing away from the front of the building, another following seconds later.

"Plan B," Grace groused.

"But Grace, we do not have a plan B," said Fatima as she drove the streets of Vancouver rapidly.

"There is always a plan B."

Grace nervously inspected Ahmed in the rear seat. His attention was on the road ahead.

"Ahmed do something …return fire or something," demanded Grace. "Shoot the tires out." Even as she said this she knew it was a very "Hollywood" thing to say. She could shoot the tires if given enough bullets and a stable platform but then again she was an assassin with marksman skills. Ahmed was an electrician.

The bus was not as agile as the mini van and it began to slip further and further behind.

Grace always had a plan B. She just rarely briefed others on it.

Grace explained, "Plan B is explosives and they will throw them out soon."

Sure enough the explosions came, but not when expected. As the bus approached a bridge, it suddenly exploded in a ball of bright orange flame. Pieces of the bus interior flew off in every direction, stopping cars in both lanes near the burning hulk as it slowed to a stop. Plan B stopped the pursuit as seven hostages and two terrorists died in a fiery blaze.

Chapter 5

The Canadian men's hockey team defeated the U.S. in the finals 3-2 in overtime. The French men's team did not compete. The fiery explosion effectively decoyed the police chasing Grace's little white van. She had Fatima turn and twist their way deeper into the Vancouver suburbs and finally into an industrial estate. There they torched the vehicle in an abandoned warehouse. Then the three terrorists split up to make their way back home.

Grace preferred to strike out on foot. She knew some back hidden routes around the area and after an hour arrived at the chosen spot to rejoin Janus. He waited impatiently for her with arms crossed and clenched fists.

"What the hell happened?" he hissed as soon as she swung into the passenger seat, venom dripping from every syllable.

Grace looked Janus straight in the eye and turned her head in that little look that implied 'I know better than you' and said, "Jafer and Bashir happened, that's what. Get us out of here and I will explain on the way."

Janus put the car, a used Toyota Camry he bought earlier that day, into gear and sped east.

"Your," she emphasized the pronoun, "explosives expert got his wires crossed and instead of creating a diversion with an explosion from the back of the bus...." she paused and shuddered ever so slightly.

Janus finished her sentence for her. "The bus exploded and was the diversion."

"Ayoha." Allowing her anger at Janus to take over, Grace answered "yes" in Arabic through clenched teeth. She hated when he finished her sentences. It happened more and more lately, the longer they were together as a couple.

Their escape plan took them to Toronto. It was a long cross-country drive, mainly on back roads. This gave Grace some time to contemplate their relationship.

They met in Afghanistan and then traveled to Libya for the liberation there.

She knew people who knew Janus. He was easy to meet. He liked western women and in Mazar-i-Sharif there were not many.

The trick came not in getting involved with him personally-that was easy. The time consuming part was getting into his organization. But she played her small part in Afghanistan and eventually her help gained his trust. She was accepted and her role grew even bigger when they escaped to Libya.

There they worked as a team-sort of. He was still in charge and she still stayed in the shadows for her own good reasons, but they interacted more as a unit then as a commander and foot soldier. In Libya his love for her became more pronounced and open as opposed to the hidden lust they shared in Afghanistan.

Grace wanted to stay in the Middle East but Janus wanted a bigger role in AQNA and thus he accepted the current mission without talking to her. She resented that and it showed in many aspects of their new life in North America. Janus would live to regret that decision sooner rather than later.

***

Sean looked out at the perfect torrents of rain pelting the bay window of Ralph's three-bedroom house on Lakenheath Air Base.

Typical English weather for February. About every 30 seconds another wave of rain, pushed by the punishing North wind, would slam into the window.

It was amazing, Sean thought, how the weather forecasters change their semantics every day to communicate the same thing. Partly cloudy with a chance of rain. Sometimes sunny with partial clouds. Other times cloudy with periods of sun. Occasionally it comes out as rain with equal periods of sun. None of these word conundrums described the weather tonight. Tonight it was wet, wet and wet.

Sean walked back to the poker table via the kitchen for a snack. He found a few boneless chicken wings and potato chips with French onion dip, his favorite dip in the world. He was constantly amazed at Ralph's house. Here was a married, forty-something, high school principal on a U.S. Air Force base living in a four-bedroom "McMansion." The USAF always tried to match family need with their housing allocations. The highest-ranking officers got the biggest houses due to their rank. RHIP as the saying went: rank has its privileges. However, a school principal getting this huge place, that was different.

"Ralph, remind me again why you rank such a large house with your practically single lonely body?" Sean teased. Ralph's wife traveled extensively for her job and was never at home; they had no kids.

"I have pictures of the general's daughter," replied the witty African-American.

"Wait a minute, he doesn't have a daughter," yelled someone listening in on the conversation. Six of his other compadres were in the midst of a break from cards, some relieving their beer filled bladders while others did a delicate dance around the food counter. The two still at the table – the biggest losers of the night so far – unconsciously counted their chips and reviewed past mistakes.

Eight people made up the poker group. Sean formed it when he arrived at Lakenheath 18 months ago. It consisted of Sean's flight crews: Sean and Emile; and Mark and his pilot John, since they flew together they also partied/socialized together. The other four members were outside their immediate circle. Ralph, the high school principal at Lakenheath, James, one of the maintenance officers who lived near Sean and two other aviators, Brad and Sammy. Of the eight invited, only six or seven usually came on any given night. They tried to play once a month and rotated who hosted, but with deployments and the holidays they ended up playing about eight or nine times a year.

The house rules were always the same no matter who hosted the poker night. Dealer calls the game. Dealer antes for everyone-this is so no one has to argue about who or who did not ante for the game; it was entirely the dealer's responsibility to make sure the pot was right at all times. Three raise limit per card. The stakes are small. It is nickel ante poker with max quarter raises until the last card when the raise can go up to a half dollar.

Sean liked the stakes. Nobody could lose more than $20 in one night. The buy-in was $5 and then eventually someone would start to lose and have to buy-in for another $5. Everyone at the table then gave him grief for "slapping a little leather," i.e. opening up his wallet to get the $5 bill out. That was far worse than losing the money. The humiliation of having to admit you lost your initial stake was bad. Doing it twice was embarrassing. Doing it a third time meant your mind was elsewhere.

The games, as decided by the dealer, were usually seven-card stud, five card draw, Texas Hold'em or Omaha. Five-card stud went out of style 30 years ago when Bill Boyd dominated the game but once a night someone called that too, in honor of Bill.

Minutes later everyone rejoined the game.

Sean sat across from Emile. She wore a bright orange Jimmy Buffet T-shirt proclaiming a change in attitude. Tight jeans and black ankle boots completed her outfit for the night. Not that Sean was looking or anything. She was more like a sister to him.

Mark called Texas Hold'em as his game. I hate this game thought Sean. Mark dealt two cards facedown to each player. Sean held an ace of diamonds and a queen of hearts. A strong start, not as good as a pair, but still high cards.

Emile and Ralph both bet blind-before they could see their cards, as is the custom in hold'em poker

He glanced across the table at Emile.

Her pile of chips was considerable. She played poker pretty well…for a girl. She noticed Sean's attention and smiled back at him revealing a single dimple on each side of her face. They were only visible when she flashed a big wide happy smile. Her dark John Lennon glasses obscured her blue eyes. What was she thinking?

She bet 10. Ralph 15.

Her blond hair looked a little darker as it flowed beside each ear trapped a bit by the glasses. Totally into the game, Emile paused long enough to blow him a kiss with just her lips.

"Hey Sean, while we're young." came from the player to Sean's left, their maintenance officer friend James.

The fake kiss shook Sean out of his trance; the words shocked him to attention. How long had he been staring at her?

"Call," and he put in a red and white chip. They always played with poker chips instead of actual money. Sean insisted. Chips made it easy to count who made or lost money at the night's end. Plus, at such low stakes, it gave the game more of a professional feel. White chips were a nickel and red chips a dime.

Everyone else called.

"Pot's right," determined Mark and then he dealt the flop. The ace of spades, five of hearts and ten of diamonds.

"Did I mention the ice queen cometh?" announced Mark.

"You mean Tally?" asked Sammy from the far end of the table. "She's coming to play tonight?"

Sean kept quiet to see what happened with Mark's little news flash.

"No, but word is she is transferring to the Bolars next week. I'm going to be her assigned WSO since John is leaving next month."

Emile glanced at Sean to see his reaction. There was none; he kept his eyes down on his cards. His wayfarer sunglasses rested on top of his head. He pulled them on for "special" hands. Dressed in a faded black biker jacket and tight ripped blue jeans, Sean was the picture of comfort. He even had a bit of a five o'clock shadow going. Emile guessed he shaved early on Friday morning. Probably before leaving his girlfriend's house and had not shaved since. Now by Saturday night he was starting to look like the wolf man.

She knew it was Sean's way of rebelling against the Air Force. He hated the short hair rule and no beard. Even though he did look damn good with his short cropped hair just touching his ears and the thin longish mustache. Still he pushed the limits during the week and let it all grow out on weekends. The squadron wives rumor mill – the strongest intelligence source on base – said Sean was in a relationship with an enlisted girl. The signals were not so good on where she worked. Most put bets on a tough, attractive maintenance girl; still others thought it might be one of the female security police. Emile knew it was the girl in the command post, but "Rider" swore her to secrecy.

Now Emile drifted off in her thoughts. Only love could hurt so bad. She felt something for Sean. So far she convinced herself it was just a motherly instinct. Lately she was not so sure. Why would she want to become mixed up with Sean? He was handsome, but most "bad boys" were, weren't they? Sean's problem, she thought, was that he loved all women. He loved enlisted girls who were supposed to be off-limits due to fraternization rules. He loved married women, or so he told her. Perhaps he just loved women who were unavailable.

"Why is Tally coming to the 492nd? Why can't she just stay in the Panthers?" Emile asked with a hint of jealousy in her voice as she scanned her cards again. Jack of clubs and nine of spades. Three card straight with two cards to go. Not looking too good.

"She needs to get out of there and fast." Now it was Sammy speaking up. Sammy flew in the Panthers with Tambra. He knew more but, Emile knew he would not divulge it, no matter how hard they pressed.

Brent, Sammy and James folded after the "turn" when Mark revealed one more face up communal card.

Mark looked at his cards after dealing the queen of hearts. His two clubs, a nine and five, did not look as strong after the flop and turn. He knew his pair of fives was not going to win the hand. He needed another five "in the river" and was not willing to pay to see it.

Emile surveyed the remaining players. Ralph was to her left. Nervous when it came to cards, but strong when it came to his job as principal. One of the squadron wives told Emile all about Ralph. He handled the parents well. Most seemed to genuinely like him. The students, well most, thought he was fair. Some hated his guts and some adored him. That was always the case though.

Ralph played poker in his "lucky" Boston Red Sox cap. Although a regular on the Sean poker circuit, he missed quite a few games due to his school duties. Sean organized a poker gathering every month and the host rotated. Since Ralph volunteered to host this month, the game was at his house and he provided the food and beer.

This marked the second time Ralph hosted. Both times, he went over the top in his food and beverage selections. Tonight, the steamed shrimp and crab legs were a big hit. He seems to be over-compensating for something, thought Emile. Maybe he's a little nervous around aviators since most of Sean's crew were F-15 flyers. Chasing that thought away was Ralph's drumming fingers, his "tell." Emile made a note to drop out if she did not hit on her straight next card.

Emile's eye drifted back to Sean.

He may have been a smooth talking ladies man extraordinaire, but when he was around all of the alpha males of his group, he was more reserved. Confident, just not cocky.

Emile knew he had been raised in Charlottesville, Virginia, a true southern gentleman with his "Yes ma'am" and "No ma'am" and "Sweet tea please." But after growing up in the Piedmont region of Virginia he had escaped, or so he thought at the time, to Colorado for enrollment in the USAF Academy.

Emile met hundreds of Academy grads over her short career and they all fell into two categories. The first were the straight-laced, by-the-book geeks who had no social skills whatsoever. They thrived in the structured learning environment of the USAF Academy in Colorado Springs. Unfortunately, they rose the fastest in the ranks due to their endless brown-nosing of field grade officers. These were the USAF "Neidermeyers." They worked hard but that was it. There was nothing else in their boring lives.

The second group were the hell-bent, whiskey-drinking, party animals who enjoyed the academy for what it was: a ticket to an Air Force commission as an officer – often with wings attached to it. They refused to stop living and took every chance to enjoy life to the fullest and socialize. Quick to start a party and usually the last to leave, they took life one day at a time and lived each day as if it was their last. Sean, bless his heart, came from this last group.

He had a shit-eating grin on his face. Emile knew the look. He had either two pairs – probably aces or queens or either fives or tens. The board did not lend itself to a flush since there were only two same suit cards showing. In this case, the best a player could have was four hearts, two from his hand and the two hearts showing. How the betting went would tell much.

Finally, Mark checked on her right side to start the bidding. From his beady eyes, lanky frame, perpetual smile and boyish good looks, everything about Mark screamed friend, not boyfriend. They had spent a week in France for a squadron ski trip at Christmas. Sean backed out at the last second and left Emile committed. She had only signed up because Sean was so enthusiastic to go. He blamed it on sickness, but Emile, who watched him closely, saw no signs of it.

Anyway, Mark and Emile spent much of the trip skiing together and partying afterwards with the squadron. Mark's fluent French impressed Emile. They got their meals quicker, jumped ski lift lines easier and had a great week of snow, booze and mountains. Nothing magical happened. If anything, she thought Mark might have a bit of a drinking problem. Tonight just confirmed it, as he was already four bottles into Ralph's Old Speckled Hen case.

Mark checked, so he was no threat.

"I'll bet," said Emile. She swirled a few chips around and plunked down a red and a white. "Fifteen."

Ralph raised her 25. Sean called and Mark folded like the cheap paper plate he was using to hold his chicken wings.

Emile knew Ralph was her opponent in this hand - he either had two strong pair, three of a kind or a straight. She called as well, betting on making her straight. Mark rolled over an eight of diamonds to make Emile's straight (8-9-10-J-Q). A very strong hand. A quick check confirmed no one could have a flush. Likewise, four of a kind and a full house were out of the question. A straight was the best hand possible and only two other straights were better than hers.

Emile opened the betting on the last card with 20. She did not want to scare away any money.

Ralph looked at Emile and frowned.

What the heck does she have? She is not betting too much. Maybe she has two pair. Then again this is Emile. She's good at cards.

She was of Scandinavian descent, of that he was positive. Blond hair that seems effortless but always straight, never curly. Wide, thick, red lipsticked lips that beg to be kissed but hold back once too often for his taste. Most noticed the dimples, but Ralph settled on the nose. A little larger than the rest of the features on her small, beautiful face. She was quick to smile and forgive, but laughed with a snort on occasion that made you do a double take. She was plump for an aviator. No, that's not fair, he thought. A big-boned, Scandinavian trick of the light because she dressed in layers often and early in the colder months. At 5 foot 6 she was slightly shorter than everyone but Brent, who was her height and a little defensive about it.

Ralph did not know Emile very well. In fact, his only impressions of her came from the card games or occasionally at the officers club. He found her intimidating because of her excellent card skills. On breaks in talks with the other guys they all said she was a sweetheart. Reminded them of their sisters. Had a heart of gold.

Ralph noticed something early on when playing with Emile. Most other players at the table waited for good cards, and then tried to make the most money from those great hands. Emile did that and more. She loved to take poor hands and manipulate them into a share of the pot for herself. Whether that involved out-maneuvering her opponents, shaming them into staying or bluffing them into folding, Emile didn't seem to care. She loved winning; it was her vice. She raised when she should fold and called when she should raise.

"Your twenty and I raise thirty. That makes it an even fifty for you Sean. Or a candy bar if it makes you feel better to put the betting in perspective," egged on Ralph.

Sean looked at Ralph and smiled sarcastically, then turned back to Emile. Neither player was giving anything away.

Ralph was cold, his face a mask. Emile smiled and fiddled with her poker chips. She was up to something. Sean had two pairs, aces and queens, but something didn't feel right. He was being set up.

"I'll call. Here's your Snickers bar Ralph," he said as he put two shiny, rarely used blue chips into the pot, happy to see their cards for just 50 cents.

Now it was just up to Emile to call. She had them right where she wanted. Ralph's 30 raise left her the opening she needed and all the information about her opponents. Ralph should have raised the roof so he only had two pair or maybe three of a kind. Sean was just hanging on like a dead man walking. Two pairs at the most.

"Your thirty, Ralphie, and fifty more *boys*." She said the last with a cowboy accent. She was hot tonight.

Ralph hated to be called Ralphie. They all knew it and she was doing it intentionally to goad him. He was beginning to hate Emile.

"I'm in," he said and threw in two blues, stabbing the table with his finger. Emile abruptly turned to face him as his chips hit the table, anger briefly flaring on her face. She heard him mumble the B word just under his breath. She started to raise her finger at Ralph, shaking it like a club, but thought better of it. Sean did not react; maybe it was just the Comrade Bill stout beer she was drinking.

"It's just a candy bar Ralphhhhhhh," Sean taunted without the "ie."

"In or out Rider?" asked Ralph impatiently.

"In…. All in!" shouted Sean, smugly pushing in the last few chips he had. It was win or slap leather.

Mark declared the pot was right. Since the boys called Emile, she showed first.

"Straight to the queen boys. Read'em and weep." She flipped over her two down cards casually.

Sean moaned. "Makes my two pair look mighty small." Now he remembered why he hated hold'em. It was all about the flop. You could be sitting pretty but then lose it all simply because of the communal cards. Hold'em is more trickery and cunning, more bluff and betting.

Winning at hold'em depended less on the cards and more on the skill, character and courage of the bettor. In small stakes games like this, it was truly hard to bluff anyone out unless you played some kind of all in stakes where if you lost you could not play anymore. This was a friendly game and because of that the limitations prevented true hold'em strategy.

I hate wild cards and communal games. Why can't we just play seven stud every hand?

"Son of a bitch," said Ralph, slamming his hand down hard on the mahogany table. His three tens were no match for a straight.

Unfortunately, Sean had to ask the banker, Ralph, for another $5 in chips. In the lull that ensued to count out Sean his new stake, Mark posed a question to the group.

"Guys," he said, darting his eyes to Emile, "and gal. Anyone have a problem with me asking Tally to one of our little card soirees?"

He continued quickly, "I mean if I am paired up with her, it might be fun to play a little with her." Sean glanced nervously at Mark. Mark finished by adding, "So to speak."

"Now you want her playing cards with us?" asked Emile, still raking in the large pot. "She has a husband, in case you don't remember. The JAG on base. You want to invite the top prosecutor and his wife to play illegal cards with us?" she asked incredulously.

"Who said anything about her husband? Besides I hear they don't get along too well," said Mark. "Anyway she loves to play poker. I heard she played at the Academy. Did you know her at the Zoo, Rider?"

"Nope. We never met. She's a few years older though. I think I was a first year and she was finishing up. I heard about her." A smile creased Sean's lips for a split second. "But my lips are sealed." He mimicked locking his lips shut with a key.

"You know what my momma always used to say: If you can't keep a secret...." He paused to let the others finish one of his favorite sayings. In unison they all shouted, "Come sit next to me!"

Laughter broke out, relieving some of the tension. After a short time, they agreed that *if* Tambra became crewed with Mark and *if* she knew it was an invite just for her and not her stuck up JAG husband, then she could come play one night as a sub and as a try out.

Toronto, Canada

Grace stumbled upon Janus' extracurricular activities by accident. Her neighbor, Mrs. Simpson, just happened to make a passing comment about the absence of anyone at home to let in their cat last Tuesday.

Grace loved cats. Everywhere she spent any amount of time she had a cat. Usually a trip to the animal shelter found a suitable feline that just needed some love. Grace loved cats because they made her more outgoing somehow. She also suspected they made people live longer. Grace had no illusions her cats would prolong her life, however. She envisioned a short life span and she was going to enjoy it for as long as it lasted. She took one day at a time and lived every day as if she only had six months to live. Death seduced Grace but had yet to win her over.

Perhaps her lack of family led to her passion for cats. Parents dead. Brother dead. She missed her family, although they were often in her thoughts. Well, her mother and brother were in the good thoughts. Her dad was the stuff of nightmares. The place you put people who abuse you.

But it was just Grace against the world now.

She queried her neighbor about the cat. Grace worked every Tuesday night from 6pm-2am. Mrs. Simpson admitted gleefully, since she had a secret to share, that Grace's boyfriend always left every other Tuesday from 8 pm till 11 pm. He always returned with a smile on his face, before Grace made it back home from work.

Grace acted as if she just remembered where he went and convinced Mrs. Simpson it was nothing to worry about. She also promised to take better care of Commodore, their cat. After Mrs. Simpson left, Grace's mind went into overdrive. Where was Janus going? Who was he seeing? Why was she not involved in any of this? She had a sneaking suspicion she knew why, but needed time to prove it.

Lakenheath, England

After the poker game split up around 11pm, Ralph asked James to stay for a bit. Ralph had James sit. He could tell the young man was nervous.

"James, after our last talk I spoke with a friend and he gave me this to give to you." Ralph, gravely serious now, passed him a brown envelope. James' eyes began to tear as he opened the envelope. Inside was a lifeline: Five thousand dollars in hundred dollar bills.

"But I…I mean…."

Ralph shut him up with a quick wave of his hand.

"We both know you have a gambling problem. Remember, I am your friend. I'm the one who found out about your big problem and here is the fix for it. All your debts to that betting establishment can be paid off with this money."

Betting in England was legal. Several betting shops were on every high street in most decent sized towns. They took bets on almost anything and had odds from the big casinos in the States for sports like baseball and American football. James was in deep to some bad characters, not the shops themselves, but it was a minor point. He was a gambler and needed to get the "family" off his back once and for all.

"But how can I pay you back? It will take a while."

"Don't worry about it right now. I have a friend who is writing a book on the maintenance side of things. He likes to have insider knowledge of how things work. He may ask for some little details about things in the maintenance world. I told him you could give him insight." Ralph smiled and leaned back confidently.

"Nothing classified though. I can't give away classified details," protested James.

"No, nothing like that," insisted Ralph. Had James known where to look he would have seen a subtle blush creeping into Ralph's face and neck.

***

Brent had other plans for after the poker game. He had
arranged to meet a "friend" who lived and worked in Mildenhall,
and ten minutes after he drove off base his car rolled into the sleepy
village.

Her screen name was "Peaches." Definitely not her real name,
thought Brent. She and another girl operated out of a rented flat on
the outskirts of town. They alternated days or, more precisely,
evening and nights. The best part about the older apartment was
the location between Mildenhall and Lakenheath Air Base.

This was his first time. A friend at the squadron casually slipped
hints that he visited once a month "for a good time." Brent called
from a pay phone off base to arrange the meeting. Dragons did
summersaults in his stomach. His palms felt wetter than when he
walked in the typical English mists. Parking away from the
apartment so as not to attract any attention, as if a lone male
walking around at this late hour would be normal under any
circumstances, the aviator approached the boudoir and reached to
ring the doorbell. As he pushed the buzzer he saw the curtain
flicker by the living room window and then the front door opened a
crack. Peering inside, Brent saw nothing but darkness and a slim leg
curving around the doorframe.

"Hi, Tommy," a sultry voice welcomed him. Of course, he
hadn't used his real name.

"Hi," he responded timidly as he snuck into her lair.

His hour ended up being just 35 minutes, but he was very
happy when he left the two-bed room flat. Peaches counted the
money he left for her skills in communication and massage. Of the
200 pounds, twenty went to the maid who cleaned up, twenty went
towards the rent and utilities and eighty went in Peach's pocket.
The remaining eighty British pounds went to her protector, who in
turn paid half of that to his boss. Most of that money eventually
found its way back to Grace and AQNA.

Not only are terrorist groups involved in the drug trade and
human trafficking but also in extortion and prostitution. AQNA
even made some of its money through charitable giving. In some
cases, their Birmingham members posed as bogus charity workers
using familiar charity cups asking for donations to various relief

organizations. Some of that money did make it to the charities. Most did not.

Toronto, Canada

The next Tuesday Grace drove toward work at her usual time, but doubled back and watched the apartment from a stakeout position hidden down the street. Arranging for her co-worker to swap shifts was easy. Grace feigned going to night school and asked if the friend would take a few shifts every other Tuesday. Eager for more work and money, the younger woman readily accepted, even agreeing to let Grace use her car for the four hours she was at class.

Janus left as Mrs. Simpson described, right at 8 pm, and drove to a very seedy part of Vancouver. Grace followed him stealthily. He did not seem too concerned about anyone tracking him. He entered an apartment complex and went to a lower floor apartment.

Grace locked her friend's car and moved beside the window of the apartment Janus entered. The curtain obscuring the window was hung up on the ledge and allowed Grace a small view of the inside. She peeked in and from Grace's vantage point she could see everything. Sure enough about two hours later he emerged and returned to their home. When Grace arrived back, ostensibly "from work," Janus mentioned nothing about his nocturnal pursuits.

Grace did the same thing two weeks later. Again Janus ventured away from their apartment and visited someone whom she knew nothing about.

Chapter 6

CIA Offices, Seattle, Washington

Hope stood behind a lectern waiting for the rest of the law enforcement invitees to straggle in. She adjusted the sleeves of her white blouse, pulling them out further from her black blazer. In a statement towards an anti-establishment look, Hope wore a blouse with an open collar instead of her normal button down look. Her black skirt rested just above the knee, also non-agency; but she was away from the East Coast and wanted to show off a little. It highlighted her mile long legs.

She wanted to keep the attendees involved in this discussion. Hope thought speeches should be like skirts…they needed to be long enough to cover important stuff but short enough to keep everyone interested.

Her assistant nodded everyone was present and, clearing her throat once, Hope began.

"Ladies and gentlemen, welcome to the Central Intelligence Agency assessment of Northwestern US. and Canadian threats." With that, she dimmed the lights and marched through her presentation.

"As you all know the Rogers Arena in Vancouver Canada was attacked a month ago. Seven French hostages as well as four security men were killed. Four terrorists from the AQNA were also killed.

We believe the group, an Al Qaeda offshoot in Yemen, is still operating in this area. Apparently our drone strikes have been causing some damage to the group. Our intelligence indicates the group in Yemen split up, either through attrition due to our attack missions or due to a philosophical difference. In any event, about thirty known members, several high-ranking, migrated to North Africa through Sudan, Tanzania and Kenya. From here, operatives tell us they have joined forces with other Al Qaeda cells to form Al Qaeda in North Africa."

"Don't you mean Al Qaeda in the Islamic Maghreb?" came the first question from a high-ranking official within the FBI office.

Hope shook her head sympathetically. "Not really. The Maghreb group does work with the AQNA, but only when it suits them. The AQIM attack Algerian forces and want to create an Islamic state. AQNA encompasses AQIM and Al Qaeda in Libya, Mali and Sudan. If you recall, the Mali war that the French recently fought was against Al Qaeda commanders. These Arabic-speaking leaders had their own bodyguards and ate different foods. Basically, AQNA led the Mali locals in their war. The same thing is happening in Algeria, Libya, Nigeria and other countries in Africa."

Hope smiled, when she did her eyes seemed to narrow, but radiate just as much energy. The look, and she used it often, gave her the appearance of staring directly at everyone in the room.

"Bear with me as I fill you in on some history of the group that we think is on the West Coast now. There is Al Qaeda central and then regional identities of Al Qaeda. The regional groups are linked with senior Al Qaeda leaders, but regional group offshoots usually are not hardcore Al Qaeda members. This is the situation in North Africa. AQNA has close ties to Al Qaeda central. AQIM does not."

"What other events have the AQNA organized?"

"The Benghazi attack on the U.S. diplomatic post which killed four including the Ambassador, the taking of the Algerian gas facility Ain Amenas which killed 43 hostages, the Mali war. They are involved with the trafficking of narcotics to Europe from Latin America through the coup-ravaged West African country of Guinea Bissau." Hope reeled off ten more attacks before saying, "We are classifying AQNA as third generation Al Qaeda and they could be the deadliest version yet."

She paused to let her words sink in to the audience. She had their attention.

"Many countries in the region are too poor to supply funds and (or) troops to regional peace forces, even towards commitments they have previously agreed to. Additional cracks in these peace initiatives occur from political disagreements between the states within the region. Morocco and Algeria fight over the Western Sahara as we speak. Finally, the geography of North Africa affords great protection to groups trying to hide from spying eyes.

"Frankly, we have given up on eradicating them there for the time being and are concentrating our assets on stopping their imported terrorism." Hope clicked the next slide in her PowerPoint presentation and showed a picture of Janus.

"This is the cell leader believed to be operating in the Northwest. Our intelligence hits are in Seattle but he could be anywhere along the seaboard. His name is Abdul-Nur Ramni, also known as Janus and he has direct ties to Cleric Mikaeel. Janus rarely gets his hands dirty. He is the moneyman and the brains, but not the muscle."

The picture of Janus showed him in a blue oxford shirt and black cargo pants leaving a nightclub. His look was intense. Janus stood at medium height, well toned yet not a weightlifter by any means. He looked like a rich, bright, spoiled Arab who often went to the tanning booth.

Hope stopped briefly to allow the room to fixate on Janus then she clicked to a black slide with details but no photograph.

"He has a second in command known by the name of Azrael. That means Angel of Death in Arabic. She is his muscle and enforcer. We do not have any photographs of her. What we do know is she is in her late twenties, about five foot seven or eight, athletic and thin. She has a dark complexion and dark black hair. She is a trained assassin, skilled in the art of garrote, knives and poisons. She shoots pretty darn well too."

One of the men in the room made a testosterone-filled joke along the lines of "sounds like my kind of gal" which Hope ignored as she pressed on.

"We estimate the cell consists of eight to ten people. Mainly men who either were here or came in over the border from Canada." This bristled the egos of the Canadians in attendance and Hope quickly smoothed their feathers. "By the way, the most current intelligence we have about Janus comes via the Canadian Security Intelligence Service, who briefly intercepted a possible cell member in Montreal before he...." Hope scanned the room quickly to see if anyone was going to need debriefing later because of their clearance level, but she knew everyone present and their need to know authority. "Expired due to heart failure."

Her mind flashed back to that day two weeks prior. Hope sat at a rectangular desk facing an Arab man who sat not facing her but at a ninety-degree angle. Across his chest ran two black cords with swirly wires. Around his left arm a blood pressure-like cuff rested.

Both hands rested palm down on black mats specifically designed for the chair. Electrodes ran from all of these pressure points to a device on the back of the chair. From here it sent information to Hope via secure Wi-Fi. She sat with a laptop open in front of her providing the lie detector data. Her subject, Tarif, could not see any computer screens. Hope walked him through a series of questions about his name, address and nationality. He answered these naturally and without hesitation. He was a willing witness at this point and not a martyr for the cause. Tarif, which meant "rare" in Arabic, provided transport for the terrorist members. His pay for the job was substantial. This was how the CSIS identified Tarif and his activities.

"That last briefing point has not been released to the general public," Hope continued. The last thing Hope wanted was to antagonize her counterparts in the CSIS. They had enough trouble from the Canadian media who, at one extreme claimed the CSIS were too aggressive in their tactics (Hope thanked her God every night the Canucks were aggressive), and at the other criticized them as "sloppy." The CSIS could not win and did not need any more bad press coming from their neighbors.

Hope finished her briefing 10 minutes later with a warning.

"They have money but not an infinite source; they have weapons but again not an infinite pool. They are dangerous and elusive but not perfect. Please report any possible leads to either me or my supervisor at Langley. Thank you for your time."

Toronto, Canada

Two weeks after discovering Janus and his strange bi-monthly visits, Grace knocked on the door of the first house. A tall, blonde woman, who looked to be about 21, if that, met her. Loud music blared from her stereo in the apartment. Florence and the Machine's "Kiss with a Fist" reverberated off the far wall. The music had not leaked outside with the door closed; Grace admired her insulation. She had a tube top on and a loose-fitting brown skirt. She did not invite Grace in but instead wanted to know who she was and why she was knocking on her door at 8:30 at night.

Grace flashed a quick police badge she kept for just such occasions. Flash an official looking badge and take the upper hand by putting the other person on the defensive.

The young woman stammered and denied Grace entrance to her home claiming she needed a warrant. Which Grace did need if she wanted to search this woman's apartment under the guise of a policewoman. Instead, Grace backed off. The woman had done nothing wrong, she said. Although Grace suspected she was breaking several vice laws with this apartment. No, she told the now-frightened woman, the police were looking for a man. She showed her a picture of Janus; the woman said she saw lots of men before realizing that was incriminating.

Grace gave her a disarming smile that said "it's okay, just us girls chatting here."

"Now that you mention it," said the girl, eyeing Grace. "I do remember him from about a month ago." The girl seemed to be debating whether to say more, and Grace smiled again.

"He was here for two hours," she continued finally. "No tip. Liked his woman submissive. Very creepy."

"Sounds like our man." Grace shuddered. It was all true. "Have you seen him before or since last month's meeting?"

"No, he gave me the impression I would not see him ever again. You know the type." The girl was speaking freely now. "Promise the world so you will go a little extra on the blowjob and the in/out then as soon as he gets off he cannot stand to hang around. Only this one did hang around, but only to humil me. You know what I mean?"

Puzzled, Grace frowned and replied honestly, "No, I am afraid I don't."

The young girl leaned casually against the outside corridor wall, relaxing more, her long legs exposed by the slit in her skirt.

"Well he stayed but not for round two, instead he wanted me on my knees and then he just kind of shouted dirty names at me for the remaining time. Things like 'dirty whore' and 'filthy slut.' But he did pay upfront and…" she giggled, "he came early so we had lots of down time."

"Now that I know about," Grace admitted. The working girl would never know it but the "policewoman" she was talking to knew Janus' problems all too well. The woman asked Grace one final surprising question.

"I am thinking about getting a gun. You know, for self-protection. A girl needs to take care of herself. Any recommendations? My boyfriend might get me one for my birthday."

Grace definitely had some opinions on that subject and she was more than happy to share them with the girl. What was the best handgun for a woman? That was a tough question these days. Unfortunately, gifts from men fell into two equally bad camps in these situations. Grace saw this happen all too often. The first camp bought guns that were "lite" i.e. supposedly easy to handle and with less recoil. Unfortunately, these weapons would not get the job done when a 250-pound drug crazed rapist was attacking and thus were not the right weapons to possess. The other scenario involved husbands "handing down their old guns" to their wives. In these cases, the guns were inferior for various reasons and were being replaced by the man and "gifted" to the wife with the rationalization she would not be using them except in emergencies anyway. This meant the women did not practice with the guns and thus were deprived of experience with their protection.

The men who were buying the women a gun should ask the same questions they themselves ask before purchasing a gun. Whoever the shooter is (man or woman) what is the largest caliber that can be handled well? In Grace's professional opinion, something larger than a .38 Special was good. However, equally important was what platform the shooter could best operate under stress and correct for malfunctions, i.e. a great gun that worked perfectly at range may not be the best if it malfunctioned routinely or was inaccurate when fired in a less than perfect environment. Grip size was a factor as well. Small hands often required small grips and vice versa. Yet another determinant is the situation in which the shooter might use the gun. Home protection does not require a small concealable gun. In that case, larger sized guns would be appropriate. However, in the case of a weapon you wanted concealed, that situation limited realistic options. And if you do want to conceal the pistol, how will you carry it? That will determine the best choice too.

Often if the caliber and gun type are such that the recoil is painful then the shooter will not practice with the gun. Usually so-called "lite" guns were called Ladies guns (like the Smith and Wesson Airlite) and had less weight to absorb some of the recoil, ultimately making the gun harder to handle. Grace advised unskilled shooters (anyone who was skilled should select their own gun and not ask for someone else to do it) to buy something they felt comfortable practicing with on the firing range. If they are with someone, such as a partner, try and make sure the partner is comfortable with the weapon too because they may end up using it as well.

Grace preferred a full-sized, custom Browning 1911 with thin grips. Hers cost over $5,000 a piece from a Swiss manufacturer. She had three made. The high capacity magazine gave her a 9+1 capability (thus nine bullets in the magazine and one in the chamber). The semi automatic weapon provided an excellent concealed weapon to carry with a slim width and easy to draw feel. Utah even named the 1911 as its official firearm. That had more to do with John Browning's relationship to the state more than anything but it always amused Grace. Best of all the 1911 accurately places .45 ACP cartridges at desired targets. It costs a lot and does not have as much finesse as other guns but to Grace it worked and worked well in tight spots. Light weight and functional were buzzwords Grace used to describe the 1911. Thin and flat, it simply was her take everywhere, do anything, weapon. She hated the loud report and the muzzle rise but both things were old hat to her now. Practice, practice, practice and a muzzle suppressor helped. Of course a silencer did not really silence the gun's noise; it just muffled it a bit. Unlike what Hollywood always showed in the movies.

***

Grace knew all about computers and the computer she shared with Janus, in particular. Grace and Janus used their computer together to "Catfish." They were Internet scammers who fabricated online identities and entire social circles to trick people out of passwords, money, information, etc. Most people "catfished" to get people into romantic relationships. Often it was older men trying to get younger girls. Grace thought it was a dreadful practice, especially when played on innocent children who had problems at home and just wanted someone to be their friend. Janus and Grace did it to form a network of unsuspecting accomplices.

Grace went home and used the extra time attempting to break into Janus' computer account by finding his password. He changed his password every two weeks and she had to break the code each time. She was unsuccessful that night but tried again a few days later. This time she got in.

She also went to another "prostitute" Janus visited and went through the same question and answer session with her. Same modus operandi. He was two-timing her when she was supposedly at work.

She made a note to stop having sex with him since she found out he was not using a condom with these new friends. The key was to prevent it but not so he noticed. Even sex with a condom was not 100% safe sex, but at least a properly worn condom reduced the chance Janus caught an STD from one of these "girls." He was risking infecting Grace.

From observing Janus when he received instructions from his superiors within the Al Qaeda North Africa organization, Grace knew how he communicated.

Janus and his superior both had access to the same Gmail account. Janus' superior would leave an email message in the account draft folder. He would not send it. Janus then logged on to the account the next day and looked at the draft and then created his own draft as a reply. Then he deleted the first draft from his boss. Sent emails could be analyzed or intercepted or traced. Draft emails sat in the account. Unless you knew the account and the password you could not get to them. Snooping government eyes would never see the draft email messages.

Grace had the password. It was his sister's name and birthday backwards. Now that she had it she had access to the draft messages. This gave her access to Janus's communications.

Chapter 7

Charlottesville, Virginia (Seven years earlier)

Hope and Grace were sorority sisters in Chi Omega at UVA. Hope met Grace's brother, Tim Matiseni at the University of Virginia. He was a fourth-year student like Hope, but his major was Religious Studies. Although an unlikely couple, one thing led to another and in April he invited her to Foxfield, a horse race event that involved much drinking and partying.

Tim took Hope to his fraternity's tent.

Three weeks later, much to the chagrin of Grace, Tim and Hope were dating.

Hope spoke with Grace about it privately before the couple announced it to the sorority. Grace swore she was okay with it and gave her blessing to them. Hope and Tim dated for the rest of the semester and into the summer months. Although they became closer during the summer while living in Charlottesville, things became trickier as the summer came to an end. Hope had a job lined up with the CIA and was just waiting for her chosen start date to arrive. The CIA recruited her while she was in her third year at Virginia. Such a move was not unheard of but was highly unusual. Her double major in International Law and Arabic Studies put her in the top 1% of her graduating class. The fact that she could speak and write Farsi did not hurt her cause either.

Tim originally thought about the priesthood. His strong Catholic upbringing on his mother's side influenced him, but four years of partying at Virginia changed that avocation. He wanted to do good works but not limit himself to the seminary and all it entailed. Grace helped to talk him out of his seminary plans too, and the time with Hope sealed his fate. Hope showed him he could have a fulfilling religious life while still having a very active social life.

However, in the end, Tim and Hope talked and both agreed a long-distance relationship was not going to happen. Hope was determined to serve her country, probably as a field agent in the Middle East. Tim wanted to help others and perhaps do missionary work but not necessarily in that part of the world. They stayed together until Hope left in early August.

Tim went to work for a major charity for several years where he met his wife, Val, after which he turned to missionary work.

March Toronto, Canada (Present Day)

Grace clicked open Janus' email account to see the latest from his superior called Jeddah, after the Saudi Arabian city on the Red Sea. Arabic filled the screen.

Grace, who was fluent in Arabic, Korean, Chinese, Spanish, French and Danish, had no problems reading it. Spanish she learned from her mother and Danish came when she was living in Copenhagen as a child. Arabic and Korean were mastered in college as part of her Middle Eastern/Foreign Studies degree. That college education, on occasion, really paid off. The latest Draft message said:

Janus
Peace be with you
O sends regards. Five acceptable losses. North America too hot. Regroup to European targets. Contact TBD.
Jeddah
Punishment

The last word seemed out of place. It made no sense. Grace then opened Janus' last reply by going into the temporary files of his word processor program. It took a bit of time but she eventually got there. He too had an out-of-place word to end the email.

Grace copied both messages to a memory stick. Later that week, after observing Janus when he went into the email account, she noticed he referenced his old faded Koran.

Janus was pious when he needed to be, either in front of troops/martyrs or with his superiors. However, in the Western countries he did as the Romans do. Drinking their whiskey, eating their pork and more importantly to Grace, fucking their whores.

The next message from Jeddah was ominous.

Janus
Allah is great. Azrael is becoming a liability.
American intelligence sources suspect her aid.
Advise your next move. Begin preparations for
move to Europe.
Jeddah
Transgressors

Grace now pieced together that the last word was a code word they used to confirm each other's identity each time they posted a message in the draft section of the email account.

Afghanistan mountain region (Two years earlier)

Grace sat with the Bedouin tribe. She wore a long black hijab with bright orange trim. Of course she also had on the headscarf, which covered her face. She liked this aspect of Islamic culture since it helped her get around without being noticed. As a Westerner hiding her sexuality, identity and skin color this outfit provided perfect concealment.

Her visits to Tim and Val were always unannounced. She came from Mazur i Shariff in the north, but could not reveal that to anyone. Arriving involved a helicopter, rickshaw, motorcycle and sometimes a lift on a NATO Humvee.

Tim was her rock. He stabilized her. When Grace was younger she overheard her father talking with her mother and he said Grace was slightly bipolar. She looked it up. Characterized by extreme mood swings. She brought it up to Tim but her older brother just gave her a big hug and told her she was who she was and she was special all the same. She always remembered their talk and how it helped her press on.

She liked Val too. They both got along remarkably well. Val was a kind, caring woman and she loved Tim deeply. Grace saw it in her eyes.

Today the tribe was celebrating a wedding. That night all families gathered by a grand bonfire. Grace's brother Tim and his wife Val sat across the fire from her. Their missionary work offered many traveling opportunities to different parts of the world. Grace cajoled Tim into coming to this rural part of Afghanistan once she learned of her own assignment here. They did not acknowledge their kinship. Grace insisted on that. Instead, they claimed to be alumni from the University of Virginia, which was true. It just so happened that Tim was two years older than Grace. That made her time at UVA both harder and easier.

The tribe lived in and near the Ajar valley in north central Afghanistan. Deh-e-Mianeh, Balch Creek and Kohe Ala were all tribal herding areas in the Ajar valley located in Bamyan province. They lived near the Ajar Valley National Park, originally a nature reserve for the Afghan royal family who had used the area for hunting, especially the ibex. It became a national park in 1981 but the recent fighting had deteriorated most government support and services. Poaching was a problem, particularly the ibex or wild goats. The tribe used the goats for hair, meat and milk along with their skins to create water and wine bottles.

The tribe members used oil and kerosene in homemade candles. Tonight someone mentioned a fuel tanker had broken down a short distance from the celebration site. The families had rushed to the site to take some gasoline. It was the Bedouin way to take advantage of life's unexpected gifts. Hundreds of the tribe's people swarmed the stalled truck. What they did not know was that a rival tribe had sabotaged the truck. Sand placed in the fuel tank forced the truck to fall out of the convoy on a nearby highway. Several hours passed and the ANA guards assigned to the truck had long since gone home.

Villagers cued in an orderly line siphoning gas from the side spout. A little here, a little there. Many did not have gas cans as such, but instead brought coffee cans or water pouches too old to use for drinking water and now served other functions. Tim and Val did not participate but did go with the villagers to the tanker. They warned them repeatedly not to "take the American gas" but their cries of concern were not heeded.

Grace watched the drama unfold from a safe distance not wishing to be seen with large groups of people. She visited Tim and Val when she could but did not involve herself with village or valley politics. She had her own secretive reason for living in Afghanistan, one she did not share with Tim.

High above them, unheard because they were orbiting 20 miles away at 30,000 feet, flew two F-15E Strike Eagles. Their orders were to destroy a damaged oil tanker and kill as many Taliban raiding it as possible. Intel had been tipped off that the Taliban disabled the vehicle and was now using it to equip their warriors for a Molotov cocktail raid against an Afghan village sympathetic to the government.

In actuality the "tip" came from the rival village that had seen the Dehquangala village rise in power in the 12 months since Tim and Val's arrival. The couple brought in fresh ideas for agriculture and sanitation. They arranged for U.S. military vets to vaccinate the village herds and provide classes and education for the children. That meant more visitors, more gifts and more prestige. The rival village of Sare Sahr had lost some of their prestige and the tribal elder knew how to seek revenge. He gave his Afghan army friend the tip.

The tanker was stopped outside Dans La Vallee d'Ajar.

Strike 01 and 02 checked in with their controller shortly after takeoff.

"Wolfhound, Strike 01 checking in as fragged Bullseye 090/135."

"Strike 01, Wolfhound has you loud and clear. Call when ready for tasking."

The lead WSO made sure his pencil was ready and 9-line paper ready to fill in.

"Strike 01 ready to copy."

"Strike 01 1, 2 and 3 NA. 5894. Destroy disabled fuel truck. N 35-36.222 E 067-37.278"

The controller continued "expected threat small arms and AAA, no friendlies in the area, no run in restrictions. TOT ASAP."
The WSO read back the important details and then proceeded to come up with their plan of attack. The Ajar valley ran east and west but the main road ended in the western valley section, so they planned their attack axis from the west over the least populated area.

The term "Destroy" meant the crew had to make sure no collateral damage would occur from the attack. In other words, responsibility rested on the crew for not killing innocents on the ground.

Strike 01 acquired the tanker in his sniper pod and noted the mass of shapes crawling over the tanker.

"Wolfhound, Strike 01, confirm no friendlies in the target area. I have upwards of fifty contacts in or on the target."

"Strike 01, Wolfhound is unable to ID squirters at this time."

"What do you think Rider?"

Sean thought about the situation long and hard. The tanker was easy to find but all of the bodies around it made the hairs on the back of his neck rise up. Something was not right. He had a ton of combat time under his belt, much of it here and in Iraq, and this did not seem like your normal milk run.

"I say I am not hitting the pickle button and dropping a ton of iron on people who are a) not shooting at anyone and b) who do not seem to be hurting anyone. Let's turn back the tasking and go find something we can do."

"Wolfhound Strike 01 is unable to drop on this target due to ROE considerations."

"Wolfhound copies Strike."

Wolfhound sent a message informing the mission tasker of a large mass of unidentified bodies near the target and requested verification. Hope received the message. She had ordered the original mission. Now she called her source again.

"Khaleel, I have reports of a large group of people near the tanker. Are you still observing it? Are you sure they are Taliban?"

Khaleel spoke quickly in hushed tones. "Yes, ma'am. I am about a hundred yards away and…," he paused, "they are all Taliban. Of that I am sure. I can see them all even though I am hidden in some rocks. It is very dangerous for me here. When will the bombs come?"

"You are positive Khaleel. They are enemy Taliban."

"Yes, of course Taliban. Many of them. You must strike them a blow now!"

"Ok. Bombs should be there in…" She checked her computer screen. There was another flight scheduled to check in with Wolfhound in 5 minutes. "Ten minutes. Get to safer ground now."

Hope again tasked the crippled tanker for destruction, not knowing her information was deadly wrong.

Khaleel did not end the call. Another man who listened to the call with headphones did so. Khaleel was not watching the melee below him at the tanker. Instead, he was frantically trying to figure out how to escape the clutches of his fellow tribesmen. The tribal leader knew Khaleel was working with the American CIA and used it tonight to feed them information that suited his purposes. Khaleel, to his credit, refused to go along with the plan, but when his entire family was threatened with death by stoning, his resolve wilted.

Suddenly, two villagers grabbed his arms while the chief placed a cloth over his mouth. Khaleel struggled valiantly but it was no use, the chloroform overwhelmed him. He was knocked out in less than 10 seconds.

The opposing chieftain spoke: "Quickly, take him close to the tanker and leave him under a blanket. I want him eliminated. I do not want any witnesses who can put us with this terrible NATO massacre."

They supported and carried Khaleel as best they could. The chloroform started to wear off so they dragged him closer to the tanker. Finally they put him down and covered him with a blanket in some trees before discreetly knocking him out one last time. Then they left the tanker periphery and ran as fast and as far as they could. Meanwhile the opposing chieftain watched with satisfaction from a safe ridge outcropping above.

Grace felt uneasy about the situation at the tanker. Something was not right but she could not put her finger on it. The festive wedding party was all around her and the people sang and danced while they waited, only adding to the surreal picture.

The far off sound of jets tipped her sensors into overdrive.

"We need to leave here now," Grace shouted. "Get your people. Let's go!"

"We only have about twenty more people waiting to get some fuel from this old truck. Just one more minute."

Grace slipped away from the tanker fuel frenzy to make some phone calls. She needed to find out what the heck was going on. She stepped behind a large rock to shield her from the music coming from pipes and drums carried by the revelers.

The French Mirage 2000D fighter jets checked in and received the exact same tasking as Strike. No mention was made of the two hundred people milling and cueing around the target. The French aviators did the same pre-attack tasks. Both WSOs used their high resolution targeting pods to find the crippled fuel tanker.

Few Taliban were in the area and none at the tanker. The target run for the French fighter jets was uneventful. Both WSOs saw the people at the tanker but the young WSO in the lead aircraft failed to prevent the release. Maison 51 flight dropped two 500 pound laser guided bombs into the fuel truck.

Both bombs released and instantly saw the different laser beams, one from each aircraft, targeting the center of the tanker. In the cockpit, the counter showing time until impact slowly ticked down. With just 10 seconds to impact, the older, more experienced WSO noticed all of the smaller figures in his targeting pod.

Grace heard the bombs whine as they accelerated into the target area. She stood up and screamed, "Everyone run! Get away!"

No one could hear her above the din of the party. She was too far away to warn even Tim and Val. The last thing she remembered seeing was Tim waving back to her laughing.

Inside the Mirage 2000D, the older WSO saw their mistake immediately. "Shit! Those are kids down there and families!"

Thinking quickly, the aviator slowly moved his laser spot off the tanker and away from the crowds. His bomb impacted in the woods north of the tanker and, while doing some damage, did much less than it could have. Unfortunately for Khaleel, the woods were where he slept. He perished instantly.

The younger aviator, however, kept his laser spot steady on the tanker. He did adjust his spot ever so slightly away from the tanker center. The result was spectacular as his bomb impacted the tanker, exploding its contents in a fiery envelope of heat and pain.

Everyone at the tanker and within fifty feet evaporated in the fireball that spread outward and upward. Those who did not perish instantly sustained terrible burns. Tim and Val were sitting on a rock 37 feet from the tanker. Of the 127 in the area, 53 died instantly, 18 died within a week of their third-degree burns and eventually another seven would expire. Only 49 survived. Val and Tim were not among them.

Grace witnessed the bombing but ducked instinctively when the first errant bomb hit in the woods. The second bomb hit the tanker a split second later. The rock had saved her life. A second later and she would have died too.

Lifting her body from the protected rock shelter, a smell struck her instantly upon reaching the man-made clearing. Pyres of burnt flesh and rising wisps of smoke marked the locations of families, sweethearts and little ones. Fires raged out of control. The truck was a mass of twisted, mangled metal larger than the human debris but no less crumpled.

Grace swore vengeance on whoever had done it, good or bad.

Later, a little digging revealed the jets were French and the team assigned to provide security for the region at the time was the 48th Security Police based out of Lakenheath Air Base. Grace never told anyone she was present that night. She buried what was left of Tim and Val and moved back to the north. She was never mentioned in the after-action report NATO did when it investigated the massacre.

Grace dreamt always of that fateful night. The nightmare haunted. It did not help that she carried a constant reminder of Tim's death: a small scar above the left elbow where her exposed arm extended past the rock protection. The burns were terrible. The scar was a visible reminder to finish her revenge.

Tim's loss was the lowest depression she ever felt. She missed him desperately like the desert misses the soft, wet petals of rain.

Toronto, Canada (Present Day)

A week after finding Janus' message from Jeddah Grace began to use computers in other buildings she cleaned to log onto Janus' account while she worked. She needed the information every day now since the messages were coming quicker and to a resolution. She tried to time it to when there was football on the ESPN cable channel. Not American football, of course, but what the Americans called soccer. Janus loved the game and was a Newcastle fan from his days there. This way she knew he would not be on his account as he would be absorbed in the game.

When she saw Janus' reply to Jeddah she was stunned. She doubled up her efforts to crack the code Janus and Jeddah used to verify each other.

Jeddah
God is great
Plans are underway to eliminate the problem known as Grace. I move to Europe in April. Will contact you about possible summer targets later.
Janus
remember

Grace had determined the words ending each email came from the Koran version Janus had. It was his codebook. They skipped ahead 11 pages every time and started with the bottom right word on that page and then moved one sentence up each time while jumping 11 pages as well. If Grace was right, the next word would be "manna." She waited and watched. The next draft email would be from Jeddah in the next few days. Could she wait? Was her life in danger now? Janus was acting strangely.

Chapter 8

CIA Headquarters, Langley Virginia

Hope anxiously drove the two hours from Langley to her home in Ruckersville, Virginia. The speed limit on U.S. Route 29 was 65. Hope set her cruise control at 70 and passed more cars than most on the road. It was mindless driving; Hope weaved in and out of the slower traffic and reflected on her role in Grace Matiseni's mission.

The meeting with her supervisor did not go well. Hope reviewed the questions and her answers

"What exactly is Operation Barbarossa?"

"Barbarossa is the process where we, the CIA, attempt to place an undercover agent in a terrorist cell with the objective of taking cell control or advancing to upper management within the organization. The ultimate objective is to gain control of the cell's targets in order to better suit U.S. interests."

Hope continued when her boss did not interrupt. "If a cell can be manipulated to do the work of the U.S. in a clandestine manner, so much the better. For example, if the cell will assassinate a key leader who the U.S. also wants eliminated, then their purpose is similar. It is based loosely on the principle that my enemy's enemy is my friend. If the cell cannot be 'tricked, coerced or manipulated' into an act of terror that works for the U.S. in some way, then the cell can be intercepted by intelligence provided by information from the mole within it."

"And how does Grace Matiseni fit into all of this?"

"Simple. Grace is our double agent in the Al Qaeda North Africa cell. I placed her in a position to gain the confidence of certain known members of that cell. She did with flying colors and now is the second in command. Their leader is a man named Abdul-Nur Ramni, code-named Janus by his superiors. Janus is responsible for the July seventh 2007 London bombings and the Madrid bombings. Of course, those were before Grace joined. Recently they are responsible for the Vancouver attack on the French men's hockey team."

"And how are eleven dead and a major terrorist attack on Canadian soil a positive for the U.S. or the CIA?"

Hope composed herself and battled back from his accusing tone. "Imagine how much worse it could have been, had it not been for Grace. Have you read the report on Vancouver? Our estimates are that she single-handedly saved the U.S. and Canadian teams. I shudder to think what might have been if we did not have her imbedded with Janus. Even Grace cannot be everywhere all the time. She admits things spiraled out of control in Canada but she thinks it will be worth it if she can stop an even bigger event."

Hope held something back from the director. Grace claimed the bus bomb was an accident, but Hope knew Grace better than that. Grace never trusted others. She did everything herself.

"What about her history?" It was not a question but more of a statement from the director thumbing through Grace's file. It was rather thin.

"I see here you two went to school together at UVA and were even in the same sorority, Chi Omega."

"She was studious but secretive."

He continued to skim her file and paused and looked up at Hope. "Is this right? Says here she is bi-sexual."

Hope nodded and quickly added, "I dated her brother in college."

The director smiled under his glasses and made a mental note. There was more to that but it could wait.

"And what of her family?"

"Both parents are dead. Mother was Chilean. Father was fifth-generation Italian-American. He served in the diplomatic service-several postings, most notably Copenhagen, Denmark and London, England while Grace grew up. Parents tragically killed in a car crash while Grace took Asian and Middle Eastern Studies at Cambridge. She subsequently transferred to the University of Virginia."

"Why transfer and why to UVA?" the director interrupted.

"Activities unbecoming a Cambridge academic and because Virginia had the exact same studies she had at Cambridge. She speaks fluent Korean, Chinese and Arabic along with English and Danish. And she's no slouch in Spanish either," volunteered Hope. The director was about to ask about the incident for her expulsion when Hope knowingly continued.

"She failed an exam and then attempted to blackmail a female professor into changing her grade. There was also a fire."

"Why would any school take her after that?" asked the director.

"She was having an affair with both her female teacher and the husband of her teacher. Her dismissal was hush-hush. Turns out a male teaching assistant who had the hots for Grace and the female teacher ended up grading the failed test. So it was quite a love triangle."

"I don't even want to know about the fire. Continue," instructed the director.

"Entered CIA just after graduation, two years of advanced training before field work. Only sibling, her brother Tim, killed three years ago in Afghanistan."

"Orphans make the best agents," muttered the director.

Hope ignored him and continued. "Three years as a field operative before assignment into Operation Barbarossa. Two years off the grid inside AQNA. She is currently number two behind Janus in the most active cell."

"Tell me something I could not read for myself in her folder Agent Rausch."

Hope squirmed in her chair. "She's twenty-nine. Intelligent, cunning and has a wild streak. Excellent street sense and can blend into any Asian or Middle Eastern environment. She has a passion for arson."

"Obviously!" snorted the director.

Unfazed, Hope continued. "She is sassy and classy at the same time. She appreciates people who perform well. Even if the task is simple, she thanks them. She loves animals." Hope started to mention that Grace had a butterfly tattoo but thought better of it.

The director crossed his leg, resting his ankle on his other leg's knee and then grabbed the lower half of the top leg with both hands. Leaning forward and looking Hope squarely in the eye he came to his decision. "I want this over and done. Get her back in the fold and do it quick."

***

Grace flew to Fort Lauderdale, Florida the next day. Arriving, she quickly joined one of the cruise ships making their annual transatlantic journey. The big cruise liners left the U.S. in April after cruising the Caribbean in the winter and transferred to Europe for the summer season. She had hired on as a Costa Rican maid. Background checks for housekeeping staff were nonexistent. The cruise lines figured, rightly so, where could they go? Everyone was stuck on the ship and their wages came at the end of the cruises. Of course, Grace did not care about the wages; she just wanted to get to Ireland without flying. Flying brought more possibilities of detection than an innocent cruise ship.

After 14 glorious days – more like slave labor at sea – and some wild crew parties below deck, Grace bid farewell to her new friends. She disembarked the ship at the port in Dublin where she had a few connections from the old IRA days and stayed a few nights in various locations. She did not stay long.

She did contact Ahmed once he entered the United Kingdom. She informed him that Janus wanted him to take a more active role now that he was at the 3rd level rank. AQNA started with an organizational system that listed a member by the number of missions they had completed. For example, level 2 meant they had completed one mission. This system failed shortly thereafter when members started to realize few people reached level 3; after proving they were competent on the first mission, most received suicidal tasks on their second. Recruitment suffered. Changes occurred.

AQNA changed to the current system of apprentice (new member on first mission), 2nd level (accomplished 2-4 missions), 3rd level (5 or more) and master (planner of missions). She told Ahmed to meet the contact in Luton for Janus and organize the cells to come to Wales.

Grace took the ferry to Holyhead from Ireland. From there she rented a car under an assumed identity and drove deep into Wales and her meeting at Betws-y-Coed.

Betws-y-Coed, Wales (Memorial Day weekend)

Sean navigated the numerous curves and jinks in the road towards Betws-y-Coed, dodging the occasional pheasant or sheep. Tambra lounged beside him in shorts and a tight t-shirt. Sean's Blue BMW 320i M Sport convertible spent the past four hours driving from Lakenheath to their Wales destination. Memorial Day weekend meant four days off for the two fliers. They had Memorial Day Monday as a holiday and then the Wing had a family day on the Friday before. So they found themselves leaving Friday morning at 9 am after Sean picked Tambra up at a village a few miles away from where she lived. A friend allowed her to park at her house while she was gone. So no one in the village would see Sean with the married Tambra, whose husband was away on business in Germany for the long weekend.

The retractable top on the BMW was for vanity more than convenience for two reasons. The English weather did not afford many great sunny summer days and Sean's work schedule meant that he was not around for those good days when they did shine on the island. There was a reason why most aviators call Lakenheath "Lakenpain." Deployments half way around the world for half of the year were not uncommon. Twelve and fourteen hour days were the norm. Any chance to take a break was a welcome respite.

Tambra had suggested the getaway. She was dying to get away from East Anglia and Lakenheath for a few days and the Memorial Day weekend was perfect. Most base personnel stayed close to home and celebrated the long weekend with American-type activities, thus decreasing their chances of being seen by unwanted, nosy eyes.

Tambra did not love her husband anymore. That was a foregone conclusion. His abuse was well documented but he was protected due to his position within the USAF. As the JAG, or Judge Advocate General, he was responsible for prosecuting offenders at the base. Of course not unexpectedly, her immediate bosses had neglected her cries of abuse. The abuse had been minor when compared to recent big-name cases. Her husband had threatened her life, choked her, placed a knife to her breast, but he never did anything that left a lasting mark. Sometimes she had bruises, which quickly healed and could be explained but never scars. Nothing that could be proven. Her husband was a smart, manipulative, evil man and she knew it.

Crossing the Welsh border at 1 pm the couple stopped in the village of Conwy. After a late lunch, Sean took Tambra on a two-mile scramble up the mountain named after the town.

Sean led Tambra out of Conwy by a northern sea walk. He navigated between some housing developments and guided her across the railroad tracks to begin an ascent of Conwy Mountain. The trail was wide and well-traversed. After a short climb, the trail became more of a path and the gradient increased. Both aviators were used to exercise as part of the Air Force's "Get Fit" campaigns. The oldest joke of the Air Force for aviators in two seat aircraft was, "I do not have to be the fastest officer in the Air Force. I just have to be faster than the other aviator in my airplane if we are shot down."

Tambra thought her forty minutes of hiking had finished upon reaching a broader trail that looked as if it went more east-west along the mountain spine.

"Are we at the top now?" she asked expectantly.

"Not even close, but we are at a great lookout point," he said, clasping her hand and leading her a few meters off the trail through tall wispy reeds to a small clearing that rested in the side of the mountain facing the Isle of Mann, far in the distance, and the Irish Sea. Once they were nestled into their secluded spot, Tambra looked around and noticed the rocks and reeds pretty much blocked anyone from noticing the clearing, just big enough for the two of them to stretch out before falling down another gentle slope off the front edge. Behind them, towering rocks and the mountain shielded the spot in the leeward side. Sean pulled a blanket out from his backpack and laid it out like a bullfighter preparing to meet his opponent.

A beautiful, sunny and surprisingly calm day afforded them great views of Great Orme and, beyond that, the Irish Sea to the north.

"After you, Madame." He exaggerated the invitation to lie down with a sweep of his arm.

Tambra summoned her best Scarlet O'Hara accent and twanged out, "Why, thank you, kind sir."

They plopped down in a fit of laughter that helped break up an uneasy tension that existed between the two at the start of this weekend journey. Sean knew Tambra's troubles with David had increased. He intentionally did not bring the subject up on the drive but felt like it needed to be discussed at some point during this trip.

They both soaked up the early afternoon sun and propped their heads up on their backpacks to watch the few boats that sailed the Irish Sea. Tambra mimicked Sean's position. At some point Tambra turned and whispered into Sean's ear. He looked at her with expansive eyes and a sheepish grin, but nodded enthusiastically. They were both naked within 30 seconds. Not a record for him but quite impressive given the fact that they were 2000 feet up and had just hiked forty minutes. Their lovemaking was fast and furious. Sean did not know if it was Tambra or the fact they were outdoors, but he liked it. They cuddled afterwards, dressed and napped, falling asleep in each other's arms as the sun's rays hit their upturned faces.

"Tambra," said Sean after they woke, "it's none of my business, but why do you stay with David?"

Tambra looked away. Sean knew the basics. He had done some research after their first date. After he saw the bruise on her back.

Domestic violence was on the rise. Recessions always led to a rise. There usually were two main reasons: arguments over money or over the kids. Neither fit Tambra and David. They were DINKs-Dual Income No Kids. Tambra was a party person and David was a controlling, sadistic jerk who liked to play mind games with Tambra and inflict just enough bruises where they were not seen in public. Sean saw the results of David's slapping, shoving and hitting in private. He wanted to beat the living shit out of the guy every time he saw the bruises. But they were in places he should not be seeing.

When Tambra spoke it was in a weak voice Sean had never heard before. She was scared.

"I'm not a masochist Sean and I don't love him anymore. He lost that a few years into the marriage. Now, I honestly fear I will always be at risk if I leave him. He tells me it too. He swears if I leave him he will find me. And I know he will. I...."

She stopped and her face froze in a mask of fear that Sean saw in other places, unexpected places. The Madrid subway bombings or at the London bus bombings. Those victims all had the same sad, tired look.

Terrorism and domestic violence have the same definition. The loss of freedoms, self-sufficiency, safety and emotional stability are all objectives terrorists hope to achieve. Domestic violence is terrorism with individual victims. Domestic violence is intimate terrorism.

Tambra remembered reading one time that redheads have a lower pain threshold than brunettes or blondes. She used to blame herself for not being "tough" enough. That was when she was weaker mentally. The article said redheads were something like 20% less resistant to pain. Maybe that was her problem. Not a chance in hell. Other husbands did not degrade and inflict such pain on their wives. Tambra just chose poorly. The fact that she was a Catholic and did not believe in divorce just added insult to her injury. Even if she was not afraid for her life, her religious upbringing kept chaining her to him. Ultimately, she was afraid of what he would do to her if she did divorce him.

It had started about a year and a half into their marriage. First came the verbal abuse. Looking back it was all so innocuous. A slow build up and accumulation. Then came the physical abuse. David was sucking the life out of her. He was controlling. The kind of man who was quick to promise and slow to deliver.

"Please don't bring it up again," she said to Sean. "It's my cross to bear. And this has been such a great start to the weekend. I don't want anything to jeopardize it." Tambra continued to stare off across the sea. Sean was just hoping his comments had not already spoiled their time together.

Tambra and Sean spent the afternoon exploring Mount Conwy and then drove back to their B&B that evening.

Traveling south from Conwy to Betws-y-Coed, Tambra found the winding, narrow Welsh roads exciting. At times they thought a passing car might run into them to avoid another vehicle in the same lane. The danger the road presented helped to remind her of the real-life danger she faced every time she strapped in an F-15E to go fly or met the ire of her husband. One was a known risk, the other an uncertain fate.

Just before the major road into Betws-y-Coed, Sean turned left and drove up a well-maintained paved road marked "Angels B&B." Right below it, in older paint, was "Hawks Camp Ground" with a symbol of a tent. A third of the way up to the B&B they passed a field on their right. Weeds sprouted up in various areas all around the large campsite and one massive wet spot lay in the center, inviting all who came near to a thorough soaking. Three simple tents sat beside each other on the far side of the field. The road meandered and switched back for half a mile more before reaching the lone house on the hill. A new sign proudly proclaimed "Angels B&B - Heaven on Earth." Four large bay windows fronted the side nearest the road overlooking the valley in which one of North Wales' most popular inland resorts rested. Four rivers met here. Actually one, the River Conwy, met its three tributaries flowing from the west, the Llugwy, the Lledr and the Machno. Betws-y-Coed owed a lot of its buildings and existence to the Victorian age and the Snowdonia National Park, in which it resided.

The bed and breakfast was outside the town proper. Sean had used it before, but Tambra did not need to know. It was within walking distance to the town but up a side road and perched on top of a hill, so few people came to the B&B except guests.

It was perfect for their rendezvous. A quiet weekend away together and nowhere near the base, so the chances were small that anyone who knew them would see them together.

***

Grace loved Wales and her return brought back memories of long weekends and a summer away from college. Betws-y-Coed, sitting in a beautiful valley in Snowdonia National Park, was the ideal location for summer outdoor activities. Walking and hiking are popular. The town had numerous craft and outdoor activity shops and drew the most visitors of all of Wales. The nearby Swallow Falls, lush woods and wonderful mountains that surrounded the village, all provided numerous options for getting outdoors and experiencing the countryside. Swallow Falls was one of the prettiest spots in all of North Wales as the river Llugwy cascaded down into crags and smaller streams or chasms. Perhaps most striking were the isolated cascading waterfalls, mountain top lakes, enchanted river pools and ancient bridges which all served to enhance the area's beauty and secrecy.

Just as Victorian artists had come to the area and formed artist colonies giving Betws-y-Coed its eclectic ambiance, so too had Grace escaped the cliquish ways of Cambridge. No one cared who visited or stayed, as long as they were peaceful. These days it was a mecca for hikers and free spirited hippies. It was perfect for Grace and her conspirators.

Contrary to this stereotype, the main street, Holyhead Road, beamed with inns and bed-and-breakfasts, many of which were quite costly. Of course, money was no object to Grace, but obscurity did have a cost. Every few steps a shop specialized in outdoor clothes. The tourist center provided maps and advice on day trips but none of the Jihadist were going anywhere near these public places, except Grace. Grace visited St. Michael's church, a 14th century monument and one of the oldest in Wales. Then again everything in the United Kingdom was old. You could hardly throw a crumpled beer can without hitting someplace that was older than the US.

Nearby Grace stopped at the Pont-y-Pair (Welsh for the Bridge of the Cauldron). Built in 1468, it currently fought foamy, frothy water that buffeted against the structure from a recent heavy rain. Numerous trails started or ended at the landmark. Just a mile away was the Miner's Bridge on the road to Capel Curiq, where miners crossed the river via a steep ladder as they went back and forth to work each day. Capel Curiq boasted of the Ty Hyll or the Ugly House. This name came not from any homely patrons or owners but from the huge, uneven boulders that formed its walls.

Grace wanted to be seen but not noticed. So she visited some of the local sites simply to blend in with the other tourists. Wales was so lovely and open and sparsely populated. The landscape suited her well. The forest and streams calmed her.

Scholars do know the Romans invaded Britain in AD 43 and just thirty-five years later the conquest of Wales was complete. The occupation did not affect the Welsh much, as the Romans remained concerned with their roads and hill-top forts. Christianity, sheep and metal-working were fixtures in the area by the time they left in AD 383.

After the Romans left, much of Wales was overrun by the pagan Anglo-Saxons and the Picts of Scotland and the Irish. This was the period of Arthurian Legends. But Wales became separated from their Celtic cousins in Cornwall.

Eventually slate quarries and woolen mills became the order of the day and the basis for the local economy by the 19th century. Today, those quarries and mills were closed but agriculture and tourism had risen up to fill the populace needs.

After her evening hike in the chilly Welsh drizzle, Grace knew why the traditional Welsh cuisine was heavily dependent on butter and cheese. She stopped at a 15th century inn frequented mainly by locals, which had its roof at road level. The stone cottage sat on a riverbank and the recent rain-swollen river beside it made more noise then she expected. Outside the inn was dark and foreboding but inside the main eating area was a complete contrast with a bright roaring fireplace at the near end.

She did not have to duck her head to miss the low ceiling beams but a quick glance around the restaurant told her at least one of the locals probably did. To start she ordered a dish of Welsh rabbit, or rarebit. Rarebit consisted of cheese sauce with a slight mustard tang poured generously over buttered toast. For her main entrée she went with Glamorgan Sausages (Selsigen Morgannwg) also known as "toad in the hole." This traditional vegetarian dish consisted of leek, mild mustard and Welsh cheese in caramelized onion gravy. The sausages were strictly an optional bonus.

Leaving the restaurant Grace studied the foothills and mountains surrounding Betws-y-Coed. The Glyders, Moel Siabod and the foothills of the Carneddau range made for excellent cover for their upcoming meeting and training exercises. She was pleased they could meet here but worried a bit about the camping that her followers would have to endure.

Grace did not mind camping. She just preferred not to do it unless a job required it. She had lived off the land on numerous occasions and still did it every now and then just to stay fit enough and balanced enough to do it. But camping in a god-forsaken campsite (she picked it for its remote location) with nine men was not her idea of fun. Especially if it was not necessary. She could blend in. So she did. The others of her cell could not just blend in and thus they were resigned to camping at Hawks Camping grounds. After a relaxing dinner she slipped back into the camp in the dead of night and went over their plans for the UK.

***

The house stood on top of a flat hill overlooking the village. Four prominent bay windows adorned the front. A small patio with five Adirondack chairs facing the downward slope marked the left edge of a well-worn sidewalk to the front door of the B&B. The door was large, red and welcoming.

Kristy, the owner, met them at the door and showed them to their room. The largest room in the B&B was on the top floor. Tambra gasped at the view from their bay window and made small oohing sounds when she went to investigate the bathroom.

Kristy spent a few minutes explaining the elaborate dance ordering breakfast entailed. Every night before bedtime guests were asked to sign up for their breakfast choices. Guests were given a long list of homegrown ingredients from which to choose for their omelets or pancakes.

"Waste not, want not," chimed Kristy.

Sean could almost smell the salmon, sausages, bacon, mushrooms and tomatoes.

"But then you...." The owner caught herself before finishing her sentence. She had almost said but then you know all about our great breakfasts Sean.

"I've never had the pleasure of visiting your establishment before," Sean corrected her before she could say anything else. Both grimaced at her slip and cringed to see if Tambra noticed, but she was absorbed in admiring the en suite bathroom grandeur and antique four-claw bathtub.

Whether Tambra caught the lie or not, she was not letting on. Sean knew he might pay for that later on. They both fell asleep soon after Kristy left. Neither had the energy for any lovemaking as the sun, wind and previous rendezvous had taken its toll. Sleep came easy for them.

After a 45-minute nap and a hot, shared shower, the couple slipped downstairs to go into town for dinner.

"No, you don't have to walk down the driveway," offered Kristy when queried about the walk into town. "The best way is the path through the woods. It is half the distance since it is a straight line as the crow flies. Out the front door, down the hill into the woods at the signpost marked foot trail. Eventually you will come out at a clearing on the opposite side of the field or camp ground depending on who is describing that piece of land," she chuckled. "Into another section of woods, again sign posted, then to the main road. Cross it and follow the path to the suspension bridge and then you are in town at the train station. You can't miss it." She paused then asked, "Where are you heading for dinner?"

"The Bistro," replied Sean, still a little worried Kristy would give away his secret about visiting here last year with someone else.

"Great choice!" she beamed. "Go past the train station, to the river then turn right. The Bistro will be on your left, just before the first main bridge on your right."

"Thanks."

They followed Kristy's directions down the hill and into the woods. The temperature was still quite warm from the day's sunlight. A month before the summer solstice in Wales meant the sun did not set until after 9 pm. The sky was bright and the wind light.

Exiting the woods, Tambra decided to ambush Sean.

"So, you have never been to this B&B before?" she asked.

"No, never. Why do you ask?" Sean answered reluctantly after too long a pause.

The path now took them by the campground and Tambra glanced over at the tents she had seen earlier on the drive up to the B&B. They were right beside them now and she observed three tents, one a smaller single man tent and two large ones that could sleep 5-6.

She continued to interrogate Sean.

Laughing, she said. "How did you find out about this place and know to book the Bistro? That seemed like the right choice in Kristy's opinion."

They were walking down the path hand in hand and Tambra thought she heard a strange language coming from the tents. Sean continued speaking, not noticing the tents or the conversation from the campers.

"Well...I have a friend..."

"Just one?" Tambra interrupted teasingly. Wrapping her arm around his waist as they continued their journey past the campground. She strained to try and pick up the words from the hidden campers. It sounded like Arabic.

"Ha ha. No, this one is actually at the travel service on base and she..."

"She?" Tambra squawked a little too loudly and pulled him to a stop. Sean cringed as soon as he said it. Stupid. If you are going to lie, at least don't bring another woman into the story.

They stopped right beside the tents. The conversation in the tents ended but a few more words passed before someone hissed out a "sshhhhhhhh."

It was Arabic. Tambra would bet her life on it. She served two tours in the Middle East. One in Afghanistan and the other in Iraq. She knew Arabic when she heard it.

"Wait a minute. Don't get all jealous on me just because I mention another woman." Sean was trying to recover from his faux pas and had just made another one by using the word "jealous." Tambra hated that word.

Standing there beside the tents, with the strange, hushed Arabic and now Sean's thoughtlessness, Tambra felt the moment was awkward on many levels. But the last thing she wanted was an argument.

"Forget it," she said as she dragged him away from the tents. "Let's go." She looked back over her shoulder in time to see a man exit one of the tents. He looked at her menacingly and she got a good look at his face. He wore glasses. Bizarrely, Tambra thought the glasses were sexy. They conveyed intelligence. But it was a strange custom for an Arab man. He removed them as the couple turned and walked away. Who was he?

Chapter 9

Betws-y-Coed, Wales

They walked into town and found the Bistro quite easily. La Bistro Jordan was a small homey place with a large central room and one smaller alcove. Candles adorned every table and the menus were in both Welsh and English. It was comfortable and special without being too pretentious. Just what they wanted for their getaway.

Tambra could not help but replay the image of the man at the tent. She knew him from someplace. An icy chill went down her spine as the waiter placed her main course in front of her.

Could it be? She remembered a photo of a suspected terrorist that the UK intelligence hinted was in the East Anglian area. It was in her husband's briefcase a few weeks ago. Her husband always enjoyed showing off his work to her. This time it may have been worth something.

She remembered the man now because at the time she thought his eyes were cute with the glasses he wore and she remembered him clearly because of his attractiveness, despite the glasses. This was the same man. To that she would swear. She never forgot a face, especially a good-looking one. They both were tanned, of Middle-Eastern descent and, although she never saw him speak, she was sure he was the leader who hushed the others who were speaking Arabic in loud, quick tones as she and Sean approached unannounced earlier.

But that complicated things. If he was a terrorist and she spotted him then she should call the base and report it to their Intel team at the squadron. They would then pass it on to the UK authorities to investigate. That, in and of itself, was not the problem. The problem came when it inevitably got back to her husband that she had reported it. Her husband would have to know at some point. If she called it in anonymously it would not have the importance as if she called it in personally to Sal, their Intel Officer. Sal could not keep it anonymous. Tambra knew Sal and he was a stickler for the rules. Tambra ate her lamb, but obviously her thoughts were elsewhere.

Sean took her inattention as a sign she was still upset. He did not want this to hang over them the entire weekend. His father always said honesty was the best policy, and although he found exceptions to almost every rule, this time he needed to set the record straight.

As the waiter brought their dessert – his a chocolate tart with homemade vanilla ice cream and hers the Crème brûlée – Sean looked at her and said, "I am sorry."

Tambra thought Sean regretted ordering the tart. He always second-guessed himself on his food choices. Mistaking his apology for an excuse to try some of her Crème brûlée, she pushed hers over toward him and offered it freely. He laughed and then frowned shaking his head.

"No, I mean I am sorry about not telling you I had been to the B&B before. I came here last year." There it was out in the open. Let the chips fall where they may, just hopefully not on him.

"Oh that! I know." She smiled mischievously and stuck her tongue out proactively just before she wrapped her lips around the spoon with the crème brûlée. "Mandy something, right?" She looked down, pulling the now empty spoon out of her mouth slowly, her doe blue eyes blinking innocently.

Shocked and awed at the same time, he stammered, "But on the walk down you seemed…. I mean you got mad and…well."

With a wave of her hand and a pert little smile the event was over. Her attention was back to Sean and the wonderful weekend he planned.

"Let's forget about it. Tell me what we are going to do tomorrow."

After dinner they stopped in a few more places for nightcaps and ended up walking home quite late in the dark. Tambra suggested they take the road back to the B&B even though it was farther. She had no desire to be traipsing around in the woods at night and did not wish to pass the tents with the man whom she should report. Better to sleep on it, she thought.

***

Grace appeared a few hours after Sean and Tambra went to bed. She would have slipped into the campground unnoticed, except after the incident with the American tourists this evening; Ahmed did not want any more surprises. So he set up a schedule whereby one remaining man would be out of the tents and alert to any intruders. As it was, his sentry did not see Grace in time to stop her from sneaking up behind him and surprising him. He reached for a knife but she kicked it away deftly and drew her own pistol with a silencer just in case.

The noise from their scuffle did bring the other men out of their tents and Ahmed as well, with his gun drawn. Grace had the drop on him, but, not wanting to get shot by her own people or embarrass the now-elevated number 3, Grace put her hands up slowly in the moonlight and whispered the password she had told them to use for this day.

"Behold the moon rises and the sun hides."

Ahmed responded with "Better to see in the night than be blinded in the day."

Accepted by the others, Grace turned to a more formal welcoming.

"Brothers, peace be with you." And Grace prostrated herself momentarily. She hated doing that but the religion expected it. In unison the men replied, "And also with you," as they too bowed down.

At just after midnight Grace did not worry too much about being seen or heard, but she still posted a sentry (a different man than the one she had surprised, to be sure). Inside the larger tent, the men gathered, waiting for her to speak. No women were here tonight. Grace justified their absence by saying the logistics of separate tents was too hard. She left the two other women in the terrorist cell behind. One was Fatima from the Vancouver operation. Grace discretely asked Ahmed how Fatima was coping after their last mission. He told her she was doing well considering all she had been through.

The reality was that Grace kept the women out of the Wales meeting on purpose. There are two types of terrorist males: religious nuts and bad men. The latter just want to inflict pain. Grace wanted to protect these women as much as she could so she kept them close to her when she was able or even better, away from the action as much as possible.

Ahmed did well to get three AQNA cells together in one place on such short notice. She expressed her pleasure with his successful assignment before outlining the plan.

Grace always liked to praise in public and criticize in private.

"I have word from Janus about our next mission."

The three cells Ahmed organized sat before her eagerly awaiting instructions. One from Birmingham, one from Ipswich and a third from Milton Keynes. They all converged here because today marked the start of operations. So they packed up their meager belongings before going where Janus would send them. The day had come to strike a mighty blow at the Americans and British who corrupted the Muslim world.

The men were too professional to guess at their next objective; instead they squatted in stony silence as Grace gave them their orders.

"We have two possible targets. But only Janus and I will know both." She paused for effect, scanning the eyes of each man present.

She read their minds.

"It is not that Janus does not trust you...he does. It is simply a matter of operational security. The fewer people who know of each location the fewer who can reveal it, if captured."

Grace called the names of three men and told them to go with Ahmed. The others she briefed on her part of the plan. Grace and her team were to be the backup cell and attack an USAF base located in East Anglia. There were two possible targets: RAF Mildenhall and RAF Lakenheath. The choice of which one to attack and when would be hers, and hers alone, as the main operative in the field. Janus had complete faith in her. Ahmed would take his team and hit the London target. Grace would be involved with the planning and execution of both attacks but would remain isolated from the London attack in order to lead the air base attack.

***

Sean woke before the sun came up. Tambra slumbered peacefully on her side. Sneaking out of bed, Sean grabbed some clothes and his running shoes. He dressed outside the room in the hallway.

Why do I have this claustrophobic fear of being in a relationship? I cannot wake up in the same bed the morning after with a girlfriend. Why?

Sean knew the underlying reasons. His dad died in a paper mill accident when Sean was five. Attractive mom left with three children and no job. The family moved to a smaller house and mother started working as a maid in a nice hotel and a second job as a hostess at the restaurant.

Sean's memories become a little fuzzier here. His mom would only keep a boyfriend for six to twelve months. At about that time in her relationship, she found out the men in her life did not want to marry her with the three-kid baggage that came with her. Accepting this fact, she began to use her boyfriends for gifts, money, and good times. Next came the habit of dropping her boyfriend before he could drop her. Sean admitted he picked up this trait from his mom.

Love them then leave them. That was Sean's motto, too. It had worked for 29 years.

Later, after a ninety-minute run, he met Tambra at breakfast downstairs. She knew his quirks and idiosyncrasies and allowed them. Her own closet was full of skeletons, so she did not go peeking into anyone else's.

Saturday was just as nice as Friday and they climbed Snowdon, the highest mountain in Wales. For dinner that night they dined at a local hotel on the main street.

Sean performed the same ritual Sunday morning. He was gone when Tambra woke up and showered. Only this time it was raining in the morning hours. Luckily it cleared shortly before they met for breakfast.

Tambra strolled onto their balcony and lit a cigarette. The death stick was her release. Inhaling she sucked the burning nicotine into her lungs. It hurt and felt so damn good. She was going to die anyway, one way or another, so why deny herself this simple, ugly pleasure?

But where was Sean? He couldn't have gone running in the rain, could he? Was he that desperate to get away from her?

Sean asked her to quit smoking for him and she had. He hated smokers. The smell reminded him of his mother. Not that he hated his mother; he loved her. But the smell of cigarettes in the car made him choke growing up. He almost threw up every time he thought of it now. Apparently his mother took up the nasty habit after his dad died. It killed her twenty years later. Lung cancer took away his mom when he was in his twenties.

Even though she kicked the habit cold turkey for him, Tambra still had occasional lapses. Like now, when she was a little stressed. Sean did show up a short time later. He explained that he was up early and went to read downstairs. It was his rationalization and she let him keep it.

By now the tents were gone. Tambra asked Kristy if she knew who the men were but she said she had not known anyone was there. She went on to comment that the so-called campground was more of an eyesore run by a rather cheap owner who was not well-liked in the area. The B&B owners had been trying to buy the land themselves but the owner kept asking for a ridiculous sum of money for the small clearing and so they just lived with it on their back door.

The food Saturday night had been good and the service exceptional, and they found themselves back at the Bistro for their final night's dinner on Sunday. Only this time Tambra's mood was lighter. The man in the tent had moved on and although she felt a momentary pang of guilt about not calling it in, she rationalized that he was probably not the one from the pictures anyway.

Office of Special Investigations (OSI)

Over the past six months as assistant chief of security at RAF Mildenhall, Major Kate Healy liaised on occasion with the Office of Special Investigations. The OSI tended to be secretive and kept to themselves. They called you when they needed you and were seldom available. So it was with a little trepidation that Kate walked into the OSI five minutes early for her 8 a.m. meeting. Did they know her secret? Everyone had secrets, right? It was just a question of finding hers and determining if it really mattered. Unconsciously, she chewed on her left index fingernail after sitting in their conference room for what seemed like an eternity.

She dressed in civilian clothes as directed by the invitation. Black skirt over the knees, white blouse and matching black blazer with stockings and comfortable black pumps, not too high but enough to prove she was a woman. She crossed her arms, providing a protective barrier across her chest.

Invitation, yeah right!

Director Stevens had requested she stop by first thing Monday morning, but failed to say why when he telephoned Saturday evening.

It was the first time she had a direct phone call from the chief of OSI, someone she had not met after six months of coordinating with them. It was usually another agent and rarely the same one. She sensed the agency was going through quite a lot of turnover with many established agents leaving recently. Budget cuts had hit every department, even security.

Director Stevens kept her waiting exactly eleven minutes. When he did walk in, she was about to burst with anticipation.

"Good morning, Miss Healy. I am Director Stevens," stammered the older gentlemen as he entered the room. Kate's official Air Force photograph, which he had memorized, did not do her justice. She made an instant impression on him with a quick smile and stood smartly to take his hand.

"Nice to finally meet you, sir."

"Do I detect a Caribbean accent? Faint but just there in the background?"

Kate blushed and let her dimples show. It had been a long time since anyone caught her on that. She must be nervous. This man was sharp and to the point. "Yes, sir. From my mother's side. She is from the Virgin Islands. Saint Thomas."

"Beautiful place. Do you visit often?"

"No sir, my family lives in Charleston." She added "South Carolina" then realized it was a stupid follow up since the director obviously knew where Charleston was located.

He gave no indication of impatience, but instead got down to business.

"Please sit. May I call you Kate?"

Kate noted he sat opposite her with nothing between them. Most supervisors place a desk between them to give them an air of superiority.

"Yes, please… sir," she muttered, surprised at the informality. But also noting he failed to offer her the same courtesy.

"Kate, we have a problem…" He let the words hang like a noose twisting in the wind. Kate ran through all of her problems. Most were minor, one was major. Was she about to be kicked out of the Air Force? She gulped and nodded sheepishly. Acids began to build and flare in her stomach. Kate crossed one arm over her body and touched her other arm.

"There are reports that someone at Lakenheath is a sexual predator. I want you to do a little snooping for us."

Kate exhaled a little too loud. It was not her they were investigating. Instead they wanted her to be the investigator. Who watches the watchers popped into her mind.

The director continued by outlining who it was they suspected and how he wanted her to proceed. When he finished, he sat back.

Now it was Kate's turn to take the offensive.

"If I agree to this assignment." The director raised his eyebrows in disbelief that she would even suggest declining. "It will be a little awkward for me to snoop at Lakenheath while assigned to Mildenhall," she protested.

"I realize that," he replied with the beginning of a grin. "You do not know it yet but you will soon be reassigned to take over the 28 SP Detachment here at Lakenheath. That position will help you nose around easier."

"Am I getting this assignment because of my skin color?" She did not mean to be so brazen with her question, but it just came out.

The director laughed her accusation off effortlessly.

"No. A nasty little affair has been uncovered and all involved are being reassigned. You are next in line since both the commander and deputy commander are involved."

"I see."

"And it gets better. You were a cheerleader in your past so we will make sure the teacher in charge asks you to be a volunteer. That way you can be closer to the students on the squad."

"You have thought of everything, haven't you?"

"I try, Major Healy. I try."

"I may know of another way of getting close to the perp. Suspected perp," she corrected herself, "socially."

"I have complete faith in you"

Kate agreed to take on the role of undercover investigator. The director made it painfully obvious that her volunteering was expected. The idea of a promotion did not hurt either.

***

Hope boarded a flight from Washington Dulles to London Heathrow dressed in a grey suit coat, loose fitting white blouse, tan comfortable slacks, and easy-to-slip-off shoes. She loved to sink back into her seat with her Bose noise cancelling headphones, take off her shoes and relax. Flying long distances was one of the few times she could relax. In her lap were working papers. Hope looked around the economy class cabin through her large opaque tinted glasses. She admitted to herself everyone she saw looked suspicious.

The cabin was half-full. She looked everyone deeply in the eyes as they boarded or sat. No one smiled. It troubled her. She vowed never to fly again but knew that was an empty threat.

Maybe it was just the people in economy class that scared her. In years prior, agents would fly in business class but recent budget cuts made that a low priority.

Every passenger wore ear buds or stared at laptops. Hope had both. She hated airline food but liked catching up on all the movies that she had little time to see when she was on the ground. Her boyfriend, a local district attorney in Charlottesville, rarely wanted to go to a movie. Their dates tended to be elaborate affairs that either involved attending a public function in a well-dressed manner or sneaking away for a one-night bed and breakfast getaway in the Blue Ridge Mountains. Both suited Hope when she had the time. She just wished they could do more mundane things sometimes.

Hope loved football and baseball and anything to do with her two favorite teams, the New York "Football" Giants and the Yankees. Born in Bar Harbor, Maine she later moved to New York and grew up worshipping the Giants and Bronx Bombers. The NFL season was in the doldrums of summer, but America's pastime was in full swing. Hope glanced at the USA Today and smiled noting the Yankees were tied for first with Boston for the moment.

Her team needed a relief pitcher desperately, but seemed unwilling to invest the money to get one.

Her boss sent her to bring in Grace. That meant she had to find her and then communicate the orders from the director. If that was not enough she also had contingency plans for if Grace refused the order to come in from undercover. That had happened a few times over the years too. Her trip across the pond promised to steal some of her personal private time.

10,000 feet over Scotland

Sean looked down through the scattered cloud deck at the Scottish highlands and lochs below his aircraft. That was one good thing about flying in England. If you had the fuel to come to Scotland, the low flying was stunningly beautiful. Of course, getting through the typical Scottish cloud decks was the other side of that coin.

Sean led a two ship today on a routine training mission. The plan was to fly low level to practice an attack on a bridge near Oban. The forecast was not too bad but they needed to go around some summer cumulonimbus clouds to get to their start point. The clouds, shaped like anvils, so prominent with thunderstorms, peeked above their flight path reaching upwards of 25,000 feet.

Sean waggled his wings to catch Tambra's attention and signal her to close up the formation spacing. Prior to his execution wing flash Tambra's Strike Eagle was as far as two miles away. Now she flawlessly maneuvered her jet to close formation, within twenty feet of Sean's F-15E.

It took thirty-five minutes to fly up from Lakenheath. The fighters did so at a high altitude (above 30,000 feet) to save gas. They did the same on their return journey. That meant a lot of droning time, flying straight and level with the autopilot on. The void was often filled with conversations between crewmembers or occasionally music piped in by an unauthorized communication patch cord and MP3 device.

Sean picked up the conversation they had been having earlier in the flight. He sat in the front seat with his arms crossed, hands gripping his upper arms. The autopilot peacefully flew them on a trajectory north.

"Emile, do you think I should do my ops checks differently?"

"Are we back on the accident again Sean?"

"No." He did not sound convincing.

"Sean we have been over this a dozen times. There is nothing *you* could have done differently that would have prevented the accident on the Libya raid."

"Em, you have to say that. You're obligated to because you need me sane enough to land this thing when we get back to the heath today. But work with me on this one. What if, from now on, I ask if CFTs are feeding?"

"Sean you know the standards read that if a wingman says same then they are feeding the CFTs as expected."

Emile was worried about Sean. Despite his outward appearances, he seemed conflicted inside. Over the past two weeks he had been in what she called his bargaining mood. He always seemed to be saying "what if this" or "what if that." He was trying to negotiate with his subconscious and justify what happened.

The flight path direct to their let down point put them on a collision course with some clouds ahead. Sean momentarily disengaged the autopilot and resumed aircraft control. He threaded the needle between some wispy cirrus clouds skirting the nearest anvil by a good thirty miles. He did not want to come anywhere near the potential thunderstorm clouds with his formation. Popping out on the other side of the cirrus he spotted their let down point. No clouds interfered with a clear descent.

"Check the area with the radar for any bug smashers, Em," Sean referenced the affectionate Air Force nickname for private pilots.

The civilian, slow-moving airplanes were a hazard to a fast-moving fighter flying low to the ground with less room to maneuver.

As they descended, Emile used the APG-70 radar onboard to sweep the low level start for radar returns. None appeared. As an extra measure of safety, she activated the F-15E's AAI system which electronically sent out reference signals to identify other aircraft squawking an identification code. One such hit popped up on her radar showing up as a diamond.

She concentrated the radar energy there and seconds later found the slow moving plane at 1000 feet.

"Strike flight, slow traffic three miles north of entry leg. Altitude one thousand," announced Emile on the discrete frequency used to communicate just between aircraft in their formation.

Sean keyed the mike and transmitted their intentions to the Scottish Military air traffic controller monitoring them: "Scottish Mil, Strike 01 flight is happy to go on route."

A sweet female Scottish voice came back with, "Roger Strike 01, altimeter at Lossimouth is 29.85. Monitor appropriate frequencies and squawk 7001."

"Strike 01, wilco."

Sean and Emile put their conversation behind them and concentrated on the mission before them, flying over the Scottish lochs and valleys at 500 feet and 500 miles per hour. Unfortunately weather prevented their training delivery. Roughly twenty minutes into the low level Sean commanded the flight to route abort in order not to enter the low clouds obscuring the target area. Although the F-15E was designed for flying "anywhere, anytime," Strike Eagles did not fly low to the ground intentionally in the weather. It was a risk the Air Force did not wish to take with fifty million dollar aircraft on practice sorties.

After they leveled off at 33,000 feet and the autopilot took over to fly the jet back home, Sean had some time on his hands.

He brought up the accident again.

"Maybe I should have stressed the contingencies more in the combat flight brief that night. I may have pressed too hard."

"Everyone wanted to be there Sean. We're all big boys and girls."

"I know. It's just easy to be brave when you have nothing to lose. You know what I mean. The married guys – they have a wife and rugrats to think about."

My philosophy has always been if it's dumb, dangerous or different then step back and reasess what you're doing. But I didn't that night for some reason. Was I trying to prove something? Did I press because I wanted the most combat time? Was it something else?

"What if I had turned back the mission because the fuel margins were too thin?"

"Then you would have been the first aviator to turn back that mission. You know as well as I do that we flew almost fifty of those missions before the accident Sean. We had to if we wanted to be in the fight. Flying from Aviano to Libya and back took numerous air-to-air refueling hook-ups and some good piloting skills. Dog Fifty-two," said Emile, intentionally avoiding the lost pilot's name for fear of speaking ill of the dead, "did not fulfill his wingman contract with you. It is not your fault." She was adamant in her defense.

"But..."

"But nothing, Rider. Get back in the game or get out of the way." Her last comments were meant to shake him out of his funk. When it did not appear to work, she tried another tact.

"Can I fly us back home?"

Sean did not take long to think about it.

"Sure. Your jet, but only if you hook us up with some tunes for the return trip."

"What do you want to hear, sweetie?" asked Emile in her most seductive voice.

Her voice worked. His mind wandered for a few moments. Returning, he begged, "How bout some Salt-N-Pepa?"

"'Push It.' Coming up."

"Better warn the other guys."

"Strike 02, prepare for WSO flying."

"We're already there, One," came Mark's reply. Whoever was flying the jet usually made the radio calls.

Emile punched in and cranked up the hypnotic rap song. When she did, Sean started to gyrate and dance with his hands in the air. Emile did the same, leaving the autopilot on a little while longer to watch Sean flail. Strike 02 bobbed up and down, a mile away, dancing unintentionally to the beat of "Push It." Sean and Emile jived inside their jet and laughed as Strike 02 weaved and careened around the sky.

When that song ended and Rush's "Fly by Night" came on with its long guitar rifts, Emile turned off the autopilot and grabbed the control stick. The aircraft bobbed up and down when her untested hand took the jet.

"Better make it two miles, Strike 02," Sean directed. Tambra took quick control and moved Strike 02 further away, then gave the jet back to Mark.

Both jets, now 2 miles apart and flown by the backseaters, did a wild dance to the music. Sometimes moving in opposite directions like uncoordinated kittens, the aircraft pushed south toward home.

Sean coached her and did not think about anything else all the way back to Lakenheath

***

Eight hours later, Hope landed in rain and a low overcast at London Heathrow. Immigration was a breeze and she smiled at the efficiency in which the agency arranged for her weapon to accompany her. Hope used a Glock 19. The 9MM weapon was easy to reload, only weighed 21 ounces empty and just felt right in her hand. The Brits were a little gun phobic so the staff officer at customs politely warned her that use of her firearm was prohibited under all but life or death situations. Hope smiled helpfully and nodded enthusiastically. Not that she believed a word of it. A gun on her person meant she was responsible for using it, not some paper pusher at a cushy desk in Heathrow.

The first thing she noticed was the lack of attention she received. No one met her as she left Customs.

This did not come as a surprise since no liaison officer contacted her after she phoned MI6 about her visit. It was as if she did not exist. Such was the state of coordination between the services these days. High-level activity got all the attention, but because of the demands from drone attacks and other high-profile missions, the other duties seemed lost in the shuffle.

"What we have here is a failure to communicate," Hope muttered under her breath as she hailed a quick taxi downtown to the center of London. She chose the Doubletree by Hilton at Westminster since it was only three blocks from MI6. In fact, the hotel stood beside the home office, which rested behind MI5, which faced the Thames River. Hope settled into her stylish, modern hotel room. She selected a king suite. She loved king beds. Her fitful sleeping habits, as her current boyfriend would attest to, usually resulted in all covers on the bed ending in disarray. A large bed allowed her to toss and turn, containing her gyrations like a pen for a wild pony. Unpacking her carry-on bag but not her suitcase, Hope went to visit MI6 after a quick shower and lunch. It was 2 pm when she walked in the front door of England's Security Service.

People often confused MI5 and MI6. MI5 was responsible for protecting the UK, its citizens and interests from any major threats to national security. MI6, or the Secret Intelligence Service (SIS), operated around the world and was responsible for gathering secret intelligence outside the UK.

MI5 was headquartered in Thames House on Millbank; MI6 sat beside the Vauxhall Bridge on the Thames east side about one block south. Hope had a short walk.

After a brief sit in the immaculate waiting area, a well-dressed man approached. She gave him a quick once-over as she stood to meet him. He was slightly shorter than Hope. She guessed 5 foot 9 inches. His rugged face appeared as if a smile had never passed over it. He had little to no hair on the front of his scalp. This made his head appear to be slightly larger than normal and very oval in shape.

His attire was all business: a black, single-breasted coat, white buttoned down shirt, and thin black polka-dot tie. Although with his hands tucked unceremoniously in his pockets, it defeated his stylish look. Black patent leather wing tip shoes completed his ensemble. Trim and lean with some scars probably hidden by the suit. Hope liked what she saw: large nose, probably broken on numerous occasions; large ears that appeared even bigger with his lack of frontal hair and a five o'clock shadow that would do justice to any man. He looked tough but not cocky, worldly but not beaten down by the weight of the world.

But best of all he had no hidden look. Instead he stared Hope straight in the eyes.

"Miss Rausch?"

Hope cringed unconsciously when she heard his accent: a slight Scottish brogue. Why did she cringe? It was just a very masculine accent and a deep voice. It was almost as if he could see through her.

"Yes. And you are?" she fired back, putting him on his heels a bit.

"Connor Ackson, at your service." Now he flashed a smile that attempted to win her over. It did. She sensed it was real and he wanted to start off on the right foot with her. The smile faded just as quickly as he began to quiz her on what she hoped to accomplish in the United Kingdom. She gathered that smile rarely made an appearance but when it did it was worth waiting for.

Connor escorted her to his office on the third floor. He impressed her when she saw it was a corner office with windows.

"I see you do not have many non-business things in your office, Mr. Ackson. I approve." That sounded a little too bitchy so she quickly followed it with an apologetic, "I mean, I'm the same way back at the agency."

He nodded and pointed out a seat for her. She noticed he did not sit until she did. A gentleman spy. One soccer photo adorned the wall. He noticed her inspection.

"Some mates of mine in college."

"Which position do you play?" asked Hope. It was now her turn to impress him.

"Defender and that was years ago. Nowadays I limit myself to darts at the pub."

She doubted that by the way his white shirt fit under his jacket. He was fit and lean but she expected no less from an MI6 agent. Connor simultaneously conducted his own recon on the woman sitting in front of him.

Blond with a simple ponytail worn up high. Stunningly attractive. Green eyes that matched her kelly green dress with black accents. Minimalistic sandals and a small black clutch purse.

Where does she keep her gun?

"How do you know about football? Sorry, I think you Yanks call it soccer."

"Four brothers, three older and lots of sports at my house."

"Let me guess: I peg you for a surfer girl or baseball tomboy."

She rewarded him with a smile. "Close, but no cigar. Beach volleyball. I was tall and lanky growing up, so as much as I wanted to play softball, I was terrible at it," she said, crossing her legs seductively and unconsciously.

"Somehow I doubt you are terrible at anything."

She blushed and directed the conversation back to business deftly with, "How much help can I expect from MI6 in trying to catch Janus and his terrorist cell?"

"What you see is what you get."

Hope could not hide the twinge of disappointment in her eyes. She expected as much, but had hoped for more. This terrorist group was expanding and getting more dangerous by the day. They had to be stopped.

Connor sensed her disappointment and tried to bring her down gently. "You know I do have some experience to offer. Former SAS, degree in criminology at the University of Dundee and... "

A hint of that smile.

"I play a mean bagpipe."

"Really?" she asked as she uncrossed her legs and patted her skirt playfully.

"Ah nooo," he replied with a heavy Scottish brogue. "Afraid not, but I *can* play the radio."

He would do.

Recovering quickly she answered, "I look forward to working with you."

"Right. What's our next move?"

Lakenheath Air Base, England

Sean pulled into the base post office. This was his last stop before heading into the squadron for duty today. As soon as his car door opened the pungent odor of pigs and their associated offal flooded his nostrils. Nothing like a June day in East Anglia to put things in perspective. Wind from the west, he guessed, striding into the quaint PO box-filled rectangle. Sean escaped and evaded his way to his own container on the lowest row. Sean chuckled at the irony of how the PO boxes near the floor almost always seemed to be handed out to the tallest individuals and the top boxes always went to the short people. It was as if the post office gods were playing a joke.

Sean bent down to roll his combination through its required paces and was rewarded with the familiar click and pop of his door lock releasing. He peered in and retrieved several letters when he heard the soft-toed rhythm of flight boots on the stone floor. Sean glanced up in time to see Emile towering over his prone form. With a smile on her face and three white envelopes in her hand, she had struck a determined pose reminiscent of her field hockey days.

"Em, you are the only person I know who likes to get bills," he teased.

She shrugged impishly. "Hey, at least it's mail and well, I do kind of like the efficiency of paying and getting credit for this kind of…what?" She finally noticed Sean had not moved since she began her diatribe.

"What?" she demanded her voice rising ever so slightly.

Sean's distraction came from a small trick of light from the hallway window. Emile's head tilted left and the sunlight from the window framed what looked like a halo over Emile's head. Her body appeared tight in her flight suit, filling every available inch of fabric in a subtle, sexy way. Her smile was her best feature, thought Sean. She could make or break someone's heart. *I wonder what she looks like out of uniform?* Sean shook his head and the halo disappeared. Emile was the kind of girl he hoped to marry. Not the kind of girl he wanted to bed just for the sex.

"Nothing, just lost in my thoughts," he answered, standing. Flashbacks to his best birthday ever flooded his memory. Blessed with June 21st as his birthdate, the summer solstice and longest day of the year, Sean had many memorable celebrations. But his favorite had to be when he was in pilot training at Laughlin Air Force Base in Del Rio, Texas, seven years ago. He golfed with his roommates in the morning, ate lunch at the club, then took a quick trip down to Lake Amistad ("friendship" in Spanish), for an afternoon of sailing and swimming with some nurses from the hospital.

Why is it we always remember our best and worst birthdays but none of the ones in between?

Sean stood quickly, bringing them face-to-face and unexpectedly close. Emile blushed a bit and stepped back first. Sean lifted three greeting cards to dispel any tension, showing them proudly.

"Unlike you, Missy, I am excited about real mail. Birthday cards to be exact."

"Who are they from? And since when does a forty-year-old get birthday cards?" she joked.

"I am sure they are from all my girlfriends." Sean began to itemize them: "Let's see. Yep, this one's from Nicki, an old flame in Charlottesville where I grew up. A mystery card with no return address, but I am pretty sure I know who sent that one." Emile saw that it had no stamp, simply an MPS in the corner. That stood for Military Postal System and it meant it was mailed from someone in the military who probably worked at Lakenheath. That meant the girl at the Command Post or perhaps Tambra?

Sean looked at the last one closely then it was his turn to blush.

"Hey, this last one is from you, Emile!" He used her real name instead of her call sign, Bambi, or her shortened name, Em. He touched her arm as they walked out and turned to her earnestly.

"Thank you, Emile. It means a lot to me. I will save it for my actual birthday though, on the 21st."

She smiled. Not sheepishly but confidently this time. He was being honest with her. She could tell. Emile spent so much time with him she knew his signs. His nostrils flared when he lied. In fact, many people had that same trait, but it was very pronounced with Sean. She wondered if his girlfriends knew.

"Come on, there's an intel brief at the squadron in five minutes. We can't be late."

Sean and Emile arrived together and slunk into the back row seconds before the brief began. Sean did have time to stop for popcorn from the squadron bar. Senior Airman Sal Hutchins gave the monthly intelligence brief in the squadron vault. He began with the highest threat to the base and the area.

"Latest information places multiple AQNA cells in England at this time. Here are photos of the cell's possible leaders."

Photos of Janus flashed on the screen. Next came a photo of Ahmed.

"This man is Ahmed Wasem. He is linked to the Vancouver French Hockey team massacre."

Tambra gasped loudly. Some fliers around her turned to see who exclaimed. Tambra feigned a cough to cover her surprise but Sean heard and saw enough not to be fooled by her chicanery. Sean saw fear glide over Tambra's face.

The picture of Ahmed confirmed what Tambra already knew. She remembered the man from her trip to Betws-y-Coed. He spoke and stared at her and Sean from the campsite. Tambra recognized him after their visit but only because of a dossier on her husband's desk at home. She had hesitated and ultimately did not report him. Her reasons were purely selfish. How could she explain a Memorial Day weekend trip to Wales when her husband was away on business?

***

Sam Hendricks

Hope stopped at the front desk to make her dinner reservation only to find a note waiting for her. Hope read it and burnt it after reaching her room.

Meet me in Camden market Saturday at 1 PM. Come alone. I have information to give for cash. Azrael.

Chapter 10

Little Venice, just north of the center of London, formed where the Grand Union and Regent's canals met and a sea of shops, cafes and stalls spilled out to entertain and encourage every type of shopper. Grace loved it for the colorful markets and the huge crowds. It was the perfect place to meet someone without a tail.

Winding streets and dark alleys were filled with Goth or alternative fashion boutiques that competed with restaurants, pubs, theatres and bars for the hard-earned coin of the realm. Once only a weekend market, Camden Market was now a seven day a week entity. Grace told Hope to meet her at 1 p.m. on Saturday, the busiest time of the week. Grace was already there and followed Hope down some narrow alleys to make sure she was alone. She was. And so it was that Grace met Hope on a restaurant bench deep in the heart of Camden Market.

This meeting would be tricky. Grace needed to pass information to Hope but on her terms not the CIA's. Plus Grace did not want anyone else to know she was working for the CIA. She knew there would be many people who eventually would hear their conversation.

Grace kept Hope waiting fifteen minutes and did not approach until Hope had both hands wrapped around a burrito from the Mexican stand.

Hope prayed she did not spill any juice from the meal on her suit or on the microphone she wore. The agency would want to hear this conversation and even Connor and Scotland Yard, too, if she could approve it through the proper channels. An AQNA operative willing to trade information for money. Quite a coup for the agency. Even it was just all smoke and mirrors and created by Operation Barbarossa.

Grace watched Hope for a few minutes from a hidden vantage point on a roof just above the restaurant. Crowded House's hypnotic "Weather With You" played in from her earbud. She loved the song; it reminded her of those early enjoyable months in Cambridge.

"Why so grim, Sunshine? You look as if your pet goldfish just died," Grace ribbed as she slid into place beside Hope, who had just bitten into her burrito.

Hope looked at her expectantly, glad to see her, but flashed her that scathing look that only a woman can give to another woman when they expect them to talk with their mouth full.

After carefully swallowing her bite, she wiped her mouth with her napkin. Now it was her turn to keep this woman waiting. Turning with the sophistication her burrito did not provide, she said, "Oh, I don't know. I get a message to meet the number two terrorist behind AQNA and..."

"I need money and for money I will provide you with the information you need."

"To stop your organization's acts from happening?"

"Actually that's your job."

"Wow, it's that simple, huh?"

"Pretty much."

"Why can't I believe you?"

"Oh, but you can Agent Rausch. You can."

"How do I even know you are who you say you are?"

Hope knew who Grace was she just could not admit it. Doing so would jeopardize Grace's cover. The money aspect of this was all part of the show. Why else would a suspected terrorist sell out her jihadist group.

Grace knew Hope was wearing a wire. It was standard CIA protocol. She also knew someone within the British government would hear the recording. Discretion was the better part of valor here.

"Don't play games, Hope. You will lose if you do. Pay me Five hundred thousand dollars; I want forty ten-thousand dollar bills and twenty five-thousand dollar bills. Place them in a brown envelope and leave it taped under the park bench that faces the equestrian statue of King Christian V in Kongens Nytorv in Copenhagen, Denmark. Tomorrow at five p.m."

"And if I *can* come up with your half a million dollars?"

"You will have a clue to preventing the next 7/7 on British soil," Grace added for the benefit of whomever the UK government assigned to listen to the tape. "Always a pleasure, Hope."

"I wish I could say likewise," sneered Hope. When she failed to hear anything behind her for a long minute Hope ventured a peek. No one was there except some Goth teenagers.

Bury St Edmunds, England

Emile answered her door, not expecting anyone this early for the bi-monthly poker game. Tambra stood in the doorway wearing a long brown skirt, white blouse and black knee-high boots.

"Poker night has gone formal," snickered Emile.

"Shut up," Tambra said as she entered Emile's quaint apartment above the Bury St. Edmunds Arc Shopping Centre.

She and twenty others like her lived in the relatively new two-bedroom apartments. Emile kept the larger bedroom for herself and turned the smaller one into an office/guest room. That left a freakishly small kitchen for the poker feast and tiny living area for the poker table.

"I just came from the school. Do you want some help or not?"

"I've just spent the last two hours working feverishly on this place. Can't you tell?" Emile asked hopefully.

Looking around, Tambra warmly replied, "Emile, it looks great!"

Over the past few months Tambra had moved deeper into Emile's social circle. It started with Tambra's transfer to the Bolars. Then she became crewed with Mark. Two months ago, she came to their April poker game at Sammy's house and everyone agreed to invite her as a permanent member to replace James, their maintenance officer friend, who was deployed for a few months. Everyone liked her fun, can-do attitude. Even Emile admitted she was pretty cool to hang out with.

Emile liked Tambra but there was something amiss. Her alarm bells still sounded every time they met. Not a vicious, "she is out to get you" kind of warning but more of a "watch out girlfriend" type claxon.

Puzzling. I need to keep an eye on her tonight.

Spreading her hands innocently and with a warm smile, Emile pleaded with Tambra to stay, help and she would not say another word about her outfit. She helped her cause by pouring Tambra a beer from the pin (mini keg) she had on tap. The UK kegs held 20 liters, approximately 36 pints or 4.5 gallons of beer. Emile had a friend who worked at a local microbrewery and provided her with one on request. It was a very cost-effective way to drink with a large group of people as long as everyone wanted to drink the same type of beer.

Giggling, Tambra said, "That's more like it."

Tambra volunteered at the local secondary school in Bury St. Edmunds. Every other Saturday she was free, she tutored the children in reading and cognitive skills. Tambra explained, while they set out the chips, dips and nuts, that tonight was a parent-teacher conference and she attended to meet some parents and speak with them about her more special children. Tambra specialized in motivational techniques to help students succeed.

"There is a book out that I swear by, it is Sarah Armstrong's *Teaching Smarter with the Brain in Focus*. Most of my lesson plans incorporate some ideas from that book. It really helps me create situations in the classroom to engage my students so they comprehend better and achieve more. Armstrong refers to them as brain-boosting tools for teachers, and they work."

Emile appreciated the help setting up but also suspected it was just as much for Tambra to get out of the house and away from her husband. As such a visible couple, their troubles were a poorly kept secret.

Sean arrived fifteen minutes early, so he and Tambra chatted at the table while counting out the poker chips. Emile peeked in on them twice to make sure everything was alright. Each time she did she had the distinct impression she intruded on something private. They both seemed embarrassed and yet happy. She stopped looking in after the second visit. It was as if she was not welcome in her own home. The feeling did not sit well with her and she ran to the door when the chime announced that another player had arrived.

Mark, Brad and a cute dark-skinned woman stood on the open landing.

"Em, this is Kate Healy recently transferred to Lakenheath from Mildenhall. Kate now runs the Forty-eighth Security Police squadron. Kate, may I introduce tonight's hostess with the mostest, Emile Bergren?"

Now Emile remembered: Sean had asked if, as a favor, he could invite Kate to the game. A messy firing of the colonel in charge of the Lakenheath security police unit and his second-in-command, a female lieutenant colonel with whom he fraternized, brought Kate to the command position a few days ago.

The fraternization between officers, even those in a supervisory position, might have been overlooked, but because the SP second-in-command was married to another officer, things got ugly. Thus it was that Kate took command of the unit that suffered two self-inflicted losses. Both commanders were well-liked and had hidden their relationship very well. Emile knew through the grapevine that Kate was going to have an uphill battle. The security cops on the flight line were not happy about losing their bosses.

Kate was in the game for Sammy, who called from Scotland where he was stuck with a broken down F-15E. Kate was just a "friend" of Sean's. He swore to Emile that Kate was not one of his girlfriends. Emile believed him, but as with anything Sean, there was probably more to it.

Emile quickly evaluated the newcomer as they all entered. Kate wore comfortable newish jeans and a white oxford button down shirt over what looked like a brown camisole top. Her black hair curled like a bubbling brook onto each shoulder and framed a face that could talk a twenty-dollar bill off a beggar. She had a flat nose and large lips, but they seemed to fade into the background when she flashed her radiant smile. The gladiator in Emile quickly measured her up as 34-26-35. She might be trouble with this crowd. The night would be interesting.

Introductions were made and seats taken as Ralph arrived a few minutes late. The game started with everyone all smiles and grins.

An hour later most money was where it started. There were no big winners or losers yet, although Sean had fewer chips than anyone and Kate was down a bit too. Finally the deal returned to Emile and, as she anted for everyone, she declared the game while looking deeply into Sean's eyes.

"Seven stud, hi-lo, roll your own, Louisiana rollback."

Sean smiled at Emile and with much sarcasm teased her with, "You know I love you, don't you, Em?"

She had chosen his favorite game. On the last hand, Sean's deal, he had been too wrapped up in the moment and picked "pass-the-trash," also known as "screw your neighbor." He won the hand and it helped him steady his dwindling money pile, but now Emile took pity on him and threw him another lifeline. She truly was too good for him.

"I have a silly question, but what in the heck is 'high lie, roll your own joint, Louisiana hot sauce'?" asked a bemused Kate.

Sean jumped to the rescue before anyone else could help the damsel in distress. Explaining the "best hand and the worst hand split the pot – hi-lo – instead of two cards down and one up, all three are dealt down and the players choose which one to show and well… Louisiana rollback means the players pick their best five cards and, in an effort to get more betting, roll back each card one at a time with betting after each card. So it really is a piece of cake."

Kate stared at Sean with a deer-in-headlights look. After a few seconds she simply shook her head and nodded. She was not doing too well. She was almost halfway to running out of her first stake.

Emile shuffled the cards quickly. She never lost a card and never once looked down. She had a poker style few possessed. It was as if some hidden strings forever linked her small hands and the cards.

Ralph caught Kate staring at Emile's dexterity with the cards and leaned across Brad to whisper in Kate's ear.

"Spooky, huh. She says she played a lot in college. But I think she is a reincarnated Victoria Coren."

Kate looked at Ralph long and hard, then, realizing her error, flashed a bright smile and turned away quickly.

Ralph was enthralled by Kate. He could not stop looking over at her. He felt his pulse increase.

Why is it that all women flirt with me? I have a charmed life.

Kate opened her mouth to say something but couldn't tear her eyes away from Emile's card prowess. Emile scanned the players to make sure everyone was ready. Once she finished shuffling, Emile asked Sean on her right to cut.

"Thin to win," he declared as he took a little cut of the cards.

Emile snapped out the three cards to each player like a riverboat gambler and recapped the game. Eventually everyone rolled one of his or her three cards face up.

Since it was rollback at the end, Tambra started things off wisely with a "check" followed by a check from Mark.

Tambra wanted to hold back and not reveal her good hand too soon. Thus her coy check maneuver.

"Five," declared Ralph.

"There's always one," muttered Sean at Ralph's rejection of a free card for everyone.

"Yeah and it's usually you," Emile fired back.

Brad folded and the rest stayed in.

Now the remaining three cards for each player would come face up and when Emile dealt each card she included a commentary.

"Lady for the gal," said Emile as she dealt a queen to Tambra.

"Bust card to go with your hook, Mark." It was a large card ten of diamonds to pair up with his seven already showing.

"Duck to go with the five, nice low. Never scoff a duck," as Ralph got a two to go with his five.

"Pair of Cowboys for the lady," meant a king to pair up with Kate's other king.

"Bullet with the six to my friend from C-ville," she said as she dealt Sean an ace to go with his six.

"And the dealer gets a jack-me-off, no help." Emile got a jack to go with her eight.

Her voice seemed far away as her magical incantation flowed around the table.

"Pair of boys bets," Emile said to a reluctant Kate.

Another round of betting saw Mark drop out, and Emile's hands flew over the felt cloth especially placed on the table for the night. After five cards Emile showed J-8-6, Tambra Q-6-10 all hearts, Ralph shows 2-5-9, Kate K-K-7 and Sean Ace-6-J.

The next card was the last up card.

"Eight of diamonds for Tambra, no help with the flush."

"Bullet for the headmaster. Nice low. You can thank me later. Don't forget to tip the dealer and the wait staff at the end of the evening."

Sean saw Emile wink at Ralph after her last comment. She must be getting a little tipsy, he thought. Good for her.

"For my new friend this evening, a five. Sorry Kate, no more boys available."

"Sean, do you want it from the top of the deck or the bottom?" Emile teased.

"You know I always like it from the top," laughed Sean, eyeing Tambra and then, when she looked away, he snuck a glance at Kate to see if she got his double entendre. She did and smiled wickedly.

Emile saw his move too and felt a stab of pain where her heart used to be.

"A bitch for Sean." Venom dripped from her mouth as she said it.

"A hook for the dealer…how convenient for my straight."
Tambra Q-6-10 (hearts) and 8 diamonds
Ralph Ace-2-5-9
Kate K-K-7-5
Sean Ace-6-J-Q
Emile J-8-7-6
Everyone paid to play and Emile gave everyone a card face down. Again they all bet and no one folded.

"Now the real fun begins," smirked Emile. "Pick your five cards to play and place them in the order you want to reveal them. Remember this is high-low split."

Emile continued, "The first card is always free here. Show your first card."

Tambra revealed her queen of hearts, Ralph his ace, Kate surprised with her five, and Sean turned over his six.

The betting and revealing cards continued with no player backing down. Only one card remained hidden.

Emile recapped before the last round of betting started.

"Tally shows Q-10-6-9 all hearts. Possible flush. Ralph 5-4-3-2. Nice low or maybe a straight or both ways? Kate is a bit of a mystery with 7-5-4-3. Does she have a 6 and the straight or an ace or duck for the low hand? Interesting, dear. Sean 6-4-3-ace. Do you have a duck and the perfect low or a five and the straight as well?"

Emile paused and said, more to herself than anyone, "What the heck am I doing in this game?" She had 5-6-7-8 showing.

Emile pointed a finger at Tambra and said, "Looks like Tambra and the Queen bets."

"Fifty" and Tambra put two blue chips in.

"Fifty and I raise Fifty." Ralph placed four blue chips in.

"What the heck. It's only money right? I call" claimed an exasperated Kate.

"Sean have you grown a pair in the last five minutes or are you going to fold?" Tambra teased him from across the table. Every so often he thought he smelled a whiff of her perfume. Light Blue by Dolce and Gabbana. Cedarwood and jasmine filled his nostrils each time he caught it. He could also see a hint of her black lacy bra thru her white blouse when she rose up to reach across the table for betting. His excitement for what would come later tonight had him underachieving at the table.

"In and raise you all 50."

"Em, I think that is 150 to you," Sean stated, oozing with sarcasm.

Sean reflected on Emile's transformation during poker night.

Emile, in a word, was modest, honest and hesitant. She was the picture of you-first manners. She had beautiful, trusting instincts that could find no fault with anyone. Yet when she sat at the poker table, all vestments of her quiet mentality come off. She sipped her light beer impatiently. Her neat and ordered world was completely the opposite at the table. Her chips stood not in neat stacks but were stirred into a maelstrom of reds, blues and whites. She was a player. She played to win.

Emile casually tossed in twenty red chips. "Your 150 and why not take the last raise and make it 200 total. Oh and twenty reds in protest so whoever wins will have to divide that mess."

Tambra put in her 150 remaining, Ralph put in 100 as did Kate and then Sean called with 50.

"OK, declare. Remember take two chips under the table come up with one closed fist. Then we show what is in our fist. If you have no chips you are going for low hand only, one chip is high hand only and two chips means going both ways-but you have to win both ways or you lose everything. You can use your other two cards if you go both ways. Good luck gentlemen and better yet ladies." Emile always put that little luck spiel in. Sean made a note to ask her if she had ever been to Las Vegas.

Everyone complied and put a closed fist on the table. Then opened them to reveal their decisions. No surprise Tambra went high, Ralph surprised everyone with a rare both ways call, Kate went low, Sean went low and Emile went high.

Again Emile took control with "Lets do the low hand first. Show your last card."

Kate had 2-3-4-5-7.

Sean rolled a two for the perfect low. Kate started to protest that it was higher than hers because of the ace but Sean cut her off like an adult telling a child there was no candy right before dinner.

Emile felt sorry for the newcomer, but the house rules were quoted before the first card was dealt. Their house rules made the ace low in cases of low hand, so ace-2-3-4-6 was the perfect low. The rules also stated if you went both ways (attempting to win both the high and low hand) you could use any combination of five from your seven cards.

"You were playing against a stacked deck, Kate. Not only did those two have perfect low hands, but you were playing with the wrong information. I am sorry" Emile consoled.

Emile truly was sorry. It was terrible luck to lose against two perfect low hands. Emile knew the odds in poker and the average winning hand for low hand was 9-6-X-X-X. And the average winning high hand? Emile smiled thinking of three eights and how much better her straight was. She should win half the pot easily.

Laughing, Kate blew it off. "Heck, I can lose everything twice over and it's still cheaper than going to the movies. And here I get chicken wings, pizza, quiche and delicious brownies."

Emile beamed at the compliment to her refreshments and nodded in appreciation.

Ralph also had a perfect low with an ace and then a six from his other two cards.

"So far Sean gets a fourth and Ralph gets a fourth for sharing low hand. Ralph, I think I know what you have for a high hand." Emile played it out a little bit. She knew he had a straight 2-3-4-5-6 but she had a higher straight 5-6-7-8-9 so she wanted to twist the knife a bit.

"But my little old straight to the nine beats yours," she said and with a flourish she rolled over her remaining card.

Sean's "Hallelujahs!" started seconds after she showed her nine.

A hint of a smile crossed Emile's face as she said "I admire your guts, my friend. But since you went both and did not win it both ways, you lose everything. Sean gets the low hand share now."

"You were damn lucky, Rider," grumbled Ralph.

"Better lucky than good, I always say," gloated Sean.

Emile was just about to rake in her share when Tambra called out meekly, "Not so fast, Bambi," in her best matronly voice.

Sean cringed whenever Tambra called Emile "Bambi." He knew she hated the call sign. Sean never used it. Emile thought it was a sign of weakness and felt like everyone in the squadron thought she was somehow not up to the task of flying in a high performance aircraft. She needed to get over that irrational fear.

Tambra turned over her own surprise as the eight of hearts completed her flush. Emile shook her head. The odds of a flush in seven-card stud were something like 1 in 500.

"I believe the high hand is mine. Sean and I get to share the pot." She smiled at Sean. Emile leaned back and watched them split the pot like greedy crows over a dead carcass.

"You know poker is America's game," was Tambra's only comment during the division of their loot.

Sean's reply convinced Emile the two were up to no good. "Yeah, sex is good but poker lasts longer."

They were cheating all right. But not at poker.

***

The poker game ended at 11:15. Ralph and two others had wives or families so they usually begged off at 11. Ralph lost most nights. Tonight was no exception. Down $7, he said little before making his way to his car. He checked under his seat to make sure the package was still there and started his journey through Bury St. Edmunds.

Ralph arranged for the drop between 11 and midnight. He was important enough to warrant a window for his drop off information. He had demanded that concession and they had given it to him. This way he could attend the poker game and then drop off his packet of information on his way home. No one would be the wiser.

At first his handler just wanted little bits of non-classified information. Teacher work schedules for the weeks ahead or the budget for the school's upcoming year. Nine months ago when he started feeding information it was all a little bit innocent. Recently the information escalated. Now it was a school diagram including a schematic of the southern gate. Last month it was a layout of the fuel truck depot. He got that from James with relative ease since the man owed him for getting him out from under his gambling debt.

He headed for the fish and chip shop on top of the hill by the train station, parking just out front. Normally the fish and chips shop would be heaving on a Friday night but not until the young people came out of the nightclubs and pubs. So at 11:30 it was still early and not too crowded. Ralph made his way in and ordered his fish and chips. The order came soon thereafter, wrapped in wax paper to keep the grease in. He sat on a bench outside in the warm night air. The fish was plentiful, the chips greasy and mushy. Eating and finishing in a hurry, Ralph turned and walked down the dimly lit street toward a waste bin on the corner. Deftly he balled up his leftover paper bag and then swapped it with another identical looking wrapper he removed from his jacket pocket. He tossed the wrapper into the bin on top of the other foodstuffs and swiftly returned to his car, never daring to look back and see the homeless man rummaging in the bin. The information would make its way to Grace tomorrow.

Arriving at Lakenheath Air Base at midnight, Ralph slowed down as he approached the south gate. He dimmed his lights and rolled down his window to show his identification to the gate guard. Lightly guarded at this time of night, the British police guard working with the American security forces waived him through after a cursory look at the ID card. Instead of heading home, Ralph parked at the dark, empty school.

Unlike the school days where children would be running down the halls, laughing and giggling, tonight the school was deathly silent. Ralph's shoes made a slight clacking as he strided confidently to his office. His door was slightly ajar but no light showed through. He pushed the wooden barrier open slightly with his foot and saw her sitting, arms folded on the couch. She stared at him with deep, dark, angry eyes.

"You're late," she accused, gathering courage from somewhere inside her.

"So what," he replied. His tone and sharpness left no doubt in her mind who was in control of their relationship. Crossing the small, somewhat cramped room, Ralph turned on a desk lamp as he sat behind his large mahogany desk. Not for the first time in his stay at Lakenheath, he wondered who the fool was that ordered such a large desk for such a small office. It dominated the room leaving no other space for the normal clutter of a principal's office. His filing cabinets were in an adjacent office so that he could at least have a large vertical locker for his wardrobe.

She leapt up off the couch. Her enthusiasm for starting her
chore hid the seething hatred for what it had become. Ralph swung
the chair away from his desk to face her approaching form. His eyes
were cold.

She lived on base with her mother. Her father left them when
her mother deployed to Germany five long years ago. He was not
military and finally could not handle the moves and the fact that her
mom was the breadwinner. It was an easy decision for her mom to
accept the assignment overseas. She and her daughter would leave a
bad relationship and start over, moving from the U.S. to England.

Cindy wore what he had directed her to for this rendezvous.
Tennis shoes. Always tennis shoes. The guy was an archetypical
schoolgirl misogynist. This month's request was the Lakenheath
Cheerleaders' outfit. Red and white skirt to the knees. Cheerleader
top with "Raiders" blazoned across her chest. No bra. He insisted
on that most months. She removed it in his office when she came
in. He knew she did this and had a video camera hidden in his
office to film such things and their encounters. It was blackmail
insurance against any possible fallout. Of course, he had played his
little power trip maneuver on over a half dozen girls so far and
none had complained. He suspected they loved the power they got
by getting off the top man and getting some perks associated with
his power as well.

In addition to entry on the cheerleading squad, other benefits
included permission for school trips that were above and beyond.
For example, last year's special trip to Paris for the Renoir
exhibition at the Musée de la Garde. He went as a chaperone.
Unfortunately his wife could not make it. On that one he was
almost tempted to invite two of his "sex slaves" to his room at the
same time for a ménage à trois. He had chickened out at the last
second, fearing that if they knew without a doubt both were
involved it might give them confidence to fight back somehow
against him. That was the last thing he needed: for the two girls he
was currently "cultivating" to wise up and unite.

Kneeling in front of his chair, Cindy placed her hands behind
her back and waited for his instructions. She swallowed and looked
up at him trying to put on her best "holier-than-thou" face. He was
not ugly but older. Cindy thought about their encounters afterwards

and she liked to describe him as having a middle age balcony over the toy store.

Ralph parted his legs and inched his bulk forward so his buttocks rested on the front of the chair. He nodded to her and their ritual began.

Cindy and her mother transferred from another base several months ago. She was a cheerleader at her much-smaller school. Now, at the larger Lakenheath, she found her chances were slim to none of making the cheerleader squad next year.

Cindy was easy to trap. He called her in one day after school for a school dress code violation. It was her first offense and he explained it did not need to go on her official record. If only she would do something for him. He manipulated her into sending him a picture of her topless. Her full facial profile was in the picture. No doubt who it was. As instructed, she had written in red lipstick across her chest the word "whore." Ralph told her it was her punishment for inappropriate attire at school and if she did this all was forgiven and no formal notice would appear in her records.

Sexting was not that big of a deal around school. Cindy and most of her friends did it. The girls were a little more conservative. The boys would snap a photo of their "junk" as they called it and send it out into the circle of friends. As long as it stayed among the few that were actively doing it, then no big deal. Everyone knew not to post it on Facebook or Instagram or anything like that. Most knew it could be a crime. They saw the warnings on television via the American Forces Network (AFN), the military satellite network of TV, that sexting could be prosecuted as child pornography. But then again, dope was illegal and so was underage sex, but some kids did that too. It was all a protest against the establishment and the future they were leaving for this generation.

Cindy sent the picture and then everything spiraled downhill. Next he blackmailed her with the picture saying it was a much larger offense and she would be expelled for the semester if word got out. But he did give her something in return for her efforts. He guaranteed she would make the cheerleading squad and she did.

She was his. And he made sure she knew in perfectly clear terms what would happen if she told anyone about what was going to happen between them. Cindy was trapped. She wanted to get the perks but now found it came with too high a price.

For his part Ralph expected nothing less than complete dedication from his "girls." He played basketball in college. As an athlete on campus he received a great room, spending money and lots of perks. The basketball team did very well for such a small school and invitations to lavish parties became the norm. Eventually Ralph just came to expect such gifts. In his mind he was entitled to them.

Even his girlfriends at that time were entitlements, or so he thought, from his performance on the court. In actuality, the women he dated were other athletes or cheerleaders. Female athletes in training are more likely to date another athlete simply because of the familiarity with a training regime. But Ralph did not know this. He thought the babes came with the room, food and fame because of his special skills. He became narcissistic early in life.

Natalie was easier to manipulate. Ralph caught her using marijuana in the girls' locker room after school one day. From that day forward she was his to twist and use. Neither of them knew it but she was also funding the terrorists in a small way. Her money for the drugs went to another student who in turn was distributing for another man. This other man took his profits and paid a percentage to a man named Nasir who provided the drugs. Nasir provided some protection and intelligence to this man about the English law system that attempted to thwart his illegal activities. Nasir used his profits to support his terrorist activities, which included AQNA. The world truly was a global economy. Unfortunately that not only applied to food and products but also to prostitution, drugs and terrorism.

***

Grace did not trust anyone-especially snitches. Ralph was betraying his country and the base he lived on. She loathed Ralph but relied on his position and information to help with her plan. She ran surveillance on Ralph a few weeks earlier. Getting on the U.S. air base was child's play to her. The school doors were chained with pad locks at night. There was not a key in the world that she could not replicate.

Sam Hendricks

She set up a small remote-controlled, motion-activated, hidden camera and microphone to spy on him in his office. A week later, after reviewing the tapes one day, she found his indulgence with Natalie. Shortly after that she watched in horror as he corrupted Cindy.

PART II

The Romance

Sam Hendricks

Chapter 11

Copenhagen, Denmark

Hope and Connor sat together on the short flight. She was quiet, lost in her thoughts. He enlightened her on the customs of Copenhagen.

Reading from his pocket guidebook, "Did you know that June 23rd, St. John's Eve, is a night of celebration before the feast day of St. John the Baptist? Bonfire night had been a public holiday until the 18th century. The Danes had a tradition of celebrating holidays on the evening before the actual day, thus the night of June 23rd was bonfire night. It was the day where the medieval wise men and women would gather special herbs needed to care for their people for the remainder of the year. These modern day doctors built a large bonfire to keep away the evil spirits that night."

"Interesting," was all she could muster while glancing at him amused at his boyish enthusiasm. "Interesting," she repeated still elsewhere.

"I wonder if she picked this date for a reason?" he asked. He continued not bothered by her inattention.

"In modern-day Denmark all across the country speeches, picnics, songs and even an occasional straw witch go with the bonfires. The fairly recent addition of burning a witch made of cloth and straw was the last act of the evening. In fact, it says here Bonfire night in Denmark is truly one of the most captivating family events of Danish culture."

Hope did not hear his last sentences instead she answered his question from earlier. "This woman does everything for a reason. We have to expect the date is significant."

Just as Grace had arranged, Hope and Connor arrived in Denmark on June 23rd, St. John's Eve.

Copenhagen was alive with activity. Bonfires raged in many popular street areas such a Nyhavn and Stroget. Students roamed the city celebrating their recent graduations. It was a beautiful midsummer weekend in the middle of the Copenhagen Jazz Festival. All of this added to the ambiance of the city.

Hope's plan was to find Janus by following Grace once she took the money. Unfortunately, that task became much more difficult with all of the increased activities throughout the unofficial capital of Scandinavia.

"If we want to catch this terrorist, why don't we have more resources to do it than just the two of us?" asked Connor as they walked down Stroget, the pedestrian street that led toward the center of town and Nyhavn.

Hope turned to answer him, slightly irritated at his arrogance.

"I don't see any other Scotland Yard resources here in Copenhagen. Besides, everyone has a budget crunch these days so assets are limited. We just have to catch Janus ourselves."

Her support in the field was limited but she had assurance from her boss if she found Janus, a phone call would bring the Danish special police.

"Bloody hell," Connor answered, as they passed a sexy lingerie shop. Typical male, Hope thought, watching his head swivel around to get a second look.

"Don't tell me you're a British prude, Connor."

Connor flashed a smile at Hope to stall her and then snuck one last look at the fading sign for the shop.

"Naw," he replied in his best imitation of a Southern accent. "I just like my sex in the bedroom or on the telly. Not in a shop!"

"Right," she exaggerated and let his innuendo hang silently before directing them both back to the mission.

"Remember we are looking for his second in command, Grace Matiseni, AKA Madison or Maddi Gonzalez. She is raven-haired, about five foot eight. Her hair is cropped. She has an athlete's build. Darkish complexion so that could narrow things a bit here in the Scandinavian capital."

She checked her Glock 19. The 9 MM bullets could stop any threat and she liked the fact there was no external safety. The quick and easy reloads of her 15-cartridge magazines gave her comfort. It was 7.28 inches long and weighed 30 ounces loaded. Security services used it the world over.

The 9 MM cartridges designed by Georg Luger in 1902 are also called Parabellum (derived from the Latin *"Si vis pacem, para bellum"* meaning "If you seek peace, prepare for war."). Hope loved that phrase.

"Brown eyes. Intelligent, cunning and with a wild streak."
Connor dodged the late evening shoppers as he fired back.
"Sounds like you know her pretty well."

"Tracked her for over a year is more like it," spat Hope, hate in
her eyes. Her emotions were real. The truth about Grace and her
connections to Hope were lies. Hope did not like the way things
were going with her undercover agent and wanted to reel her in
now.

"What nationality is she?"

Hope did not want to lie to Connor so she decoyed him a bit
with her next answer. "She is not really from a nation but
imagination. Her imagination is what we have to worry about. She
is a free lancer. Not a dedicated radical. She wants money now but
who knows what she will want in a month."

The summer solstice had occurred just two days earlier so
midsummer night was quite short. Today the sun would not set
until 10pm and allowed for just six and half hours of official
nighttime. In reality much of that "nighttime" was not real
darkness.

Hope and Connor arranged to have an envelope of money
taped under a park bench in the center square. Hope observed from
one side, Connor from the other. Connor would trail any suspect
with Hope following a short distance behind.

The square had a major thoroughfare running north-south on
either side which merged into a "V" on the south side of the square.
The east side route went one-way north and the west side went one-
way south. Leading away from the square on the west side were
numerous pedestrian streets, including Stroget the main shopping
street. Nyhavn branched off from the square to the east.

Nyhavn was a center of entertainment and on midsummer night
it was one of the busiest in the area. Nyhavn, or "New Harbor,"
was a 17th century waterfront in Copenhagen. Stretching from
Kongens Nytorv, the "Kings New Square," to the harbor front,
Nyhavn was a large canal with many historical wooden ships. The
north, or sunny side, included numerous brightly colored 17th and
18th century townhouses, bars and restaurants, which faced the
harbor. Even in the cold Scandinavian winters, some strong-willed
individuals sat outdoors with a beer, blanket and heaters provided

by the establishments. Tonight that was not a worry. Temperatures swelled to 25 degrees Celsius, a balmy 76 Fahrenheit.

They watched the drop area to see who would pick up the money. Both expected Grace to pick it up or Janus. An hour later their waiting paid off. A short, dark-skinned woman with black-cropped hair plopped down on the bench just long enough to reach under it and rip away the envelope then bounced up and began walking away.

Connor announced the pick up into his two-way microphone on his cuff link, standard Scotland Yard issue these days. He began to follow her as she weaved in and out of the crowd of revelers.

"I've got Grace heading east from the center square towards Nyhavn. She has the package."

"Copy. Follow her, but not too close. I want her to lead me to Janus. He is the objective!" Hope lagged behind so as not to give herself away to Grace as Connor followed.

Connor followed her for the next two blocks, hanging about a block behind. Hope hung back cautiously, observing and beginning to sense something was wrong. Connor was too good-looking to be missed. Tall, broad-shouldered and with a neatly trimmed beard, he stood out simply because he did not stand out. That's some commentary on today's society.

The pursuit of his target was not easy. She kept looking back behind her every few hundred yards and stopping to look in shop windows to see behind her. Nyhavn was a mob of people. Some stopping to chat with others eating, some drinking by the pier. His target soon left the bustle of Nyhavn.

Connor reported every turn and every stop. In each instance he would be away from the target while Hope continued slowly closer. Then she would notify him when the target resumed her journey and Connor would continue the pursuit. They both drifted further into the city. Turning and walking. Finally, after about four more blocks, the target stopped and put on a red beret.

Loud music blared from a large open truck filled with banners, balloons and students as it roared by on the street. The students yelled and waved at Connor as they passed.

To add to the madness that is Bonfire night, the Danish schools usually have their graduations on or about the same time. Luckily the schools stagger their graduations throughout the weeks but quite a few schools have graduations on Bonfire night.

Graduation classes are usually small, close-knit groups of 20-30 teenagers. On the day of their graduation a large party or lunch is held at the school. Afterwards the students leave to board their "lastbil" or truck. Most of these trucks are classified as small flatbeds. The students "pimp" the trucks with inflatable devices, posters, placards, balloons and bed sheets with slogans.

For the next 24 hours they proceed to visit every student's home. Accompanied by loud music, hooting, hollering and joyful fun, the truck full of students winds its way through Copenhagen, stopping for an hour or less at each home. Once they arrive at a home, the hosts, mostly proud parents and family, provide food and drink. After visiting everyone's house the students, many very inebriated, stop at their final destination - a party barn or location for the night.

Grace remembered these scenes from her childhood growing up in Copenhagen. She chose this place and this time for a reason. She had strong friends in the city who were valuable allies both in and out of government. Some were even in the shadowy underworld.

So it was that evening as graduation buses whirled around Copenhagen every few minutes. The buses honked their horns as the graduating students hung out of the rails with bottles of beer and signs begging for cars to honk if they liked the graduates. Some girls, as the night progressed, became more generous with the amount of skin they showed. Some boys did as well, although the sight of a male mooning did nothing to improve the bonfire night antics.

Every student who passed the upper secondary school examination received his or her student cap. All students wore white caps with their colored ribbons on top. Most girls wore a white dress or top. The boy's attire varied too much to generalize.

Hope thought to herself that this was too easy. Grace was being too blatant. Hope slowed and began to look around her, trying to get her bearings. Where were they? Why was the target leading them this way? Why the hat and why now? It was an obvious way to track someone; the target did not want them to lose her.

Hope should have keyed her microphone and informed Connor but she hesitated for just a few seconds. She wanted to try and find Grace herself. Her first sense of foreboding came when she caught a whiff of cinnamon.

Grace had found her.

Hope felt a gun in her back.

"Glad to see you again, Agent Rausch. Do be a good girl and do as I say. I would hate to ruin your St. John's Eve with a bullet to the head. Go left and down the stairs. Let's have a drink you and I, shall we?" Hope obeyed and stepped down the narrow stairs into an underground bar called Velvet Underground.

The bar was dark and loud music played from an old video jukebox in the far corner beside the hallway to the toilets. The bar counter was long and wooden and ran along the right side of the establishment as you entered. Hope had to duck her head on the last step. Grace did not.

A few eyes turned to watch the ladies enter but they soon went back to celebrating. Six or seven students stood at the far end of the bar away from the entrance singing and dancing a bit, but mainly drinking on their bar crawl. Connor continued to follow what Hope now knew had been a decoy.

"Take the first booth on the left, Hope. Nice and slow. You know the drill." She sounded happy to have Hope in her gun sight.

Grace swung effortlessly into the booth across from Hope and held her pistol underneath the table.

"Please don't make me use this," she nodded her head towards the gun without taking her eyes off of Hope.

"Order us two Carlsbergs. Don't worry, I'll pay. I seem to have recently come into some cash." Grace smiled at her own humor. Hope ordered the drinks from a passing waitress. The drinks arrived quickly and the two continued their conversation.

"So tell me, what information have I bought today?" asked the skeptical blond agent.

"Focus on the August Beach Volleyball tournament."

"Any particular date?" asked Hope.

"I think even you will be able to figure out which day to concentrate on, Hope."

The insult included a tip, and Hope knew it. It must be either the finals or a day when a celebrity or dignitary was supposed to visit.

Hope took in Grace's features as she outlined some aspects of the attack. Grace somehow looked younger than Hope expected. Was she trying to look great for her boyfriend Janus?

Grace had both hands underneath the table holding the gun over her white skirt. Hope remembered seeing her shoes just under the plain cotton skirt: black high top Converse All Star Chuck Taylors, or "Chucks" as the kids called them. They were the most popular brand of shoes in Copenhagen. She had seen over a hundred in the past hour alone.

Hope did not know it, but Grace had her reasons for giving away Ahmed and the London attackers. They were a decoy for her mission. She did not want them to succeed since she was not there to control the damage. She definitely did not want Ahmed anywhere near her next target. He asked too many questions lately: Where is Janus? Why has he not shown his face to us? What can we accomplish in London?

No, Grace wanted Ahmed caught and hopefully killed. His action would serve as a smoke screen for her main attack as she extracted revenge on the Americans who let her brother die.

"So, Agent Rausch. I would focus on the execution command via the cell network and try to find Ahmed while you're at it," she continued. "And one more thing. This one is on the house. Another attack is coming, but I cannot tell where yet. It may be another cell that I am not in charge of..." She hesitated then said, "I think it will be a few days after the volleyball attack. I have heard some chatter about the town of Bury St. Edmunds so I think it will target a UK asset there. I will try and get you more info."

Hope had heard enough. She wanted to get Grace. Raising her hands, she interrupted Grace and asked, "May I cross my legs. Or will that draw a bullet from you?"

"No, by all means do. I always enjoyed seeing your legs, Hope." It was the answer she expected and she sighed with exasperation while putting her hands back down. She crossed her legs and, in doing so, touched the transmitter device in her front right skirt pocket. With a little luck she'd activated the front mike button and their conversation was now broadcast to Connor.

Hope tried to distract Grace with a little flattery. "I think I have all that, but who is the decoy target we, or I should say, my partner Connor, is mistakenly following? She has the money too, I might point out."

Hope took a sip of her beer to ease any fear Grace may have of opening up to her. They were just two girls out having a drink, except of course, one had a loaded Browning 1911 pistol pointed at the other.

"Oh, she's just a friendly look-alike who is distracting your boyfriend... from Scotland Yard isn't he?" Grace lapsed into a British accent. "Or is it MI6. I can never tell with those British types."

Returning to a whisper, she continued, "And the money has been transferred five times by now, my dear."

***

Connor closed in on his target when he heard their conversation, spinning her around abruptly while saying, "Grace" as if she were an old friend.

Back in the bar Grace beamed, "But I must admit, she's not as good looking as I am."

Connor gazed on a goddess. She smiled and gave him a Danish grin, saying, "Jeg har aldrig modt dig, Sir."

He did not understand her but gathered it was something along the lines of a very friendly "Who the hell are you?" He flashed his badge and placed her under arrest, leaning her against the Illums Bolighus department store nearby. He frisked her first for the envelope and Grace was right: it was long gone.

The decoy, soon after the pick-up, had turned to look around casually and flipped the envelope a short distance to a person coming directly in front of them. This person then flipped it into the waiting open newspaper of another accomplice walking in the opposite direction behind yet another accomplice. The three other accomplices then performed two more transfers to further complicate tracking before joining Grace in the bar. The two men and a woman were now standing at the bar and drinking. Grace used local friends in Copenhagen, not cell members. This was her game, not AQNA.

Connor had but a split second to make a decision. Arrest the decoy and be unable to support Hope or turn the useless decoy lose and try to find his partner.

Hope made his decision for him.

She looked at Grace's untouched beer. "I see you're not drinking your beer Grace. Maybe the Velvet Underground has margaritas? Shall I ask the waitress?"

***

Connor released the decoy then quickly accessed his iPhone for information on the Velvet Underground and the quickest way to get there. He hailed a cab at the nearby taxi stand and in his best Danish-English asked for the Velvet Underground.

His cab travelled a short distance before it became ensnarled in the traffic jam caused by the student graduation buses. Connor found himself surrounded by the loud party trucks or angry residents trying to get through the traffic jams the students caused. Handing the cabbie twenty Danish Kroners Connor exited and began to run towards the Velvet Underground-fighting the crowds out enjoying the night.

***

Grace laughed and declined with a shake of her head. "No, I wouldn't want that showing up in my CIA file, now would I? Speaking of files. Yours says you pack a Glock 19. Where is it? I know you're wearing."

Hope slowly and carefully pulled open the left side of her blazer to reveal her holster.

"I probably ought to have that. See, I am feeling a bathroom moment coming on and I wouldn't want you shooting me in the back. Now would I?"

Grace motioned for the gun. "Grip first under the table and with your left hand."

Hope obliged.

"Good, Hope. See, you *can* work well with others," she mocked. "I promise to give it back, empty of course, when I return from the loo."

Grace saw her friend move from out front of the underground bar. He entered and nodded to Grace behind Hope's back, signaling that Connor was on his way in.

Hope, you infuriate me more than anyone I know. But I love the way you work. I don't know how you did it but you got the cavalry to come to the rescue.

"Time for that bathroom break. Just sit quietly and I will be right back." Grace slipped off the booth just as Bon Jovi started to sing "Blaze of Glory." She backed her way into the crowd at the far end of the bar and ducked down the hallway towards the bathrooms. Connor slowly entered once he heard Grace say she was going to the bathroom. Seeing Hope, and that she was in no harm, he approached her.

"Drinking without me?" he asked.

"Shut up!" she snapped. "She has my gun. Any way out of here?"

"No, no exits in or out other than the front door."

"Give me your spare piece and let's get this over with."

Connor reached down and discretely pulled out his ankle gun, giving it to Hope while he hid his own as they made their way to the hallway. The bartender pushed a button behind the bar and the jukebox started up with a popular Danish song for graduation. Frankie Goes to Hollywood began the steady heavy toe-tapping beat of "Relax." The students, energized by the music and their beer, began a wild flailing dance. The other occupants at the bar joined in from behind and Hope and Connor were squeezed and delayed.

Connor had a rather sleek blond Danish girl gyrating up next to him. He seemed to be enjoying himself and Hope had to drag him away. They entered the dimly lit hallway to the restrooms and passed a young female student wearing nothing above the waist. She was very intoxicated and very happy. She winked at Connor and he stopped and pushed against the wall to allow her to pass.

The men's room was the first door on the left. The women's room was the next door on the right. A private employee's the only other door at the hallway end. Suddenly shouts of joy and hoots of hurrah sprang from the bar as the young topless girl entered. The jukebox song seemed to crank up even louder.

Connor checked the men's room while Hope waited. He returned, satisfied that no one was in there. Hope slowly opened the women's door and peered in. Small but clean, the room contained two stalls, one useless urinal and no windows. Grace was not present.

"She's gone," spat a frustrated Hope.

Grace knew Copenhagen like the back of her hand. She had lived there for two years with her parents when her father served as a minor diplomat, and was comfortable blending in. Hope knew this.

Connor opened the employee's door but it contained no windows, just a few kegs of beer. They walked back into the bar to hear the drunken Danish girl, who now wore a friend's shirt, bragging about something as several people tried unsuccessfully to shut her up.

In Danish she told her friends, "She gave me five thousand kroner for my hat, gown and shirt and a thousand more to walk out here topless. I love that woman!" Her comments were not completely understood by Hope but her gestures back down the hall tipped them off as to the outcome.

Hope and Connor rushed back down the hallway.

"She got that girl's clothes but escaped somehow out the back. What's behind this building?"

Connor tried to remember the layout the iPhone showed him when he put in the location. Hope burst through the employee door and now looked everything over with a more detailed eye. Scanning the walls and the floor she saw what she missed before; dust everywhere except in front of a bookshelf.

"I think this leads to the large square in front of Nyhavn and near Magasin department store."

"Quick help me with this." Hope looked for, and eventually found, a quick release lever that opened the bookcase into the room revealing a narrow unlit corridor. In the distance they saw a shimmer of light as Grace slipped out and onto the street. Darkness returned just as Connor used the flashlight on his iPhone to illuminate the corridor.

They made it out onto the street corner in time to see Grace, now dressed in a white shirt, skirt and cap, disappear into a crowd of hundreds of singing, cheering, and chanting graduates in white running around the statue in the square. Some were just starting their run; others were milling around and still others rushed back onto their waiting party trucks or busses to move on to another drinking stop. The cap on Grace and her upturned collar concealed her face well. She blended completely.

Grace mingled and then went left with another group onto the biggest waiting bus she could find, just as it was pulling away from the square. She did not care where it went as long as it was away from the center of Copenhagen. Peter Gabriel's "Big Time" blared from speakers positioned on either side of the bus. Students gyrated to the beat. Other students looked at her innocently when they noticed she was not in their class. She started to answer in flawless Danish, then realizing her new alias, slipped into some Americanized Dansk.

She explained to them that she graduated from the American school for diplomatic students and they were celebrating the same way. She was just lost, separated from her friends. She feigned a little inebriation and soon had all the friends she could hope for. Everyone took care of her for the next few hours as they had two more stops before their big party at a friend's summer home on the shore. Perfect, Grace thought, and I will give one of these guys a graduation night to remember. Now she just had to pick the least drunk, cutest and most intelligent young man of the group.

Hope's Hotel Room, Copenhagen – (Five hours later)

Hope awoke with a heart-stopping startle. Blessed with the ability to almost instantly wake up, she could not figure out what woke her in her darkened hotel room. She sensed something or someone inside the room. Instinctively she slowly moved her hand under her pillow.

Rats!

Her backup Glock 19 was missing. She placed it there before going to bed, as was her ritual. Now, she heard her intruder. A soft, gentle, almost apologetic cough came from a chair repositioned against the wall.

Suddenly a light broke the blackness. A bright beam shining directly into Hope's face and blinding her just as her eyes were beginning to adjust to the darkness. Her uninvited guest pointed a tall reading lamp at her, obscuring the light outline of Grace where she sat dressed entirely in black, legs crossed, her Brown 1911 resting casually in her lap.

"Hello, Hope." Grace paused to survey the room, shaking her head in dismay at the extravagant accommodation.

"How's my favorite CIA agent?" Grace continued.

"I'm your *only* CIA agent, Grace, so put that gun away." Hope silently and gracefully slipped off her covers while watching for any movements to stop her. If allowed, she was going to get out of bed.

Grace saw the silk covers begin to slip away from Hope's body. Grace knew it was a calculated move to distract her, but she was not falling for it. Not now. Not ever.

"Tsk...tsk...tsk...No, I think I like you right where you are Hope." Grace paused for effect for several seconds. A truck rumbled by outside on its way to an early morning delivery. "In bed. And yes, while technically true you are the only CIA agent I currently know, that is irrelevant to this discussion. Do you still wear those little blue...?"

"Get to the point, Grace." Hope cut her off.

"Ok, why all the skullduggery?"

"Would you believe the CIA does not like all the computer time you have run up on this one?'

Grace stifled a giggle. She had sent in several adamant requests for processing time from the Langley computers. And it paid off when they discovered the code Jeddah and Janus were using. She could never have uncovered that on her own. Hope had approved the requests so Grace knew Hope was stalling.

"Try again Hope. I need something better than that."

"The old man wants you to come in. He wants Janus arrested and you to come back into the fold. That is why I am here."

Grace began to laugh.

"What's so funny, Miss Matiseni?"

Between more laughter, Grace spit out, "Janus is dead."

Chapter 12

Grace flashed back to that fateful week which led to Janus' demise.

She did not hesitate. That night, while Janus lay soaking in the bathtub, Grace offered to scrub his back. The faintest hint of cinnamon came from a small stick in her mouth. Slinking into the bathroom in her sexiest lingerie, she leaned over the tub to rub his back, relaxing him further. She noticed his erection and smiled at her abilities even as she slipped the garrote around his neck. With his eyes closed in meditation, he never had a chance to recover from the tight wire. Blood flowed into his bath, turning the murky water into a pinkish pig red.

The next draft email came from Jeddah on Saturday. It was two days too late.

Janus,
Expedite disposal of girl. Expect contact to be Luton
Mosque.
Inshallah
Jeddah
manna

Grace assumed Janus' identity via the draft emails. She had the codes and the connections. Either this would work or not. She typed it up and hit "Save Draft" a few days later.

Jeddah
Peace be with you.
Girl disposed of. Heading to Europe. Will contact
Luton. Have found new girl as a patsy.
Janus
blood

She got her answer the day before she left for Europe.

Janus
God is great.
Your discretion on target(s). Meet two cells at
Betws-y-Coed on weekend of May 25. More to
follow.
Jeddah
angel

***

Focusing on Hope's hotel room and the present, Grace smiled at her situation. She now ran the cell acting as if she was Janus. She deceived both the CIA and AQNA.

"Grace, the director is closing Barbarossa and calling everyone back in."

Grace waited patiently for more.

"We lost an agent in another cell and the man does not want more exposure."

Shaking her head, Grace pled her case: "I am too close to something good here, Hope. This is cancelled over my dead body."

Hope had the good sense not to utter the obvious cliché but her facial expression and body language conveyed the message all the same.

"Hope, women should be running the CIA. We are better compromisers and sure as hell better listeners."

"If it makes you feel any better..."

"It doesn't. Continue."

"I disagreed with his assessment and tried to talk him out of it." Hope changed the conversation direction. "You really beat us like a drum today. That was a nice exit."

"Thanks. Your signal to your lover boy was a neat trick too."

"He's not my lover. You should come back to Langley and see the gadgets they've come up with in the two years you've been away. I think you have been away too long Grace." She did not mean for it to come out as hard as it sounded.

"Maybe I'll stop in some day. Hope, I am not going in now. If I do, something worse will happen. The attacks will still go on without me."

"I know." They would continue, but without Grace if Hope had any say in the matter. If the director wanted her back, it was her job to make it happen.

Grace saw Hope's nostrils flare. Hope was lying. Time to leave. Grace moved out of the chair towards the door to the balcony and yanked the lamp plug from the wall, plunging the room back into darkness.

Grace had worn a patch over her left eye. It was an old trick. She called it her pirate eye. By keeping the left eye completely covered she preserved her night vision in that eye. Much like someone who wakes up in the middle of the night and needs to go to the bathroom. If you turn on a light to see, you ruin your night vision and then, when returning from the bathroom when the lights are off, you end up stubbing your toe. If instead you cover one eye and keep night vision in it for the walk back in the dark, you do not stub that toe.

After turning off the light, Grace made her way quickly to the French doors and onto the balcony. Checking the restaurant canopy that rested below her, she hopped over the railing with one fluid motion. The drop of ten feet felt like an eternity but she hit the slanted strong tarp of the restaurant below and slid gracefully over the edge, landing on the sidewalk below. Two accomplices on either side protected her flanks. They all reached the waiting car by the curb within 15 seconds of Grace bidding Hope adieu.

Hope recovered just in time to see Grace and her associates speed away into the early morning. Hope was, in fact, wearing both pajama bottoms and panties underneath. She always did when in the field so she could react quicker. She should have expected something like this from Grace.

"Damn that bitch! She took two of my guns in less than twenty-four hours!"

To her pleasant surprise, Hope later found both guns neatly tucked away in her hotel room closet.

**

Grace spent the rest of the early morning huddled around a dying bonfire, on an isolated beach, west of the Danish capital. Her friends, associates really, left her alone, sensing her desire to reflect. "Stew" may have been a better adjective to describe her funk. She sat cross-legged in a yoga pose, back against a small berm, a warming blanket draped around her bikini-clad body to help ward off the slowly evaporating night's chill. Her recent soak in the sea jolted any thoughts of sleep from her mind.

What is it about Hope that so infuriates me?

They were close from college.

I'm past that now.

Grace tipped her head to one side to watch a singularly stubborn ember float high into the sky and disappear in a wisp of smoke and a crackle. Her dazed gaze caught the stars that made up the constellation Pisces just above the horizon. How appropriate. Pisces: victimized and moody. Grace was moody now. She became more despondent with the passing time.

I sacrifice.

That was her mantra in life. Since her brother's tragic death.

I will sacrifice everything.

Not hard to explain, really. After seeing her brother and his wife die horribly in front of her, Grace accepted that she was to blame for their deaths. And why not? She selfishly asked them to come to Afghanistan, so that she could be closer to them while there on her CIA-sponsored missions. She knew something was amiss that night when she caught the whine of the aircraft high above them, but she dismissed the warning sign, caught up in the rapture of the wedding party. If there was a Supreme Being, he had punished her – not by injuring her or taking her life – but by making her witness her brother leave this world.

She had sworn vengeance.

"Vengeance is mine, I will repay them." Grace quoted the book Tim used to carry with him. Of course she twisted the phrase a bit. Instead of God taking his vengeance, Grace became the avenger.

She sighed, thinking of all the trouble she had gone to in order to steal the NATO report about the mistaken bombing. All that trouble and it said nothing of interest to her. She wanted to know who and why. It said neither.

After Afghanistan, she returned briefly to Langley before her next assignment. It was then that she discovered, through her own employer, and only *after* sleeping with someone close to the top, that the French had done the bombing and that an American military police force was responsible for security in the region. Her nerdy computer friend had proven very helpful indeed.

She swore that day that she would have her revenge on the French aviator who led the mission, the person who ordered the bombing and the commander of the security forces. It would take time and money, but she had plenty of the first and was working on the second. And so it was that she came to use her position in her current organization to her advantage. The person who ordered the bombing would not pay this time. Their time would come though. Instead, with a prod here and a nudge there, she goaded Janus into attacking the hockey stadium when she knew the French team would be present.

The bus following her van as they made their escape in Canada did not "accidently" explode. Grace went over the wiring herself beforehand and made some modifications. The phone she used to communicate with them was a two-way signal device. Grace set it off herself. She killed two birds with one stone. Terrorists eliminated and a little bit of revenge for her.

Let's see how the French people feel when their own innocents die in a fiery bombing.

She did feel a little jolt from the mission and the results. But her joy was short-lived. She chided herself for foolishly going off track. She wanted the ones responsible. To make them pay.

Janus no longer followed her hints and suggestions so easily. He had lost interest in her but when he received instructions to eliminate her, she had beat him to the punch.

Now it was time to get back on track. She manipulated her resources for the bigger target. If the CIA could use terror groups for their own purposes, why couldn't she?

And the half a million dollars she now had. That kind of money would make all the difference for Grace. She planned to go rogue after this and money like that would start an assassin off in style. Of course, after her connections laundered the money she would end up with less than half that amount.

Was it not the best piece of thievery? She remembered something similar from a play she performed at Cambridge. *Women Beware Women*. For some strange reason the powerful play popped into Grace's head.

Bonfire night, and here I am sulking and thinking of college plays.

Chapter 13

Grace and the AQNA had a problem. The zealots who were willing to blow themselves up for a cause were not the sharpest knives in the drawer. The intelligent terrorist wanted to live to fight another day. But to do that you needed foot soldiers willing to do the bad things. So the smart lived and the dumb died but it was awfully hard to get good help.

Suicide bombers provided a limited return on investment. They kept dying. You spent six months training them and then they were gone. Too much turnover meant no experience built within the ranks and no leadership from having "been there and done that." It was tough on morale too, at some point. Grace was growing more weary of this job by the day. But soon it would all be done.

Lakenheath Air Base, England

Thursday was "Blues day." The Wing Commander declared that all Air Force personnel were to wear their official Air Force blue uniform. Aviators included, unless they were flying or conducting a simulator mission, in which case they were allowed to wear their flight suits. It was not such a big deal with the "shoe clerks," the aviator's affectionate term for the administrative staff who ran the Air Force from behind a desk. Aviators hated to wear the blue uniform.

There were some advantages, though, thought Sean from his vantage point on the bed of a certain 21-year-old enlisted woman. She exited the bathroom, her raven-black hair up in a bun on top of her head. Sean frowned, forced to imagine what her hair looked like when released from that infernal restraint. Residual heat from her hot shower left drops of moisture along the dark glasses, which framed a young determined face. Sean did not have long to wait. Wordlessly her nimble fingers release the strands and she shook her entire body, gently unfolding her luxurious, wavy hair.

"Ta-da," she announced with a flourish and leapt on top of the semi-naked Sean. Hitching up her skirt, she unbuttoned her blouse and revealed a sexy French lace sling bra from Victoria's Secret. Sean's body gave away his excitement and she turned to gently slide off the rest of his flight suit. Sean leaned up towards her, supported by both of his arms.

"Do you want some of this?" she teased, cupping her ample breasts before releasing the bra's clasp. Freed from their nylon netting, Sean took a nipple in his mouth anxiously. Each of her breasts could fill a large wine glass. Sean never seemed to forget that, especially at dinner or social drinking functions. It was his weakness: a woman with beautiful breasts.

"I thought we were meeting friends tonight at Imagine?" Her pouting lips indicated she wanted to go out and not stay at home.

"We are. I just..."

"Yeah, I know what you're thinking."

Imagine was a unique nightclub in Newmarket, some ten miles from the air base. DJs played loud, lively music, and with drink specials every hour it was the place for hen and stag parties so it was always packed. Of course, two full bars and outside seating along with a huge dance floor didn't hurt. Newmarket was the hottest party town in the area due to the local horse races and the clientele they brought in.

Sean and Laura snuck into Imagine through a side VIP entrance. Sean knew the bouncer and did not want to wait in line with Laura. He was not ashamed of her. But dating Laura was technically illegal, according to USAF regulations. Some rules were not enforced. Fraternization among the officers and enlisted was frowned upon. And if an officer took it too far, like flaunting it in public, then someone could cause trouble. Laura knew this. Sean was very up front when they started dating. Theirs was not an exclusive relationship. She knew about Sean and his habits. She dated him for the thrill of being with an older, experienced man. The fact that he was forbidden fruit just added to the adventure.

Sean knew she would be trouble if anyone important found out about them. But then again, no brass ever came out to the club scene. Sean liked the thrill of Laura, and the adrenaline rush of pushing the envelope on the ground was almost as good as flying an F-15E. Flying was better than sex, but just.

Sean scanned Laura's perfect backside as she walked seductively in front.

If you obey all the rules you miss out on most of the fun.

They pushed their way through the late-night crowd to a back table where Mark and Emile sat with red, fruity slushy drinks.

"Homer, my man. You look slightly better than death warmed over," kidded Sean as he slid beside Mark. Mark's eyes were already glazed over, evidence of his support for the drink specials before midnight.

"Me thinketh thee dothest protest too much," snickered the inebriated man clumsily attempting to quote Shakespeare. Emile gave him a motherly pat on the back while eyeing Laura. Sean pulled Laura into the chair beside him and introduced her as "a friend." Emile knew that was his euphemism for girlfriend or, as far as she was concerned, persona non grata. She regretted coming out already.

Laura wore a navy mini-dress with pink pumps. But the obvious focal point of her outfit was the plunging neckline.

Mark did a double take when he finally noticed Laura.

That's the command post chick, isn't it? Man, Rider has balls the size of church bells.

An awkward silence filled the space between Sean and Emile. Luckily for Sean, or so he thought, someone appeared to break the spell.

"More dance partners!" exclaimed Kate as she sauntered up to their table dressed in tight skinny jeans and a sexy black camisole held up by wafer thin straps. Gyrating her hips seductively against the table to the start of "Groove is in the Heart" by Deee-Lite, she reached across and pulled Sean onto the dance floor, much to the dismay of Laura.

Kate threw a shout out over her shoulder as Sean took her hand, "Watch my bag Em, please?"

The salt in Emile's wound was this: not only did she have to watch the love of her life dance with someone else but she also had to babysit that woman's Anya Hindmarch handbag.

"Oh joy!" Emile plastered a tight-lipped smile across her face.

"Sean you're playing with fire," warned Kate as they reached the dance floor.

"Who me?"

Nodding at Laura, Kate continued, "You know exactly what I mean."

"Is this an official reprimand from the new Lakenheath SP Commander or a tip from a dear friend?"

"Does it matter?" she parried.

Sean dismissed her warning with a knowing smile.

While they moved, Sean took time to recon the bar. As if two women at the table were not enough, Tambra sat on the far side of the room with a hen party for one of the ladies from the Legal office.

Meanwhile, Kate's attention was similarly diverted. Her eyes kept wandering to the group from the school. Ralph seemed to hold court with a harem of young teachers. And she felt Laura's piercing eyes like a high-powered laser into her back the entire dance.

When they returned to the table Laura was absent. Kate sat beside Emile.

"Ok you two: the question of the night is this. If you could only have one DVD on a deserted island, which one would it be?" asked Emile. "I said Monty Python and the Holy Grail. I still find funny things that I have not seen before. Mark said Star Wars, the first one." She rotated her index finger beside her temple, giving the international signal for crazy. He caught her in the act and made like he was going to take away her strawberry daiquiri, but she froze him in his tracks with a puckered up kiss from her Ferrari red lips.

Sean lost track of the conversation, suddenly hypnotized by Emile's luscious lips. They really were a highlight to her beauty, full and delicious.

"Definitely has to be Casablanca for me," sighed Kate sipping her raspberry daiquiri.

"Hopeless romantic," commented Sean just loud enough for everyone to hear.

"And what about the great Rider," Kate egged him on.

"That's easy." Sean paused to draw them all in a little closer. He wanted to drink up the perfume from Emile and Kate together. A mental picture began to form.

Stop It!

"Jaws." They all looked at each other confused. Why would he pick that movie? Before anyone could question him, he explained.

"That way I would be content on the island, happy not to go in the water."

They all laughed. They couldn't really argue with his logic.

Laura flitted between Sean's table and some friends from the base. But Sean did not dance exclusively with her. Instead, he found himself asking Emile to dance. Laura had begun to hang onto him too much. Or so he told himself.

Emile enjoyed the attention, whatever the reason. At one point they entered the dance floor halfway into Emile's favorite dance song, "What I like About You" by the Romantics. That was a short one and ended way too soon for Emile. The DJ spun that into a slow song and since they were already there and it was jam-packed, they stayed and danced cheek to cheek, though perhaps a little farther apart than the other couples.

"You're gonna get me into trouble, young lady," he accused her. She is like a hurricane, thought Sean. Beautiful yet dangerous, a large presence with unknown potential.

"With whom?" she grilled, enthralled with the closeness. She was right. But Sean didn't know his own heart. The façade of Laura to hide Tambra was getting old. Every time he glanced at Tambra she gave him an icy stare. She didn't like watching him dance with other people, especially Laura. So he found himself dancing less with Laura as the night progressed and more with Emile. That was his rationalization.

Tonight Emile was truly stunning. Sean watched her as he swayed her full figure to the rhythm. Emile was smartly dressed in a black dress that revealed her figure in all of its glory. Gazing into her baby blue eyes, Sean realized Emile was gorgeous.

Emile felt something with Sean. Their timing was perfect to the slow song. He did not take his eyes off of her and a good tension lay between them. Electricity was in the air. Something inside told her this was dangerous. Summoning her liquid courage, she leaned and whispered in his ear.

"I don't want a friend, Sean," she said quietly. "I need a lover."

There was a momentary pause in his dancing. He hesitated for a fraction of a second before regaining his rhythm. Sean was completely surprised to hear this. At the least, that she would admit it.

"I consider you my superior," he whispered gently back into her ear. He caught a hint of her expensive Thierry Mugler perfume. Sean knew women's perfume. This Bergamot, Vanilla and

Coumarin scent was unmistakably Angel, the popular perfume in the heavenly-shaped shooting star bottle. Very fitting for a female aviator.

"Sean. I want you to take me seriously. As an aviator and as a woman." Her body moved ever so closer to him.

This is wrong. Emile is a good girl. Hell, she may even be a virgin.

That thought had never occurred to him before.

"Em, I'm not sure this is a good idea."

He wanted her attention and lately began to see her in a different light but this was not the place or time for anything to start.

Emile noticed his hesitation. Mistaking it for rejection she quickly left his embrace as the song ended and began to fade away. Their moment was over.

Why was it in life that you can't pick who you love? Love stinks. Sean and I are like fire and matches.

Music blared from the speakers around the packed dance floor. Table service dwindled as the club reached capacity so Mark and Sean pushed their way through the sweaty bodies to the bar.

"So, are you excited about next week's live weapons mission? We're scheduled for Friday, right?" asked Mark while they waited.

"Oh yeah. Stoked!" Sean lied. He was dreading the flight and felt with every approaching day the weight on his chest got heavier. It would be the first time he released live weapons from his aircraft since that fateful night last year when he lost his wingman. Mark did not know Sean's fears and naturally assumed he was excited about dropping real weapons instead of the BDU-33, the little blue practice bombs they dropped on a daily basis.

"Any word on what our load out will be?" asked Mark.

Sean feigned enthusiasm. "I have my sources at the weapons load barn," He said, referencing where they built the bombs before loading them on the F-15Es. "My bet is GBU-12s, GBU-54s and …" He paused to tease Mark for a bit.

"JDAMs?" asked Mark.

"Think bigger."

"AGM-130," offered Emile, enjoying being a spoiler to Sean's game as she passed them on her way to the ladies room.

Later, Mark sat behind a wall of beer bottles on the table, slurring as he spoke. Emile leaned on his arm and asked, "Haven't you had enough, Mark?"

"Me? No, ma'am."

Then he spoke the words they all were thinking.

"You think I have a problem, don't you Bambi?" Emile bristled beside him, but he continued. "I drink. I get drunk. I fall down. What's the problem?" Laughing, he launched into his favorite joke as everyone else exchanged a knowing look.

"How is flying an F-111 and masturbating the same?" Mark slurred.

"I'll bite Mark. How are they the same?" asked a sympathetic Kate, who had not heard this joke.

Enjoying the attention from Kate, Mark finished with a loud flourish.

"They're both great while you're doing it but you're ashamed of it afterwards."

***

Finally, toward midnight, Tambra joined the table and sat talking with the group. The outnumbered men sat and listened passively as the subject turned to women in the Air Force.

"Does anyone else have any issues working within the testosterone-filled, male-dominated aviation field?" asked Laura, impressing those who did not really know her or her college-level educational background. "I see it all the time. We are second class citizens and not promoted as fast as the men either."

The ladies exchanged emphatic head shakes.

"You know women work twice as hard as men. Especially as aircrew, to be equal," stated Tambra as she mentally castigated the two men at the table.

Emile got nods from the other ladies with, "You cannot imagine how much extra I do just to be considered the same."

"Women bring a lot to the table," announced Kate, sipping her drink as her gaze drifted away to Ralph and his group.

"Yeah, like waitresses," Mark piped in obnoxiously.

The silence after his comment was deafening.

"Don't you get it?" he laughed again at his own joke. "Waitresses bring a lot to the table..."

"Mark needs to go home," said Sean. It was more an order than a statement.

But Emile was already handling him. Her natural mothering instincts were kicking in.

"Okay slugger. I am heading back to Bury St. Edmunds. Can I get you to walk me back to my car? I need a big strong guy to protect me on the drive back, so I can give you a lift home." Emile had stopped drinking right after Sean rebuffed her.

Mark knew he was a few sheets to the wind and needed to get home somehow, so he graciously accepted her offer.

As they drove home, Mark only said one thing before falling into a deep slumber.

"Em, I know you've heard the joke about Sean."

"Which one is that, Mark?"

"Sean is so afraid of commitment that he won't even open an email if it has an attachment." And he laughed himself to sleep.

Drunk as Mark was, his words were still like a dagger to her heart. There was too much truth in the joke.

***

The terrorists originally set up their stakeout to watch the Lakenheath SP squadron commander and his deputy. Their demotion left Grace's team scrambling to monitor the new commander, Kate Healy, but the men did not sense a great deal of worry from Grace about the disruption to her plan. This calmed their fears. Grace knew she could use the information about the former commanders soon after the attack anyway, so all was not lost.

Dakhil reported on their surveillance of Kate, the new Base Chief of Security. Not only were they watching Kate but Grace arranged for Fatima to hire on with a cleaning company that serviced Kate's house. Fatima let Grace in with her one day for cleaning. The two of them swept the house for electronic surveillance devices. They found nothing in the kitchen, bedroom or bathroom, but the living room and office had a video camera that was activated with motion.

Kate rarely went out with others from the base. She was by all accounts a workaholic. She'd recently started to play poker with friends, but had no discernable boyfriend. She lived in Cambridge and frequented a different pub on the rare occasion she ventured out. There did not seem to be any pattern to the pub visits other than the third Tuesday of every month, when she went to the same pub every time, the Rose and Crown. Other than that she worked long hours and occasionally partied hard with a core group of friends.

Grace decided to pay a visit to the Rose and Crown the following Tuesday. She entered about 30 minutes before Kate and instantly knew Kate's secret. Everything But the Girl sang "Missing" from the jukebox. Dakhil would be blind to all the signs, but Grace knew from experience what secret lurked behind Kate's pretty face. The pub seemed to be a hangout for women and men of diverse backgrounds.

Grace knew she would have to work fast. The attack was just a week or so away. Grace waited and watched quietly but made enough eye contact and occasional banter with others who sat near her to blend in. One conversation with a particularly chatty redhead revealed the true meaning of the Rose and Crown. The redhead also could not help but gush over a certain American who lived in Cambridge and came here frequently. Grace knew she had her woman. The redhead did not seem to know Kate well so Grace feigned interest until Kate walked in with a friend.

Kate showcased her fantastic skin in a black wool mini dress with a deep V neckline. The skintight, short-sleeved Debenhams edition dress highlighted Kate's toned figure. A low ponytail and black leather ankle boots completed the sizzling look. Her friend sported black knee boots, stockings and a lacey black mini dress. Both were comfortable with the surroundings and the atmosphere, but not with each other. Grace sensed that they were just friends and that the Asian woman was new to the pub. She garnered much attention and Grace's new friend, the chubby redhead, confirmed she had never seen her before.

Grace watched the evening unfold as the two women chatted and ate dinner over a few small glasses of wine. Kate's companion seemed at times uninterested in Kate, especially when others made eye contact with her. Grace saw the bartender send over a few complimentary wines for them from others in the bar. Few of those comps made it to Kate. She seemed to be in a lower orbit than her friend and knew it, accepting her lower status with style.

Finally, Grace made eye contact with the two ladies but intentionally lingered on Kate. For the first time all evening, Kate flashed a smile that lit up the room. Grace caught it and responded, mouthing the word "Finally." They both laughed. Eventually, after buying both ladies a drink, Grace sauntered over and joined them.

Kate warmed to Grace immediately. Her friend seemed less pleased to have someone else at the table. Grace spent the next few minutes paying more attention to Kate then her friend. The Asian woman seemed truly stunned that someone would be more interested in Kate than her. Twenty minutes later, after finishing her drink, she quickly dismissed herself from Kate feigning a headache.

Grace introduced herself as Helen, the lonely wife of a diplomat in London. She claimed to occasionally visit friends in Cambridge and decided to venture out tonight. Kate lied equally well, claiming to be Judy, the wife of an American academic teaching in Cambridge. When Grace pressed her a bit about the college, Kate politely refused to answer on the grounds it may incriminate her. And Grace parried the same when Kate brought up questions about her mythical diplomat husband. Kate seemed to enjoy the attention and Grace was happy to give it.

"Would you like to go someplace," Grace turned to survey the crowd, "a little less...coed."

Kate tried to keep a straight face but snickered as she replied, "Tell me what you really think Helen."

Grace shrugged and used Kate's alias too. Looking into her eyes she said, "Judy, I like your company, but I'm here so infrequently I can't afford the luxury of parlor games.

Kate was taken aback by Grace's bluntness, but she was also flattered. Besides, her "date" had ditched her.

What the heck! Live for the moment.

"Do you have any particular place in mind?"

"You mean besides your place or mine?"

Grace answered a little nervously. It was a strong comeback and she did not want to scare off her little fish.

"How about my local pub. It's a few blocks from here. On my way home," she added.

"Perfect."

Kate did not take Grace home that night. They parted with a quick kiss on a dark road two blocks from Kate's flat. But she did let Grace take her to a hotel after their second date a few days later.

Their lovemaking produced a few surprises like Grace's small green and blue butterfly tattoo. Kate had smacked Grace on her right ass cheek, asking playfully, "Any deep meaning to your tramp stamp?"

Grace faked a grimace of pain and stated cryptically, "Some people get tattoos as a bold, symbolic gesture. Others get one in a drunken, drugged or double-dog-dare-fueled moment. In each case, they last a lifetime. Better the former than the latter."

Kate noticed she had not answered her question. She had been tempted, once, to get her own tattoo. It would have been a tiny ladybug on her neck or ankle, but she chickened out. Suddenly, seeing a little bit of sadness in the eyes of the woman before her, she was glad she had not taken the ink to skin way back when.

They arranged a third date for a week later on Thursday.

Now Grace would know where Kate was and be able to snatch her quickly, when needed, on Thursday night before the attack. No need to trail or stalk her; instead Grace just wooed her.

Bury St. Edmunds

Emile walked through Bury St. Edmunds as she did most Sundays on her way to St Mary's church. Although her Air Force dog tags said she was Southern Baptist, she found the Anglican service at St Mary's suited her just fine. Part of the Benedictine Abbey site, St Mary's was renowned for its magnificent hammer-beam wooden angel roof.

Entering from the main entrance, Emile was struck by the long aisle. That aisle and the huge west window seemed to give the interior an otherworldly feel. Although she had her choice of three morning services, Emile opted for the traditional 11 a.m. service. Every Sunday she marveled at the choir. No women were allowed in the choir, just alter boys and a few men. It was such a sharp contrast to the Baptist choir she sang alto in growing up.

It reminded her of the male-dominated world she fought on a daily basis in the USAF. She worked twice as hard as her male counterpart yet got little to no recognition. Some thought that, because she was a woman, her flying spot was given to her due to a quota system. It was difficult to handle the glass ceiling as a young woman. It was emotionally challenging, but at the same time it gave her the determination that had helped in recent months when her superiors gave her lesser assignments.

Emile knelt in her pew. Hers was heated. Early on she realized the front half of the church pews were heated by a small radiator system. The remaining back pews were freezing cold, and had effectively converted her from a back row Baptist to a front row Episcopalian.

Today's service was the Holy Communion. This meant a little longer service, but Emile enjoyed the ritual.

How would an alien race react if they listened closely to the rites said before Communion?

The pastor recited and the congregation repeated, "Eat of his body and drink of his blood."

Would they think we were cannibals? Well, we did literally say we were going to eat his body and drink his blood.

She smiled, imagining Count Dracula saying, "I want to drink your blood".

Why am I here? I find comfort here. Why? Is it the trappings of religion that comfort me or the actual teachings that give me my moral compass?

Yet others of her faith sometimes looked at different religion's teachings and interpreted them literally to suit their agendas. Emile wondered if the world might be better off without religion and with more good old honesty and neighborly courtesy. Or did the world need religion to guide the people into those common courtesies? She did attend regularly so there was some link or purpose for her.

My faith is important to me because it is what determines who I am and is part of my family upbringing. And how I raise my own family. Which means it is important to my choice of partner in marriage-if that day comes.

Emile took Communion at the rail and admired the stained glass window on her walk back to the pew. The windowpanes depicted biblically significant events: Samson, David and Goliath, Jonah and the whale, crossing the Red Sea. Nothing compared to

Emile's own emotional struggles in her relationship with Sean but she took comfort knowing sometimes the good guys won.

After the service, Emile exited through the north door, bypassing the usual shaking of the pastor's hand and strolled behind the Bury Cathedral to the Abbey Gardens. Reaching into her pocket she pulled out her iPod and headphones. Pete Townsend crooned to her. Apropos, she thought. "Let my love open the door." The dreamy melody lifted her up.

She had asked Sean to meet her in the rose garden at 12:15 pm. He was not part of her Sunday mornings. She regretted that more than she cared to admit.

Poking her head into the hedge-sealed enclosure, she spotted him sitting on one of three memorial seats.

During World War II, nineteen airfields sprang up in the flat local fields for use against the Germans. The USAF used most of these. In fact, by 1944 15% of the population in Suffolk was American. The rose garden has special significance to American fliers, past and present, since there is a memorial to the 94th Bombardment Group there.

Sean stood as she approached. He was struck by how beautiful she looked in her simple church dress; the anxiety he felt since she had first proposed this meeting hummed inside of him. Why did she want to meet? Why here? He worried he had offended her in some way on Thursday, but he knew he had been mostly sensible that night. After all, he'd had to fly Friday.

Emile smiled as she approached, but Sean detected sadness in her he'd rarely seen. He moved to hug her but she shifted away and motioned for him to sit beside her.

She is so beautiful. Why haven't I noticed that sooner? Or did I just push it away?

For Emile, her mind was made up. She had been playing this moment over for an eternity, it seemed. Sean was here, now, and she had to speak or she might never be able to tell him how she felt. Anxious, Sean interrupted her thoughts.

"Em, you look great. First Thursday night at the club and now your Sunday best. You dress up nice." As soon as he said it, he cringed. Somehow the words did not come out as he intended. Why was he suddenly nervous around Emile? He never had these issues around the other women in his life.

Blushing, Emile ignored the compliment.

"Sean," she began, suddenly curious about something. "Why can I never get you to come to church with me?"

"Aw, Em." He laughed self-consciously. "Based on previous experience, I just don't think the good Lord cares too much for me. Besides, the Bible has some serious flaws in it, you know?" As soon as the words came out, he regretted them. Would he insult her religion, now, too?

Emile pushed back her shoulders in a defensive stance.

"You don't even know the Bible," she said. "How can you say that?"

"I didn't reject the Bible without first reading it. What kind of person do you think I am?"

Shaking her head, she gave him a faint smile and pressed on.

"I really didn't invite you here on a Sunday to get into an argument about religion. Never mind that stuff. I got sidetracked." She paused, shaking off the thought, gathering herself for something. "Listen," she began again. "Sean. I really enjoyed Thursday night. Honestly I did."

The concern on his face almost made Emile stop. He leaned forward slightly. "But? But what, Em?"

"I can't do what I did Thursday night. Sean, you have at least one girlfriend." She plowed on before he could protest. "And I know of one or two others that are not legal, if you know what I mean. Thursday," she said, hesitating and uncomfortable. "What I said was a mistake. And I'm sorry, but..." she looked at him with hard eyes, resolved. "I won't be a notch on someone's bed post."

"Em," Sean began, startled. He had thought about the night – about them moving together on the dance floor and her words, hot in his ear – far more than he could admit to her. But this was Emile. What could he say to her? "Em," he tried again. "You're someone to marry, not to sleep around with."

He startled as she stood abruptly, pounding her fists against the light cotton of her Sunday dress.

"Sean, goddamnit. That's the most unfair thing you have ever said to me." She looked down at him, her eyes pleading. "Don't you realize that puts me on an impossible pedestal I can never come down from? You have me permanently locked away!"

Stunned, Sean watched her, speechless as slow tears rolled from her blue eyes.

"It's almost like you want me to be one of your girlfriends but get no benefits. A friend without benefits."

She knew she wasn't being quite fair. What had Sean ever promised her? What had he ever said that would make her think they could be anything more than friends, more than partners? Quickly, before the emotion could overtake her, Emile finished her thought.

"I believe if you truly love someone you will reveal your secrets. I'm revealing mine, Sean. But you, you have more secrets than anyone I know."

Sean sat stone still, baffled by her emotion. He had hardly thought of Emile as he thought of most women. She was his partner, his WSO. She was Emile – smart, faithful, good Emile. But she was more than that to him. He suspected it but barely knew. Confused, injured by her hurt, he moved to console her, but the choice was wrong; she moved away.

"Em, what do you want from me?" he asked, frustrated. "I felt a connection Thursday night. I can't hide that. Maybe I want to see what more comes from it."

Emile shook her head. If only it were that easy.

"Sean, you need to be honest with yourself and me before anything else." She paused, sighing. "I don't want to be part of your harem."

Sean nodded, staring at her small hands that seemed to tremble at her sides. She sat again, as far from him as the bench would allow. This was tearing her up and he hated himself for it. Emile's belief system was family, faith and friends. But what did he believe?

Emile felt a wave of emotion sicken her stomach. She had laid herself bare, and for what? Would Sean suddenly confess his love and change his whole life for her? She hoped he would, emphatically. But now she felt foolish. Thursday night had not been some prelude to a real relationship, and certainly not on her terms.

Beyond talk, Emile stood up and quickly excused herself. She did not look back at a stricken Sean as she exited by the same route she entered, through the Cathedral entrance. In the Cathedral courtyard she spotted five chickens roaming free. Rumor had it that the priests tended to them but allowed them to wander aimlessly. Normally seeing them made Emile very happy. But not today.

This was indeed a day for firsts. Retreating back to her flat via a circuitous route, Emile was not up for explaining her tear-stained face. No, the only solution for this problem was popcorn, wine and music. Those three things had always solved any problem. Maybe, thought Emile as she reached for the wine opener, they could put a dent in this one.

Sean watched her retreat, mesmerized by every step she made. He was confused. Not just by her actions but by his as well. She loved him. He could see that now. Maybe he knew it before but just ignored it. Maybe that was one of the reasons he slept around-to keep her away from him. Was that wrong? It felt like a mistake now.

Was he finally ready for a real relationship? What would that mean? She obviously wanted to get him to church. How did he feel about that?

One thing at a time slugger. Don't get too ahead of things.

Standing, he still felt butterflies in his stomach from the emotional meeting with Emile. *Why do I suddenly have indecision when it comes to this woman? Strange.*

He had some thinking to do.

Chapter 14

Thursday Night, FIVB Volleyball Tournament, London England

So much for getting any support from the home office. After Hope reported her contact with Grace and the unsuccessful attempt at capture, the CIA basically said she was on her own. No other field agents were available to assist her. Connor did not fair much better. He was able to convince MI6 of a possible threat and arranged for protection for the intended victims. But they already had a security detail and the venue was well tested and had impeccable security features. Both agents were on their own.

Hope knew the attack date once she reviewed the guest list. Prince William and Kate, the Duke and Duchess of Cambridge, were due to attend the Friday night ceremonies. The royal Couple picked Friday because they did not want to interrupt the opening ceremonies.

Hope and Connor caught a break when the intended targets announced to MI6 their visit Friday was cancelled thus removing them from the equation. Both breathed a little easier in the knowledge that the VIPs would not be involved.

The royal Couple did not announce their cancellation to the public. They planned to do so at the very last moment. This gave Hope and Connor a chance to catch the entire cell on Friday.

From Grace they knew the event would be the London Volleyball tournament. Sponsored by the Fédération Internationale de Volleyball (FIVB), sixteen two-person teams came to compete in a round robin tournament for four days. There were separate men's and women's brackets. Four groups of four teams each. Each team played a game against each group opponent. Then the top two teams from each bracket played in a single elimination tournament to get to the finals.

The four days' events were broken down into three periods and separate tickets were sold for each four-hour period. So Friday started with a 10 a.m. to 2 p.m. period then had a 3 p.m. to 7 p.m. period and finished with an 8 p.m. to midnight session. Since

Thursday included the opening ceremony and a few matches, it only had the late session from 8 p.m. to midnight.

Tonight they tracked Ahmed and tried to find his other agents. Hope and Connor were surprised to see him show up at the venue Thursday.

The tournament would last throughout the weekend, providing Londoners with another great weekend of beach volleyball. The 2012 London Olympics first introduced beach volleyball to the London masses.

Entry was by ticket only, which cost anywhere from 30 British pounds for the cheap seats on Thursday, to 500 pounds for the best seats in the house on Sunday for the Championship. Ahmed and his team all had tickets for Thursday and Friday evening.

The event was set up just like the London Olympic Beach Volleyball venue at Horse Guards Parade. Located on the Prime Minister's doorstep in Central London, the Horse Guards Parade provided an iconic location for beach volleyball. Two entrances were for spectators. One on the north side by the Mall and another from the south side via St. James Park. Guests could exit from the north entrance or leave by a walkway towards Westminster. Those with elevated seats were afforded a view of Whitehall where most of the governing of Great Britain was carried out.

Once inside the Horse Guards area, there were two catchment areas where visitors were "held" until the courts themselves were cleared of the previous match's spectators. One by St. James Park Lake and one by the north entrance, before the food court around the volleyball courts themselves. There was no need for clearing on Thursday evening since there was only one session planned.

Hope scanned those coming through the turnstiles at the south entrance and Connor watched the north entrance. Both were looking for Ahmed, since Grace said he would be the leader. They had his cell phone number and a good idea of where he was, most of the time. But he was tricky and, on more than one occasion, gave them both the slip. Now they waited for him to come to them.

Hope saw him first. She radioed Connor about her sighting and directed him to enter the facility and pick her and the suspect up visually inside the enclosure. Hope followed Ahmed from a safe distance as he made his way deeper into the facility.

***

Ahmed wanted to do a dry run through Thursday exactly as they would tomorrow night to work out all of the last second details.

Shari and Manny walked into the volleyball enclosure first, arm in-arm through the North gate. The two lovebirds were not stopped at the metal detector for their weapons, but instead Shari had to enter again because of her jewelry. She wore it intentionally to attract attention to her, as Manny went through without hesitation. After removing her gold jewelry she re-entered the metal detectors and passed without delay. Once inside and hidden from immediate view, Manny gave Shari a small package that he carried in for her.

Shari and Manny walked around the facility observing all security personnel. As expected, a heavy police presence existed outside the facility and at the entrance gates, but fewer policemen walked inside the park. Instead, unpaid volunteer stewards made sure guests arrived at their seats successfully. Shari counted just ten policemen and women inside and most were at the immediate entrances to the grandstands on the south and west side of the courts. She texted a simple number to Ahmed to indicate how many they saw.

Ahmed glanced down at his Blackberry and smiled as a text of "10" appeared. The number was lower than he expected.

He was the mastermind. He would watch and direct. If needed, he could step in as the fifth element. The original plan was supposed to be six attackers. Five men and one woman, with Ahmed one of the five men but in a supporting role. Unfortunately, one man was in hot water at the mosque and thus deemed too dangerous an asset to bring along on the mission. His detection or detention would ruin everything, so he was scratched from the operation and no one else could replace him at the last second. It was an aspect Ahmed did not like.

Ahmed entered the area last. He had Jason go through the south entrance first. Of the three men entering this way, Jason was the most Western looking. Talil trailed him 10 minutes later via a different metal detector at the opposite turnstile. Neither had problems entering. Both men wore jeans, tennis shoes and a polo shirt. Jason wore a red shirt and Talil wore bright green.

All three men spent a considerable amount of time slowly
working their way into position. The matches started at 8:30 p.m.
with a women's match between the USA team of Ross/Kessy and
the Brazil duo of Antonelli/Rocha. Next at 9:30 p.m. came the last
match of the night between the men's teams from Germany and the
Netherlands. The opening ceremonies took place at 8 p.m.

Jason reached his assigned spot opposite Shari at 8:45 p.m. Talil
became the last to slot into position at 8:52 p.m. They didn't want
to raise suspicion by being in the same place too long. So the two
on each side occasionally would signal to each other and change
places. As Big Ben struck nine o'clock, all five-terror cell members
felt their adrenalin rise and the palms on their hands begin to sweat
from the unbearable wait. They almost felt the same emotion of an
attack during this dry run. Seconds became minutes of anticipation.

The Duke and Duchess of Cambridge would enter through
either of two special gates: The north gate opposite the courts
where the crowds were to exit after the events (as opposed to the
north central gate where fans entered), or the south gate opposite
the courts. The east side was walled up since it faced Whitehall. And
the west side contained a minor food court with souvenir shops and
had the major artery into the ramp around the courts from the
enclosure area. The ticketed volleyball area consisted of a west side
enclosure containing exhibitions and practice volleyball courts and
the eastern section which contained the main volleyball court. This
volleyball court ran north south with grandstands on the west and
south side. The east and north side were relatively shallow (no
second story stands) so guests could enjoy the view of Westminster
Abbey and Big Ben.

Hope and Connor both rested at the volleyball court's NW end,
outside the grandstands, in clear view of Ahmed. The 20,000 strong
crowd cheered behind them. Small snippets of the Clash's "Rock
the Casbah" revved up the crowd in between serves and a DJ
interjected with exultations to pump up the fans.

Ahmed relaxed casually beside a sausage stand, looking directly
east down the entranceway towards where the royal couple would
enter. His Blackberry rested to his right on the small table where his
overpriced meal sat untouched. He could see Jason in the distance,
on the closest corner of the oval that formed the volleyball courts
and seats.

Talil was obscured but further up ahead of Jason. Unlike most of the small crowd milling in the walkway outside the stands, the two men faced away from the action and the DJ's noise and towards the ramp.

They both chewed Khat. The drug became a habit for them from their training in Somalia. They could still get it in England but since it was lesser known among the drug options, they had to go to the Somalian sections of large towns like London to get their fixes. The drug heightened their senses and made them more alert. Of course, the side effects would kick in sometime later but they were unlikely to be on this earth then. Instead they would be in heaven with seventy-two vestal virgins.

Shari lounged innocently against a lamp post. Ahmed could just make her female form out in the distance. The warm summer night provided an unexpected heat wave for this night match. Shari swished her red linen silk skirt to fan herself. It was a sign to Ahmed they were ready. Manny, her partner today and in life, stood behind a banner that proclaimed the London Mayor's good deeds; he was nervous.

All the terrorists were in place. They had all trained extensively with their weapons but none expected the targets to show tonight.

Ahmed was just about to cancel the practice run and have his crew leave the park area when he noticed a headline on an electronic billboard nearby.

ROYAL COUPLE TO ATTEND OPENING NIGHT OF VOLLEYBALL

Ahmed blinked and made sure what the title said made sense. He checked his Blackberry and saw a twitter post from a close aide to the couple who confirmed they were canceling Friday and attending tonight.

Luck was with Ahmed when the gate closest to him swung open at 9:08 p.m. His four-person crew was in perfect position.

***

Hope saw the same message Ahmed saw. Her reaction was simple and direct.

"Aw, shit. Connor we have a problem here."

"I just saw it. I'm on it. Calling my friend to execute the comm plan now."

"What the hell are they thinking?"

***

The royal couple did heed the warnings from MI6 but instead of cancelling they decided to attend on a different day with less advance warning and a minimal security presence. Their advisors assumed this would mitigate the threat and still allow them the publicity opportunity required. They did not inform anyone of their new appointment until the last minutes before arrival. It was a complete surprise.

Six men and two women made up the royal couple's security detail. Two agents waited in the royal seating area, standing guard over their seats. Six escorted Prince William and Kate onto the grounds; two on each side about ten feet away and a lead agent thirty feet in front and another trailing the entourage by about the same distance. Kate's lady-in-waiting followed just beside her on her right and they discussed the various upcoming events. William's friend and family solicitor accompanied him. By entering through the special gate opened just moments before, the entourage bypassed security with their guns. The couple insisted on a low-key entry and finally persuaded all involved to allow them to come in after play began. The disruption was expected about 15 minutes into the first match.

The royal couple also asked for no fanfare until they made their way into the royal seating area. They did not want their arrival to disrupt the competition until an appropriate time.

Ahmed did not dare set the attack in motion yet. Too many armed policemen were outside the venue, with access into the facility as the special gate opened. Instead Ahmed waited until the royal entourage was well inside the venue and the gate safely closed behind them before contemplating sending the command to execute the attack. The gate closed and the additional police remained outside. Ahmed breathed slightly easier. But the delay did give Connor the time he needed.

As the couple passed from his view Ahmed pressed the green send button on his Blackberry. This text message would go to the other terrorists alerting them to attack the group that just entered.

Hope and Connor heard the signal beep in their ear buds indicating Ahmed had attempted to send the command text. They began to move swiftly toward him in order to arrest him. They both hoped Connor's ex-girlfriend's stunt succeeded.

Earlier that day Connor met with his ex-girlfriend and explained the favor he needed. Connor's IT friend tried to figure out a way to block just Ahmed's signals from transmitting, but that could not be arranged, so she simply shut down the entire Blackberry network based on his attempt to send out a signal. It was like splitting an apple with a sledgehammer but it worked as the entire London Blackberry network collapsed.

Connor now owed her big time but it was worth it. She was a high-maintenance divorcee with two children but very well preserved for her mid 50s.

Ahmed looked down at his Blackberry, momentarily basking in the glow of his triumph, but frowned when he saw the message it presented him.

"Your message could not be sent at this time. The network is down."

He pressed the resend button, acid building in his throat at the thought of failure so close to success.

Again the machine scoffed at him with the same network is down message.

Ahmed glanced up and saw the last security detail pass out of view, walking around the curve in the courts that blocked his vantage point. He also saw two individuals walking with purpose towards him. They looked suspiciously official and one, the man, looked too much like a policeman.

Thinking quickly to help himself escape, Ahmed decided his best course of action was to go on the offensive. What was it the Americans so loved to say? The best defense is a good offense.

He ran toward the two approaching people yelling at the top of his lungs in Arabic, "Allahu Akbar" over and over again: "God is great." Unfortunately for Ahmed, the music at the volleyball courts had just cranked up and the Clash was singing their chorus at the same time.

All four terrorists were surprised to see their targets appear tonight but they were ready nevertheless.

Shari and Manny did not hear Ahmed, as they were the farthest away. But Jason, the closest cell member to Ahmed, heard and reacted. Turning to shield his action he pulled his small, bamboo blow tube from within the folds of his shirt. Quickly discarding caps off each end and checking to ensure that the blow dart preloaded earlier was working, he spun slowly. He got Talil's attention and both men spun towards their target. They faced the security detail as it passed and blew their darts toward the closest security guard.

The blow darts could hit accurately from 20 yards depending on the skill, lung capacity and barrel length. They only needed to hit slow moving targets five or ten feet away. It was like shooting fish in a barrel. Once the darts took out the security members, the terrorists planned to take their machine guns and spray the crowd to kill as many as possible, starting with the young royal couple.

Both darts hit the secret service members squarely in the arm, sinking an inch into their skin and injecting a quick acting poison. The two burly guards each felt the pinprick, turned and raised their pistols to fight the threat just as their nervous systems reacted violently to the drug injected into their systems. Both men tripped as their legs gave out and hit the ground in a spasm of activity.

The drug their darts were dipped in was Etorphine, sometimes called M99. It is three thousand times more powerful than morphine. The terrorists extracted it from Oripavine or the poppy straw of opium. Often used to immobilize elephants and racehorses, vets like it because it is fast-acting and has a known, fast antidote, diprenorphine. Etorphine is fatal to humans. Instant effects are dizziness, nausea and paralysis.

Poisoned darts are used widely in jungle areas around the world. Grace gave Ahmed the idea when she met him in Wales. Often plants are sources for the poisons, but frogs and poisonous fish also supplement the poison drugstore. Antiaris toxicaria, for example, a tree of the mulberry and breadfruit family, is commonly used on Java and its neighboring islands. The sap or juice of the seeds is smeared on the dart head on its own or mixed with other plant extracts. The fast-acting active ingredient (either antiarin, strychnine or strophanthin) attacks the central nervous system causing paralysis, convulsions and cardiac arrest.

Their two companions on the other side of the formation did not know of the attack until they saw the two men crumble to the ground. The loud crowd noise, cheering a hard spike, served to blunt the noise of Ahmed's additional warnings. Likewise, Shari and Manny could not hear it either but upon seeing Jason and Talil spring into action, so did Shari and Manny only slightly later. The two security guards closest to Shari and Manny were a woman and man team. Each terrorist faced another of the opposite gender. Both raised their blow dart pipes and aimed.

The two secret service members on the left side of Prince William now turned, upon seeing the threat, as Jason and Talil stepped forward to grab the ownerless pistols clattering on the ramp as the previous guards writhed in pain before death. The female opposite of Manny leading on the left front dropped to one knee and shot twice at Talil as he reached for the gun. Her shot penetrated his heart and killed him instantly. The other bullet hit him in the left shoulder. The other guard felt a dart enter his buttocks just as his own shot went toward Jason.

Ahmed instructed his team to aim for the arms or buttocks for fear they might be wearing body armor. It was an unnecessary precaution. They were wearing only lightly protected flak vests. The policemen's shot at Jason missed vital organs, hitting the right thigh and sending him to the ground in agonizing pain, but not before Jason retrieved the pistol in front of him.

By this time, the Duchess and her assistant stopped, shielded by Prince William and his friend. The four of them dropped to the ground as the gunfire erupted from their security detail.

The small pistol shots were not registered by the crowd due to the loud pulsating music from the DJ.

The royal couple, and what remained of their security team, were now in the shadow of the upper stands and hidden from view. The only people on the eastern ramp leading to the stands were the Jihadists. The others fled rapidly once the shots occurred.

Connor and Hope drew their weapons when Ahmed began his rant and rushed towards them, thinking he was a suicide attacker, but the gunfire from behind stopped them.

Ahmed saw his team begin their attack. Hope and Connor turned, fearing the worst, torn between arresting Ahmed and turning back to help prevent the attack. Ahmed made their decision easy. He stopped just fifty feet from them, pivoted and ran toward the exit. Hope hesitated but Connor made the command decision.

"Forget him!" he shouted sprinting back the way they came. "Back to the royals. They need our help!"

The music from the DJ stopped abruptly. The crowd hushed awaiting play at the volleyball match when more shots rang out. This time the crowd heard the gunfire. It would take them a few seconds to realize what and where the shots were coming from and then a few more to panic. The gun battle would be almost over by then.

An injured Jason fired all seven rounds into the two closest forms threatening him: the male guard who shot him and the now-limp form immediately in front of him. All seven shots proved redundant; the male security guard he hit across the tarmac was also hit from behind by Shari's dart.

Three remained of the security team: the lead man, the female in front of Manny and the trailing guard. The trailing guard rushed to protect the royals while firing from his hip. He hit Jason, who was searching the security bodies in front of him for a magazine in an attempt to reload his pistol; the machine guns they expected to pick up from the security detail were not there.

Connor and Hope zigzagged through the gaggle of panicked fans. There were four or five people fleeing the shooting back on the ramp. Some did so successfully. One did not. They all interfered with any chance Hope and Connor had of firing at the assailants.

Connor ran into one of the few spectators in the arena who was not watching the volleyball match. The woman, in her forties and rather large, heard the gun fire and instantly ran in the opposite direction.

If she had kept running straight, all would have been fine. Instead, when she saw Connor, and then Hope, approaching her she moved to get out of the way, colliding head on with Connor as he also swerved.

Hope did not slow down to help him but instead charged ahead toward the royal entourage.

Connor fell to the ground, trapped under 200 pounds of flesh. He finally rolled her off his body but in the process dropped his gun and she fell on top of it. He dismissed it and continued on seconds later.

Shari was stunned by the attack's ferocity and suddenness. This was not what she had expected. The plan was simple enough. They should have surprised all four of the security team closest to them and then taken their machine guns to finish off the other two security personnel. But instead their attack went off piecemeal and at a moment's notice because their targets appeared during the dress rehearsal. And the police they were killing did not have machine guns as planned.

Stumbling in the "fog of war," Shari rushed to the guard immediately in front of her position and picked up his pistol. Gunfire to her right from the trailing security man and in front of her from Jason had so far kept her from being hit.

Shari kneeled, grabbed the gun and turned towards the trailing security member. She fired five times in quick succession, not aiming as well as she should have. Practice was one thing; live firing was quite another, especially under pressure. Firing a pistol versus a machine gun was quite a different experience.

Four of her five shots were wild and missed; the last hit her enemy just below his heart. He spun and fell out of the action. His flak jacket may have saved his life, but did not prevent him from injury.

Meanwhile Manny, realizing the deteriorating circumstances, rushed toward the only gun available-the female guard in front of him.

The security woman heard Manny approaching from behind. But she had choices to make. She was on one knee, facing away from him when suddenly she turned to her right to eliminate Shari's threat to the royals.

"Get down! Everyone stay down," she yelled, seeing her boss, the trailing team member, fall when Shari's fifth bullet found a target. Taking careful aim at Shari's midsection, she squeezed the trigger just as Manny leapt onto her back. The bullet intended for Shari's back hit her right bicep from behind forcing the gun from her hand as she crumpled in pain.

Both Manny and the female security agent tumbled to the ground. Above her, Manny had an advantage; the agent tried to buck him off but Manny grabbed her head with both hands and slammed it into the pavement. She stopped moving as blood slowly dripped from a gash over her right eye.

Shari turned toward the scuffle, cradling her arm and trying to stem the blood from her wound. She saw the last remaining security team member, the front agent, rushing back towards the ambush.

The loud music and roaring crowd had covered the battle sufficiently until the shots rang out. It was then that he turned and realized he was out of position, too far in front. His anticipation of the logistics of getting the group into the stands and to their box had led him to lose track of the prize he guarded behind. Now he made up for his missteps by making a radio call for help and rushing back to the mayhem around the royal couple.

"Manny, lookout! Behind you!"

Hearing Shari's warning, Manny rolled the unconscious female security woman up to shield himself from the oncoming lead agent.

The lead agent saw the exchange of gunfire between Shari and the trail agent and the fight between Manny and the female agent. He raised his weapon to shoot Manny but could not get a clear field of fire with the other agent's body between them.

Manny took advantage and easily shot the rapidly approaching agent twice in the chest and once in the face using up four bullets. Manny was the best shooter of the terrorist group; he surveyed the area slowly. The security team had finally been neutralized. They were all dead or unconscious. The terrorists had only a few precious moments before more police arrived on the scene.

Connor and Hope were too far away when the royal couple entered. Their sprint towards Ahmed first robbed them of precious seconds needed to intercede in the gun battle just played out.

"Shari, see if you can find more weapons," Manny commanded, standing and slowly advancing to Prince William, Kate and their aides all cowering on the ground. The tiny unprotected group was not what Manny expected. The royals were not flat on the ground, but instead were crouching low on the balls of their feet. The Duchess was protecting her lady-in-waiting who was lying on the ground with her hands over her head. The Prince's friend stood slowly to block William from the approaching threat.

"Get out of the way, man. I have no beef with you. I am after the royal couple," Manny stated matter-of-factly to the older man 20 feet away. Manny knew he was running out of bullets now.

"No bloody way, mate!" said the aide defiantly.

"Have it your way" said Manny. He casually aimed the pistol between the man's eyes when a movement on his left grabbed his attention: a flailing, screaming tall blond running up the ramp towards him.

Hope yelled, "Nooo!"

Hope had run fast, faster than Connor.

Manny quickly assessed the combat environment.

The situation is falling apart. Ahmed is nowhere in sight. He has ditched us or been killed himself. I only have an injured Shari left of my team. There are no machine guns. There will be no grand hostage-taking situation. I think I have two bullets left in this gun. Maybe one more, maybe one less. This crazy woman needs to be taken out.

Before Manny had time to shift his gun, shots rang out. The running woman was hit twice in the chest and fell to the ground. Turning, he spied a slumping Shari who had used the last ounce of her energy to prop herself up and take Hope out.

Finally, something is going right today, thought Manny.

Smiling wickedly, he shot the Duke's friend in the chest. The older man fell back, stunned. Prince William caught the falling man and cradled him in his arms as he lowered the weight to the ground. The Duchess quickly moved, putting herself between Manny and her husband, the future King of England.

She shouted out in fury, "You bastards!"

Manny kept his gun pointed at her.

Connor saw Hope fall, but he could only run past her in his goal to save the royal couple.

Chapter 15

Manny saw a balding man running towards them. Probably the blonde's partner, he surmised.

One bullet left but more where Shari is and the royals do not know how many bullets I have. I will take out this newcomer running, bluff my way to Shari's gun and finish them off.

Manny turned away from the Duchess and took aim at Connor.

Connor watched the terrorist turn and point a gun at him. Connor had no gun.

Hope had a gun, but it was too late to go back and take it off of the dead woman. The only play left was to keep running and hope the terrorist missed.

Just as Manny started to pull the trigger, he sensed movement within the royal group. It distracted him slightly and his first bullet just missed Connor, whizzing past his right cheek. Manny felt but never heard the three bullets from the gun that the Prince fired, peppering his body.

Connor leapt and hit Manny's falling body. The bullets had hit the terrorist's right temple, his right shoulder and his right side. Connor tackled the dead man and used his body to cushion the fall.

Prince William, while appearing to cradle his friend and obscured by his wife, had actually reached to recover the gun from the fallen trailing agent who came to try and cover the royals. Once secured, he motioned non-verbally for the Duchess to step slightly to her right, which presented him a clear field of fire to Manny.

As Connor got to his feet, he looked at the Duke with admiration and nodded.

The Prince said simply, "I *do* have some weapons training myself remember."

The Duchess of Cambridge fought valiantly to stem the blood loss from her husband's friend, her dress stained with the dark red of the chest wound.

Moments later, eight more royal protection detail members arrived on the scene to whisk the Duke and Duchess away. Kate sobbed and pleaded for someone to get an ambulance for William's friend, refusing to leave his side until one of the team took over caring for his wounds.

Connor looked down the ramp at the limp form of Hope. Neither leg moved in the pebble gray trousers. But her head was slowly moving from side to side. Connor ran to her.

Hope tried to sit up but fell back. Connor skidded to a halt beside her, going down on both knees. Her hand waved in circular motions around her chest.

"Hope, you're alive!" said Connor as he cupped her head in his hands. Checking her wounds, he miraculously found there were none.

With deep breaths, Hope motioned again to her chest and said, "Bullet... proof... vest."

Connor helped her into a sitting position.

"Much better," said Hope and she reached under her black suit coat to touch the metal jacket she wore.

Connor smiled and said, "Ned Kelly saves the day."

The horrified look on Hope's face meant Connor's joke did not go over well.

He referred to the nefarious Australian who wore the first "ballistic suit" to protect him from bullets back in 1880. Of course, he was a gang member, or revolutionary, depending on whom you talked to about the subject.

Hope's vest was a custom fit. Often a woman, or even a large man, had a hard time getting a good fit with body armor or bulletproof vests. Hope's was a perfect fit after years of adjustments. The level three lightweight vest was well-concealed under her white blouse and black blazer.

Hope opened her blazer and parted her blouse to reveal a black Kevlar vest and two holes where the bullets were stopped.

"I'm gonna have some bruises," she said.

"Yeah, but consider the alternatives," scolded Connor.

"How are our HVTs?"

"The high-value targets are on their way home. Safe and sound. Wills saved my life with his shooting." Connor explained quickly what she missed while she was out cold.

It was Hope's turn to smile. "Good thing gun control only applies to the..." She coughed and took a deep breath. "Commoners, eh?"

Police began to filter in and block off the area.

"You okay? If so, I am going to check on our bad guys. Maybe we're lucky and get a survivor."

"Sure. I'm fine just a little winded."

Connor made his way back to the battle area.

Hope called after him, "For the record, you run like a girl."

"Whatever, my American Amazon friend."

"I kicked your ass getting to the royals and what did I get for it? Two shots in my belly," she guffawed, doing her first and last impression of comedian Mike Meyer's Fat Bastard, the Scotsman.

Connor waved her off dismissively with his hands behind his back as he walked away. Hope could not help but wonder what might have been if they had not been here or if the terrorists had more people. Just Ahmed, who escaped into the night, would have been enough to tip the scales and turn this into a gruesome outcome. Luckily it was all over now.

Later that night, both Hope and Connor entered the small, dimly lit room in the basement of HMP Belmont, or as it is more commonly known, Her Majesty's Prison High Down. Located in south London, Belmont is where MI5 and MI6 do their dirty work in regards to terrorists or those suspected of terrorism. The good news for those working deep below the prison was the public never would know of the operational aspects of the floors. The bad news was that often the most undesirable and despicable people visited their establishment and they needed to be catered to, though not in a good way.

Shari had survived. The other three terrorists did not.

They were on slabs in the mortuary. Shari saw them when they brought her in after attending to her wound. She could see the faces of Jason, Talil and, of course, Manny. She saw them even now when she closed her eyes. But she astutely realized there was no Ahmed.

Either he survived and escaped, or was dead and they were not letting her see him. Of course, there was another explanation: perhaps he was captured alive. But she doubted that possibility. She saw how he acted and planned. He knew what he was doing.

A man and a woman entered her room. The woman was attractive, young and alive with energy, but she seemed either troubled or injured, with a limited range of movement. She looked familiar. At the last second Shari realized she had shot this woman at the volleyball event.

The man was balding, older yet more reserved. British.

Looks almost like a BNP poster boy.

No, Shari scolded herself.

They don't let them in the force. Or do they?

"I would stand, but my handcuffs keep me chained to the arms of my chair. My apologies." She did not nod in deferment but instead stared at each visitor in turn, cold and hard. Her directness hinted at strength and character.

Hope watched the prisoner.

This woman almost killed me. If not for the vest, I would be lying in the mortuary with four of the royal couple's security team.

Hope thought of the Prince's lawyer friend who did not survive either; he had passed away on the operating table.

British accent with Brummy dialect, thought Connor. No trace of African influences. Another homegrown terrorist. This time from Birmingham.

"We can help with that arrangement, Shari," Hope suggested confidently as she took her seat in a much more comfortable leather upholstered chair. She placed her fingertips together to form a prayer symbol and saw the weakness in Shari's eyes when she used her real name to address her.

Shari recovered her composure quickly. "And what does an American with a token British bulldog want from me?"

This one was quick and intelligent. What a waste, regretted Hope. She could have been someone they could use at the agency. She was a good shot.

Hope's bruised ribs confirmed that. The dart she used was not poisonous like the others. Instead hers was a powerful knockout drug, but not fatal. So the security man she sunk her dart into did not die at her hands, but only after Jason pumped a few rounds into his unconscious body.

Did Jason suspect Shari was not going to use the poison? Was that why he shot her target? Hope would have to think that one through later. In fact, as luck would have it, both of the individuals that Shari shot with a gun had lived: Hope, and the trailing security detail member who Shari shot in the left torso. He would be in the hospital for a few weeks, but was out of critical condition and would recover.

"Look, no one has tortured you, yet. Those are my orders." Hope let the unspoken threat hang in the air. Then she played her ace in the hole.

"We know all about Janus and the Angel of Death." Hope intentionally looked away from Shari but instead relied on Connor as pre-briefed to observe her reaction.

She definitely hit the mark with that one, noted Connor. Slight shifting of posture in an uncomfortable cold metal chair. Pupils increasing in size and a small, almost imperceptible, right-leg twitch. She was part of their group.

Connor cleared his throat to indicate what approach they should take next. Cough was one avenue, chair adjustment was option two, and clearing the throat was the best option.

Hope pushed back her chair, stood and got in Shari's face quicker than Connor had seen anyone move in his life. She was like a tall, lanky gazelle. He made a mental note to check out more about beach volleyball players. Hope spit out a threat to Shari.

"You will rot in the worst prison this country has and no one, and I mean no one, knows about it. No lawyers, no human rights activists and no contact. You know why?"

It was a rhetorical question but Hope was so intense and so in Shari's face at the moment that the young woman could not help herself from asking meekly, "Why?"

"You tried to kill the royal couple." Hope's lips curled into a nasty scowl. "Nobody wants to have anything to do with you. If you just curl up and die everyone will be a lot happier. The authorities are more than happy to look the other way in your case so that this little problem goes away.

"Hell, they are even thinking about allowing my government, yes the good ole US of A," Hope acknowledged Shari's observation of her origin and profession, "...to crank up a plane for rendition. Guantanamo Bay. How'd you like to go to Gitmo Shari?"

Hope saw a flicker of fear in Shari as the terrorist smiled menacingly. Hope read her as the kind of person who smiled when upset or afraid. Terrorism was one thing, especially if you had a system of rights to back you up and no death penalty. But going to Gitmo – that was a whole different ball game.

Hope moved behind Shari and stroked her face gently. "The guards will love you there." Hope placed her other hand on Shari's backside just as Shari began to imagine what the consequences of her actions might be. Shari jumped at the contact. This would not take long.

Four hours later, Hope asked Shari questions while Connor watched from behind a two-way mirror. Shari sat in a comfortable chair in front of Hope but was turned away at a 90-degree angle. In this case, Hope looked at the right side of Shari's face. A blood pressure cuff rested on Shari's left arm. Her right bicep had a bandage from her gunshot wound and the doctors suggested this arrangement because of her injury. Two curled coils of wire ran across the front of her chest. One over her breasts and one just below them. The chair she sat in had flat armrests that were for her hands. Hope placed her hands flat, palm down and attached small clips around each finger of her right hand.

"This is a lie detector test, Shari. We will do this first to get a baseline about how accurate the information is that you have provided to us, and then I will give you sodium thiopental which, as you know, makes you tell the truth. There is no way you can lie to us when it takes affect. Finally, I will administer another polygraph test to confirm it a third time. Shall we begin?"

These were all lies, but Hope was not about to tell Shari this. The polygraph test was unreliable. The drug was highly unreliable. Often the subject would confuse fantasy with real-life. Hope found the information was about 60% correct. The real information often came because the individual believed they were under a truth drug. What a way to run a spy agency, Hope groused.

Hope started the lie detector test with a series of irrelevant questions in which Hope knew the answers. Agents in MI6 were scouring the Internet, government databases and going door to door anywhere Shari was known to have lived in order to find out more about this particular terrorist.

Everyone was falling all over himself or herself to help Hope and Connor now that they had saved the royal couple from death.

"Shari how old are you?" Hope asked

"Twenty-five"

"When will you turn twenty-six?"

Days ago Shari would have answered never. Now she replied, "On December tenth"

Hope asked these all up front so she could get a baseline of what truthful, easy answers looked like with Shari. She monitored her computer screen to see what a correct answer meant on her readings.

Next came the comparison questions that had an indirect relationship to the terrorist attack/group but in which Shari was expected to lie. These set the bar for lies or untruths.

"Where were you born?"

"Pakistan." Shari lied. She was born in England. But Hope told her to lie on this one.

Hope saw a slight elevation in Shari's blood pressure and her respiration rate increased significantly.

As soon as Shari made a quick, small gesture of touching under her nose when lying, Hope noted that for future use as a tell with Shari.

Finally, Hope began to ask questions about the information Shari provided to her and Connor earlier.

These questions dealt with the terrorist group's actions and by comparing them to the previous questions they could catch Shari in a lie. If her response matched the irrelevant questions, she was telling the truth. If the answer was like a comparison question, she was lying to them.

"What was the plan?"

Shari explained, a proud gleam in her eye. "The plan was simple: We had tickets for Thursday and Friday as spectators. We all slipped through the metal detectors with blow darts. We were going to use the blow darts on the security detail to neutralize them and take their machine guns, kill the Duke and Duchess and as many visitors as we could."

All her vital signs showed this as a true answer.

"So you planned your attack for Friday?"

"Yes, we had tickets for Thursday as a practice but we thought the VIPs would be visiting on Friday. We were not as prepared for the attack to go off tonight."

"Why do you think you failed in killing the Duke and Duchess?"

Shari pondered this for several seconds before answering, "We were one short. If Ahmed had been willing to sacrifice his life and join the fight we would have succeeded."

"Did you mean to kill these people or just incapacitate them?" She knew her darts were not poison unlike the others.

"No, I did not mean to kill anyone" Shari pleaded. Hope saw her blood pressure and respiration fluctuate slightly higher but decided to give her the benefit of the doubt when Shari's finger lightly touched her nose. Hope marked the answer as a lie.

Shari gave them one more piece of information. This is what she negotiated with to prevent being sent away to Gitmo.

"I do not know if this is important or not but my boyfriend Manny was friends with another man in the area. Not London, but in East Anglia. There may be another cell operating nearby. Manny expressed an unusual interest in a town called Bury St. Edmunds."

"Go on," prodded Hope taking notes.

"I asked if he wanted to visit it one weekend and he quickly said no. I am not dumb. I think his friend lived there and another cell is there as well."

Hope noted from her readings that Shari was telling the truth.

Unknowingly, Shari had confirmed Grace's earlier information. Hope and Connor were soon on the M11 towards East Anglia and Bury St. Edmunds. Hope and Connor wanted to get there as soon as possible. Something was going to go down in Bury St. Edmunds in the next few days.

***

Thursday night was an elaborate dinner at a restaurant of Grace's choice. She wanted to take Kate to Midsummers, a two-star Michelin restaurant in the heart of Cambridge, but Kate begged off, arguing it was too visible and her husband might find out. Kate was beginning to worry her wonderful romance with this woman was getting too big to hide from the Air Force and her nosy co-workers. So far their fun had been restricted to small dive pubs and a hotel. Dinner at the most famous restaurant in Cambridge was too much.

Grace knew all of this, but acted as if she did not care about her husband finding out. She wanted to impress Kate tonight with her sincerity. The restaurant suggestion and then the cancelled reservation calmed Kate's fears.

Of course, Grace did not intend to go to Midsummers with her either. That was the last thing she wanted to do on the night before her grand ops. It was an elaborate bluff and it worked.

Although she never admitted it to Kate, Grace knew Cambridge quite well.

Grace suggested an alternative: takeaway Thai food brought back to their secluded bed and breakfast. Kate brightened at the Thai food suggestion. It was one of her favorites. Soon they were headed for the bed and breakfast with a Thai green chicken curry, chicken Pad Thai, spring rolls, wontons and prawn crackers.

The cottage was by the River Camb. It was more of an upscale cottage than a bed and breakfast. It had a porch overlooking the river, a living room with a simple flat screen TV with Sky satellite, a small kitchen off to one side and, behind the living room, a bedroom with a large king-size poster bed and an ensuite bath with a large, white, old-style claw foot bathtub.

Grace was the perfect host. Dinner turned out to be quite good. Grace had only two glasses of wine – non-alcoholic wine that looked just like the wine she offered Kate. After dinner they made love, which Grace taped with a hidden camera. In the afterglow, Grace served Kate her final drink of the night, spiked with GHB, also known as the date-rape drug. The odorless, light-colored powder made Kate's wine taste slightly salty, but she did not notice.

Kate collapsed fifteen minutes later. She felt the twinges of uncontrolled movement and grabbed Grace's hand.

"Something's wrong. Help me!" she exclaimed frantically.

"Nothing's wrong," cooed Grace. "Don't panic."

"What the...?" Kate stammered as the room began to spin and fade to black.

Grace silently squeezed her hand to comfort her for the few short moments before she lost consciousness. Kate tried to squeeze back but could not; her limbs went limp.

Chapter 16

"You promised t...o...pr...o.... tec...m...e," Kate mumbled as she slumped to the floor. With the hours Grace had before the others arrived, she arranged Kate for some compromising photos and videos, in various positions and states of undress: topless, bottomless and completely nude. Some involved toys like a strap on around her hips; still others had Kate tied, bound and blindfolded like a sex slave.

Some featured Grace, her face obscured, with Kate beside her in a pose, face slightly turned so you could not see her closed eyes. You never knew when something like this would be useful, thought Grace. As long as the asset stayed alive, blackmail was a powerful tool.

Grace wore a blond wig for the photographs and she would keep the disguise for the next phases of her mission. Anything and everything to keep the other side guessing.

By midnight, Grace had Kate ready for her interrogation. Grace would try a civilized approach first and, if unsuccessful, would hand her over to the brutes that usually did this sort of work.

Kate's hands hung above her head, cuffed to the shower railing; her legs were immobilized by a bar with straps at each end. She wore white satin panties and a bright red ball gag protruded from her pink lips.

Grace slapped her to wake her from her drug-induced stupor. It took three slaps hard across her pretty face before her eyes, shuttered for so long, sprang to attention. Kate looked down at her bound body and recognition flickered in her eyes. That emotion was hope. Kate hoped this was an elaborate sex game between the two of them. On their second date, Grace had introduced Kate to some soft scarf ties and Kate responded enthusiastically, both to being tied up and to reciprocating. The scarves were harmless, easy to slip out of, but still represented a form of bondage that Kate found attractive. She claimed her orgasms with Grace were the strongest she had ever had. Grace had no doubt about that.

The hope in Kate's eyes flickered and died when Grace caressed her cheeks but produced a seven-inch butcher's knife.

"No my dear, no foreplay tonight. I need answers and I need
them now. Or else my crude but efficient friend here, the butcher's
knife, will be my instrument of torture." Grace ran the flat blade
side along the curves of Kate's hips. In a rare burst of energy after
the drug, Kate mumbled several profanities into her ball gag while
glaring at Grace and twisting her body away from the blade.

"Listen carefully, my sweet Kate."

Kate's eyes focused a bit at the use of her real name.

"Yes, I know all about you Kate. I am going to make this very
easy for you, my darling." Grace moved aside to reveal a laptop on
the bathroom countertop. She pressed enter and began to play the
collage of pictures and videos she had just created of Kate. Kate
stared and trembled as the revealing posed pictures appeared. This
was a nightmare for Kate.

What did this woman want?

Then the video of that night's lovemaking appeared on screen.
That hurt the most. It was tender and, Kate erroneously thought,
special.

Somewhere in the house distinctive cow bells clanged as Paloma
Faith belted out "Can't rely on you." Grace smirked at the irony of
that as she loosened the gag buckle and let it fall around Kate's
neck. Kate gulped for air and licked her dry lips.

Kate sputtered, "Let me guess, we can do this the hard way or
the easy way, right."

Grace stared at her like a vet would a horse about to be put
down.

*Do people really say that? Who in their right mind goes with the hard way
over the easy way?*

Laughing, Grace scolded Kate. "No. We're just gonna do this
my way. I need the password for the South Gate at Lakenheath.
You give it to me. I let you live and go free in a few days. Simple."
Grace tempted her with a smirk. She had a strong feeling Kate
would not give up the password. After three nights with her she
knew Kate was a proud, tough and, most importantly, loyal woman.
Too bad, thought Grace. She could use someone like that in her
line of work. Grace suspected pain would be the only outcome
tonight.

Kate refused unceremoniously by calling Grace a fat bitch.
Grace spent the next hour working her over slowly. The pain was

intense but left no mark that could not be covered up with clothes. Grace inflicted small cuts on her body in key places: on her scalp, behind her ears, along her breasts, along the hip lines. To add to the ambiance, Grace put on some mood music. Duffy wafted out with her catchy and appropriate song "Mercy." Life truly is better with a soundtrack, thought Grace.

Grace eventually put down her tools and straddled a chair to watch Kate twist, spasm and bleed.

Kate nodded in submission. Her head hung down in exhaustion, wrists strained in her cuffs under the weight of her body. The pain in her thighs was long past excruciating from the tension of her spread legs and the whipping, cuts, slaps and water torture from the shower.

Kate's ball gag was long since removed so Kate could hear herself scream. Grace motioned with her hands for Kate to give her the information. "The password, please."

Kate's grimace of pain shook Grace a bit. She had suffered well for someone not trained to withstand torture. But this was still the easy stuff, thought Grace. She shuddered at the thought of Ahmed or Ralph with Kate.

Kate paused, gaining some modicum of dignity. Raising her head slightly, she gave away her secret: "Rhinoceros."

"Really. Are you sure Kate? Because if you are lying to me, I will hurt you even more." Grace flicked her whip to Kate's exposed thigh. Kate screamed in pain, each small cut sending shock waves through her system.

Grace left her for a few minutes as the Eurhythmic's "Sweet Dreams" began to play from the stereo. Kate began to fade out from the pain. She heard clips of a phone conversation as she dropped in and out of consciousness. Straining against the cuffs and the spreader bar, she rattled more than moved coherently.

Grace appeared at the bathroom door, shaking her head in disappointment.

"I know that is not the password, Kate. Such a shame. Now I must turn you over to my associates and they will be less forgiving than I."

Grace picked her way over to stand beside Kate. Grabbing a handful of hair she jerked Kate's head back to get her attention.

Grace whispered now; screaming at Kate had taken its toll on her voice.

"I already know what the password is." That was a lie. "We just need you to confirm it and I can let you live." The last part came out more pleading than she intended, but at this point she did not care. Time was running out for them both.

Kate summoned every last ounce of energy and spat at Grace. It missed, landing on her own torso, slowly rolling down Kate's belly as she passed out.

Good for you, thought Grace. She had never seen a pretty girl look so tough.

Checking her watch she decided not to try and pry any more information from this turnip. What was that phrase, trying to get blood from a turnip? Her mother always said that.

Grace tidied up Kate but was surprised a short time later when Dakhil appeared with an unwanted guest. Ahmed came with news of his London attack. This angered Grace. They could all see her face suddenly flush with emotion when he explained that the royal couple surprised everyone by attending a day earlier. Fortunately, they were already in place, but they were unsuccessful; Ahmed told them he was the lone survivor.

Grace paced the floor.

Of course Ahmed survived. He always survives to be the thorn in my side. He is the smartest group member I have and I am running out of ways to get rid of him.

Her strategy was falling apart. Surprise was ruined.

They turned on the TV to see information about the attack. The royals were mentioned but not prominently. The newscasters were confused since the planned royal visit was scheduled for Friday. Instead the newscaster speculated a gunfight may have broken out at the volleyball event between a gang and armed police. The royal couple were in the "wrong place at the wrong time". No mention of follow on attacks in Britain were discussed.

"So far, so good. If the Brits are keeping a lid on this then maybe they will not share it in time to prevent my attack tomorrow." Grace pondered aloud. "We shall see."

"A car approaches slowly," announced Dakhil from the front window.

"Red Volvo. Probably with the lights out. Parking just some distance away," she guessed.

"Yes, who is it?" he asked releasing the safety from his weapon.

"Easy." She whispered, calming him with her tone. "It is our American mole. I contacted him."

Ralph flashed his headlights several times five minutes after arriving. Grace did the same with the house lights and Ralph was admitted without much fanfare.

Grace knew him from her surveillance of his home and school. She liked to know who was giving her information and why. He was a high paid snitch that wanted to leave England but on his own terms and not in handcuffs due to his indiscretions. Grace suspected he wanted to use the cell to get rid of some loose ends and to make him out to be a hero in the end so he could reclaim some glory. He was a classic glory hound thought Grace.

She was not surprised to see Ralph make an appearance. She knew why. Earlier in the evening, under interrogation, Kate had confessed to working undercover in an investigation against Ralph. The OSI asked her to snoop and try to find information about him. They were concerned about allegations of his relations with underage children under his care. Grace detected no subterfuge about the other things. So far dipping his wick jeopardized things, but had not compromised them.

But Ralph was ruined or was about to be soon. Ralph knew the clock was ticking on him. He suspected as much and when Grace informed him of her latest intelligence he was willing to go even further than he originally planned.

The moment he stepped into the bathroom it complicated things. He would want to kill Kate tonight. If she saw him, and she would when he tortured her for the password, in his mind she would have to die in order for him to continue with his silly, twisted existence. But Grace had plans for Kate to help them get in the gate. Now that some of the element of surprise was gone she needed every advantage she had.

Grace left Ahmed in charge at the cottage. He and Dakhil had express orders to interrogate Kate for the password but they were NOT to kill her. Grace carefully explained to everyone, especially Ralph, that Kate alive was a key part to getting on base. She warned

Ahmed not to let the American hurt Kate and warned Ralph that
she would castrate him herself if he messed up her plans.

At least no physical damage that is. Ahmed smiled at that
thought. Grace didn't relish leaving Kate as vulnerable as she was to
these three men, but she had to be at a certain Fire Chief's house by
4 a.m. Cambridge was 30 minutes away from Mildenhall and she
had other arrangements that needed processing before she could
get the ball rolling. Due to recent events, timing was crucial.

Later, early Friday morning, Grace discovered that Ralph had
sprained Kate's arm. Ahmed had stepped in and prevented Ralph
from killing Kate, but not in time to stop the gross injury.

"I need her conscious, you stupid prat," she scolded. Gently she
cradled Kate's arm. "She is no good to me trying to get in the gates
if she is unconscious due to pain from your stupidity!" Her mission
was a marathon, not a sprint. She needed everyone and all the
pieces in place when she wanted them.

***

Sean stopped by Kate's flat late that night. He had just broken
up with Laura. It was not quite as tearful a confrontation as he
expected. She had taken it in stride but he could tell she was a little
hurt. For once, he had told the truth: He thought he loved someone
else.

Sean thought it strange that Kate was not home. His good
friend was usually at home this late at night. He thought of Kate as
his rock when it came to issues. He wanted to talk to her about his
emotions and what he should do next with Emile.

I hope she is having fun wherever she is.

***

The Fire Chief of Mildenhall lived in the village. In fact, he lived
two doors down from the police station. People thought the
proximity to a police station guaranteed protection. They were
often wrong. In many cases, these same houses were robbed more
often than other similar houses. Why? Because the robbers knew
the police would be elsewhere or, at the very least, it created a false
sense of security in the homeowners, so they did stupid things like

leave their doors unlocked or windows open. Grace smiled as she crouched beside the back door to the home.

Jonathan Myers was no such fool. Elaborate alarms crisscrossed his two-story Victorian house on the high street. He did this to protect Annie, the wife he loved dearly, and his precious 17-year-old daughter, Sally. All three slept peacefully on this fateful Friday morning, blissfully unaware of all the precautions and procedures Grace had gone through to get into position at 4 a.m.

Turning her head to avoid ruining her night vision through NVGs, she waited for her chemicals to do their job.

This is my favorite time of the day thought Grace.

This is a time when the world is asleep. And I prowl wide awake.

She imagined who lived in the houses she drove by and how they slept. It was a fun exercise. Preparing her for the nocturnal activities at hand. The soothing sound of Neil Diamond in her earbuds singing "Amazing Grace" helped keep her heartbeat at an even pace.

Jonathan was smug. He thought of almost everything, but left a weakness in his castle. Grace had realized it just a day into observing the family.

Their orange tabby Maine Coon came up to Grace on the back porch and purred. Grace stroked her and warned her to watch out for the hot burning lines that now streaked down the door forming an extension of her cat flap.

Whispering into the cat's ear, Grace apologized and explained. "Sorry Samantha dear, but I need a little more room than you to get in." The fiery burning stopped abruptly and the small rectangle Grace had created around the cat flap began to teeter forward.

Grace deftly caught it from her crouching position before it hit the bewildered cat. Samantha pranced, unfazed, into the kitchen; Grace barely squeezed through the rectangular crawl space behind her.

No electronic eyes scanned this room. Because of Samantha and her nocturnal activities, it was the one room without protection. Grace looked through her Night Vision Goggles into a dimly lit kitchen.

NVGs are dual eyepiece devices, which take night images and intensify them. The picture that users see is green, and often fuzzy, but ultimately NVGs turn nighttime into a daytime-like picture. Too much outside illumination, from the moon or artificial lighting, is detrimental to NVGs. Often they perform best in low illumination situations. Grace wore a new technology called CORE (Ceramic Optical Ruggedized Engine). It produced a better NVG image due to the use of a ceramic plate instead of glass plates. The technology would be out soon but for now Grace liked having a leg up.

The control panel for the alarm system rested across the room on a wall off the porch. Grace rubbed her gloved hands as she mentally practiced entering the code. The more I practice, the luckier I get, thought Grace, remembering the phrase from someone in her past.

Grace punched in the code.

2-4-6-8.

Not quite the enigma code Britain was most remembered for. But that often happened. People bought elaborate systems, set them up and then felt so secure that the code to deactivate the system was left as the factory code (often 1-2-3-4) or worse, the owner's anniversary or birthday. Hours of human observation had revealed the punch pattern and an examination of the keypad revealed the code.

Two green blinking lights indicating that the system was armed and functioning disappeared. The system was deactivated and awaiting instructions. Instructions that would never come today.

Grace made her way silently through the old home, round each habitation, hovering like a wraith.

Jonathan, Annie and Sally all slept in separate rooms. Jon's snoring dictated his removal from the family bedroom years ago. So Grace had an easy time finding him. Take out the main threat first, she always said.

Creeping into his "man cave," Grace saw him sleeping face down in a heap of covers. Why do some people sleep face down, thought Grace. She always slept face up. It helped her be alert quicker upon waking and oriented her and the pistol she slept with underneath her pillow. Forward, left and right were the same place every time she awoke. Routine was the cornerstone of good fundamentals.

Jon dreamed of Victoria Pendleton, the great British cyclist. They were both riding a two-person bike on their way to a secluded spot by the lake. He visited the lake often with Victoria.

Suddenly the image disappeared, replaced by the feel of cold hard steel as a pistol with silencer touched his ear. Darkness still surrounded him. He began to sit up, but a sharp impact to his back forced him onto his belly again.

He was just about to complain when a whisper silenced him.

"Shut up and listen if you want to live," hissed his assailant.

Wild thoughts ran through his head. The intruder wore a device on their head that blinked with a twinkling red light. The person was a she, he thought, based on the tone and inflection.

"Tell me the code word to enter the American Air Base Lakenheath. Think and answer carefully. I have the answer and want only confirmation. If you lie...you and your family die."

Jonathan was no hero. He had no allegiance to the Americans. He thought they were nice enough chaps and he loved their barbeques in the summer with great U.S. beef, but nothing was worth harm coming to Annie or Sally. Hesitating only to make sure he remembered the correct word, Jon said:

"Eclipse. The word you want is Eclipse."

Grace smiled underneath her mask. He was just quick enough to not be lying.

Ralph's report stated that while trying to probe for the codeword innocently at last month's BBQs on base, Ralph caught the SP commander exchange a heated glance at Jonathan when he let it slip that Bonnie Tyler protected the entry to Lakenheath. Ralph did not dare press further but he surmised it had something to do with one of her hits. That meant "Total Eclipse of the Heart"; or "Holding Out for a Hero." His best guess was heart, hero or eclipse and since the first two were more common, he surmised it would be eclipse. Now Jonathan had confirmed it on the first try.

Grace was glad something was going to plan. But she had to be sure. You never succeeded if you did not put 100% into it. So she cuffed Jonathan around his wrists and ankles and went to get the gals.

She led both women into the room, one at a time. The child went in first, then the mother, to let the situation sink in. Both had their hands zip-tied behind them and duct tape over their mouths.

It was amazing how many uses Grace had for duct tape. It could bind people's limbs, tape their mouths (especially if wrapped repeatedly around their heads) and held bombs in place magnificently. She made a quick mental note to have her banker in the Cayman Islands invest some of her significant assets in 3M and Duck brand. Although she quickly dismissed the notion after remembering that the US. Government recommended it in their disaster preparedness information after the attacks on 9/11. So the boat may have sailed on the company's success by now.

Too bad.

She had Annie kneel beside her daughter. Her breathing was shallow and increased in intensity when she saw her father incapacitated on his bed. He turned to try and see her but she was directly behind him at the foot of his bed.

Grace turned off her NVGs and let her eyes adjust, as the women sobbed inconsolably. There was no time for modesty so the ladies came dressed as they were. Annie wore light blue pajama pants and a thin silk blue pullover top. Sally wore only baby blue hip hugger panties. Her young pert chest protruded defiantly. Grace pulled Jonathan around so he lay on his side and stared at his two family members. Annie began to sob looking back and forth between Sally, her innocent daughter, and her trussed up husband. Grace turned on a small flashlight and illuminated the two women from behind. The beam partially blinded Jonathan. Before he diverted his eyes sideways he saw his daughter's condition and semi- nude body. He could not remember the last time he'd seen her naked. It was probably four or five years ago. His face flushed with embarrassment.

Grace wasted no time before asking him her question again. She wanted proof it was indeed a truthful answer. There was no better confirmation of that than with a threat to a family member's life. Leaving the light on a stool behind them, she smacked Annie on the ass. Annie jumped as the cold leather glove struck home. As Annie straightened, rising from the slumping position of her bum on her ankles to standing straight up at the knees, Grace pounced.

"What is the password? Tell me truthfully or I will hurt each of them. In front of you. Slowly."

Jonathan panicked, not understanding if this woman wanted another password or the same code word he honestly provided earlier. He stammered involuntarily.

Grace roughly pulled Annie's top over her head, exposing her chest as well. Her sobs increased and her head began to shake up and down and she sobbed through the gag imploring her husband to comply, "Yes! Yes!"

To her credit, Sally rested on her knees and stared straight ahead. She finally accepted the situation and expected to die any moment, so her mother's torment meant nothing to her at this point. She was a blank canvas with small tears streaming down her face.

Grace felt some small compassion for the girl. Then smiled at the teenager.

Hey if you can't enjoy your work, why do it?

Jon blurted out his answer again.

"Eclipse. The word is eclipse! It will get you on base." Grace nodded at his sincerity this second time and knew he was telling the truth.

All pretense of danger was now removed.

"Because you did not lie to me Jonathan, you and your family will live. My mother always told me never to lie. And you have honored her with your actions, so I will give you a sedative and let you sleep through all the fun."

She switched off the flashlight and turned her NVGs back on. She tried to minimize the light to avoid unnecessary detection.

She returned Annie's blouse to its normal position and tucked it in her pajama bottoms.

Grace turned her attention back to the mission.

No, no time for such things. Focus on the task at hand.

She had each of them drink a glass of milk mixed with a strong sedative that knocked them out within minutes and would keep them asleep for the next 12 hours. Grace returned each member of the sleeping family to their bedrooms and removed their restraints and gags.

In Sally's room, she found a chunk of gum on the bedside table. Sally chewed it right until bedtime then took it out before going to bed. Grace took the wad of gum.

Grace crept out of the house. She thought about setting the alarm again and then thought better of it. No use risking something going wrong with it later and the alarm possibly going off. That would be just her luck.

She went out the cat flap and then returned the section of back door so it stood where it normally would. To make sure it stayed in place she took the gum and used it at different places to hold the flimsy door in place. It would hold long enough to fool anyone glancing that way. And Grace chuckled to herself. Forensics would have a field day analyzing the gum for DNA.

Lakenheath Air Base, England

RAF Lakenheath sat 4.5 miles northeast of Mildenhall village. Although an RAF base, Lakenheath was home to 5,700 active duty USAF service men and 2,000 British and U.S. civilians. The base had nearly 8,000 people on it at any given time. The host wing, the 48th Fighter Wing, was known as the Liberty Wing.

Sean was leading the sortie today and briefed the other three members of his flight on what he expected to happen and when. He covered the takeoff and landing phases, the "coming and going." He talked about contingencies, the "what ifs," and then finally got to the meat of the matter: how they would employ the live weapons on the aircraft. It was Sean's first flight with real weapons since the accident and he was not taking any chances.

In stark contrast to typical British weather, the day promised to be bright and sunny with little or no wind. Perfect for flying and bombing.

After the briefing, Sean allowed each aircraft crew twenty minutes to do their own crew coordination briefing and get geared up in life support before meeting at the operations desk for last minute updates on the weather, airfield status and flying restrictions.

Tambra stood to leave with Mark, and then hesitated. "Mark, I'll meet you in life support," she said. "I need to ask Sean something."

"Okay, we can talk about the weapon release on the way out to the jet," offered Mark.

"Em, our crew coordination brief is standard, just like always. Give me a few minutes here with Tally and then I'll meet you in life support."

The look Emile shot Sean told him she did not like the fact that their crew coordination brief on their live fire exercise was going to be discussed in the "bread van" driving out to the jets. He nodded understanding but waved her away anyway. She shook her head in frustration and turned on her flight boot heels, brushing Tambra slightly as she walked out. The move caught Tambra by surprise. Sean hid his grin.

Pouring a little salt on her open wound, Tambra called to Emile, "Can you grab the door on your way out, Bambi?"

Tambra realized then that Emile blamed her for this ill-timed deviation and she was right. It was not the time to do this but she had to or she might never get up the nerve again to do it.

"What's up, darling?" asked Sean after the door closed behind Mark and Emile's departure.

"Sean, it's over. I have enjoyed your company and the 'friends with benefits' thing was great, but I am stopping it here and now." Tambra folded her arms across her chest.

Sean stood, puzzled.

"Don't." Tambra placed her hands on her hips in a defiant stance and continued. "Don't give me that boyish imp of a grin that says 'she's broken up before but we'll get back together again.' We won't. This is really it. I have decided to leave David."

"And, when I do leave him, I cannot afford to have anyone else in the wings. Do you understand?"

Sean watched and listened. His relationship with Tambra was strange. They were not dating because she was married. Sean dated other women, but not Tambra. They hooked up only when it was convenient for her. At those occasions he dropped everything because he liked being with her. Maybe it was because he knew it would never lead to anything.

Age was not a problem. Sean just turned 30, she was 35. She did have a higher rank than him. She was a Major whereas he was just a Captain.

"Yes Tambra I understand, if that's what you want."

"That's what I want, Sean."

Sean attempted to give her a hug. She wanted no part of it. This had to be a clean break or she might falter.

"No, Sean. No hugs, kisses, or signs of affection."

She moved further away from him, but plowed on with her speech.

"This will not be like last time. This is it."

Sean spoke one of the few Arab words he knew "Khalas" which meant the end or finished.

Tambra smiled at his pronunciation and reciprocated a better sounding "Khalas."

Tambra felt a small tear form and quickly left before she was overcome by the emotion of breaking up with the only person in the world who knew her well and still loved her. But despite all the recent pain with her husband and the emotional loss she just suffered, she was happy with her decision.

Instead of going directly to the life support room to put on her flying harness and get her helmet, she ducked out onto the patio and bummed a cigarette from one of the enlisted folks.

She gave up cigarettes years ago but occasionally broke the habit and lit up. She told herself this would be her last one. She was right.

Chapter 17

Bury St. Edmunds, England

Hope and Connor slipped into Bury St. Edmunds around 9 a.m. Parking in front of the historic vine-covered Angel Hotel gave them a perfect location to scout the medieval city. East of the main parking lot were the Abbey Gardens. They climbed gently west via Abbeygate Street, also known as the High Street to locals. After two hours of prowling the town, nothing caught their attention.

Hope's cell phone rang: "New Sensation" from INXS. Hope spoke rapidly and excitedly. She finished the short conversation and grabbed Connor by his arm, dragging him back towards the car.

"Shari remembered something else. She said Lakenheath village was more significant." They spun out of the city and onto the A14 towards Lakenheath.

***

Due to recent U.S. deficit reduction cuts, the military faced "across the board" 10% cuts from its budget. Luckily, Congress and the President eventually allowed the military to make the cuts themselves, surgically and strategically, versus taking an axe and simply cutting everything arbitrarily. When the time came to make the cuts the USAF decided to fly less and do more training in the flight simulators.

Crews now flew on odd days. So one set of aircrew flew on Mondays and Wednesdays and the other crew flew on Tuesdays and Thursdays. Fridays were for whichever crew got shorted during the week due to maintenance or weather cancellations. This reduction in flying hours also led to formed crews. So now a pilot and a weapon systems officer were paired up and flew the majority of their missions together. The cuts ended the luxury of mixing up crews to get different perspectives.

On the preflight of the aircraft Sean and Emile walked around the jet checking to make sure no safety pins remained. Emile checked the weapons, Sean the aircraft. Both checked fuels, hydraulic levels and the amount of chaff and flares the F-15E carried.

Emile patted the three GBU-54s mounted on the left CFT. The Boeing-crafted Laser JDAM (LJDAM) was a smart bomb that could guide to a GPS coordinate using satellite guidance or follow a laser beam into a target. The laser option was a primary option against a moving target. The Air Force wanted to modify an existing weapon and give it more capabilities. The GBU-54 was developed by adding a laser seeker to a 500-lb GBU-38 GPS guided bomb. The dual capabilities made it ideal for either a stationary or moving target while ensuring minimal collateral damage.

Emile made sure all the laser seekers' had the correct codes. Today's bombs were made with 1625 as their seeker frequency coding. The laser seekers stuck out from the front end of the 500 pound ordnance and were covered with a plastic hat to prevent damage to the seeker head during taxi. The armament crew at the "last chance" inspection removed them when the two jets came to rest at the end of runway parking area.

The GBU-31A on the right CFT was a GPS weapon only. It could not fly to a laser spot like the GBU-54. That did not prevent it from getting its own attention during the preflight. Emile made sure the bombs hung securely to the aircraft, the traditional tug on the weapon guaranteed this. She also looked at each wing and fin of the weapon. A bent fin could seriously disrupt the trajectory of a weapon in flight.

Both types of weapons were called "smart" bombs because they could hit precise coordinates using GPS navigation systems. They were "launch and forget" meaning once they dropped off the jet no other aircrew actions were required.

Next she stepped to the bomb fuses and made sure everything there was correct. Many of the arming safety wires and pins, usually accompanied by a bright red flag as a reminder, were removed but one or two still remained to guarantee the aircraft's safe movement around the airfield before takeoff.

The aircrew still had some steps they needed to perform to get the bomb off the jet, but making sure all the safety pins and flags were in until they were supposed to be pulled, and then that they were pulled before takeoff, was an important task for the ground crew and aviators.

The two crew members climbed into the cockpit and the crew chief assisted Emile and then Sean with their ejection harness buckles and belts. Once they were all strapped in, the crew chief left the airplane and moved in front of but to the side of the aircraft so he could monitor the engine start sequence.

Sean reflected for a moment before starting the Jet Fuel Starter (JFS) of the big F-15E. Nine months since the fateful accident.

Everything preventing him from flying in combat was accomplished: an accident investigation board, simulator check ride and clinical evaluation. There had been no repercussions. He could get back to doing his job. All he needed to do now was get through this flight with live weapons and execute a live drop. After that he would be mission ready.

The clinical evaluation may have been the hardest of the three obstacles. Over the past three months the psychologist, a fairly attractive lady with short black hair and large dark glasses probed Sean about his childhood and life as a fighter pilot. He told her about his father's early death, his mother's problems and even delved a little into his love life.

But it was his dreams she seemed to focus on. Recently Sean had one recurring dream involving Sean taking a test at the Air Force Academy. He could see the school buildings clearly and the Rocky Mountains behind the school. He was in a classroom by himself taking a test. But he was naked. He looked down from above on his own nude form.

The desk was too small. His tight muscular form barely squeezed into the wooden desk and under the lap top front. From the side, his muscles tensed in his thick legs, rippling down them in rivers of flesh and sinew.

He could not see the test title. Glancing at the clock in the classroom front, he knew he only had five minutes to complete the exam. As Sean flipped through the pages to see what remained, he noticed some questions in a foreign language he recognized as Arabic. Suddenly the bell rang and a teacher mysteriously appeared. Her big round glasses detracted from the brown hair that hung casually around her ears. A white blouse was tied just below and barely covering her ample bosom, exposing a tan midriff. The woman's brown skirt dropped to just above her knee and when she leaned forward, the slit on the left side revealed black thigh-high stockings and black pumps. She reminded Sean of the teacher in a video by one of those old metal rock bands.

In a sexy voice, she declared that time was up, but when Sean reached her desk to hand in the test and ask for some leniency, the teacher did not notice his Adonis-like nudity, or his lower regions, which had clearly come to attention in front of the sexy instructor. She was joined by his wingman, the one who perished in the Libya mission and neither took notice of his naked body standing before them.

The Air Force shrink told Sean the dream meant several things.

The test itself represented the fact Sean was being put to the test. It was an anxiety he was facing now. Perhaps he felt he was not up to the challenge or had apprehension about flying again with live bombs or in a combat scenario. These things happened. It also could have been a fear that Sean did not meet other people's standards for going to war.

Sean's nudity indicated that some action of his was drawing the wrong type of attention to him. He wanted to be noticed but was going about it the wrong way.

Sean was using psychological projection. This was a defense mechanism where a person subconsciously denied his own attributes or emotions, which were then ascribed to other people.

She pointed to two such instances; the first was with Sean's relationship trauma. Since Sean's mother could not maintain a steady relationship, Sean took that as his role as well; but Sean did not acknowledge this character flaw. Instead, in his mind, everyone cheated if they were single. So he projected his own mantra of "treat 'em mean and keep 'em clean" on everyone except himself. Sean blamed others for his lack of commitment in relationships.

His second projection occurred in relation to flying. In Sean's mind everyone else flew a little too recklessly. They needed to be watched and monitored, but not Sean. That was why he lost his wingman in Libya. His wingman was a loose cannon. It was not that Sean flew too close to the edge at times and asked for the maximum effort at all times. It was not that Sean demanded too much and gave little support. No, the others demanded and gave little, not Sean.

She claimed he was still traversing the five stages of grief or loss. He had gone through the first three stages, denial, anger and bargaining. That left his current phase (the fourth): depression and eventually acceptance.

His sessions with the shrink were now over. He passed his evaluation last week. The last words she said to him were, "It is up to you to accept the demons inside you and correct them or continue to let them delude you."

She liked referring to everything as a demon. Perhaps it was her Asiatic background. Sean had not given it much thought since he left her. Not until today and he had to strap himself into an 80,000-pound killing machine.

Fighter pilots were like insurance policies. You always wanted them paid up and current but you never hoped to use them. If you did cash in that policy, it meant you lost something precious, which was not good. But the thought that something good was coming "to back you up" felt good too, in a way.

Although most fighter pilots felt like that, many yearned for the thrill and adventure of combat, especially the young aviators who had never "been there and done that." Not Sean. Sean had combat time under his belt – over 200 hours on 43 combat sorties in the F-15E, the time split fairly evenly between Afghanistan, Iraq and Libya during a tour of duty at each remote location. But he wanted – no, he needed – to get back on full status. If the balloon went up today, he wanted to be the one the boss turned to for results.

Sean gave the crew chief in front of the airplane the signal and pulled the JFS knob. Instantly the Jet Fuel Starter began to spin within the aircraft. Sean and Emile heard the JFS whine as it sprang to life and provided their intercom, communications with the crew chief, and fire protection circuitry, which Sean checked.

"Warning AMAD Fire! Warning AMAD Fire!"

"Just testing," came Sean's reply. "Ready on two, chief?"

"Yes sir, fire guards posted, fore and aft clear. You are clear to engage on number two." This mantra from the crew chief told Sean that a ground crew member stood by the fire bottle ready to come if there was a fire, both the front and rear of the aircraft was clear of any people and objects, and Sean could safely engage the engine to the already turning JFS.

Sean started #2, the right engine. The Pratt and Whitney 229 engine roared to life seconds after the jet fuel poured into the titanium engine bay. Sixty seconds later the #1 engine on the left revved at 69% or idle thrust.

With both engines started, it was time to go through their pre-flight checks. Again each aircrew performed their checks like a well-oiled machine. Sean checked the engines, hydraulic gauges, flight controls and instruments. Emile set up the avionics they would use for their flight and checked the systems and weapons they were to employ.

Twenty minutes later, both Strike 01 and 02 taxied out of their assigned parking spots on the Charlie ramp and waddled their heavily armed jets down the taxiway. Their 20 MPH snail's pace ensured no mishaps in the obstacle course of vehicles, men or equipment on either side of the taxiway.

Strike 01 rolled into EOR and took the first available spot on the south side arming area. Strike 02 rolled to a grinding stop on their right side. Strike 01 bounced twice to a halt.

"Sean's going to have to take that one to the shop if he keeps riding those brakes like that," commented Mark.

"Give him a break. It's his first live sortie back since the accident," defended Tambra.

"I thought he was cleared last week and flew once already."

"No, it was his simulator check ride he passed last Friday and he was weather cancelled on Monday and maintenance cancelled on Wednesday."

The arming crews plugged in their communication cords.

"Sir, this is your armament troop, can you hear me?" asked the ground crew.

Sean grinned inside his oxygen mask. Time to get back into the game and have a little fun. His crew chief had told him, just before pulling the chocks, there would be a young airman on the headset for his arming and Sean should show him every courtesy. The crew chief then winked and gave him thumbs up; Sean understood perfectly. It was Sean's favorite prank.

Sean gave the airman a thumb down signal, "Nope, chief I cannot hear you."

"Really?" he asked surprised. "I checked everything before you arrived and it all checked out good."

Sean had to physically "go cold mike" (when he turned his microphone off so neither Emile nor the ground personnel could hear him), straight himself of the giggles and then resume his discussion with the crew chief about how he could not hear him.

"No, no. I don't know what you did on your check-out son, but I cannot hear a single thing you say. Are you sure you are on the right frequency?"

It still had not dawned on the young airman what Sean was up to.

"I am supposed to be on three, Sir, and that's what I am on."

"Ok, if you're supposed to be on three and I cannot hear you, then it must be a bad cord. Better get another one from your backup."

"Roger that. Standby, sir." The young airman went to his superior off to the side of the jet and explained that he could not hear the aircrew. Emile remained silent the entire time. She had seen Sean pull this practical joke about five times now and did not think it was particularly funny. She let him go this time without any admonitions since it helped calm him a bit. Sean knew the light bulb went off in the airman's head when he smacked his forehead just before explaining to his super.

At least he got it then.

Sheepishly, and chuckling as the entire team smiled at him, the armament troop returned with a small smile. He plugged in again and asked, "Can you hear me now, sir?"

Sean burst out laughing. "Sorry chief, I still cannot hear you."

"Good one, sir," Now all three had a good laugh, including Emile.

The airman continued, unfazed, and asked if both the aircrew were away from any switches.

Sean assured him they both were and, as added insurance, they both placed their hands up in the windscreens where they could be seen.

No aircrew wanted to be responsible for an injury to the people running around a jet trying to arm it up for takeoff. It was bad enough having to be near a jet with two running engines, but these folks had to go underneath the jet and pull the safety pins and covers from the weapons. If an aircrew moved a switch erroneously, it could zap a human with dangerous radiation in the case of a radar, or hit them with an airplane part (a stabilator, flap or aileron) in the case of flight controls.

While the arming crew did their magic, Sean looked over at Strike 02 and gave it a quick inspection to make sure their weapon loadout was correct and all their panels were closed and secured. Basically just a motherhood item to make sure nothing was out of order, since they were about to take the weapons loaded beasts into the air in a few minutes.

Strike 02 bristled with a Mark 84 2000 lb. bomb on their left pylon (farthest most on the wing) and an AGM-130 on the other side of the airplane on station 8. Both aircraft flew today with an AXQ-114 data link pod on their centerline station 5 or just underneath the aircraft between the two motors. Strike 02 carried it to drop the AGM-130 but Strike 01 carried one simply because maintenance had yet to download it from an earlier flight with EGBU-15's.

Both pilots wore their own Helmet Mounted Display (HMD). The HMD provided the capability to cue aircraft weapons and sensors while looking outside the aircraft. Traditionally weapon and sensor cueing were accomplished by looking down into the cockpit or for the pilot to look through the HUD (Heads Up Display). Now the HMD allowed the frontseater to look outside the aircraft and see through a series of symbols and color coding, information that previously resided inside the cockpit. This allowed for easier eye contact with both friendly and enemy forces airborne and on the ground.

This was accomplished by providing a faceplate over the helmet that projected the symbols when the field of view of the helmet looked in that direction. It had revolutionized the F-15E in terms of data information. Unfortunately, the back seat of the aircraft did not have a HMD. The Air Force felt there were so many other duties that involved the WSO being "heads down" that the cost of the HMD for the backseater was prohibitive.

Emile thought about their last real meeting on Sunday. They had flown twice since the Abbey Gardens conversation and neither had brought up their discussion.

Discussion. Right. I doubt if Sean felt like it was a discussion. More like a one sided pronouncement from me. I am so stupid. Why didn't I just keep my big fat mouth shut and not declare my feelings for him. Things are kind of weird between us now. I wish I could undo everything.

Sean was trying to figure out how and when to tell Emile that he had broken up with Laura and Tambra. He did not want to talk to Emile about it until he had split up with the other women, so that meant being evasive about things until now.

I don't want to do it while we're in the jet. I will wait until we land and then ask her out to dinner. I'll tell her I have something to tell her and that we need to be alone.

Satisfied with his plan he glanced around the cockpit. He stopped at the fuel gauge making sure the fuel was feeding correctly. Next he observed the telelight panel to make sure no system warnings were displayed.

Sean was quiet and distracted and that was not what Emile wanted to see from him on their sortie today. She did not realize some of the distraction was because of her and their last meeting. She tried to get him to open up while they waited for the armament crews to do their duties outside the airframe.

"Sean, you seem pretty different today. A little distant, what's up?"

Sean heaved a loud sigh but did not say anything. The only sound was the occasional drag on the oxygen system as each of their valves creaked back and forth. The sound reminded Emile of someone trying to breathe through a stopped-up nose. Finally Sean broke the silence.

"Em, why is it I can handle everything as a flight lead but get butterflies in my stomach when I think about dropping live weapons again?"

"You're asking me? I get nervous just thinking about a check ride. You...you breeze through life as if you're on a golden parachute. I'm surprised you're having issues with the live weapons drop. It's your last hurdle before becoming a full up combat ready flight lead again, right?"

"Em, I listened to what you said to me last week in the Bury Gardens. Remember what you said about keeping secrets?"

Emile gulped. He had listened to her and perhaps taken some of it to heart.

"Emile, I am going to tell you a secret. I am deathly afraid to drop live weapons. It has been building for a few weeks now and the aborted attempt this week just postponed my angst. There, I said it."

This was quite a revelation to Emile. She realized it took a lot of guts for him to say that to her before the flight. She also double-checked to make sure the tape recording device was not on. Usually aircrews only taped the important part of the mission, so conversations going and coming from the low level or bombing ranges did not get recorded.

He had listened to her when they had their emotional scene Sunday. She sat a little taller in her ejection seat. She was happier at this admission simply because of the intimacy it implied. But still concerned about the nature of his conflict.

Emile thought about her next words carefully.

"Sean, you can do it. It's just like riding a bike. You never forget and it is no different than dropping ordnance in the simulator or in the jet, but from the training armament page."

Sean was not buying it and neither was Emile, if she was honest.

"It's not the same."

"Aw, Em. It's something in my head. I know it's an irrational fear. And if you tell anyone else it is my fear I will disavow it and never speak to you again, but…"

A loud twang announced the airmen had connected back to their communication system.

"Sir, both aircraft are armed up and ready to go. We will see you on the ground in about an hour and a half."

The airman's comments jerked Sean out of his reflection and back to the present.

Time to take this huge metal contraption into the sky.

Sean acknowledged the young man and then returned his crisp salute as the jets pulled forward and then hung a right 130-degree turn to point at the runway. Both jets accelerated like pigs from a standstill and the extra run-up in power he needed surprised Sean. They were loaded with 3,500 pounds of explosives.

"Strike push three aux." This commanded Tambra to automatically change her radio frequency in the auxiliary or backup radio to tower frequency, Channel 3.

"Strike check."

"Two." Tambra's acknowledgement was crisp and quick. You always wanted to sound good on the radio. Sean's philosophy was this: the entire flight could be a disaster but if you sounded good on the radio, then something good came out of it.

"Lakenheath Tower. Strike 01 flight of two ready for takeoff Runway 24."

Staff Sergeant Brian Henderson in the control tower cleared Sean's flight for takeoff with "Strike 01 flight, winds 250 at 15 knots cleared for takeoff runway 24. Contact departure channel four." The SSgt appreciated the clear weather conditions and the orderly flow of jets taxiing toward the runway. Things were running smoothly today. That would all change in a matter of minutes.

"Strike 01's cleared for takeoff. Push four."

After that radio call, both WSOs changed the aux radio to channel 4, which was departure frequency. The WSOs did most administrative duties in the jet. This allowed the frontseaters, or pilots, to concentrate on flying the aircraft. It was a good system that had worked for more than 25 years, ever since the Strike Eagle rolled off the assembly line for the first time in 1988.

Sean inched his aircraft onto the 9000-foot long runway first and centered it dead in the middle of the 150-foot wide concrete strip.

Strike flight performed a rolling takeoff. Both airplanes would take off separately with 20 second spacing between each takeoff. Neither jet would stop on the runway.

"Ready?" asked Sean.

"Good to go," came Emile's standard reply.

"Departure Strike 01 flight, rolling. Request traffic service." And with that Sean pushed both throttles into military power.

The throttles had four primary positions: off, idle, military and afterburner (AB). Aviators used idle power to slow the aircraft; it was the lowest power setting without turning an engine off. Between idle and military there are no detents, or specific settings, just various RPM percentages. Military power was considered high power and if a little extra power was needed and you are willing to burn much more fuel for that boost then afterburner is selected.

Sean went from idle to mil by pushing the throttles forward until they reached the first detent or lever restriction. Checking everything looked good on his engines, a second later he pushed the throttles beyond the manual stop or detent into afterburner. The crew could not feel it but the engines went through 11 different stages of afterburner as the airplane accelerated rapidly.

"Good swings, good fuel flows," came Emile's lone comment on the engine's status. That was good news. Bad news would have been communicated with a directive "Abort!" then the reason for the abort.

"One hundred knots," were the next words out of her mouth seconds later indicating they were now past the point where they could safely abort if one of their tires blew.

"Committed," this meant they were past the point where they could safely abort the takeoff for anything. They were now "committed" to the takeoff. This all happened in the span of five seconds. Sean pulled back on the stick and the nose wheel lifted off the ground and then the main wheels were off and they climbed away from the runway. Sean lifted the landing gear handle and retracted the flaps. Around the base the roar of the escaping jets cascaded off the buildings in a cacophony of booms and rattles.

"We're clean," was Emile's confirmation of a successful landing gear and flaps retraction.

Strike 02 did the same 20 seconds later and both aircraft climbed into the sky south of Lakenheath.

***

The first thing they had to do was cut the phone line into the firehouse. No sense in letting the possibility of a real-life fire call ruin their plan. Not that either Lakenheath or Mildenhall fire squads got many calls. On average maybe one a day, usually at night for a cooking fire.

Over the past few months, Grace had managed to get two terrorists "inside," as cooks for the fire stations. As always, integrating into this society was easy if you accepted the menial, unwanted jobs such as cleaning, cooking or serving.

Each of the infiltrated terrorists let in two friends through side doors while the firemen ate lunch. They would be the muscle with weapons in case plan A did not work.

Chili was the food of choice. Faysal and Hasan made it and served it at exactly 11:15 a.m., laced with the strongest knockout drugs at their disposal. Six men collapsed unconscious at the Lakenheath village station. The chief was a different story.

As it was, the chief was late getting his chili. Luckily, he did not notice his own men as they ate, slowly becoming more groggy and incapacitated by the minute. He was distracted with his monthly reports and grabbed his food and dashed back to his office. But a quick glance in his office revealed he was not eating. Grace was on a very tight schedule.

Hasan called to the chief and asked him to look at something in the lunchroom. He reluctantly answered the call and received a pipe wrench blow to the back of his skull for it. Now all seven were rendered unconscious and the terrorists quickly stripped them of their uniforms and carried their limp forms into a storage room, locking them all in.

Mildenhall was not much different. The chief had called in to say he would be late, so lunch started without him. Actually Grace had one of her accomplices call in to another of her terrorists at the station who cooked the drugged meal. He faked the call from the fire chief Grace had so efficiently subdued. The five remaining men sat down for lunch at 11:15 a.m. as well. However, one man left to work on a piece of equipment. The four large men fell unconscious shortly thereafter, but a communication error left the untargeted fireman alone for a minute or two. Just enough time for him to note the cut phone lines when he tried to call out to his girlfriend. Running back into the kitchen, he collided with the three terrorists moving his slumped colleagues into the storage room. He fought back, punching one of the men until Zamil pulled a gun. They tied him up and left him in the storeroom with the others.

Grace glanced at her watch after receiving the call from Ahmed telling her they were ready at Lakenheath. It was 11:28 a.m. The entire operation to remove the firemen and replace them with her people took 13 minutes from start to finish. Now they waited.

Airborne near RAF Lakenheath

The civilian aircraft was a Cessna 172, the most common civilian aircraft in the world. Lakenheath had once had an aero club, but it closed 10 years earlier. The number of civilian traffic crossing into the Lakenheath control zone had increased over the years as more airspace restrictions went up over London down to the south.

With London becoming more fortress-like in its airspace
restrictions, it naturally drove the pleasure craft further away from
the big airports like Heathrow, Gatwick and Stansted.

In any given week, 25 civilian aircraft passed overhead
Lakenheath. The controllers would try to get them not to do it,
since the fast jets flying into and out of Lakenheath were a potential
hazard, but, legally, the slower, smaller traffic could transit with a
radio call if done enough in advance.

Today the control tower had one such civilian plane inbound.

Charlie Victor Romeo 571 had taken off from Cambridge at
11:30 a.m. this morning. Its flight plan was to fly to Norwich and to
do so it would transit Lakenheath airspace for seven minutes from
11:42 a.m. to 11:49 a.m.

Staff Sergeant Brian Henderson paced the control tower. Now
that the last F-15Es had taken off, Brian could relax a bit. Unless
one of them had an emergency and returned early, the tower had at
least an hour before more work was needed controlling returning
aircraft, other than the civilian traffic scheduled in a few minutes.

CVR571 slowly trundled across the British skies. The bright sun
was a rarity, although East Anglia did have the best weather of any
part of England. Today was chosen for many reasons but the
forecast for sunny skies was one of the main ones.

CVR571 made contact with the Lakenheath tower.

"Lakenheath tower, Charlie Victor Romeo five-seven-one
requesting permission to cross your control zone at one thousand
eight hundred feet in five minutes."

SSgt Henderson acknowledged the call and granted the light
aircraft permission. Now that all of his Eagles were airborne, it was
no problem allowing a civilian plane into the control zone.

***

Motaz calmly flew the aircraft on a steady course towards
Lakenheath. Grace predicted it would be easy and he never doubted
her, but surely it would not be as easy as this. The controller had
given him permission. His months and months of flying lessons and
practice were paying off. He had acquired his private pilot's license
legally in France over two years ago. The French were lax in so
many ways, he thought. But here he had not risked practicing his

flying for fear of raising suspicion. So, for the past month, he had practiced on video games. It was truly amazing just how realistic those games were. The terrain and visuals were good enough to prepare him for this mission and the Google maps of Lakenheath showed the location of every building. Insider information from the principal and their two menial labor workers provided everything else he needed.

Taking his eyes momentarily off of his instruments, he noted the time. 11:40 a.m. All was going as planned.

PART III

The Attack

Sam Hendricks

Chapter 18

Lakenheath Air Base, England

Lakenheath Air Base was oriented primarily north-south. The base was west of the A1065 road, halfway between Mildenhall and Brandon. The village of Lakenheath was located west of the air base. Mildenhall town was south of the airfield. The runway and aircraft shelters were on the northern side. The infrastructure buildings sat on the southern portion of the base. The Base Exchange (BX), commissary and administration buildings all rested in this southern area of the base.

Nadia hummed a familiar tune in her car. She was parked approximately 100 feet from the entrance to the fuel dump at Lakenheath. She faced the dump entrance, which had an electronic steel gate that swung open slowly as fuel trucks entered or exited. The entire fencing around the fuel dump also consisted of this reinforced Kevlar plating. This was not Nadia's first time here. She ate her lunch here every other week, each time watching and timing the gate opening, measuring the distance from her location to the gate and observing the fuel trucks inside and their schedule.

Nadia worked as a cleaner for one of the local companies. It was easy to find the job. Many British often complained about the foreigners who came and took jobs from them but in reality many British did not want to do those lower class jobs for the pay and long hours that came with them.

Nadia was a natural born British citizen but because of her complexion people often thought she emigrated from the Middle East. She saw the same stereotypical beliefs and behaviors over and over. Often a natural born Brit who applied for such jobs would take it just long enough to fulfill whatever work obligation they needed to do in order to qualify for their next round of "benefits." Other times, the Brit would accept the job but then fail to turn up on time the next day and the next and eventually would have to be let go by their employer. But having reset their "work" clock it would qualify them for more money for being on the dole. The socialized system of paying them more to not work than to work in England was hurting the British work ethic in many cases. Nadia knew of some who took advantage of the system. Many from the neighborhood where she grew up were benefit frauds, but she also knew many immigrants from Eastern Europe and the Middle East who loved the UK and the work and opportunities they found in the United Kingdom.

Nadia waited patiently. Her stomach was in knots. Every few moments, she reached to touch the Koran she had brought with her on this mission. Touching it gave her a sense of calm, even if just for a few precious seconds.

A fuel truck approached and she watched as the rectangular gate slowly swung open. Glancing inside the fuel enclosure, she saw exactly what she had prayed to Allah she would see today: fuel trucks lined up row after row, with big black hoses snaking from underground connections. From her vantage point the scene looked like giant caterpillars with small flies buzzing around them.

Men in green Air Force coveralls swarmed around the trucks, checking gauges and manhandling the hoses into position. The waiting empty fuel truck pulled inside and the gate swung shut, blocking Nadia's view of her target.

Her iPod alarm went off at 11:40 a.m. She jerked to attention. Now it was an automatic green light. Due to the problems with the London volleyball attack last night, and their over-reliance on radios and smart phones, especially the Blackberries, their plan had changed. Grace had chosen to use communication out signals. So unless she heard otherwise by phone, then everything was a green light to go. No phone call before 11:40 a.m. meant that from now on her mission went ahead. Now she had to wait for her opportunity and that meant more stomach cartwheels.

Her anxious minutes of expectation paid off. She saw her accomplice sneak up to the gate on time. The plan originally was to just drive a cleaning van full of gas and assorted chemical cleaners – very combustible ones – into the first fuel truck that left the compound. That fuel truck target would be full and the explosion great enough. But Grace refined the plan and determined that a clean strike into the fuel compound would have a devastating blow to the base and create a larger distraction from the real attack. Normally the gate only opened for entering or exiting fuel trucks. In both cases, the trucks would serve as a barrier to her from the center of the fuel dump. However, Nadia observed on one occasion the fuel driver got out of his truck and pushed a button on a panel beside the gate. Later investigation at night revealed a manual override opened the gate once a series of codes were entered in the keypad. It was the Air Force backup system.

Fatima, her accomplice, entered the key code they had received from James, the maintenance officer. Ralph used his "author friend" as a cover and said he wanted to get a look inside one night for authenticity. James protested it would be the last information he could provide or else he would have to report Ralph. Ralph agreed and only received this information relatively recently. He suspected James gave him the code before it was to be changed; his confidence level on the information was not high. But to everyone's surprise, it worked.

***

Fatima arrived an hour before the attack and used a fake identity card as a cleaner that Grace had procured for her. She parked well away from the fuel dump and waited. When the time came she carefully drove behind the fuel dump and left her car running while she snuck up to the fuel gate panel as stealthily as she could.

She entered in the code and said a silent prayer for success.

No alarms went off, so she pressed the manual override button. The light on the panel turned green and the gate began its slow progression open. Fatima risked one quick glance toward her friend Nadia in the waiting van and then hurried back to her car.

Nadia gripped the steering wheel harder and revved her van engine. This was it.

She gunned the engine, accelerating as fast as the big van would allow, and sped from her concealed observation area onto the road approaching the fuel dump. The men working that day paid no attention to the gate opening. Several suspected it to be a returning fuel truck from the flight line. Six of the ten refueling bays were loaded with fuel trucks taking on their precious cargo of JP-8 aviation fuel. Each R-11 refueling vehicle held up to 6,000 gallons (30,000 pounds) of fuel.

Nadia's Jiffy Cleaners van sped to the now-open gate. Her practice on a deserted country road paid off: Her timing was near perfect. She knew she only had fifteen seconds before the gate opened fully. How long it stayed open on a manual override was anyone's guess but her objective was to be at the gate 16 seconds after it started to open. Adrenaline put her ahead of schedule. The speedometer hit 40 MPH as the opening gate rapidly approached in her windshield. 50 MPH and she swerved violently to the left to avoid the gate, as it was not completely open.

Over-correcting for the veer to the left, she turned the wheel hard right and took the bulky van into a right swerve bigger than the left jink. Both right side tires took the bulk of the van's weight as the momentum almost tipped it over.

The men inside the fuel depot scattered like ants as the speeding van entered and accelerated the fifty feet to the refueling trucks.

Nadia's instructions were to aim for the center of mass or center of most of the trucks. That objective was now out of reach. After bringing the van back onto all four wheels, she simply released the wheel to stop inducing any more torque and let it speed up towards its collision. Nadia closed her eyes and muttered one last prayer as her suicide van impacted the second fuel truck from the left.

The van and fuel truck exploded simultaneously, creating a fireball outward and upward of fifty feet. The blast was so large it reached the outer perimeter wall and the Kevlar outer surface deflected some of the blast back into the area. Both fuel-laden trucks beside the impacted vehicle went up in near simultaneous explosions, nanoseconds after impact, contributing to the fireball. Fiery debris landed on the fourth fuel truck in the line and it soon went up in a smaller burst of flames. All four drivers died instantly, along with six ground personnel trapped in the blast radius. Those men would have gladly chosen their fate over what was in store for the nine others who fought off burning clothes as they ran away from the site.

The driver of truck five had the good sense to remain in his vehicle and attempt to drive it to safety. Unfortunately truck five, the one nearest to the crashed van, did not wait for his relatively unscathed team to recover and disconnect his fuel transfer hoses. He panicked and shifted into high gear as soon as the fireball exploded. But by pulling away before clear he snapped the fuel hoses and allowed gallons upon gallons of fuel to spill along the concrete pavement.

As he pulled away the cloud of fiery debris landed, igniting the spilling fuel. A wall of flame sprang up and moved with a roar toward his departing vehicle. He could only watch in despair as it caught up to him and erupted around his vehicle. He jumped out of the moving truck and rolled to freedom, but the truck was a moving bomb that drove into the far wall and exploded, sending a second billowing black cloud of smoke into the air.

The last driver in truck six panicked and ran.

James, the maintenance officer friend of Sean and Ralph who was supervising and helping out in the depot, knew what to do and jumped into the cab of the truck. He watched in horror and tried to stop the other fuel truck driver from speeding off, but could not stop him. He yelled to the crew around him.

"Hit the emergency stop on the fuel pumps!" He received no response from the still-shaken men and women of the fuels section.

"Do it now!" he screamed, shaking them from their stupor. A senior enlisted man leapt to the machine, raised the cover guard deftly and hammered down on the red button with his palm.

Alarm klaxons rang out.

"Disconnect me! I need to move this rig away before it goes too," he commanded, eyeing the flames one row over from the subsiding fuel flow. Mangled fuel trucks lay in the four far rows, belching black smoke skyward.

James managed to drive the fuel truck away from the burning wreckage. Then he returned to help with the injured and direct the recovery effort.

While applying first aid to an airman who had injured his legs, James was hit by a fragment from a secondary explosion within the fuel depot. The small metal object lodged in his head. Before the day ended, James would be another casualty.

Control Tower

Airman Marino heard the roar of the explosion and felt the building shake as she looked up from her paperwork; she saw the fireball and smoke instantly.

She was in charge of ground operations today, maintaining a safe separation for aircraft taxiing or moving around the airfield to get into position to takeoff. No airplanes were expected to start up for another three hours so her concentration was on a report for the earlier morning takeoffs. SSgt Henderson, who controlled the tower, fixed his attention towards the runway west of the control tower. She watched east towards the taxiways and parking areas.

As the flash caught her eye, her first thought was that an airplane was on fire, but she knew this was further away. Perhaps on the highway that ran alongside the base?

She did not panic.

Her voice did not even raise an octave as she spoke: "Fire on the perimeter of the base or the A1065."

SSgt Henderson and Major Dillon turned just as the fifth fuel truck exploded. Major Dillon verbalized the conclusions they all reached.

"That's no car accident!" Instinctively he hit the emergency recovery button alerting the fire department. It was intended for an aircraft that was on fire or was coming in for an emergency landing, but this was one of those "not in the handbooks" type emergencies; getting people moving early might just save some lives.

Grabbing his hotline to the headquarters put him in instant contact with the wing commander or his deputy. The deputy answered curtly, knowing the hotline was never good news.

"Wing HQ, Colonel Carson speaking."

"Major Dillon from the control tower, sir. Looks as if a fuel explosion has occurred in the fuel dump area."

"Damn. How bad?"

"Bad. Multiple explosions," he replied. "But it seems contained within the walls of the fuel area."

"Keep me informed." And the deputy hung up abruptly to notify the fire department.

The Lakenheath Air Base fire department rolled out of their building within 58 seconds of the notification. Their building was beside the taxiways and near the runway, so they could respond to aircraft emergencies. They were on the scene at the fuel dump within three minutes of the call.

***

He saw the smoke and shook with joy. Part one of the attack had occurred. All was going according to plan. Noting his heading and looking out his small window towards the memorized ground references, he wished his Cessna extra power as it sped southeast. He noted the highway on his left and saw the fence line for the airfield fast approaching. That was his mark. Crossing over the north fence line, he changed heading fifteen degrees and saw the objective come into view. Grace was right and so were the video games. He could not miss it.

AQNA had been smart about the funding scheme they had Motaz use to get the money for the aircraft. They used money mules to serve as launderers for the profits from their petty crimes, prostitution and racketeering. Motaz found people who, unwittingly, laundered the terrorist's money via their bank accounts. Often the duped people were students or the unemployed who desperately needed a little extra cash. Motaz arranged to send them 5,000 British pounds. Then the "mule" would transfer it again to another legitimate account minus their 2% commission.

The individuals made some money for doing nothing at all but taking in the money one day and transferring it as soon as they saw it in their bank account. Unfortunately for these trusting souls, they were committing a crime and helping the terrorists convert their ill-gotten gains into useful cash for other things. Like renting an aircraft.

All three tower members stared eastward at the smoke and the occasional small secondary explosions that dotted the fuel area. Luckily the main gate mechanism had jammed in the open position when the fireball hit the fence. Fuel truck #6 had escaped and the fire trucks responding could easily get in.

After a moment, SSgt Henderson decided to turn back to his duty desk, resolved to not be morbidly curious about the unfolding drama on the east side. There was nothing they could do and it felt like watching a traffic accident or train wreck after the fact. Besides, he had an aircraft that should have passed outside the airfield on the northeast side and he did not see it anywhere.

Turning back to his desk he saw CVR571. It was not where it was supposed to be. Instead of being north and east of the field but still in the control zone, it was northwest of the field and heading southeast. It was lower than cleared and heading straight for the tower. Brian suspected it was off course and now trying to get a good look at the fire and smoke on the ground.

Henderson keyed his microphone speaking calmly, "CVR five-seven-one, climb and deviate south due to an oil fire on the airfield."

The pilot did not respond.

SSgt Henderson became more adamant.

"CVR five-seven-one, climb to three-thousand feet immediately and turn to heading of two-one-zero."

He wanted to divert the small aircraft from the danger area. Updrafts from the immense heat could send the small plane tumbling out of control if he got too close to the raging fire.

Still nothing back from the aircraft. CVR571 was now crossing the runway and about 30 seconds away from the tower. That was when Brian knew his world was about to come crashing down.

Recalling all of this later at a debrief, Airman Marina and Major Dillon would both report SSgt Henderson's calm order to leave stirred them into action simply because it was efficient and correct.

The tower controller owned the control tower, regardless of the fact the Major outranked him. Brian Henderson was ultimately responsible for what went on in the tower. And so when he commanded the evacuation order, everyone moved without hesitation. If he had screamed or yelled or ranted or pleaded it would not have made them move any faster and may have slowed them down in that they would have had to think about why it was in such an unusual manner. Instead Major Dillon instinctively turned to Brian while pushing Airman Marino towards the single set of stairs in the floor center.

"Go. Go...go!" directed Major Dillon as he hustled the startled Marino down the stairs, taking two at a time. She was small and lightweight and, in the end, the larger Major Dillon grabbed her and slung her down the stairs with him.

Motaz crossed perpendicular to the large runway and watched as it slipped underneath his windscreen. Up ahead the vertical control tower become larger and larger. A red beacon rotated on top of the structure. He could see the individuals leaving rapidly. One stayed a little too long he thought, as he closed his eyes in prayer.

Brian was the last to exit just as the Cessna filled the tower's west screen. He was close enough to see the calm expression on the pilot's face. The world seemed to stop as Brian watched the pilot:

his headset was off, his eyes closed and his lips moved as if saying the same thing over and over.

Motaz repeated his travel prayer, "Subhana-alladhi sakh-khara la-na hadha wa ma kunna la-hu muqrinin." Glory to him who created this transportation. Motaz never opened his eyes again.

Brian spun and jumped into the stairwell. A deafening roar echoed through the building as the plane crashed through the glass. The thunderous sound drowned all other noise as the glass came crashing down.

Major Dillon and Airman Marino ducked under a desk on the sixth floor as the tower's top cab disappeared. The airplane continued through the cab destroying it and everything in it. The aircraft's left wing caught on the support structure and spun the airplane left as it went through the control tower and out the other side.

Sgt David Foster slowed to look in his rear view mirror as he drove along the road between the control tower and a large hanger on his right. He thought he heard fire trucks approaching and wanted to pull over and let them pass if needed. Instead he saw the black pall over the area behind him. He stopped his USAF blue van.

He had just started to move forward again when he saw what looked like a Cessna minus one left wing come crashing out of the tower and plummet over the road into a parked car.

He looked up and left to where the control tower once stood; only seven of the eight stories remained. Papers and debris fluttered about the sky between where the tower cab once stood and his vantage point on the ground. As he looked on, the Cessna exploded into flames. Sgt David Foster sat, stunned. He knew one thing for sure: it was going to be one hell of a day.

Chapter 19

48 Security Police Squadron

Dina waited in the other Jiffy Cleaners van near her objective. Parked in the Morale, Welfare and Recreation parking lots, she surveyed her target. Her job was to wait for the fire trucks to roll out of their station and then execute her part of the attack. Both she and Nadia loved Grace.

It wasn't sexual. She had thought about it though. Islam did not allow such acts, but the men with whom she associated after joining the terrorist cell were not the kind she wanted to spend intimate time with either. So, she and Nadia made their desires known secretly and quietly when the moment came.

It was a love that was unspoken and a strong bond formed between the three women within this active cell. Grace chose her two fellow females for their roles for several reasons. First and primary, it was much easier for the women to get on base as cleaners, so that narrowed her choices down considerably. The second was Grace's own desire to spare them too much of the pain of killing. Grace had seen much death up close and knew these two ladies could best serve as suicide bombers with their cleaning vans.

Dina saw the smoke across the base and knew her friend Nadia was successful. She smiled knowing Nadia would enter heaven and she would soon join her there. The red blinking lights at the fire station came on, stopping traffic and warning them that the big red fire trucks would be exiting. The door to the fire station on base rolled up quickly underneath the ceiling and two fire engines pulled out and turned left. Their sirens wailed and warbled while their spinning, flashing lights danced across the roadway past shocked, stopped drivers.

Dina said one last prayer then looked right before she sped out of the parking lot. The road was clear and she punched the lumbering van's gas pedal and accelerated into the main artery connecting both sides of the base.

***

Two security police cars were already on site at the fuel fire coordinating rescue efforts. Both responded from active patrols. Now reports were coming in of a fire or crash at the control tower.

Master Sgt Diego "Chico" Santana dispatched two more cars that were on their way to the fuel depot to divert to the tower and investigate that report.

The Security Police Headquarters housed two SP detachments consisting of fifty men and women each. At times one detachment might be assigned to temporary duty elsewhere, as was the case this month. The 28th SP Detachment worked in Iraq on the last of a four-month assignment. The 10th SP Detachment was on duty and dangerously under-manned due to the summer holidays. At any given time, thirty SP were on duty. Of those thirty, one or two were in each squad car, of which the base normally used four per shift. Three more SPs were in each of two Humvees stationed either at one of the main gates or at a key location on the base. Another four worked the gates themselves with their British counterparts. Several walked the perimeter fence. That left eight policemen or women to man the HQ.

One was the duty chief in charge of running the detachment. Another ran dispatch. They had a backup at all times and five policemen formed the RRT or Rapid Response Team. The RRT were always on alert in a ready room prepared to go into action at a moment's notice. They were there for protection against base invasion, attack, or sabotage.

MSgt Santana had not called on the RRT. There was no need as of yet. A fire at the fuel depot was bad news but that was an emergency response, not a security threat. The tower incident needed investigating but until more details came back on that he was holding his RRT team in reserve.

But he did not have all of those stripes on his uniform for nothing. He smelled a rat. One incident was a coincidence. Two was a plan. And so he put the RRT on notice. This meant they prepared their gear, dressed in full armor and moved outside to their vehicles.

The Security Police building was small, strong and nondescript, except for a square wooden sign with 48 SP Squadron in the grass in front of the building and a bannered rectangular board above the entrance boasting of an award for best in USAFE from too many years ago. The five heavily armed RRT members left the building just as the noise of Dina's speeding van reached their ears.

Dina aimed for the doorway where the five policemen exited. The first three out the door saw the threat and ran left towards their armored vehicles. The remaining two policemen were just making last-minute gear adjustments. One froze dead in his tracks; the other reacted quickly and deadly. Sgt Robert "Tank" Framlin raised his M-4 Carbine Automatic rifle and aimed directly at the female driver.

He had no qualms about shooting a woman. He did not care if she was white, black, brown, Asian, Latino, young or old. All he wanted to do in those split seconds was persuade her to avoid ramming into him and his squad. His stream of bullets did just that.

Dina saw the windshield burst as the first bullets entered to her left. Glass flew into her face and she let go of the wheel in a last second futile bid to cover her eyes as protection. The van went out of control and swerved left. It flew over the curb, left of the T Junction that flowed to the front of the SP headquarters building, and slammed into the building, punching through the brick façade and deep into the briefing rooms, finally resting in the hallway leading to the dispatch room. Just as the RRT members recovered enough to begin to enter the ruined building, it erupted in flames as the cleaning van solvents combusted.

As fate would have it, if Dina had been just one second earlier she would have killed the entire RRT team. A second later and she would have missed all of the team. Dina died in the crash and missed her ultimate objective, which was to take out the RRT while hitting the SP headquarters. Instead she crippled the dispatch room. It would be another 10 minutes before anyone thought to tell the Wing Commander the SP headquarters was out of action.

***

Today Fatima worked as a cleaner. She drove slowly and purposefully from her spot near the fuel dump. She even pulled over so the American fire trucks could pass by her quickly, then she continued on her way. She arrived at the gym and entered the building dressed in her cleaning worker outfit. No one questioned her. She was invisible to the dozens of Air Force personnel working out in the weight room, taking aerobics classes or shooting hoops on the two basketball courts. She carried with her two large cleaning cases. They did not contain cleaning supplies.

After reaching the building's roof, she deposited her containers and marched back to the janitor's closet and removed a mop, bucket and supplies. She wanted her disguise to be complete if someone stumbled upon her. Then she waited.

***

The Wing Commander was having lunch at the Officer's Club with the base's various religious leaders and his staff when the fuel depot went up. He felt it from his chair and did not even bother to apologize to the group before grabbing his leather jacket and rushing out the door.

His parking spot was the closest to the front door. An obvious perk for the most important man on base.

He saw the smoke and expected an aircraft crash as he jumped in his car. Before racing to the flight line though, he called his command post on the secure radio in his car. This gave his adjutant time to catch up with him and join him in the passenger seat. As he entered, he overheard the radio chatter from the command post.

"Eagle One. Negative on the aircraft crash, sir. It is the fuel depot. Large explosion. Tower reports seeing secondary explosions and expecting casualties."

"Scramble the fire trucks and emergency vehicles. I'm on my way to the site at this time."

Brigadier General Brad "Bull" Cardwell met the fire trucks at the junction of the roads at the gas station. He wisely slowed and let them go in front to the fuel depot. He parked on the north side so as not to get in the way of any response vehicles but close enough to be able to talk to the fire chief, if needed. Getting out of his car, he heard what sounded like a small engine throttle up to an ear-splitting whine some distance behind him. He turned to watch his control tower explode in a shower of glass, sparks and metal.

Most men would have been shaken by such a display of bad luck at their place of work. Not Bull. Having seen tours of duty in

Iraq for Desert Storm One, Bosnia and then Iraq a second time, he had seen his share of adversity. Today the shit had just hit the fan on his base. He was ready.

Shouting at his adjutant over the flame's roar from the fuel depot behind him, he shook him out of his stupor with six simple words, "Find a car. Get there now!" before jumping back into his car, heading back toward the command post.

His base was under attack and he needed all of the resources to come under his control and fast. Driving while talking on the phone or radio was usually a no-no, but Bull Cardwell did it today.

"Command Post this is Eagle One. Execute lock down immediately. I say again I am authorizing Operation Lock Down ASAP."

One minute later, all gates to the base were closed as pop-up metal barriers automatically rose. Those drivers that were already on base realized the gates were closed and most turned around, knowing it would be some time before this exercise ended and they could leave the base.

The Air Force often had mock emergencies with realistic explosions that rocked the base. Although no such exercise was scheduled for today, most civilians assumed it was a test.

Outside the base, those needing to get in could not kill time elsewhere. They needed to get to work and so they waited patiently in line.

Lakenheath Village

Hope and Connor walked through Lakenheath village trying to figure out what the other cell's objective might be. Grace gave Hope some information but nothing really to zoom in on. Hope looked at the church but it seemed small and insignificant. They strolled down the high street but it contained nothing but the usual fish and chip shops, Indian restaurants and betting establishments.

Connor studied his temporary partner. She wore a blue open collared shirt with a black striped vest over the blouse and black leather pants. Comfortable sure. But what do the clothes say about the woman?

She had a cool beauty. Classic good looks. She was physically beautiful. She wanted to be found attractive, yet did not want to be judged on looks alone. The truth was that the rewards of that beauty combined with a sharp wit and intelligence equaled a million-dollar woman. She could have been an executive of any Fortune 500 company.

Hope's comments brought him back to their task at hand.

"There has to be something we are missing. Why would AQNA want to plan an attack in Lakenheath village?"

If only Grace could give us more to go on. Maybe Grace could find out who ran this other cell.

Connor verbalized exactly what she was thinking. "It makes no sense. It's too small for them. Not grand enough in the big scheme of things."

The roar of a fire truck trundling out from the station and fast approaching disturbed the quiet morning peace. Blue lights flashed. Both Connor and Hope turned to see a smiling driver manhandle the machine past them and out of the village. Grace hid from view under a tarp on the back of the fire truck watching her fellow CIA agent stumble around Lakenheath.

She's close. But too late.

Crossing the village green Hope and Connor went inside the Lakenheath village council offices and talked with the mayor.

Gate 1

Two fire trucks from Mildenhall village headed up the A1065 towards Gate 1. Their blue lights flashed but the siren was off as was the way for the British firefighters to respond. The terrorists in the fire trucks did not want to do anything that would raise suspicion. As they crested the hill prior to the base, they noticed traffic stopped and blocking their path about a quarter of a mile before the gate.

"Why are there cars stopped in the road?" Hasan asked, fear rising in his chest as their plan began to unravel before they even got on the American base.

A small fender-bender in the lane going away from the base created two opposite lines of traffic going nowhere and blocking the A1065.

"I must report this," Hasan whined as the fire trucks stopped behind the traffic, unable to move.

The driver, Musa, placed his calming hand on Hasan and shook his head. "No need Sadiq. Watch and observe."

He reached over and turned on the siren. The loud warbling noise caught the stalled drivers by surprise. Many had not noticed the flashing blue lights because they were fixated on the smoke spreading from the base. Now, with the lights and the sirens, the cars in the left lane blocking the fire trucks moved slowly further left to create a small lane down the middle of the highway. The oncoming cars in the right lane did the same to their left and the passage in the middle was just wide enough for the fire trucks to proceed, slowly but surely.

Grace had left little to chance. Each team had a driver who was to do little else but that, and a leader who had a cell phone along with more men who were shooters. The leader was to call her only if absolutely needed.

Hasan punched a number on his cell phone and waited while it dialed the guardhouse at Gate 1. Hasan had the best English accent of any of the terrorists and so Grace gave him the job of calling in the password. It was a critical task. If it worked they were in.

An unhurried British male voice answered.

"Gate 1. Security."

"This is the Mildenhall fire brigade responding to a request for assistance. Our password is Eclipse."

"Standby," his voice lowered as he turned to speak with a colleague. "Charlie, I've got the Mildenhall fire guys saying they are coming to assist. Have you heard anything about that? I know they have the fire over there but…"

Charlie's reply was muffled and too low to hear. So far it sounded like just the local Brit copper and not the SPs involved. A truck blocked the left turn lane into the gate. The vehicle could not move any further left to make room, so again Musa made a good command decision and went past the turn lane and then hung an immediate 90-degree illegal left turn into the base gate waiting area. It was bold and daring and just what an emergency responder would do when faced with the traffic they saw.

"Lakenheath, we are here to help. Password is Eclipse. Lower the barrier," Hasan repeated.

Rounding the corner, they saw the gate and the people guarding it.

Hasan alerted his team, "Get ready people, but no guns until I give the word. Remember the password should let us through."

Instead of trying to get through the cars jammed up front, the fire trucks instead pulled into the empty exit lane and slowed, but motioned for the guard to lower the barriers so they could get through.

In the gate guard shack, the two British cops were yelling at the American Security Police who were further back inside the base, talking to the stopped cars. Their M-4 carbine rifles were pointed down and away, but were at the ready. The Americans also had an M-9 Beretta semi-automatic pistol strapped to their thighs. They wore dark blue Security Police (SP) berets with a badge depicting a falcon over an airfield with the SP motto "Defensor Fortis" underneath. Their combat fatigues gave everyone the impression they were always ready for anything.

"Harry, they have the password so we're letting them in," chimed the copper closest to the two SPs.

By now an occasional car honk both in and outside the base gate, plus all the emergency vehicle's sirens, made it hard to hear much past ten feet.

TSgt Harry "Red" Reed never heard his English counterpart's words. He was talking to a mother of three about whether or not she should stay with her car during the emergency. When he nodded yes to her his British counterparts took that as a sign he agreed with them.

Both Brit coppers were facing away from the fire trucks as they entered. A quick cursory glance told them they were here and with the right password, they hit the lower barrier button for those immediately in front of the fire trucks.

As soon as the barrier started to go down, Sgt. Chris Harris knew something was not right. No one should be able to lower them without first hearing from his command post. That was procedure. The password was to get on the base in normal cases without a pass and quickly, but during a lockdown no one came in or out of the base.

"Stop those trucks!" he screamed running forward. "That's not right!!"

Musa did not even have to come to a stop; he just let off the brake and barreled on through. The first fire truck made it onto the base and zoomed past all four guards before they could do much about it. However, in doing so, the now-alerted guards noticed the strange complexion of all of the firemen on the first truck. None were white Anglo-Saxon. All looked to have dark skin and hair. The guards working the gate knew the local firemen. They had meetings with them every year. These were not the firemen they knew.

He could not do anything about the first truck, which was whizzing past him, but Chris brought his gun up and moved to block the second truck.

The second truck expected some trouble and they were ready for the first gate guards in the shack. Both British guards, dressed in yellow reflective vests and black trousers with black hats, drew their weapons and began to fire at the second truck when Chris sounded the alarm.

From the passenger side of the second truck came a hail of bullets ripping into the bulletproof guard shack glass.

Realizing their costly error in lowering the barriers, neither guard had stayed behind the guardhouse protective shield. Once past the glass, bullets tore into their unprotected bodies. Both went down with only one shot off each, both wildly high. Their actions did serve to distract the main shooter from the vehicle, and that was all Chris needed. Bringing his weapon up to his shoulder, he fired seven bullets into the fire truck driver.

Harry followed with cover fire into the passenger seat as the fire truck crashed headlong into the SP Humvee parked off the road on the right side of the gate.

"Everybody get down," Harry warned people who were just starting to exit their vehicles in a scared mob. "Take cover!"

SF members were required to know and adhere to three general orders, which formed the foundation of their duties. These orders applied to every assigned post or patrol they would ever assume:

1) I will take charge of my post and protect all personnel and property for which I am responsible until properly relieved.

2) I will report all violations of the orders I am instructed to enforce and call my superiors in any case not covered by instructions.

3) I will sound the alarm in any case of disorder or emergency.

The SP's were unable to accomplish the last two orders effectively. They were too busy accomplishing the first.

A firefight broke out at Gate 1 as Harry and Chris protected the civilians and tried to get to the three remaining terrorists in the fire truck. Unfortunately they were too far from the gatehouse to push the automatic alarm there. Instead they had to wait for a lull in the firefight before radioing back their situation.

Gate 2 (the back gate)

A lone fire truck from Lakenheath village whipped down a narrow country lane between the base and the approaching airfield. Lakenheath village had only one fire truck but was closest to the primary objective and went to the back gate at the air base. Grace took the Lakenheath fire truck. But she this meant she also had the password that she thought might be suspect.

Lakenheath was closer than Mildenhall, so her attack group left slightly after Hasan left Mildenhall with his two trucks. The plan was to reach each gate simultaneously; she wanted to strike while surprise was on their side.

Ahmed had different plans. He arranged for his group to leave a minute earlier than Grace's instructions. He wanted to hit his gate first and thus have the element of surprise. He knew whichever group hit last would face a gate warned of an attack. So Ahmed tricked his driver Musa and Hasan to get them to start early.

Grace did not know or suspect Ahmed capable of such treachery. However, she had done the exact same thing.

Wanting to hit her gate first, she instructed Uday to start their journey earlier than planned.

As it happened, both groups of fire trucks approached at roughly the same time. Ahmed's group was slowed enough by traffic to allow Grace's group to overcome any advantage Ahmed had.

So it is in all things planned. The best laid plans often come undone when the people executing them decided they know best. This was why Grace preferred to work alone.

Grace had an ace in the hole on her truck sitting beside her driver Uday. Kate was dressed in her formal dress blues Air Force uniform. She had all her medals on the left side of her light blue long sleeved tapered blouse. Her hands were tied behind her back and her dark blue skirt tumbled down to her knees; her legs were cuffed just above her black regulation issue low-heeled shoes.

Kate was drugged and did not know where she was. She was conscious, but barely. A wad of cloth was stuck deep in her mouth, trapped by a piece of clear tape.

Grace sat on top of the vehicle, hidden with two other terrorist sharp shooters, Zamil and Qani.

Although rarely used in the middle of the day, the Jason D. Nathan back gate could see significant traffic in the rush hour mornings when school was in session. Approaching noon, the traffic was much less congested there than at Gate 1. Cars quickly moved out of the way as the fire truck approached and soon Grace and her team were seconds away from Gate 2, screaming down a broad road between the wall for the high school and the family housing section on the right. It always amazed Grace how easy it would be to get on the base and do some damage as a single individual.

Grace took out a cinnamon stick and called Gate 2 from her phone when they were just seconds away. It was 11:50 a.m.

The approach to Gate 2 was almost identical to Gate 1, except the left hand turn immediately placed you at the guardhouse and there were just two security forces present.

Grace spoke her password, the one Kate had given them, just as they made the turn left.

"Rhinoceros."

She knew as soon as she said it that it was the wrong word. The silence on the other end was deafening.

Grace suspected as much. Kate was a strong-willed woman and Grace did not think she would cave in as much as Ralph thought she would. That was why she had brought her along today as insurance and that insurance paid off as they turned the corner.

Both SPs were on either side of the guardhouse, shielded by the glass. The man on the left had a phone at his left ear, his right hand at the ready on his M-4 carbine. Both carried the SP standard issue Beretta M-9 pistol strapped to their right thigh. Their stance was not relaxed nor was it at immediate attack. They projected a guarded concern as they saw the fire truck fast approaching.

Still on the phone and hidden from view, Grace continued to talk to the one on the phone. In her best imitation of Kate's voice she demanded: "This is Major Katelyn Healy. I am in the passenger seat of the fire truck approaching Gate 2. Airman, I order you to let us in to fight the fire." It was not the best imitation in the world but it was enough to distract them both for just a few seconds. She saw the other SP turn his head slightly toward the booth.

"Shoot!" she commanded to the comrades beside her who both fired off shots at the SFs. Both security personnel were hit and went down spinning backwards. She smiled as the fire truck slammed through the barricade and rattled on toward the high school.

Speaking a single one-word command in Korean, "Kimchi," awoke her ear bud. She allowed the device to play her favorite song quietly, "Dirty Deeds Done Dirt Cheap."

***

The first fire truck on the base from Gate 1 quickly came to the next intersection and went left towards the Security Police building. Seconds later, they arrived at the burning ruins.

The terrorists, dressed as firemen, dismounted the truck as one of the rapid reaction team left their Humvee with a medical first aid kit. Without turning to look at the firemen, he mumbled. "I'm glad you guys are here. We have four wounded in there. Follow me!"

Ahmed looked at the others and nodded to the Humvee while he pulled out a small pistol and shot the RRT member in the back as he walked back into the rubble of the building.

Musa grinned. "Piece of cake. I like it."

"Dina's mission here was a success. Praise be to Allah. Now, on to part two. We're taking the Humvee," commanded Ahmed.

The Humvee came with armor, more weapons and ammunition, hand grenades and they found a stinger air-to-air missile in the trunk. Unfortunately it was an American vehicle and it took a little acclimation to drive it on the left-oriented roads. As they drove off, a loud voice broadcasted throughout the base.

An echoing bass voice announced: "All base personnel. Base lock down in effect. No entry or exit from buildings allowed." It took some time but the entire base was now notified of the lockdown order.

***

The high school stood ridiculously close to Gate 2. Grace directed her driver to take the first road before the school and to drive around behind it so they would have more time before being discovered. They pulled into an alley that ran between the main school building and the rear school building. A small single hallway joined the two structures and the fire truck hid nicely.

Grace let Uday and Zamil go into the school ahead of her. She exited the truck once the others were inside, since no one had shot at them. Walking onto the fire truck foot rail she opened the passenger door and pulled out the defeated form of Kate Healy. Grasping her handcuffed hands, Grace pushed the subdued woman through the doorway and right towards Ralph's office. Inside, Zamil nodded that everything was secure. She motioned for him to get the explosives from the truck and begin the dangerous work of setting them up. Next she sent Uday to guard the teachers and children conveniently gathered in the auditorium in the rear building. Grace went into Ralph's office and sent Qani to the front lobby to watch for trouble.

Ralph waited impatiently in his office. Grace could almost see the holes his restless feet were making in the carpet.

"What took you so long?" he demanded as she entered, pushing the helpless Kate in front of her. Seeing Kate, Ralph exploded with more questions.

"And why the hell is she still alive and better yet why is she here?"

Kate tossed her head in confusion not knowing where she was, but beginning to get the sensation she was not going to make it out alive.

Grace had her own pistol hidden in her right hand behind Kate while the left hand guided the woman and pushed her to the couch.

"Ralphie, calm down. We are here and pretty much on schedule. And she..." Grace stroked Kate's hair with her left hand and shrugged. "Well, I used her to get us in Gate 2 when the password did not work."

"Didn't work ...why?"

"No time to explain. Later." She ended the discussion with the wave of her hand. "Have you kept your part of our bargain?" she asked accusingly.

"Of course," he stammered. "All of the staff and children are locked in the auditorium. There are only three exits and the two side doors are chained shut from both the inside and outside as you suggested."

"Good," she purred.

***

Wing Commander Cardwell reached the Command Post minutes later.

"Status!" he demanded.

The Operations Group (OG) commander, who responded directly to the Command Post when the balloon went up, offered his assessment.

"We are under attack!"

"No shit, Jake! Tell me something I don't know." Colonel Jake "Trap" Carson continued unfazed. "Car bombing at the fuel depot – fire is under control. Small aircraft slammed into the control tower minutes later – structure unusable for flight recovery. Casualties at..."

The Wing "King" interrupted, "I don't have time for casualty figures, Trap. We need to get ahead of these bastards and stop them."

"Base has gone to lockdown and I am expecting a predator feed any second now. All airborne aircraft have been diverted and there are no known breaches of inner perimeter toward the flight line."

"They took out the control tower! I'd call that a breach of our god damn inner perimeter!" slammed Bull his voice rising with his temper.

They both strode toward the command center. It was the nerve center of base operations. Designed for flight operations in case the Russians attacked during World War III, it now served as a war room for making combat decisions because so many sensors could be brought to bear and examined.

Bull took his seat at the head of the table as the OG brought up several screens around them on the table. One was a combination of base security cameras; another was the detection loop for the security fences. A third screen, marked "Predator Feed" in red, was blank.

"Command Post this is Gate One: we have a breach. One large fire truck with four or more hostiles has entered the base. Break. Gate One SPs involved in a firefight with an additional fire truck with three hostiles."

"Eagle One copies Gate One."

General Cardwell, without hesitation or discussion, pressed another button and announced, "All units are advised: hostiles in off-base fire trucks have breached perimeter. This is not an exercise. Shoot to kill."

"Where in the hell is that predator video? I'd like to know what in damnation is going on."

"Sir, it is coming on line now."

"How did we get a predator feed in the first place?"

The OG chimed in. "It is here for the exercise with the Bolars. They are working on their close air support missions with the predators and some British JTACS this week. Instead of running the exercise, I directed the UAV to fly over us. Took them a few minutes to reposition but it should give us a bird's eye view of the base and surrounding areas."

General Cardwell heard and processed every scrap of information his people fed him. His mind was analyzing and going through counter measures as he listened.

"I have not heard Eagle Seven on the radio for a while now. Do we have comm with them on their side channels?"

Airman First Class Laura Burnett turned from her communications console and replied. "Yes and no, sir. Yes, we are in communication with SP units One and Two at the fuel depot, units Three and Four at the control tower and intermittently with unit Five at Gate One, but they are still in a firefight with hostiles."

She took a bigger breath than was probably needed, her chest straining against the regulation light blue blouse. "But we have lost contact with Eagle Seven and never had contact with Unit Alpha."

The call sign for the Security Commander was Eagle Seven and Unit Alpha was the RRT. To no one in particular the Wing Commander asked, "What the fuck is going on here?"

Laura blushed but turned back to her duties.

"Predator is up on screen now, sir."

"Finally some good news."

But the image was not good news after all. It showed what he feared the most: another breach at Gate 2. Slowly the image moved and showed the security building's smoldering ruins.

***

In the Base Exchange, life went on as normal. Missy Barker prowled the long hallway in front of the main shops with her daughter Allison. They stopped occasionally at stands to admire art or toys or cell phones. Allison was a bit grumpy since the Lakenheath BX had fewer toys than Mildenhall. Missy attempted to cheer her up by promising her an ice cream when they got to Mildenhall later. The bribe worked and a big smile spread across the nine-year-old's face.

Elsewhere, the coffee shop baristas brewed steaming hot cups of gourmet, flavored coffee for the shoppers.

Missy watched the other shoppers pass them. Most of the Americans were overweight and not dressed very well. Tank tops, loose fitting jeans and spandex that had no business being on their flesh spoke volumes about their lifestyle. Missy, on the other hand, looked elegant in her black ankle boots, slim black pants, white blouse and leather jacket. Her blond locks, captured in a single long ponytail down her back, accented the successful woman who ran her own home business on the side. The thirty-something soccer mom was not a looker by any means but she was comfortable in her own skin, just the same. Sure, she could stand to lose ten pounds, but then again who couldn't in this age of instant gratification and drive-through, fast food convenience.

Why are Americans so fat, lazy and self-absorbed?

They were the first adjectives that came to her mind. The answer was simple: it was too easy to live on base and eat at the fast food joints, some of which crowded the food court here, elbowing good food out of the way in the process. In the greatest of ironies, cheap (and easy to access) burger and taco stands manned by immigrants looking for a new life, fried and greased their customers to a long, slow, artery clogging death. Half of the people here are dead already Missy thought, as she swiftly moved toward the exit and her escape from Little America.

Her phone vibrated against her hip. Pausing by the flower shop, she held Allison at bay and checked her iPhone. Her husband sent her a warning that a base lock down was in progress. Probably another drill, he wrote, but wanted to let her know it was coming in the next minute or so. Anxious to be on her way to Mildenhall and not wanting to accept any delay, she rushed down a side hallway to one of the doors towards the parking lot and freedom.

Missy reached the door just as a young twenty-something man with a fast food uniform blocked her exit.

"Sorry, ma'am. We just got word. BX is locked down. No entry or exit." He fidgeted with his nametag and the door bar simultaneously. Rage flared momentarily across Missy's face but she kept from verbalizing her emotions. Looking back down the mostly empty hallway, Missy pleaded in her best southern drawl as she walked close to the young man and entered his space.

"Please help me out here…Dan," she said getting his name from the fast food nametag hanging limply from his uniform. "My little girl has a doctor's appointment in fifteen minutes. We just stopped in here to look at toys to cheer her up beforehand. I have to get to the car or she will miss it."

Dan's fifteen minutes of training after work, two months ago, did nothing to prepare him for the fresh, wide-eyed look from Missy at this pivotal moment. Dan hesitated for just a second to assert his authority. They both knew his delay meant she would get through the barrier.

***

Sean monitored the radio traffic and decided to offer his services.

"Lakenheath Command Post this is Strike 01 flight. Can we help in any way?"

"Strike 01 flight this is Command Post. Contact Snake Eater on secure frequency Red eighteen." The instructions told Sean to go to a secure frequency since the base was under attack. The command post did not know who or what frequencies may have been compromised. By going "secure," now only authorized people would be on the radio frequency.

"Strike 01 wilco."

Emile punched the frequency in their radio and told Sean he was up secure.

"Strike 01 up on Red eighteen, check."

"Two," Tambra replied quickly.

"Strike, Snake Eater has you Lima Charlie. Break. Lakenheath is under attack. We have hostiles on the ground and airborne. Say weapon state."

Sean was stunned. He shook his head to get back to thinking straight. Between the two airplanes in his flight, they had three Laser Guided bombs (GBU-54's), one GPS bomb (GBU-31), an old-fashioned 2000-pound dumb bomb and one AGM-130.

7,500 pounds worth of bombs is nothing to sneeze at. Let's see if they use us. I guess this means I am back in the game.

***

"Command Post this is Unit Alpha. The SP building has been hit and Eagle Seven is missing inside."

The radio call confirmed some things the Wing Commander needed to hear. Sometimes a picture could tell a story but it did not give enough details. Bull knew human intelligence would be invaluable during an attack like this.

The attractive young airman working the SP frequency responded and passed on the General's orders.

"Roger Unit Alpha. Split up: have one Hummer support Gate 1 which is still under attack; the other is to look for the fire trucks that have breached our perimeter."

A minute later the SP voice of Alpha unit came back with a chilling reply.

"Command Post, Alpha Unit is missing one Humvee and one Jeep. We have one damaged Humvee, which is not drivable, and one member down with a gunshot wound to the back who needs immediate medical attention. The fire truck in question is here but abandoned. Looks like they have a Humvee now."

"And all of the associated equipment and weapons," pointed out the Wing Commander to everyone in the command center.

Chapter 20

The Wing Commander came over the SP frequency loud and clear, overriding the female airman's next transmission. He made a mental note to tell the airman's supervisor to talk to her about the proper fit on an Air Force uniform. Unit cohesiveness required no unnecessary distractions and her tight blouse size was causing at least one distraction…to him. He was just getting over a divorce to his much younger second wife. She was acting like a real bitch and he had serious doubts about why he married so soon after his first wife, his high school sweetheart, passed away from breast cancer.

Sometimes even I don't make the right call.

"Unit One and Two go to support the Gate One firefight; Unit Three go to the BX to protect civilians there; Unit Four from Tower go to the hospital. Break. Unit Alpha split up: send one man to the commissary and the rest proceed on foot to secure the school. All units are advised hostiles may be in U.S. Humvees, Jeeps or civilian vehicles. Proceed with caution. Protect civilian lives at all costs."

***

Ahmed, Sami, Musa, Hasan and Dakhil roared around in the Humvee and Jeep, racing to their next objective, the BX, with wanton abandon, spraying oncoming vehicles with deadly machine gun fire.

Once lockdown was initiated the only locations instantly notified were the gates. All other locations had to be notified by phone or electronically that the procedure started. Individuals relied on the Giant Voice notification. Unfortunately, it took quite a long time to make everyone on base aware of the threats present and the steps they should take.

At the BX, the Jihadists dismounted and set up the large 50-caliber machine gun on the Humvee roof. They parked in front of the chapel, which was some distance from the BX. No one was in the parking lot. Everyone cowered inside; it would be the perfect place to get hostages.

Anxious civilians had gathered in the food court outside the main shopping store. Some gathered at the three exits waiting for the expected "all clear" so they could return to their normal life. Still others paced nervously. These were the active duty Air Force members who knew there was no "exercise" or practice lock down scheduled for this week. They knew something was happening outside the brick walls they waited within. The wardens of this self-imposed prison stood behind the glass exit doors, looking outward for some sign of danger or sound of parole.

At the main entrance, some trapped Americans saw the Humvee pull into the parking lot and unlimber the machine gun. Pointing at the activity, one old man exclaimed, "They are really exercising today. Look at the black smoke in the distance and the machine guns those guys have." Without saying anything more, he slowly disengaged from the rest of the waiting crowd and made his way deeper into the BX, far away from any windows and the doors, just in case.

Pausing after assembling the machine gun, Dakihil said, "Let's see what this thing can do." With a grin, he sprayed the chapel's stained glass windows with a long flowing line of bullets. 200 rounds spewed forth in less than 30 seconds.

"That will do," he whispered.

Pulling up beside the Humvee, Ahmed, in the Jeep, instructed them to blow up the BX. Ahmed would go create more havoc at the commissary where there would be more Americans. The Jeep squealed its tires as it left, looking for easier prey with Ahmed, Sami and Hasan. Musa and Dakhil were left with the Humvee to take the BX.

***

The docile crowd at the BX main entrance saw the gunfire shatter the stained glass chapel window. Shards of colored glass fell onto the sidewalk just fifty feet away. The herd began to back out of the alcove. Seconds later, it became a stampede as dozens of civilians ran away from the main entrance. However the alcove was soon filled by more people, like moths to light, curious as to what the others had just witnessed

***

"Strike 01 has LGBs, JDAMS and dumb bombs along with twenty Mike Mike," said Sean, describing the caliber of bullets carried on the aircraft. Someone in the Command Post pointed to the BX parking lot. The predator feed showed the Humvee and the attack on the chapel front.

"Strike where are you?" asked the Ground Liaison Officer (GLO).

"Fifteen miles north, circling and waiting. We have fifty minutes of playtime," he responded, referencing their fuel supply.

"Strike, Snake Eater. Standby for abbreviated nine line."

"Strike is ready to copy nine line."

"Strike. One, Two and Three NA. Thirty-three feet. Four hostiles in a U.S. Humvee and Jeep in the BX parking lot, beside the chapel. Coordinates are to be self-generated. Multiple friendlies in the BX and chapel. Smack the Humvee. Request LGB attack. Type two control. TOT ASAP."

Emile trembled as she read back the haunting command lines for her to attack enemies on her own air base.

"Strike One read back correct," said the GLO. "Call in with heading."

***

As Musa and Dakhil made their way towards the BX building a few sporadic shots rang out from the main entrance. Security Police Unit Three had arrived, going around the back of the building and entering from the rear. The lone SP was now holding off the attackers with his M-4 carbine on single shot to conserve bullets. He did not think he could take them all out by himself but could hold them at bay for a long time.

The terrorists stopped their advance upon hearing the gunfire, ducking behind the cars in the parking lot. This was not fair. The people they were supposed to intimidate were somehow shooting back at them. They both made their way back to their vehicle and decided to shoot up the BX from the safety of their Humvee.

***

Sean quickly ran through the options available to him then briefed Tambra on the plan over the radio.

"Strike 02 take four mile spacing, shooter-cover, single GBU-54, we'll target Humvee in BX parking lot, level or dive glide."

Strike flight came in from 15 miles away. They could have come in from closer but that would have meant much less time on final approach to find their target. Typically the LGBs needed four to five miles of room to hit the target. This range gave the bomb time to come off the jet, open the seeker "eyes," see the laser energy beam the F-15E provided and have enough time to correct its course to fly to the target for a direct hit. If the aircraft released inside this minimum range, the bomb might not hit the target.

Shooter-cover is the role each aircraft would play in the attack. The first role was for the lead aircraft Strike 01, the shooter or the aircraft dropping the weapon. His wingman would provide cover or support during the attack. Strike 02 would not drop a weapon but instead would cover his lead's tail or six o'clock to make sure no one shot at him. If they did, Strike 02 could call a defensive maneuver to Strike 01. Strike 02 was also the backup laser guider in the event the shooter could not get their laser to work.

As soon as they were given the mission, Emile began to work the plane's APG-70 radar.

"Check twenty degrees to the left," she commanded.

Sean banked their fighter jet with 4 Gs in the direction she wanted.

"Rollout, mapping."

Emile spoke and Sean listened. That was the 2-seat role in this situation. Emile often described combat crew coordination as two people in a boat, duck hunting. Sean rowed the boat, but Emile did the shooting. Her job was to find the BX. When mapping any target she worked big to small. Find the large air base first. She did that easily since she already had the coordinates set up for the return to the base. The large northeast-southwest runway appeared five seconds after she pulled the trigger full action on her right hand controller.

Pressing the multi-purpose button at the base of her hand
controller froze the synthetic aperture map, a 3.3-mile by 3.3-mile
bird's eye view of the airfield. Emile moved her cursor over the BX
buildings south and east of the runway. It was easy to find since the
large hospital pointed to the BX. She zoomed in on a picture of the
BX, chapel and parking lots in between.

"There are too many vehicles in the parking lot. I can't tell
which is a Humvee or Jeep," she exclaimed apologetically.

Sean started to provide her with his opinion when she finished
it for him.

Talking to herself she said, "Use the radar to cue the targeting
pod to get some eyes on."

He could not have said it any better himself. Their crew
coordination was very good in many ways.

"Mapping complete, cleared direct," she said out of habit, even
though he had read her mind and began to slowly turn the jets
toward their target

Sean turned Strike flight to a heading of 150 and rolled out 10
miles away from their target. The F-15Es accelerated to .85 mach
and climbed slightly to 25,000 feet.

"Snake Eater, Strike flight in from the NW."

Emile moved the radar's targeting cursor to the edge of the
chapel then into the adjacent parking lot. Moving her castle switch
aft to target, she then squeezed the trigger full action to tell the
computer that was her desired target. She knew it might not be right
but by doing so the computer automatically queued her sniper pod
seeker head to look at that location. Sure enough, when she scrolled
her right MPD over to the targeting pod she saw the chapel and the
parking lot in the field of view.

"Strike 01, Snake Eater, continue."

The Command Post told them to continue with the attack but
had not given permission to release their weapons. Under type 1
and type 2 control the aircraft could not release until given
permission by a controlling agency. In this case the GLO was
watching the attack from his predator feed and could see both the
bad guys and the flight of Strike Eagles inbound to the target. He
waited to make sure the F-15Es were heading the right way to the
right target.

Slowly moving the TDC Emile scanned the parking lot for signs of hostile vehicles. Movement caught her eye and she zoomed in to find the Humvee with the large machine gun on top. The movement she had seen was a stream of bullets coming from the Humvee and hitting the BX front entrance.

The SP in the BX had good cover from his position and only had some ricochet wood fragments hit him from the machine gun blasts. Luckily, he had ordered the gawkers back before the gunfire erupted.

"Four miles to release," announced Sean.

Keying the jet's radio microphone with a foot pedal on the floor, Emile bypassed any conversation with Sean and spoke directly to Snake Eater.

"Snake Eater, confirm no friendlies in vehicles in the area. I have a Humvee firing at the BX requesting permission to drop."

"Three miles to release."

In their main radio, Emile heard Mark say, "Two same. Target is Humvee."

"Snake Eater requesting rover feed." The GLO and Command Post was attempting to see what the aircrew saw in their targeting pod video. It was a great idea, only just a few minutes late. It would take fifteen seconds to go through all the activations to set up the Data Linked signal and then a few more precious seconds to send it.

Meanwhile, Emile commanded a half action input into her trigger controlling the sniper pod and the pod went into point track on the Humvee. It stabilized her targeting pod on the vehicle. She pressed the laser fire button and noted the valid laser ranging at the top left corner: the laser was firing and strong enough to come back to the aircraft. An LGB would follow the signal if released.

"Negative rover. I need to drop now or go through dry!" Emile yelled in a rare display of emotion that rankled even Sean a bit.

"No friendlies in vehicles. Cleared hot Strike flight."

Upon hearing his flight was cleared to release, Sean checked the HUD and saw the vertical release cue marching its way down towards the pipper. Nothing like cutting it a little close he thought as he pressed the red pickle button as the timer counted down from two seconds to release to one and then :00.

The GBU-54 came off successfully.

Sean banked right and to the west, not wanting to fly over top of the BX.

Emile monitored her sniper pod to make sure it did not break track. If it did then she would have to manually put the laser back onto the vehicle. The sniper pod displayed the weapon's time of flight: Fifteen seconds remained until the weapon hit.

***

Dakhill and Musa in the Humvee heard the roar of jets and actually looked up to see the two aircraft streaking away, belly up to the Humvee.

Dakhil turned back to his task at hand and reloaded the machine gun for another burst at the BX. Just as he began to turn the loaded gun, the bomb hit.

Chapter 21

The Humvee went up in an instant. One moment the Humvee and the two terrorists were there; the next all that remained was a crater, a hundred feet long, fifty feet wide and ten feet deep. Parts of the chapel's front façade were damaged by the blast wave but it was a small price to pay.

Emile saw the impact and pointed her finger like a gun at the screen. "Gotcha."

Proudly keying the radio again she informed Snake Eater and the Command Post.

"Strike 01, target destroyed."

Cheers rang out at the Command Post as they watched the bomb impact on their predator feed. Wing Commander Cardwell nodded in admiration at the quick actions of his aircrew. Their joy at the destruction of the Humvee was short-lived.

Mark, in the other jet, was busy. Immediately after Emile's bomb hit, he took his pod to a wider field of view and began to scan the air base for any sign of moving vehicles.

"Snake Eater, Strike 02 has a Jeep moving westbound by the O Club."

***

Ahmed heard the explosion as they raced towards the commissary. He did not know what it meant but he was sure it was not good for him or his team. Speeding down the main road between the Officer's Club and some administration building, Ahmed pointed right and had the Jeep turn at the next roundabout.

"Right, then immediately left at the roundabout," he directed. But as the Jeep exited the roundabout he saw cars blocking the road to the commissary. The lone rapid response team member who ran to the commissary had quickly organized a barricade of blocking cars in the parking lot to prevent anyone from getting too close to the building. And he now stood behind the barricade with his M-4 carbine.

Confused by the cars and their order, Ahmed ordered the Jeep to slow down and approach the commissary with caution. This simple act saved his life. The rapid response team member monitored the radios and knew the Jeep was not friendly. On approach he fired from behind the cars, raking the Jeep with bullets and injuring the driver, Sami.

"Skip it. Skip it!" Ahmed yelled as he ducked under the hail of bullets. "Turn left, turn away!"

Hasan shot off a few rounds at the receding security policeman as Sami turned and exited the parking lot.

***

After they left the BX, Missy and Allison had headed for the post office. Her tale to Dan was a little white lie. She had no doctors' appointment and now spent some time on base before the gates reopened. She knew the base was on lockdown after hearing the Giant Voice message. Just another annoying drill, she thought, as she retrieved her mail and began to back out in her behemoth Suburban SUV.

Unfortunately, her stereo music blocked out much of the bombs explosions at the BX some distance away. Instead she heard a soft thud that sounded much like the exercises the military ran on the base.

Boys with toys.

***

"Strike 01, Snake Eater. Target moving. Jeep heading south away from commissary towards post office."

"Strike 01 searching."

That was Emile's calm voice letting Mark know she did not have the target vehicle in sight. Strike flight was now 10 miles east of the air base and turning west to point at the base. Emile knew they would likely end up about 15 miles away again and she would have 10 miles to find and designate the moving vehicle. A little over a minute to do it all.

Sean quickly explained to Tally that their brief was the same for the next attack. Strike 02 did not have any LGBs so Emile would drop again.

"Strike 01 flight is in from the East."

"Strike 01 continue."

Mark saved her some time.

"One from Two, I am tracking the Jeep westbound. Stare one-six-three-six."

Mark was asking Emile to use her Laser Spot Tracker (LST) function of the targeting pod. It would try to find someone else's laser beam. She activated the LST; the pod moved slightly left and a small square appeared over a moving vehicle.

Commanding a point track on the vehicle, disabling LST and zooming in gave her a great view of the Jeep as it moved west. She fired her own laser and pulled the trigger full action to tell the computer it was her target.

"Snake Eater, Strike 01, contact, target Jeep moving west, confirm passing dining hall…ready, ready now."

"Strike 01, target confirmed. Cleared hot."

"Strike 01, cleared hot," affirmed Sean.

Emile liked what she saw in the video. The Jeep was slowing to shoot at another target. The area was clear of friendlies. They had a clear field of fire. She verified good laser ranging, took one last designation on the Jeep and transferred the coordinates into the weapon.

"Two miles. Cleared to release."

"Weapon away," announced Sean as he banked south.

Chapter 22

Ahmed commanded his driver to slow down as they passed the dining hall and directed his rear gunner, Hasan, to shoot directly into the hall. It did little damage but was more of a symbolic gesture.

"Ahmed look, a big American vehicle ahead!"

Fearing the worst, Ahmed turned but instead of another Humvee or an American tank, it was a Suburban SUV, a perfect unarmed target.

"An easy target. Go...."

The Jeep began to accelerate away from the dining hall. Ahmed leaned out of his right side window and aimed his machine gun at the stopped Suburban, which was well in front of them.

***

Missy knew there was something wrong when there was no traffic going back to the main road from the post office. Even during a lockdown it took time for everyone to get the message. It was eerie. As she was about to pull out she saw the Jeep approaching ahead of her spray the dinning hall with bullets.

Seeing the gunfire in front of her, and with nowhere else to go, Missy and Allison cowered in the car.

***

Emile cursed as the Jeep began to move swiftly away. Now she had to trust the point track of her targeting pod to keep pace with the vehicle's movement. It did not. The cursor fell off the vehicle with 12 seconds left before impact. Emile saw the container around point track at the bottom left of her scope disappear. Months of training kicked in. Pressing in on the TDC changed the mode from point track to area track.

Ten seconds to impact.

Without any hesitation, she went half-action, initializing area track and moved the cursor to the Jeep.

Seven seconds to impact.

As she did this she saw the stopped Suburban further down the road. *Who was in the vehicle? Why was it out during a lockdown? Was it a friend or a foe?* She trained never to drop if in doubt of possible civilian casualties, but the bomb was already on the way.

Spilt second calculations went through her head. It would be too close. If she moved the laser spot away the bomb would still likely go long and hit the Suburban. If she kept it on target there was a chance the explosion would be muted enough to not damage the car fatally.

Five seconds to impact. The Jeep swerved left at the road junction spraying the Suburban with a hail of gunfire.

Emile kept the cursor on the Jeep as it turned and waited for the expected impact. It never happened. The Jeep continued on its new course.

Instead she heard Sean. "It's not your fault," he said. He had his helmet-mounted site on the Suburban. Emile went to a wider field of view for her targeting pod.

Where the Suburban had been, there was nothing more than a smoking hole.

***

Barely able to keep his voice from breaking, Sean reported the terrible news to Snake Eater.

"Strike 01 miss. Request immediate re-attack."

"What the hell are you doing, Rider? I just caused collateral damage. I can't drop again!" came Emile's panicked voice.

War and women, Sean thought, the best and worst of life.

"We have to Em." He paused, not knowing if his next words would work or not, but he had to say them. "Emile, this may be the worst time ever for this but... here goes. I broke up with Laura and Tambra today."

***

The GLO turned to look at the Wing Commander for guidance. Everyone in the room saw the weapon destroy the Suburban and its occupants. They witnessed a "friendly fire" incident and it stuck in everyone's throat. Was there anyone in the Suburban stopped at the intersection? If so, who were they? Why did the bomb not follow the Jeep?

With no doubt in his mind, Bull nodded yes and gave his authority to go after the Jeep again with the same weapon by the same crew. He was doubling down and, as was his style, he trusted his crews and their abilities.

A somber GLO slowly replied to Strike 01: "Re-attack on moving Jeep approved. Call in with heading."

***

Sean continued his speech after the interruption from the controller.

"I did it for you. I broke up with everyone for you."

Technically that was a little white lie since Tambra had broken up with Sean before he had the chance to break it off with her. But the intent was there so he was okay with claiming that one too. He continued his declaration, knowing time was running out on a re-attack if he could not get Emile involved.

"Now I need you to stay with me here and finish this mission."

Emile was speechless. Her hands trembled slightly and beads of sweat trickled down her forehead. It was turning out to be one hell of a day.

He said he broke up with Laura and Tambra for me. Does that mean he loves me? If so why not tell me before now.

Lots of thoughts flooded her brain in that instant.

Does he respect me? Is he doing this just to get me into bed? Could he be in a normal relationship where he stays until the next morning? Is this just a line to get me to do my job? Best not to think about that last thought right now. Or any of it for that matter. Focus on the task at hand-killing the bad guys before they do anymore damage.

Strike 01 came off target heading northbound and now turned back in southbound at 15 miles.

The Jeep headed south toward the high school. Strike flight lined up in a perfect tail aspect.

Sean heard Emile mutter, "I can't do this again."

Danger and combat brings out the best and worst in people. Sean saw this first hand in Afghanistan, Iraq and Libya. Sometimes the individuals that everyone thought were warriors turned out to be timid and weak. Others, who were not as quick or boisterous during peacetime operations, often impressed by taking a leadership role and doing brave and heroic deeds.

His voice softened as he spoke. "Emile, I believe in you. You can do this. Do it for the others still fighting down below: we have to stop them."

Those first five words were the most important. This was the first time she heard Sean say "Emile, I believe in you" and it was with such conviction. She knew he spoke from the heart. He had connected with that. It was as if he had reached down into her soul and cupped her heart in his hands and protected it. She felt warm and happy and dizzy. His voice brought her comfort. He was going to be there for her and not just in an aviator way. Something personal. She knew that now.

Women can be just as singularly driven as men. And heaven help anyone who gets in their way when they are. Emile put aside her emotions and did her job.

Emile shook away any doubts she had and designated the fast moving Jeep. The targeting pod readout showed the target as heading south at 40 MPH. This was her last LGB. She had to make it count.

"Strike 02, search for any possible collaterals out front," came Emile's call on the main radio.

Their simple acknowledgement of "Two" said so much in this tight time.

"Target is captured"

"Snake Eater, Strike 01 is in southbound."

"Strike 01, cleared in hot."

The GLO whispered under his breath so nobody else could hear it, "Good luck. You're going to need it."

Emile announced to Sean everything was ready on her end with "Cleared to release."

Emile tracked the Jeep and saw it begin to slow down.

"Bombs away!" came Sean's response. Emile cursed her own luck as the pod point track failed again due to the rapid deceleration of the small Jeep. The tracking was designed for large, slower tanks and trucks, not fast-moving small vehicles.

"Going manual," she said as she again went to area track and placed the cursor on the Jeep.

***

Ahmed peeked over his shoulder and saw the smoking wreckage of the Suburban. His eyes swept skyward and he just made out the two pinprick black dots approaching. As his eyes focused, he knew that death was possible from the two birds of prey bearing down on his group.

"Slow down quickly!" he told his driver while still looking rearward grabbing the driver's right arm to emphatically slow him down.

Improvising, Ahmed reacted quickly. "Turn left onto the field." It was the athletic track and the football field inside it. Obeying instantly, the driver slowed with hard braking allowing the Jeep to jump the curb and careen over the track into the playing field. "Hasan and I will leap from the vehicle. Hasan bring the stinger. You continue back to the road."

Passing the 30-yard line Ahmed jumped left, yelling, "Now!"

Likewise, Hasan pushed off and rolled right, leaving the 20 MPH vehicle in a flurry of activity.

***

Mark saw two figures leap from the Jeep and land mid-field, then the Jeep sped left, leaving the football field between two stands of bleachers to rejoin the road.

"Snake Eater, we have two squirters from the HVT."

Emile adjusted as the Jeep rapidly changed direction. Her pressure on the TDC was light. Too much and the laser spot would run off wildly. With five seconds left to go she regained the cross hair on the Jeep and then led it the last few seconds before impact.

Ahmed rolled to his feet and told Hasan to prepare the stinger. The bomb blast was deafening. Impacting just 2000 feet from them, the shock wave knocked them down again. The crater in the road appeared halfway between them and the school, the end of the Jeep and Sami.

***

Grace watched the fighter jet perform its death dance against her team. She shuddered and moved back from her second-story vantage point on top of the high school. The smoking debris looked a lot like the nightmares she had of her brother's death. Not a night went by where she didn't relive the carnage from that surrealistic scene. Alcohol did not stop them. Medication did not prevent them. Not even horrific additional dream material from her exploits with the CIA could displace those images. Maybe revenge could. She hoped it would.

***

The forty students in the school auditorium were hot and scared. Several teachers tried to calm them but movement was limited under the watchful eye of one of the terrorists. His machine gun and wandering were strong deterrents to any organized resistance.

One student who looked quite innocent enough did a little extra. He began with short quiet conversations with some of the students closest to him. These students were closer to the terrorist. In whispers he started to ask who wanted to try and get out. He found a few willing to try. He formed a plan.

***

Fatima carefully unpacked her cases and set up the equipment associated with the small devices. Next she removed two vials of oily, colorless liquid. The contents of the vials were sensitive. Exposure to heat, shock or flame would mean instant death for Fatima. The case carrying the vials was foam lined and had an outer shell stronger than most conventional carrying cases.

Fatima assembled her "toys" slowly and with great care. She would only get one chance at the mission. Every piece had to be properly fitted into the entire contraption or else it would not function.

Once she had her instruments of death created and the vials loaded, she waited for her signal. She scanned the road below the gym for signs of the Americans.

***

Strike flight broke to the north this time, over the air base. Sean had some action going on in his helmet-mounted sight and wanted to see if he could help in any way. The firefight at Gate 1 seemed to be over by the time he flew over it. The SP from Unit 1 turned the tide when he was able to come up from behind the terrorists fighting at the gate.

"Strike 01, Snake Eater. Target both squirters at last known location. Type Three control."

"Strike wilco."

Now it was Sean's turn to act. They were out of LGBs and the GPS jammers, activated once the base came under attack, denied him the use of his GPS-guided JDAM weapon.

The protocols for an airfield attack called for the base defensive GPS jammers to activate to prevent others from using GPS weapons against the base. In a fitting bit of irony, those same defensive GPS jammers now prevented Strike 01 from using all of their weapons to stop an attack from continuing on the base. Strike 02 had a dumb bomb, not very accurate in the best of situations, and an AGM-130.

The AGM-130 was a powered air-to-surface missile designed for long-range strikes on high-value fixed targets. It was a rocket boosted GBU-15 bomb capable of sending a visual image from the weapon back to the F-15E cockpit in order to allow the crew to guide the weapon precisely into the target. It was designed to guide into a fixed location from a standoff. Clearly this was not a situation for the AGM-130.

Strike 02 would have to sit out the action yet again and support Sean as he strafed the hostiles. The only weapon left at his disposal was the gun built into every F-15 eagle. He was allowed to attack at will because the gun was guided by pointing the airplane's nose at the target. It was rare that bullets once fired would go off course.

Unlike the LGBs. Sean only needed about six miles for his attack run so he wheeled the formation of aircraft into a 90-degree turn.

"Strike flight four mile trail, shooter-cover, gun, squirters, twenty-five degree five hundred foot HAT." Sean again briefed his wingman.

"Two," came Tambra's disappointed reply. She wanted in on the action. He could tell by her inflection she was seething at having no part in the attacks so far. Her training and attitude were chafing at the inaction but her professionalism kept her doing her job.

Hey, he thought, that's what you get for being a wingman and not a flight lead.

***

Recovering from the earth-shattering explosion ahead of them, Ahmed and Hasan stood shakily. Ahmed knew the American tactics from his time in Iraq fighting with Al Qaeda in Anbar province against the invaders. They would target both men but a moving target was easy to see. A prone man lying down in a ditch was next to impossible to see. A plan developed in his mind. He had to survive this attack and sitting out in the open was not the way to live. These Americans and their fancy devices liked movement and not old-fashioned stop and drop tactics.

Suddenly inspiration hit him. He needed to get into the high school where Grace and the others were still alive and he needed a diversion to get there.

Grabbing the stinger handheld missile – he doubted his friend could use it effectively, if at all – he pointed at the high school. "Quick. Run for the school. I will cover you with the stinger." Ahmed did not hear himself and suspected Hasan was as deaf as he. But the eventual gestures he made got his point across. The two men ran towards their next objective, the high school.

Ahmed looked behind him continually. The quickness of the American aircraft and their next attack surprised even him. The two aircraft suddenly flashed their wings and again bore down on the two men, now sprinting. Ahmed looked for cover and found it in an adjacent ditch. Throwing himself into it, he turned the stinger upwards and armed the warhead. Hasan continued to sprint across the next road and onto the baseball field.

***

Sean had both targets in his helmet-mounted site. Emile tracked them in her targeting pod as well. Sean chose the mover since he would be further along in escaping. They could always come back and get the stationary target that seemed to blend into the green TP video when he stopped.

What was the old fighter pilot saying?

How can you shoot people? Just lead them a little less than you would a vehicle.

Sean was about to strafe another human being. But this bastard was trying to kill people down below at Lakenheath and one right here in his jet, whom he truly loved.

Sean brought his formation in at 7,500 feet when they were abeam the target attack heading he wanted. At 400 knots he lined up on final approach and then pulled the F-15E down into a 20 degree inverted dive. By the time he reached that angle and then rolled back to wings level flight he was at 25 degrees nose low pointed at his target.

Sean popped out preventive flares as he came down the chute by hitting his CMD switch downwards. Small MJU-7 flares popped out behind his jet as he dived for the ground.

"Open!" prompted an excited Emile at the range where Sean could start to shoot.

Sean lined up his Eagle. Sighting the runner under his pipper he squeezed the trigger in a single one-second burst that sent 125 rounds of 20 MM bullets at the fleeing terrorist. His torso exploded into three large very separate pieces as several rounds found their target. The remaining bullets missed but all it took was one hit from a high-powered machine gun of that nature.

Emile called "Abort!" just as Sean released the trigger. Seeing the ground swell up in his full canopy, Sean pulled back on the control stick and induced a 6 G recovery, slightly more than required but he blamed it on his adrenaline. The aircraft bottomed out at 475 feet and then climbed up again to the sky.

***

Ahmed froze when the first aircraft flew over him and poured out its deadly bullets. The noise was loud but his ears were already damaged from the first bomb blast.

It looked as if God had fired a shotgun. Bullets impacted everywhere. He was too slow to target the first aircraft and his friend paid for Ahmed's delay with his life. Ahmed was blissfully spared the sight of seeing Hasan's body ripped to shreds by the bullets.

Instead he concentrated on the job at hand, since more than likely his own survival depended on this chore as well. Lining up the second aircraft, he placed the small reticle over a point where the plane would fly. Next, he released the cover for the tracker and activated it.

Ahmed held in his hands the FIM-92G version of the Stinger Man-Portable Air Defense System (MANPADS). This specific personal portable IR Surface to-Air missile weighed just 33 pounds. At five feet long and about three inches wide, it could reach a target up to three miles away or 25,000' above ground. Light and easy to operate, Ahmed had used variants of this weapon in Afghanistan but as a two- or three-man team. This was his first time using it alone.

Ahmed inserted the Battery Coolant Unit (BCU) into the hand guard and then aimed the stinger toward the fast approaching second aircraft. Inserting the BCU supplied power to the missile and the acquisition system. Once the aircraft was in the center of the site, the seeker locked on and the distinctive chirp came on, but Ahmed did not hear it. Instead he saw the green locked light appear and then pulled the trigger as he braced the launch tube on his shoulder. The launch rocket shot the missile out of the tube and well clear of Ahmed before dropping off, then the main solid rocket engine ignited, firing the missile towards it objective.

Every time he fired the Stinger he was amazed at the American's ingenuity. The SAM pushed the warhead out of the tube some distance away from the operator with a launch rocket. Ahmed instantly felt his arms relax as the 22 lb. warhead left the tube. Next came the warhead's rocket engine as it fired its solid fuel propulsion system hurtling the missile up to speeds of 2000 feet per second.

"Flare Two," was Sean's directive call for Strike 02 to expend countermeasures on their strafing run. His orders were well intended but unnecessary as Tambra fully expected some sort of tricks from the hostiles, especially after they stole the Humvee which she knew had Stingers in them. Every two seconds, with each activation of his rear cockpit CMD, Mark punched out flares. Strike 02 pulled off earlier than Strike 01 and climbed rapidly, flares popping and smoking in quick succession. But the missile was better. Stingers looked for a heat signature from the aircraft's engines. Tambra pulled the engines back to mid-power on the descent and then tapped military power for her climb. But not afterburner, which is a dead give away in terms of heat signature. Much like a motion detector on a house or room, Stingers are designed to look for heat differences.

The Stinger tracked Strike 02 using proportional guidance. The stinger seeker had a grid of 128 x 128 IR sensors. Once the jet flew away from the sensor's center it would adjust based on how far away it was from the center. The ratio of how far off and how fast it got off was calculated by the missile and it compensated by that multiplier. Almost instantaneous calculations helped the missile estimate where the aircraft would be at impact. Much like how a quarterback leads a receiver, so the Stinger lead Strike 02 as it jinked and maneuvered during its climb out from the football field.

The stinger was a passive attack weapon because it did not lock on with radar to the target. Such radar locks could be detected and a warning sent to the crew. With passive IR weapons, no such warning alerts the crew.

The best defense is proactive counter-measures such as flares and reducing or redirecting your heat signature and an active visual scan for detection of the missile threat as it approaches.

Emile saw the rocket launch from the ground streaking up rapidly toward her flight mates.

"Strike 02 break left, missile left eight o'clock."

Mark picked up the tally just after Emile started her directive call. "Break left, flare flare...oh shit!"

The flares Strike 02 produced distracted the missile enough to prevent a direct hit to the engines, but the missile did slam into the left side of the jet as they maneuvered south off target

The missile hit halfway between Mark and the left engine nacelle then penetrated the left CFT. Tambra felt a shudder when the missile hit. A small rumble sounded and then the left firelight came on.

Chapter 23

Ahmed dropped the launcher as soon as the missile came out and began to run towards the high school. He never saw the missile hit Strike 02.

***

Grace watched the bombs fall from the circling and diving fighter jets. Painful Afghanistan memories flooded back momentarily paralyzing her. The black smoke from their hits left a pall over the somber team observing from the high school. The only bright spot was the missile launched by Ahmed as it struck home against the infidel Americans. They cheered as the wounded jet retired from the battle.

***

The two remaining RRT members split up upon receiving the Wing Commander's instructions. One went to the nearer commissary. The other hoofed it in full gear the quarter mile to the high school. He arrived just as another squad car and two more SPs pulled up in front of the building amid a hail of gunfire from the school.

All three took cover behind the vehicle and trained their weapons on the high school, but did not return fire for fear of hitting a civilian. Pulling the radio from his hip pocket, the lone rapid response team member on the scene took over as site commander.

"Command Post, this is Alpha Five. I am at the high school and we have shooters inside. I believe we have a hostage situation. Number of captives unknown."

***

The discussion with the mayor was brief and unproductive. He could not fathom a reason why some terrorist group would want to attack his great village and questioned the authenticity of their intelligence. Ten minutes later, he escorted them outside into the bright sunshine at the conclusion of their meeting.

Facing south, the group noted the two pillars of smoke coming from the distance.

"What on earth is that?" questioned Hope.

"Oh dear," said the mayor, "it must be an aircraft down at Lakenheath, maybe two from the looks of things."

Hope took off in a sprint for their car. Connor followed and caught her when her high heels proved too much for running on cobblestones.

"Are you thinking what I'm thinking?" he asked, passing her and swinging open the driver's side door.

"We've been such fools. She misled us all along. It's not a UK attack but a U.S. attack on UK soil."

Connor sped east as Hope called in to her station chief to get an update.

Her station chief was quick and to the point, "Hope, the tie in might be Lakenheath Air Base. The U.S. security team responsible for Grace's brother was from there. And we just got a message that Lakenheath is under attack."

Hanging up the phone, she briefed Connor as they navigated the back road to the air base.

"After Copenhagen I asked Langley to run some cross-searches on Grace and the UK. Nothing turned up. So I had them go further and look at her brother's death and any tie-in with Vancouver. Still nothing. But I asked for another closer look with a friend I have in the branch and he found a connection. Our file on Grace's brother's death has been tampered with, that's why this did not come out sooner. We had to do some human intelligence work via face-to-face communications. Turns out the aircraft used in the tragic accidental death of Grace's brother were French-based."

"French hostages die in Vancouver."

"Bingo," she said. "I just found this out last night. But it gets worse. The security squadron responsible for that sector during the accident was based at..."

"Lakenheath," Conner finished for her.

Hope nodded and stared straight ahead, not mentioning the fact that she was the one who authorized the bombing in the first place or the fact that one of the French hostages killed in Vancouver was the brother of the French aviator who led the ill-fated bombing attack in Afghanistan.

Does Grace know I ordered the bombing? Is this some elaborate plot to get back at me? If so, why not kill me in Copenhagen? Grace had two chances if that was what she wanted.

Hope's contact did not believe Grace knew about her involvement. His recent research revealed Grace knew about the French fighters and the pilot's names. Grace probably did know the 48 SP squadron at Lakenheath and the names of the commanders of that squadron. They would be in danger now.

But ironically, the SP commanders were not stationed at Lakenheath any longer. They moved on weeks ago, due to a scandal. Obviously, Grace continued with her attack plans even though the individuals she wanted to punish would not be present.

Grace was now what the CIA called a "triple threat." She was a double agent working for another organization – in this case, herself. Hope now had orders to take Grace dead or alive, by any means possible.

"The base is under attack. Up to twenty militants in or on base. Security forces are pretty thin. Get this: the bad guys got on with Lakenheath and Mildenhall fire trucks."

Her phone rang again.

"Sir." She paused. "I think the school is the target. School on south side. Yes sir." Another long pause. "As soon as possible, sir." She hung up and started to give Connor directions.

"Go in the south gate. It normally is not open but it will be for us. Take a right and follow the perimeter road. We are going to bypass the main base and head straight for the school. My guess is that is where they are headed."

Hope and Connor pulled up outside the front of the high school, well away from the building. A security policeman in a swat outfit was a hundred yards away with his gun drawn, watching the lobby. Two other SPs in fatigues crouched behind a squad car.

Inside Hope saw a quick barricade in front of the windows of chairs, sofas, and desks. It looked like things were going to get ugly before they got better.

***

Bull Cardwell slammed down the priority phone line in the Command Post.

"What the hell is going on? Why did the CIA director just order me to let one of his CIA agents on *my* base to assist?"

No one answered his rhetorical question. Precious moments slipped by.

"Damn it. Switch our Rover feed to secure channel seven. I guess the big boys from Langley want a peek at our situation"

***

Strike 02 trailed smoke as Tambra limped away to the south. Inside her cockpit, the bright red left engine firelight caught her attention. She jinked two more times while still pumping out the flares until she was high enough from the ground where she felt no more missiles could reach her. Then she pulled the left throttle back to idle power, the lowest setting before shutting the engine down, which would be her next step if things did not go well here.

Mark was in the checklist, ready to read her the fire inflight procedure. Obviously, he had given up looking outside for other threats when they were hit and now was concentrating on getting her to do the correct steps. It was a mistake that could have cost them their lives, but Ahmed was out of missiles.

"Page thirty-two: First step is throttle idle."

"Done and the fire light has gone out." She said a short prayer, looked skyward for small miracles, and silently thanked the McDonnell Douglas engineers that made these warplanes tougher than nails.

"Step two, if fire goes out..."

"Check the system," she repeated with him as she pulled the fire warning test knob down to test the system. To the uninitiated, the cacophony of sounds that flooded the cockpit might have been jarring, but for these experienced aviators it confirmed the fire system was intact and the fire had indeed gone out. Bitching Betty repeated every fire voice warning during the test. After eight long seconds of "warning engine fire, warning engine fire" she shut up. Tambra checked both rear view mirrors and noted the smoke was evaporating.

"Strike flight, this is Eagle One." Sean recognized the voice of his Wing Commander "Bull" Cardwell and his call sign.

No authentication was necessary with his voice; everyone in the wing recognized it.

"Eagle One, Strike 01 we have a wounded bird. Retiring South. One hostile squirter dead, one active with MANPAD."

"Eagle One copies all." Bull waited to process his next order. It would be a tough one to give, but it needed doing.

"Strike, Rapcon reports unknown aircraft approaching from the East. Investigate Bogey bearing 090, 10 miles, 2,200 feet."

"Strike 01 wilco." Sean heard the broadcast from London Military about five minutes before warning all traffic to avoid Lakenheath by 20 miles. Whoever this bogey was either did not listen too well or chose not to.

"Strike 02 head south and clean up things. We will investigate and rejoin with you over Bury St. Edmunds."

Tambra waggled her wings in agreement as the radio seemed to be especially static filled with her current battle damage. Maybe some of the fire had burnt through the radio cables or antennas.

Emile locked the bogey as Sean made his radio calls. She called out a snap heading for the intercept.

The problem with the radar was it did not want to stay locked on to the little Cessna flying at 2,000 feet and 120 MPH. Made of thin sheet metal and no steel, the radar dropped off every time Emile had a decent track. The same thing happened for Sean and his radar auto acquisition modes. He finally decided to simply fly behind the bogey to see him. Flying at five times the bogey's speed made it possible to do that, but it also meant most of his tools to shoot down this threat were worthless.

Zooming behind the bogey he saw it was a Cessna, a light aircraft. Sean turned aggressively banking the F-15E into a 5 G break turn and flew 2 miles in front of the private plane and waggled his own wings as he passed in front of the target. His intention was to draw it away but it did not turn.

"Eagle One, I am eyes on bogey. No VID other than Cessna. I have tried to warn him off but no response."

"Strike 01 he is seven miles from the air base. All voice messages to warn him have failed. I am declaring him a hostile aircraft with hostile intent. You are cleared to kill Bogey bearing 090, 7 miles, 1800 feet."

Sean swallowed hard. He had never been ordered to bring down a civilian aircraft before. By now, he was above the Cessna and heading in the opposite direction. This course put him behind the slow flying threat and he quickly decided to do a teardrop maneuver in order to saddle up behind the target. The target was now at his left 9 o'clock, so he checked 45 degrees right to get some more room to maneuver and slowed his jet considerably in order to have more time on a final attack heading.

"Emile, keep an eye on that guy and talk me on to his location when we turn back in. He is starting to be a real PITA."

Emile strained to look behind her ejection seat, but by placing her right hand on the canopy she could push her torso left to get enough of a view to keep the target in sight. You almost needed to be a contortionist, Emile thought, to fly in the F-15E rear cockpit and keep the tally on targets.

"Got him." She craned her neck even further and grabbed a handhold on the canopy rail to pull herself aft slightly. "He is about five miles from the base now."

"Perfect. Hold on." Sean reefed the now much lighter F-15E into a hard 4 G turn to the left to line up behind the smaller airplane. The F-15E took off with 31,000 pounds of JP-8 but by now it was down to a much more manageable 12,000 pounds after all their attacks and low flying.

Sean could not see the airplane initially.

Emile instead called his rollout from the back seat as she followed the target through the turn and into the front hemisphere of her jet. Throughout Strike 01's turn she continually updated Sean on the bandit location by calling out its position in relationship to various points of sight within the aircraft and whether it was high or low or on the horizon. Once the jet was facing the aircraft, she transferred the tally to him. He finally picked up the flying bomb in his helmet-mounted sight after the radar momentarily locked it automatically using the guns mode of the air-to-air radar.

Guns mode is a radar system designed to lock an enemy aircraft that is close enough to shoot back at the F-15E. It automatically sets a range of 15 miles and adjusts the radar coverage to bracket or mirror the current aircraft altitude. "Going to guns" is a quick and easy way to look for a bad guy who has gotten too close.

Although the radar lock only lasted for two seconds, it gave Sean all the information he needed. They rolled out four miles at the stern of the hostile. The target traveled at 150 MPH; Strike 01 at 330 MPH after Sean slowed the aircraft with his turn and deployed his speed brake. Sean needed to get within a mile to shoot his gun, so at this speed he had less than a minute to find the target, line up for the shot and squeeze the trigger.

Sean used the speed brake to slow down the F-15E in order to stay behind the target as long as possible and thus stay out of his sight. In this case, he did not worry too much about the Cessna shooting back at him, but in practice against a slow moving helicopter or bomber they may be able to shoot him once he spit out in front of the target.

***

Ronnie "Spaz" Wilson was not moving inside the auditorium. That would have gathered unwanted attention from Hani the Jihadist who remained to guard the hostages. Instead he passed small notes between himself and other individuals who he thought might be up to the task after whispering with his closest classmates.

He was formulating a plan to incapacitate the terrorist. First he needed a distraction and then he planned to use some of the muscle at the school to take out Hani. It was bold, desperate and just a pipe dream at this stage.

Spaz scanned the room that recently became his prison. The rectangular enclosure was an auditorium in name only. Due to budget cuts and reduced manning the theatre seats were removed months ago and now simple desks and chairs dotted the large windowless room. It was a glorified study hall but it did have a speaker system for either music or school announcements.

A note came back from a student close to the left exit door. It confirmed what he already knew about the right door. Both were padlocked and had small explosive charges running along the edges of the doorframe. Their prison was booby-trapped.

Cessna

Nasir turned off his radios as soon as the jet showed up. He had used the radios only as a tool to delay suspicion. He took off from Norwich earlier in the day. Flying west on a pre-approved flight plan he trundled towards Lakenheath slowly.

First indications of his other team's success came with the radio call from London Air Traffic Control that Lakenheath Air Base had a 20-mile restriction zone in place. He smiled at the comforting thought that Grace knew this might happen. He was 20 miles from the air base then. London Control issued him vectors but he reported his navigation system was not operating properly. This gained him another 5 minutes of changing heading slightly to avoid suspicion but eventually he always crept back to heading directly for Lakenheath.

Finally London Control was not appeased and threatened him. They told him Lakenheath would shoot him down. At that point, he turned slightly away but then faked an intermittent radio by keying the mike on and off while speaking so only a partial transmission made it over the airways. Again Grace was wise in the English ways: London Control became more concerned with his loss of radios than his heading.

He knew their mission was a success when he saw the U.S. fighter jets drop bombs on their own base. Perhaps he could sneak in an attack again from the sky. Grace predicted a 65% chance of success. He plodded closer and observed the two fighter jets dive towards the airbase and a location where new smoke billowed.

Nasir exclaimed with joy as he saw the second aircraft duck and jive to avoid a missile from the ground. Could their luck really be so complete? Were the Americans shooting at themselves? The F-15 was hit and began to smoke. He heard the slight roar of its engine's vibration change to a harsher frequency and then it turned away from him and headed south. He knew the other airplane would be mad at whoever shot his wingman. Maybe he could get close enough to hit his target. Undetected meant a clear path to the BX, the largest building on base and the easiest to hit.

He knew he was in trouble when the other F-15E did not follow its injured friend, however. Instead it turned his way.

Grace had told him to leave his radios on the entire time. He monitored guard frequency. Guard frequency, UHF 243.0, was the internationally known frequency in aviation for emergencies. English was the international language for aviation so Nasir could not claim a language problem.

But he did not want to listen to the infidels anymore and so he turned them off. If he had kept them on and made just one more radio call to plead ignorance, he may have delayed Sean enough to make his target.

Nasir watched the American fighter fly past his left side at tremendous speed. It did not scare him. He was on a suicide mission and nothing could keep him from it.

Next the F-15E jet flew in front of his Cessna and waggled its wings trying to force him to turn. He did not. He knew the third time the jet flew by him would be a serious attempt to stop him. He stopped looking in front at his objective, as it got bigger. It was easy to see now.

He was five miles and a little over two minutes away. Now he needed to survive this last encounter with the big fast jet. Keeping the jet in view over his shoulder, he saw it turn slowly to line up behind him. He judged it was a few miles behind him. Grace had not prepared him for this. But seeing the plane, Nasir thought to move out of the horizontal to make it harder to shoot. He abruptly pulled back on the yoke and put the Cessna into a right climb.

***

Sean could not shoot his AIM-120 because there was not enough metal for the radar to guide the missile. His AIM-9M had no heat source to track. If it had no heat source from the Cessna, who knew where it would end up. The base was on the other side of his target so there was a good chance he would end up shooting an IR missile into his own base. That left either his gun or ramming the Cessna. Closing quickly to 1.5 miles, he was going to have to shoot using his manual gun cross and no sophisticated radar track mode.

Sean began to hum a song to relax as he saddled up to the target. It was an old Roberta Flack song with slightly modified lyrics: "Killing him softly with my gun. Killing him softly... with my gun. Killing him softly."

Pilots always joked it was like Snoopy and the Red Baron when they used the manual gun cross to shoot. Even the range was a WAG, a wild ass guess; he normally relied on the radar lock to tell him how far away he was from the target in front of the aircraft. As the Cessna grew larger in his windscreen, he estimated he was 6000' feet away and squeezed the trigger sending bullets out the right wing gun at a rate of 4000 rounds per minute. Of course, the aircraft only carried 510 bullets so this meant a total of eight seconds of trigger time.

Nasir did not know it, but he executed a perfect guns jink maneuver. Sean watched as the Cessna jinked up and away from his bullet stream, indicated by tracers. Tracers are bullets with a small pyrotechnic charge in their base. Thus every fifth bullet when fired will light up brightly allowing the bullet to be seen with the naked eye. This then allows the pilot to make an aiming correction.

Sean reacted to the jink, repositioning his fast-approaching jet back onto the Cessna. But Nasir moved again, this time into a diving left turn.

Sean anticipated the end of this new maneuver and did a snap shot. He squeezed the trigger and dragged his gun cross to where he thought the Cessna would go. It worked. The enemy aircraft appeared under the gun cross for a split second. Sean watched as the bullets arced down towards the Cessna. Then they stopped.

Chapter 24

"What the..."

Sean looked down and saw XXX in his HUD where the number of remaining bullets should have been. He banked the aircraft hard right to avoid hitting the target and tried to figure out what he was missing with the bullet count. They always flew with a full load of 510 rounds. He had one shot before the jink that should have only used about 200 rounds. That left another 300 for his snap shot.

Then it hit him; their strafe attack on the terrorist on the ground. That had used about 200 rounds. He'd only had 100 rounds when he started his last shot and the gun ran out just as he had come into zone for his kill.

"Do it again!" came the order from his backseater Emile, shaking him from his stupor.

***

Nasir shouted with glee as he escaped the deadly bullets from the American fighter plane. He focused on his objective and began to descend towards it. But he was wrong; a few bullets had hit his aircraft. The stabilizers were sluggish and not responding as they should have. He played with the yoke to see how much maneuverability he had. It would have to do.

***

"We're out of bullets. I blew it!" Sean muttered.

Emile looked over her left shoulder at the now descending Cessna. "No, not strafe him. Ram him. Last time you came so close you almost hit him. Do it again, but hit him this time." Her voice had a desperate edge to it as she finished. "It's our only chance."

Emile guessed the objective. She traced the projected light aircraft path and saw the BX directly ahead of it. "He's going to hit the BX!" she exclaimed.

Sean banked the jet into its tightest 9 G turn. Both aviators grunted as the force pushed the blood from their heads. It was part of an anti-G straining maneuver that forced the blood back to the vital organs to delay the inevitable passing out. They performed these maneuvers on a daily basis, but rarely more than 5 or 6 Gs; the 9 G turn pushed them both to their physical limits.

Sean eased back on the turn and aimed at the Cessna. This would be his last chance and it suddenly turned into a game of chicken, with Strike 01 coming in from the west and flying over the base BX towards Nasir from the east.

Smoke trailed from the rear of the craft. Maybe he had hit it after all. He decided then that ramming was not the right thing to do, but Emile was onto something. He accelerated in military power and aimed for the target.

***

Nasir was so close now at a little over a mile and a half away. Distracted by the beautiful sight of his objective, he heard the F-15E before he saw it. The jets engines strained to give it enough power to complete a quick turn but it soon rolled out directly between Nasir and the BX.

Sean accelerated quickly to 500 MPH. Now the two aircraft closed at 11 miles per minute. The four-mile gap between them took 20 seconds before they were on top of each other.

Nasir knew the American would not run into him. Well, he was pretty sure. But as the seconds ticked by, the jet showed no sign of changing course. At the last second, Nasir pushed his yoke left and down to escape the collision. A split second before colliding, Sean tapped his afterburners and pulled into his hardest climbing turn. The aircraft missed by just a hundred feet.

The F-15E climbed and the flames from the afterburner struck the Cessna's top. In addition, the jet wash struck the civilian aircraft violently. The Cessna, already in a strong left dive, shook and plunged.

Nasir fought to get the airplane flying again, but it was no use. A hard pull on the yoke only served to break the weakened stabilizer and send the tiny damaged plane into an even steeper dive. The ground swelled in his windscreen. Just before hitting the earth, Nasir thought to himself, *Grace did not know everything.*

The flaming Cessna hit 500 feet short of the BX, on the other side of the A1065 highway. Nasir survived the crash but the rear of the plane exploded into flames upon impact. Loaded with flammable chemicals to serve as a bomb for his mission, a trapped Nasir suffered a horrible and slow death.

***

Grace watched the American fighter jets from the roof of the school. When she lost contact with Musa and Dakhil she knew the Americans were successful in their bombing attacks on part of her group. Time to take some initiative.

Muttering more to herself than to Zamil or Qani, the snipers accompanying her on the roof, she announced, "Enough of this one-sided dog fight."

She continued to encourage her comrades with a quote from their beloved Koran.

"If thou cometh on them in the war, deal with them so as to strike fear in those who are behind them, that happily they may remember."

Both men replied with "Sadaqa Allahu Al-Azeem": Allah has told the truth.

Staring into the distance and transitioning to Shakespeare, Grace commanded Zamil dramatically, "Let loose the dogs of war."

If in doubt, go with quantity over quality.

Zamil reached down and fired off a red flare, aiming it so it burst directly over the security cordon crouching behind their vehicles facing the school. She left Zamil on the roof to snipe at the police out front and pin them down while looking out for other team members. Qani came with her into the school.

The responders looked up at the bright flare glowing in the blue sky, but nothing happened. No earth-shattering boom. No trumpet and cavalry attack. It just burned out slowly and floated harmlessly to the ground.

***

The signal was for Fatima. Two minutes later, a remote-controlled, mini helicopter rose from the base gym's roof. Fatima had trained with her helos for the past two months for this moment.

Manipulating the tiny control pad, the helicopter lifted off carrying a modified payload. The deafening roar of the fighter jets as they zoomed in and around the air base easily masked the blades' whirr.

Peering over the roofline edge from the gym directly towards the school, Fatima saw her objective lined up facing the school. Three vehicles used by the base security as shields while they planned what to do next.

No matter how much Fatima practiced, she could not get these delivery vehicles to be too accurate. She was hoping for more of a shock and awe type campaign.

After liftoff, Fatima accelerated the helo towards the police barrier. No sense giving away her position too early by loitering. As the small, remote-controlled device reached the nearest car, she stopped the forward movement. Before anyone noticed the enemy combatant hovering above, Fatima released the payload, a small vial of liquid: nitro glycerin.

When the vial tumbled the thirty feet, it exploded. Unfortunately for Fatima, the impact point was ten feet behind the target car.

The explosion, however, caused the RRT member to turn and face the new threat from behind. In doing so he rose up slightly, offering Zamil a clear shot from his hiding place. The rifle shot rang out; the RRT member spun around as the bullet entered his right shoulder blade. His partner collared the injured officer and pulled him to safety behind a car.

The explosion from the nitro, although impressive, was short-lived. The fire extinguished seconds after starting. Fatima kneeled behind a low wall as she nosed the helo down and pushed the speed up to accelerate the kamikaze attack.

Just as the two men retreated behind the shelter of their car, a second smaller explosion shook the area as the helicopter itself crashed into their parked car. Both men waited anxiously to see if the small eruption would detonate their vehicle but it did not. Again the fire briefly flamed hot, like a backyard grill sprayed with leaking sausage juices, but immediately it extinguished.

Fatima made sure her position was unnoticed before switching the control console to the alternate frequency.

The second helo zoomed away from the gym in the opposite direction to prevent detection. And to create an element of surprise for her second attack.

***

Tambra slammed the left throttle to idle as soon as the fire light illuminated. "Bitchin Betty" blared her warnings at the same time, "Warning Engine Fire Left. Warning Engine Fire Left."

"Mark I have it at idle and she's not…" Before Tally could finish the light extinguished. Both aviators breathed an audible sigh.

Tambra struggled with her injured aircraft. Although damaged, the bomb-heavy aircraft stayed aloft and she even managed to climb a bit on her way south towards Bury St. Edmunds.

Mark went through the labyrinth of checklist steps, notes and warnings involved with an engine fire inflight.

"She's flying and I still have idle thrust on the left engine. Need to think about getting rid of these bombs and finding someplace safe to land. Like Mildenhall or Conny," Tambra suggested.

Mark already had four different fingers marking places in his checklist and aircrew aid where he needed to reference, but did manage to recommend an easterly heading towards the channel in order to get rid of their weapons. Tambra rejected that idea because they might be needed to assist Sean since the base was still under attack.

"I am going to test the system Mark and make sure the fire did not burn through the fire detection circuitry."

She reached up and moved the switch to the test position. The litany of voice fire warnings blared into their headsets. All, except the "Warning Engine Fire Left" pronouncement. By testing the system they should have heard all of the voice warning responses; now they had to assume the fire was not out in the left engine.

"That did not sound good," chimed Mark.

Tambra scanned her engine instruments and felt a slight bang aft and left from the left engine compartment. Glancing into her rear view mirrors she saw smoke start to pour from the left engine and could not help herself.

"That's not good."

"We're smoking from the left side. I'm guarding the right. Shut down the left engine," directed Mark as he was closest to the bang and the fire. He placed his left hand on the right engine to prevent Tambra from mistakenly shutting down the wrong engine.

She pushed the left engine fire button, shut off the left throttle and finally discharged the fire bottle into the left engine. Moments later the smoke stopped, but the aircraft buckled as the engine spun down.

***

Hope prepared for another attack. She assigned the injured man on the ground with his back against the car to look out for more sneak attacks.

Taking advantage of American aviation tactics just as Grace instructed, Fatima brought the second mini helicopter in from the southeast, out of the sun.

The injured RRT man shielded his eyes and spotted the miniature aerospace vehicle just as it came around the gym corner.

"Incoming!" he shouted frantically, pointing as best he could with a bullet in his shoulder. The rest of the team stayed concealed, learning from his mistake, and turned to fire on the fast approaching attacker. It was impossible to hit such a small moving target, but the hail of bullets created a wall, which once penetrated, did damage her device. As soon as controllability deteriorated, Fatima went to plan B. Noting her little buddy was probably not going to reach her objective, she zoomed the crippled helo higher.

The good news for the base defenders was that the mini helicopter slowed during the climb, increasing their chances of hitting it. The higher altitude caused everyone to elevate his or her shot trajectories. As the helo flew closer it exploded as a golden bullet hit the vial.

But what goes up must come down and the bullets fired came back down to earth around the defenders. None were injured, but it reminded Hope of Afghanistan on the night that ends Ramadan. She saw firsthand that night how silly people with guns fired straight in the air in celebration could hit themselves or others in friendly-fire incidents.

Her work done, Fatima quickly packed up her cleaning containers. Stepping off the roof she scurried downstairs to the third floor. Just inside the stairwell was a trash bin. Making sure no one saw her; she dropped the remote control in and then added some cleaning solvents. A lit match and seconds later the bin went up in a big hot fire.

Fatima purposefully strode down to the next floor. Placing her two cleaning containers on the floor she punched the fire alarm with her right elbow breaking the glass. The ear-shattering fire alarm resonated throughout the facility. Fatima left with the mass evacuation, enjoying the look of fear and confusion from the building monitors torn between obeying the lockdown order and the need to evacuate for a fire.

Unfortunately for her, the monitors exited all gym occupants on the side away from school, thus depriving Fatima of her last attempt at distraction for Grace and her band.

Later, Fatima would escape again, slipping away from the crowd and under a fence near the base housing area. She did not realize it, but Grace had kept her out of harm's way twice.

***

Ahmed made his way to the high school in accordance with the plan. The high school was the fallback location and it would have Grace and a way out. He carefully avoided the front entrance where the police cars were positioned and snuck around to the side. Ralph's school diagram and the placement of the fire truck paid off.

Shocked to see Ahmed alive, Grace asked him about the others and nodded sympathetically when he told her of their demise.

After his debriefing, Grace assigned him to the lobby detail.

"I need you to be the rock upon which we all rely on, Ahmed. You have done well. This will be our final great moment."

He reluctantly agreed but not before extracting a promise from her to force the American war planes to go away. The attacks had obviously shaken Ahmed. Dirty, jittery, nervous and still slightly deafened, he was a shell of the man he once was.

Grace liked that. She would have preferred the dangerous man dead, but shaken was good enough for now. He was not supposed to have survived the London attack. His appearance on her door step last night was a shock. He was proving to be a liability.

Ahmed is like a bad penny-always turning up where he is not wanted. I need to watch him carefully.

Grace had watched the attack on Ahmed from the school. She agreed to his demand to put an end to the jets. This would not do she thought. Dialing in another number stored in her cell phone brought her directly to the Command Post.

She kept her demand short and sweet.

"If I see another fighter fly over this airbase, I will kill all of the children and teachers at the school. You have one minute to do this." She hung up and spread her arms wide open to Ahmed in a gesture of compliance. "It is done."

***

Watching the Cessna crash just outside the perimeter fence, the Wing Commander thought things were looking up. That's when the call came through from the female terrorist.

General Cardwell knew what he had to do. The Command Post notified Strike 01 and ordered them to an orbit point 25 miles southeast over Bury St. Edmunds. Strike 01 and a damaged 02 rejoined at the orbit point.

With the firefight at Gate 1 out and additional security police reporting to duty, Bull felt like the situation could be managed.

"All SP Units converge on the high school. Use extreme caution and coordinate your movements with Senior Master Sergeant Johnson, the onsite commander."

AIC Laura Burnett cleared her throat before her commander could continue, interrupting and correcting him.

"Sir, SMSgt Johnson called in a few minutes ago and informed us an Agent Rausch of the CIA is in charge at the high school."

Bull started to explode but stopped when his ire met the gaze of the young airman messenger before him. She was not at fault. He was mad at his security man and this mysterious CIA agent. Instead of exploding he nodded, thanked her and refocused his energy.

He allocated some of the fresh reporting force to gate security and then created a cordon around the high school.

"Nothing gets in or out, understand? People, let's review what we have here."

"All gates now secure, sir. Base is still in lockdown with assets in place at the BX, Commissary, Command Post, chapel and hospital. We now have three roaming patrol cars with two members each. The control tower is damaged and unusable for flight operations. All aircraft have diverted and landed at Coningsby except for Strike 01 flight. They are in orbit awaiting further orders. Strike 02 has an engine fire that is out and battle damage. The only known location of hostiles is the high school."

The Operations Commander paused before giving his latest information.

"We received intelligence via a text message from one of the hostages a few minutes ago, sent right before their cell phones were collected. Armed men have taken forty students and five teachers hostage at the high school."

Bull did not have any children at the school but several of his senior officers did, including the bearer of this latest bad news.

"Ok, patch me in to whoever is in charge there."

"Sir, I have you on the line with Agent Hope Rausch."

"General Cardwell this is Agent Rausch. I am with the CIA. I believe my boss called you earlier to coordinate my arrival."

"Yes, I remember, Miss Rausch," irritation dripping from his cold voice. "Now remind me again why a CIA agent is on *my* base and now seems to be in charge at the high school standoff?"

"Sir, it is a long story and time is short. Shall I brief you on what we have here?"

Bull knew she was right. Time and actions mattered, not whose authority superseded whose. But by cutting to the chase, Agent Rausch had stepped over the legality of who was in charge. He suspected her CIA badge and a working knowledge of the cell they were dealing with had gone a long way towards persuading SMSgt Johnson she should have control. All these thoughts flashed through his mind before he replied with "You're right, Agent. What have you got and what can we do to help?"

Hope breathed a little easier. These things went much better when there was no turf war over jurisdiction. It sounded as if the

Wing Commander just wanted his people safe and he did not care too much about who got the glory. She continued.

"Five to eight terrorists holding approximately forty high school students and five staff members in the high school. It is barricaded and they may have explosives. No casualties yet. They want no more airplanes overhead or else, and I suggest you make that happen."

"Done. How else can I help?"

"We were attacked here on the line from behind by miniature helicopters. I sent someone to secure the base gym but it is evacuated due to a fire. Are there any other terrorists out there running around that I need to know about?"

"No promises, but we do not think so. The rest of the base is secure and all known threats have been eliminated. So now it just seems to be a hostage situation."

"I disagree with your assessment. I know this cell and terrorist group. They do not take hostages to negotiate. They take them to blow them up later in a big display." Her words were cold and calculated and they hit him like a ton of bricks.

"I understand. What do you suggest?"

"Is this line secure?" She knew her phone was encrypted and suspected his was too, but had to be sure.

"It is," he confirmed, a little too impatiently.

She began to outline a plan.

***

At the high school they waited. Four terrorists guarded the front lobby entrance. Two were on the roof with automatic weapons and two, including Ahmed, stood behind the front desk with a small barricade in front of the windows.

Grace, Ralph and a tied up and subdued Kate remained in Ralph's office, which commanded interior school views to the lobby and the auditorium. One terrorist remained inside the auditorium guarding the students and teachers and another, Uday, busily worked on the detonator for the explosives inside the auditorium.

Grace had him wire the detonator so the explosives would detonate from Ralph's office. It was Ralph's idea, but Grace actually manipulated him into thinking it up a few weeks ago. Grace found men were easy to deceive.

As the terrorist finished up the last of his work on the detonator Grace asked, "So all will blow up from this device only?"

"Yes!" he replied, basking in the glow of attention from his commander.

"I do not want them going off unexpectedly, Uday. I want to blow them all from here at my moment of joy."

"It is as you wish, Grace." He bowed to her lightly.

She smiled at his gesture then dismissed him. "Go to the auditorium and finish wiring the explosives. Do not come here again. Stay at your post and I shall see you in heaven, my friend."

He hurried away with a smile on his face.

Ralph's position was fragile within the cell. He was an outsider who provided information. Yet he thought of himself – and Grace played up to this when in private with him – as a co-leader. His role in the operation was murky. He supplied the critical information about the base and its defenses, what little he could acquire without raising too much suspicion on himself, but Grace knew he had ulterior motives.

Ralph was very adamant they should kill someone as proof they were serious.

"She knows too much," Ralph accused, pointing to Kate. "We should kill her now and get it over with."

Kate stared at him with hawk-like eyes and switched her gaze nervously to Grace, hoping for a reprieve.

"We will in time, Ralph. All in good time," she said laying a hand on his arm. Changing the subject, she countered, "But her death means nothing. Just a brave foot soldier dying for her country." She did not look at Kate as she said this; she could not trust her face would not give away some sign of compassion for this woman she had duped and seduced.

Taking the bait Grace had given him, Ralph reacted by immediately suggesting a student be sacrificed to show their strong intentions. She readily agreed and let him go get one for their show of force.

While she waited she inspected the detonator and made sure all was correct. Behind her, Kate began to coo and make noises from her tape gag to Grace.

Grace did not turn around. Instead she stopped her work and shook her head, annoyed.

Without Kate noticing she pulled her silencer pistol from her waistcoat and spun around, firing sharply. One step later she finished the job with a blow to Kate's head from her pistol, for good measure. Kate fell over onto the couch arm. Grace grabbed the silent, limp body from behind, reaching underneath her breasts to lift her off the couch.

Earlier in the week, when she had visited Ralph, Grace inspected the locker in the corner and knew it was empty. She calculated it was just the right size to dispose of Kate's body. Dragging her dislodged one, and then both, of Kate's shoes. Grace could not help but comment to herself about the shoe's functionality for an Air Force woman. The Air Force commanders had no fashion sense.

Finally, she reached the other side of the room and dropped Kate's body to the ground, unceremoniously, to open the locker.

When she opened the door the body of Natalie fell out.

Dressed in her school uniform of light blue polo shirt, green plaid pleated skirt, dark stockings and flat patent leather shoes, she tumbled onto the floor with a paleness of death many hours past.

Ralph poisoned her earlier in the day. Her disappearance might have aroused suspicion and a manhunt.

Grace knew he was bad, but this simple cold-blooded act of murder brought him to a new level. Her level, perhaps, but she was not about to admit it.

He was different than her. Grace detected no remorse or empathy in Ralph. Whether it was genetic, chemical or his environment she was unable to determine. Grace on the other hand felt remorse for most of what she had done in her life. She was even beginning to doubt the validity of the current plan and the killing of the hostages in Vancouver.

Her meetings with Hope had sparked something deep inside her that she once had but lost in the chaos of Afghanistan and the countless other god forsaken countries since.

Embrace the chaos. That was her motto these days. She had second thoughts. Doubts even, which were never a good thing on a mission.

She stuffed the girl back in and closed the locker and left Kate to lie face down beside it.

What was I doing before Kate so rudely interrupted me? Oh yeah, the explosives and detonators.

A short while later Ralph returned with another girl. This one had a cleave gag in her mouth from a scarf tied in knots. Her hands hung limply at her sides and she calmly walked in to the office in front of a smiling Ralph.

"I've got our first victim."

Hardly your first, thought Grace.

"I did a little house cleaning as well," she smirked, thumbing back over her shoulder. "Major Healy expired while you were out."

Grace noticed Ralph now had a Glock 26 gun in his hand at the girl's back. The Glock 26 or "Baby Glock" was a 9-millimeter, low muzzle velocity, easy-to-hide gun. Unfortunately it was a poor choice for murders as it was unlikely to penetrate both sides of a body, limiting its lethality. The baby Glock was inaccurate, but convenient, and if used up close it could be deadly.

He smiled like a kid in a candy store and pushed his captive toward his desk bending her over at the waist.

"Don't move one inch Cindy," he said before asking Grace, "Is she really dead?"

Cindy quivered as she leaned over the desk, her short skirt riding up to expose her long tender legs: tears flowed down her cheeks and she gasped for breath through her gagged mouth.

"See for yourself. I do know a little something about death," explained Grace as she led him over to the body. "One shot to the heart."

"But there's no blood," he said quizzically, beginning to worry about the location of Kate's body so near to the locker that contained Natalie.

"Small caliber shot at point blank range with a silencer does not leave a big hole. She's face down now. Take a look at the hole. There will be blood on the floor."

He reached down and grabbed Kate's right shoulder to turn her over. The last thing he felt was the cool metal of Grace's silencer at the soft dent of his temple. Grace used a single shot.

He fell on top of Kate, dead instantly.

Chapter 25

"Oh, maybe you're right, Ralph. Maybe she is alive. You stupid son of a..."

Grace did not have time for this shit.

She rushed to the now-sobbing Cindy, who had just witnessed the murder of her principal. Granted, he was a principal who molested her, but still. Life was sacred, right?

Grace suspected Cindy was Ralph's other project for the year. She knew from her research that Natalie had been pregnant and Ralph forced her to abort the baby. But she was still a liability, so he killed her today and the explosion at the school would cover up his murder. Grace also knew that Cindy was pregnant and did not want to abort the baby. She discovered this when she spied on Ralph earlier last week. Ralph's plan was to kill Cindy as a hostage to prove their intentions, thus eliminating his last link to the girls of Lakenheath.

Smart man. What a creep!

Grace faced Cindy but did not take out her gag.

"Cindy, listen very carefully to me. I am going to let you go." Grace put a finger to Cindy's gagged lips and hushed her before she could mumble any questions. "Just listen and do. Go out the side door. Do not go out front or bad men on the roof will shoot you. Go out the back, but duck down so no one sees you leave. Do you understand?"

Cindy nodded agreement.

"Good. Once you are behind the building, find a policeman and tell him to tell Agent Hope Rausch this word." She paused for Cindy to understand it all. "Tell Agent Hope Rausch," and she looked deep into Cindy's eyes with as much sincerity as a lady can after she just murdered a girl's principal. "Tell her 'Alamo' in ten minutes. The front door is hot. She'll know what to do."

Grace slipped the scarf out of the girl's mouth and made her repeat the instructions.

"Good. Now let's go." Grace led her to the side door. Before Cindy left she whispered "Alamo" to confirm it with Grace and then she ran out the door.

***

Five teachers endured the hostage situation with their students inside the explosive laden room. Some comforted the students as best they could non-verbally. One male teacher, Scott McBride, was less concerned with consoling and more with reconnaissance. He caught Ronnie's attention. The burly ex-marine seemed acutely aware of the situation and Spaz's activity. Unfortunately they were on opposite sides of the room.

Ronnie was concerned about the main door. The two side doors had smaller explosives but the main door to the room had visible packages of dynamite duct taped on either side with wires running under the door out of the room.

All of the students saw Uday hook up the wires using a coil, except for the few hysterical students sobbing uncontrollably in the far corner. They were lost in their own fatal world and Spaz made no move to contact them about his plan. Uday spent the next few minutes emphatically explaining to Hani in Arabic something that Spaz could only guess was "Watch out live explosives here".

***

Ahmed was the problem. His appearance on the scene had complicated things. Her second in command was getting a little too big for his britches and Grace saw that the fight that had been brewing for months between them would likely happen today. She wanted to avoid that fight and clean up some loose ends.

Grace marched down to the auditorium. Stomping in, she picked the strongest-looking boy she could and motioned with her pistol for him to come with her. She also asked the explosive expert Uday to come as well. He protested that he was not completely finished, but she shooed his excuses away. "We have time," she said.

Back in the principal's office, she commanded Uday to pick up Ralph and take him to the lobby. He began to protest after looking at his precious detonator, but again she stopped him short.

"I will do this my way. Don't cross me, Uday. Not now."

Uday pressed her, unsure of his limits. "Why did you kill the informant?"

"He was a useful traitor, no more, no less. Besides, he was not one of our faith."

She had the strong boy carry Natalie to the lobby. The boy knew her and he fought back his tears as he lifted her body.

"Just do it," Grace said, waiving the gun behind them both.

Once in the lobby, they left both bodies with Ahmed.

"Show them to the Americans," said Grace, "and tell them we are serious. Uday, you and the boy come with me."

Ahmed began to protest and assign one of his men to be with her.

"I am an armed assassin with a black belt in karate. Do you really think I need someone to baby sit me with this ..." she turned to finish her sentence, flashing a tiger's grin, "boy?" She exaggerated the word to demean Ahmed even more. Shaking his head, he turned to concentrate on his task.

Grace motioned for her slaves to follow as she cranked up her Bluetooth earbud. Her hips swayed to the haunting guitar rifts of "Mysterious Ways" as she left the room.

***

Hope saw two bodies dumped out the front door: an adult male, African-American – she knew that had to be the principal – and what looked like a female student. The hostage situation suddenly took a turn for the worse.

Moments after witnessing the bodies, Hope's phone rang. It was a security policeman from the other side of the school. Cindy had made her way to their location.

"Put her on."

Cindy gave her the message, including the vital word "Alamo."

Hope's blood ran cold. Fear gripped her.

It was a code she and Grace had used at Virginia. It had come to be a word they would use when they needed the cavalry to come or else all hell was about to break loose. Things were going horribly wrong.

What was happening in that school? Was Grace running things? Obviously not if she sent out the Alamo message. Was it a trap to lure Hope into her killing zone? Why here and why now?

Hope only asked two questions of Cindy.

"What did the woman smell like?"

Cindy thought about it for a few seconds, puzzled. It had been a terrifying morning for the girl.

"Did you smell anything?" Hope repeated.

"Yes," the girl whispered at last. "It was…cinnamon?"

"And how long has it been since she gave you this message?"

"I came straight here," said the girl. "Maybe two minutes?"

Hope nodded grimly. Once she heard "Alamo," she knew what had to be done. Calling General Cardwell, she said simply, "Our time is up."

***

"Standby Rausch, I have them on the other line. Strike 01 execute Eagle option Alpha. Say TOT."

"That's your bailiwick, Ems."

Things were getting dangerous, thought Emile. Sean had reverted to calling her by her nickname. He only did that when he was stinking drunk or scared shitless. Strike 02 had their fire out, but in doing so had shut down one of their two engines. She didn't like those numbers.

Emile looked at her data link pod video page and shot back over the radio. "Eight minutes, give or take five seconds."

"Execute," came their commander's reply.

Back into the phone receiver, he calmly relayed, "Rausch, expect your result in eight minutes."

"I hope it's in time," she said as she stared at the barricaded school.

***

"Strike 01, I need you to hit the front of the high school. There are two on the roof and two to four hostiles inside the lobby. They have already killed two people and indications are they will kill a whole lot more unless we act. Your bomb is the catalyst for our attack of the high school to release the hostages."

Cindy had enough wits about her to brief the command on what she saw in the school. She explained that there was just one terrorist in the auditorium with the students and teachers. The lobby and roof had the majority of the hostage takers. She had no idea where the blond woman who let her escape was.

Everyone knew roughly what they were facing just not how long they had.

"Eagle One, what about collateral damage?" Sean asked.

"We already discussed that, Strike. The weapons team here thinks a hit from the south on the far north side of the building will minimize damage to the center and rear structure."

Mark chimed in on their discrete frequency, "I don't like it."

"I know Mark me either. Use a delayed fuse. Suggest 25 milliseconds. That way the weapon will be buried deep before the explosion," Emile coached.

"Roger that. Good call."

Emile piped in with a question.

"Can you turn off the GPS jammers? That way we can loft our JDAM in and minimize the damage?"

"I checked," said Command, "and it will be another ten minutes before the protocols can be overridden to turn them off and then another five minutes before all the 'trons' are cleared to use the JDAM. That's about seven minutes more than we have." Bull had his team look at every option. This was his last chance.

Sean understood what needed to be done and what heading they would come in on. He immediately swung Strike flight further south.

"Strike call inbound, pickle and give us a thirty-second warning and then ten seconds to impact. We are patching you into the ground commander, Agent Rausch, via secure communications. Her team executes as soon as your bomb hits so I need them in the loop."

"Strike wilco."

"Strike 02, did you copy?"

Tambra swallowed and keyed her mike. "Sure did, One. What's the plan?"

Sean looked out to Strike 02 and the gleaming AGM-130 on the right side of their aircraft. "Seeing how you are the only game in town, Two, you get the honor of dropping."

Inside their cockpit Tambra quipped, "Hear that Mark? We get to blow up our own base. How's that for some resume fodder come promotion time?"

"This is totally FUBAR," expressing a mounting frustration at the situation they found themselves in.

"I agree. I don't know about you…but I have a YGBSM look on my face right now."

Sean continued without waiting for her acknowledgement. "Plan is a low altitude, one thousand foot release so the bad guys don't see us coming with a south to north run in. In fact, after release Strike 01 will pull up and climb away to divert their attention from you and the bomb."

"Great," said Tambra slowly. It was all the enthusiasm she could muster.

Emile piggybacked on Sean to give Mark some needed direction. "Mark, set a delayed fuse so that when the bomb enters the front it does not go off right away. We want the weapons to collapse the front, then detonate with minimal damage to the rear of the school."

"Wilco."

Strike 02 had an AGM-130 IR variant. Known officially as the AGM-130A-12. The IR version was their preferred choice since it used the same seeker as their targeting pod. Both pictures would see the same type of terrain and features, helping Mark acquire the target easier. That made finding the desired point of impact (DPI), in this case the school's north side, less complicated.

Mark went through the laborious process of warming up the weapon and the AXQ-14 data link pod. A count down indicated two minutes until warm up was complete.

Emile did the same for her AXQ-14 pod.

While that happened, Mark entered the exact coordinates passed by the Command Post for the target and told the bomb to attempt an impact angle of 70 degrees. 70 was the highest and it would minimize damage to the rest of the building.

Meanwhile, Sean led Tambra south and then back north so they were about 35 miles away when the pod timed in and video showed up on the displays indicating Mark was synced up with his bomb. Quickly he checked his controllers and ability to control the bomb by moving the seeker up, down, left and right.

Emile saw the same and took control to verify her ability to guide if needed. He took his pod to standby and she performed the same checks he did only this time she controlled the bomb with her DL pod.

Emile became the flight's cheerleader after she completed her checks, turned her pod to standby and "gave" the bomb back to Mark.

"Mark, this is gonna be a piece of cake. Looks like you can use the cathedral tower to line up for a 340 heading into the base and school. But remember, we need to do this old school because of the GPS jammers."

Emile and Mark simultaneously went through the prerelease mantra they had worked on in the simulator months prior, when they checked out on these weapons.

Mark verified the green ready light signifying the bomb was ready to come off when the pickle button was pressed. The ready light came on after the master arm switch in the FCP was placed to ARM. It was the first time Tally did this all day.

Their attack would use the indirect method, which allowed a longer standoff range and used the DL pod to transmit signals from the aircraft to the bomb and vice versa.

Both Mark and Emile viewed what the seeker saw from the front of the weapon. Mark did not need the cathedral tower. He could see billowing black smoke from his air base in the pod video.

***

Scott McBride was five years removed from the Marines, but, "Once a Marine always a Marine". He did not like being trapped like an animal by these Jihadists. He had been duped by the principal about an assembly and then herded into the room before he or the other staff members knew what has happening. By the time they noticed the locked exit doors and tried to get out the front door it was too late.

Most of the students were terrified out of their minds. Huddled in small groups, they sat or stood by the desks with expressionless faces. They had no idea what was going on around them. Like many others they assumed a U.S. Air Force base was one of the safest places to be. They never thought terrorists could attack them here.

Scott tried to figure out the wiring for the explosives. *Where was the detonator? Were there any trip wires at the doors?*
He also made eye contact with the only student who was alert enough to catch his sublime actions. She was a Goth girl by the name of Terri. She was smart and quick.

Together they were slowly forming a plan of action too.

***

Since she was not in charge of the bomb, Emile's DL pod was in standby as she watched what Mark did. She would not guide it in, he would. But she went through the same steps in case she was asked to step in and take control of the bomb. Mark made sure he was actively "talking" to the bomb and setting the base altitude the weapon should fly to for the attack. He set 3000'; it would provide just enough altitude to get a good view of his target, but would not be so high that everyone saw it coming.

Mark's final checks involved the video from the bomb itself. He checked the nose indicator marker (NIM), which showed where he should move the bomb to hit the target based on coordinates the jet provided. A great tool unless GPS jamming was present, in which case you normally would set benchmarks or certain angles at certain times. This is what Mark would be forced to do. The video polarity looked good versus other buildings along the way, so he felt comfortable with his settings.

Tambra centered her aircraft velocity vector on the azimuth steering line. The airplane was beginning to shudder and vibrate. The winds were light. She did not like the signs the plane was sending, but she did her best to remain wings level for the release. Optimal release was 30 miles from this low but they were driving in to 28 miles to sweeten the shot. That would put them just south of Bury St. Edmunds at release. She saw the cathedral tower in the distance. She chuckled thinking this would be a once-in-a-lifetime chance to fly low altitude over the beautiful market town of Bury St. Edmunds.

Sean flew along her left side. Both aircraft accelerated to 400 MPH in order to give the weapon as much energy at release as possible. Since Strike 02 only had one operating engine the flight was limited to Tambra's maximum speed. This extra acceleration was tearing her plane apart and she knew it.

"Winds are light. Thirty miles to target. Releasing at twenty-eight miles. Guided, Level, ranges check. Good Ready," Tambra confirmed. The aircraft calculated range to the target, and the bomb did the same calculations based on its coordinates. Both range determinations needed to be within a quarter of a mile of each other or one of the systems was wrong.

Mark replied to her spiel.

"Good Data Link. Pre Nim Set. PSA Left. Cleared to release."

At 30 miles the aircraft was leaning left and Tambra was fighting the yaw by putting in a ton of right wing trim.

She saw they were in range and waited until 28 miles before pushing and holding the weapon release button and calling it on the radio.

"Strike 02, pickle."

Everyone in the flight hacked his or her clock at the "bombs away" call. The bomb came off and immediately her plane dropped dangerously low on the left side. The 2000-pound bomb had been all that was counter-balancing her damaged aircraft's weight. She had a single engine aircraft with an asymmetric load on the left wing. She should have jettisoned the 2000-pound MK84 earlier. Now she was at 800 feet, sinking and turning left over the town of Bury St. Edmunds.

"I can't control this thing." Tambra's frantic voice chilled them all.

Sean aggressively turned away from her aircraft to give her more room to maneuver. More smoke started to slip out of her damaged left engine.

Mark concentrated on watching the bomb fly out. He kept his hands on his lap as his instructor had taught him.

The bomb dropped off the aircraft and then the rocket motor fired, launching it ahead of the aircraft before it began a shallow climb to altitude. Nothing Mark could do now would help the weapon. He needed to let it get to altitude and fly straight towards the target. His job in a low altitude release was most critical during the last 30 seconds prior to impact.

But he soon realized this was not going to be his bomb to deal with. The excessive down left wing masked his DL pod almost as soon as the weapon climbed. He begged for her to raise the left wing, but her comment left no doubt to the probable outcome.

"Damn it, Mark! I m trying my best here. I can't control this baby."

Mark had a decision to make. Should he keep control and risk not being able to guide the weapon in during a critical phase later or hand control to Emile now before things got bad in his jet.

"Goalie, goalie, goalie," Mark called out sending the message that the other aircraft had to take over guiding his weapon to the target.

Emile selected transmit with her pod and came back confirming her new mission. "Guiding, guiding, guiding."

Mark reached up and pressed PB1, returning his DL pod back to standby and that's when he realized how low they really were.

The cathedral tower, the tallest building in Bury and in most of East Anglia, went by at eye level.

***

"Climb five hundred feet," commanded Emile, oblivious to their dilemma. She was not surprised by the goalie call; she and Sean had discussed the possibility as they drove out around Bury St. Edmunds, lining the flight up on their attack axis. She had a bird's eye satellite image of the high school on one of her four displays. Her target was the center air conditioning vent in the north corner of the building. As Emile concentrated on her DL screen, Sean watched in horror as his wingman peeled away helplessly, descending toward the town.

Sean wanted to scream; *Don't you realize they're falling out of the sky?* But he knew she was doing her job and doing it well. He climbed, as someone he loved descended underneath his nose. His vision of her jet became obscured with the maneuver and when he rolled slightly left to reacquire Strike 02, it was too late. Tambra was dangerously low.

***

Tambra knew how this was going to end. Her damaged plane was sinking lower and lower.

"Prepare to leave the jet, Mark. Rotate your command selector valve to normal," she demanded.

"What?" he asked, starting to assume the ejection position and removing the pencils from his flight suit pocket.

The ejection position meant putting your ass as far as possible in the back of the seat and straightening your body. He made sure his arms, legs, feet and hands were all tucked inside the seat area in order to reduce the likelihood that they would catch on something as the ejection seat fired and left the cockpit.

"Just do it and tell me when complete. That's an order, Captain."

Mark hesitated, and then rotated his command selector valve from aft initiate to normal. This meant no dual ejection – if Mark pulled his ejection handles only he would leave the plane. Normally crews fly with aft initiate selected, which meant a dual ejection would occur, regardless of who pulled the ejection handles.

"Done, Tambra. But what are you gonna do?"

The jet was at 500 feet now and she could see the elementary school in Bury where she volunteered. The jet was not turning. It was wallowing and descending. If she punched out now there was a very strong possibility of it hitting the school.

Chapter 26

Grace finished up with Uday and the student minutes later. She had the young boy turn around and then cold-cocked him with her gun. She did it with a gentle yet quick, decisive chop. He crumpled to the ground like a dry leaf on a fall day.

Grace checked the corridor to make sure the coast was clear and then she dragged his limp form down the hallway and propped him up beside the main entrance to the auditorium.

Good. Someone will find him here in a few minutes.

With that she retired back down the hall to finish her preparations.

***

"Tally you need to get out of the jet now," Sean commanded.

Tambra did not want to think about her decision any more than she had to. She let out those three fateful words no fighter pilot ever wants to say.

"Bailout, bailout, bailout!"

Mark reached for both of his ejection control handles outboard of his thighs. Grasping the handles firmly, he pulled so the handle rotated up and toward the back of the seat. Grabbing both handles also prevented his arm flailing during what was about to happen. This started the ejection sequence. Now his seat was a fully automated catapult rocket system.

The inertia reel retracted his shoulder straps pinning his body to the seat. The canopy fired its own jettison system and flew up and away from the cockpit; the noise from the wind stream was deafening. The rocket catapult fired on Mark's seat only, as his seat exploded up a rail and out of the aircraft. Almost immediately the parachute deployed and he separated from the seat. 1.8 seconds after he pulled the handle, Mark found himself pulled backward by a fully inflated parachute, drifting over the idyll of Bury St. Edmunds.

***

Sean thought his warning was just in time as he watched Mark's canopy fly open and his seat rocketed away from the jet, now trailing a smoke trail across the Bury skyline. But Tambra did not come out.

Tambra heard Mark leave the aircraft and saw in her rear view windows the powerful rocket flame that pushed his ejection seat up and away from the dying jet.

She focused on manipulating her aircraft and saw exactly what she wanted just long of the school: a large meadow butted up against the A14 highway. If only she could keep the F-15E airborne for another few hundred yards.

She did not use her afterburner for fear the yawing extra power on her right engine would slam her further left and closer to the school, and instead manhandled the limping plane with small rapid aileron tweaks.

At 150 feet, she could see the children on the playground below, pointing upward as the jet screamed over them. The Morton Hall subdivision came into view just past the meadow and highway. She did not want to plow it in there either. Holding her breath, she prayed to a god she had lost in faith years ago and nosed the aircraft into the field.

***

"Get out, damn it! Punch out!" Sean yelled. He knew in his heart she was riding the big Eagle to its grave, safely away from the town. He punched his dashboard a little too hard as the cloud of smoke and flame disappeared behind them.

The jet struck at a 20-degree attitude. She died while still at the controls.

Mark floated down in his parachute. Ejecting from 380 feet at 500 MPH was a rare feat for the ACES-II ejection seat. Tested and certified at speeds of 600 MPH and altitudes as low as on the ground, it was the best the Air Force had. Low, slow and pitched down with a bank angle was not what it was designed to do. But Mark was high enough to get a safe ejection. Mark's chute opened and he had all of 10 seconds to correct it before landing in the backyard of Mr. and Mrs. Early Goody.

One thing flashed through his mind as he drifted down. He remembered a crusty old WSO in the squadron who often claimed he always kept a staple remover in his flight suit pocket. Mark asked him why one Friday night at the bar. The WSO smiled and said, "So when you eject and are coming down in your parachute you can remove all the staples from your checklist changes and post them before they pick you up." Mark realized his checklist was indeed out of date; he had a change from two weeks ago he had not posted yet. Where was that staple remover when he needed it?

Then another thought crossed his mind.

My checklist is in the airplane.

All of Mark's training for ejection emergencies was lost in a momentary brain freeze once his parachute opened. He should have remembered "Canopy, visor, mask, seat kit, 4 line and wind" from his egress/life support training. Instead his mind was blank. The ground came rushing towards him.

Mark placed his legs together and bent his knees. He placed his hands on the parachute risers and ducked his chin. When his feet hit the ground first, he immediately threw himself sideways to distribute the shock.

Mark landed perfectly. His round parachute tumbled over the vegetable garden with a noisy flourish. The Goody's were uptown at the market, but their neighbors witnessed the bizarre scene and immediately rang up the police.

When the Bury Police finally arrived over thirty minutes later, all they found was a parachute tangled in the Goody garden tomatoes.

Mark had untangled his uninjured frame from the nylon escape suit and dusted himself off before walking to the nearest pub. He knew without a doubt that Tambra sacrificed herself to save lives on the ground. He was three pints into his recovery before anyone made the connection between him and the burning wreckage a mile away.

Chapter 27

"Command Post, Strike 02 is down. Vicinity of Bury St. Edmunds. One chute seen." Sean leaned back in his seat and sighed.

Emile's voice brought him back into focus. "Check 90 left immediately." She concentrated on the transition line (TL) at the top of her scope. It flashed at Emile now, indicating rocket motor ignition and firing. Emile searched up and down with the weapon seeker looking for the building. She was not commanding the weapon to move; now she just looked with the seeker. The first pointer was a small smoke cloud left and long of the target. That was the result of their LGB on the Jeep. Carefully she moved slowly right and found the high school.

The TL stopped flashing, indicating rocket motor burnout. The AGM no longer had self-propulsion. If it was to get to the target it had to do it on its own. The TL video jiggled a few seconds, which told Emile the rocket motor had separated, so the extra weight would not limit the bomb's range.

Sean finally caught up on his crew coordination duties by calling over the radio. "Forty seconds to impact."

Emile confirmed that with her own clock. "Lock early and update often," she repeated to herself.

Now that she had the target she could start to lock on the bomb, but she wanted to wait and achieve a high impact angle. Emile slewed the bomb seeker slightly right and found three vents in the building's far corner. Mark centered the seeker prior to release, and Tambra had lined up the cathedral tower and 340 heading: the bomb was headed directly for the target, but it was also still flying straight and level. It had not begun to pitch over and head for the building. Emile waited to lock on in order to achieve the high impact angle. Locking on early might let the bomb broach the top of the high school.

"Twenty seconds to impact," Sean announced over the radio. Inside the cockpit his nerves came through even louder.

"Em, lock on."

She waited a few more seconds and then she bypassed Transition and selected TERM at PB7. The TL disappeared, affirming the rocket motor had separated and she was in manual mode with Terminal guidance control. Now any TDC movement commanded the bomb to fly in that direction. She pointed at the vent in her narrow field of view and commanded a track. She locked short of the vent. A cross appeared slightly left of the vent, and a square appeared around it.

"Ten seconds to impact."

Emile made one last adjustment. She moved the aim point update to the center of the vent and commanded another track, updating the weapon one last time before it slammed into the school. Sean saw the impact and knew one thing was for sure: Emile had lost her "Bambi" call sign today.

***

"Ten seconds to impact," declared Emile over the radio for all to hear. But bombs, like babies, are fickle things. They are rarely on time and sometimes turn out a little different than expected. The AGM-130 bomb roared in like a freight train from the sky.

Hope and Connor and the hastily assembled assault team were expecting it. Hope even called for "Cover!" on the radio five seconds before impact. That turned out to be two seconds before the three-second early impact.

A thunderclap of epic proportions resounded throughout the base after the 2000-pound bomb hit. The earth rumbled with an aftershock for another second or two.

Shock and disorientation prevailed. The planned assault did not happen.

The weapon hit spot on. They could not have asked for better placement. The Wing Commander radioed "Shack one" on the F-15E discrete frequency after seeing the hit.

On the roof, Zamil died instantly as the bomb penetrated the building. The actual weapon explosion killed Qani when it detonated 25 milliseconds after entering the lobby. Ahmed was shielded from the blast by the barricades and front desk, but he died a split second later when the rest of the roof collapsed on top of him.

Security forces sheltering at the side and rear of the building reacted immediately, and rushed to the auditorium.

***

Hani, who guarded the students and teachers, was caught totally unprepared at the bombing of the front of the building. Already jumpy, he immediately went to go investigate, and then thought better of it. He had no idea if another bomb would hit, and crouched between some desks for protection.

But it was the quick thinking of one of the students that prevented the bloodshed. Spaz convinced two football players to use the desks in front of them as tackling dummies as part of his plan. This caused a chain reaction of desks. The terrorist heard the rumble of desks approaching and stood to see what the commotion was. The desks hit him and pinned his machine gun. He reached for the pistol in his waistband.

He turned to face the group and found no less than five people rushing him. Scott McBride and Terri the Goth came from his right, two large football players rushed him head on and a rather tough red head screamed and charged from his left.

One of the jocks took a flesh wound to the arm but they disarmed him convincingly.

McBride took the pistol from the terrorist and then without announcing anything killed him where he stood with a quick shot to the head.

His students stood stunned, none more so than Spaz whom he had signaled earlier. Some shrieked with terror at the unexpected bloodshed from their mentor.

"If he has a timer or detonator on him, he could have blown us all up. He still may be booby-trapped. So no one touch or go near him." Scott had served in Korea and knew a thing or two about subversives.

Students began to make a break for the main door when they heard the shots ring out. The former Marine fired two shots into the ceiling to get everyone's attention. He calmed and organized them.

"We're not out of the woods yet, people. Someone else may blow these explosives up and I don't want to try and get out and run the risk of setting them off. Anyone have any ideas?"

McBride stared at Spaz. Then they both looked up at the ceiling where electrical wiring was popping and spurting from the two bullet holes. Spaz smiled and eventually a grin spread across McBride's face too. Spaz started to explain his next plan but McBride beat him to it. In a baritone voice he commanded, "This is what we're gonna do people."

They all moved to the center of the room, as far away from the explosives as possible and began to open the air conditioner vent. They were leaving through the ceiling.

***

Hope reacted quickest of the forward troops. Seconds after the blast, she grabbed Connor and barreled ahead around the left side of the building. The lobby was in ruins but the side doors were still intact. Hope ran past the parked fire truck and through the side door. She faced a hallway that snaked right and left or a door ahead to the cafeteria that was dark. She went right and sent Connor left.

Connor came to the auditorium door and froze in his tracks seeing all the wiring and the explosives outside it. He checked on the unconscious student lying beside the door.

Meanwhile, other rescuers were trying to get in through the auditorium side rear doors but they were padlocked from the inside as well. The students yelled for them to stop for fear they might set off the explosives.

"Hope," Connor spoke into their communications link from the auditorium doors.

"Yeah," Hope responded, easing her way down the now dark right hallway, her gun drawn.

"We got a problem here."

Hope turned to her right and saw a door shake as if someone were running into it from inside. She crouched and prepared to shoot whoever was coming out.

"Somebody let me out. The door is locked and my hands are tied and there is a bomb in here," came a woman's voice from inside.

"Problems here too, Connor," came Hope's sarcastic reply.

"Ma'am, where is the bomb? If I shoot open the door, can it hit the bomb?"

"No," came the plea. "Hurry. It is counting down and we only have a minute."

"Stand back and tell me when you are safely away and on the left of the door." Hope knew, regardless of the woman's plea that it was entirely possible she could hit the bomb. But there was no time. She would shoot right and hope for the best.

"Connor, what have you got?" asked Hope.

"Explosives wrapped around the auditorium door and a room full of kids inside with the same."

Hope noticed the door she was about to shoot open was the principal's. She tried the door handle from her side but it was indeed locked.

"Clear. Hurry!" came the reply from the principal's office.

Hope stood, aimed and fired four shots into the lock mechanism. Not into the door handle as she sometimes saw on TV, but the lock itself. She tried it. It still did not open.

"I'm gonna shoot it again. Stand back."

Hope did not wait for a reply but aimed for the bit of lock that had not been hit. This time it struck home and the door unlatched. Hope kicked it open.

A cute disheveled Air Force officer ran out of the room. It was Kate.

Grace had knocked Kate out with the butt of her gun but had intentionally missed her with the gunshot. Kate was still groggy, but after waking she saw the bomb in the office and tried to get out of her bonds to escape. She managed to slip the taped gag off enough to talk.

"There's a bomb counting down. We only have sixty seconds. We need to get out of here." She started to run, but Hope stopped her and shook the terrified woman, removing her gag and cutting her hands free.

"Look," Hope recognized the officer's rank from her shoulder boards, "Major, forty kids in the auditorium are going to get blown sky high if we don't stop this thing."

"Connor I need you here now. We got," she peeked into the room, "fifty seconds before a Sk7b detonator takes everyone to Allah with the rest of the boys."

Running back down the hallway, Connor recounted his best Sk7b knowledge.

When the counter reached 30 seconds, a low, eerie synthesizer rhythm began to emanate from all the speakers in the school. A kind of pulsing "nana nanna nanna nnaaa." Slow at first but building into a crescendo, oscillating in and out of frequency, the sound haunted everyone in the school and even outside it.

***

"Twin entry wires. Booby-trapped for detonation unless an equal current is applied simultaneously without removal," said Connor as he skidded around the corner. He found a confused but beautiful Air Force Major looking on as Hope stood over a detonator; there were 15 seconds on the clock and the countdown was progressing.

Hope looked at him expectantly as she fingered both the red and yellow entry wires.

"Well?" she asked in a smartass voice.

"I'm getting too old for this shit," he said. "I can only imagine how you feel."

"Nice," she quipped. The counter was at 7 seconds.

"I hate long goodbyes," said Hope and she reached over and pulled out the red wire.

All three cringed but nothing happened. And the counter kept counting down.

Chapter 28

"Oh shit!" said Hope as the counter reached zero.

A loud noise exploded over the entire school. A loud crash of symbols and an even louder guitar riff flooded down. The Who blared out from the school PA system: "Won't Get Fooled Again."

Hope fell on the floor in exhaustion, laughing and singing along to the chorus, what she thought were the words "and I want to bend to my knees." That did not sound quite right and did not agree with Roger Daltrey's rendition but she continued anyway "and pray they won't be fooled again."

Just as they finished their chorus, a small bright flash erupted from each corner of the office.

Glancing around, Hope cried out, to no one in particular, "Four flash bang explosions."

Connor was the first to trace the explosions back to their source – a trip wire by the door. When Hope opened the door it set off a booby trap, courtesy of Grace. Louder combustions spread along each wall as flames ran in a spidery climb.

"Out. Everyone out before this room goes up in flames." This was definitely Grace's work. Arson was her thing. She left one last distraction for Hope.

***

Hope radioed the rest of her security team notifying them of the elimination of the explosives threat and the new danger from fire. SMSgt Johnson in turn briefed her that several students had already exited the building via the large air duct and were met by security police. One of the first was Spaz who rapidly debriefed the SP on their escape plan and the wiring of the explosives.

Hope knew the priority was getting everyone out before the fire lit off the explosives in the auditorium. But the air duct would take too long.

Hope and Connor broke down the main door to get the remaining hostages out. Luckily Spaz and McBride were right-the main door had no additional booby traps. Everyone made it out of the school before the blaze took over.

There was no time to disarm the remaining bombs; the back of the building went up in a huge fireball twenty minutes after the school had been evacuated.

After extinguishing the fire, the air base fire department chief turned over site control to Hope. She and Connor spent the next two days combing through it for Grace and the other terrorists. They found three bodies in the lobby and forensics identified one tentatively as Ahmed.

They also found a blond wig outside one of the school walls beside an open-air courtyard. In the courtyard, they found a terrorist corpse with a bullet in his brain. His burnt body almost obscured the bullet hole, but Hope's team, flown in from Langley now that she was somebody again; found it after a few days of hard work.

Hope never found any trace of Grace. She speculated that Grace was on the rooftop when the bomb hit. Video evidence identified only Zamil on the roof, but Hope reported Grace dead from the AGM-130 explosion.

***

Hope finished off the last piece of her final report.
Grace Matiseni is dead.
Hope did not believe a word of that but her superiors would like it better if that was her expert opinion. Funny how sometimes the truth was the last thing people wanted to read.

Hope knew better. She knew in her heart that, despite no hard evidence of Grace escaping, she had. Connor would laugh at her reasoning. It was purely intuition. She felt Grace was alive and a part of her was afraid that Grace would come after her next.

Hope went over the report one last time before hitting the send button, directing it to CIA headquarters.

Grace was initially assigned to infiltrate the AQNA terrorist group as part of operation Barbarossa. Her mission was to move up in the ranks of AQNA while manipulating the group's objectives to coincide with U.S. interests. If the U.S. could not use the group, then Grace was to communicate their targets to the CIA so the attacks could be thwarted.

Grace had volunteered for this assignment after her brother and his wife were killed in a horrible friendly-fire bombing attack in Afghanistan. Hope had ordered the fighter jets to bomb what her informant assured her was a terrorist cell at a broken down fuel truck. Hope never found out that her informant was actually kidnapped and killed in the attack, his family was threatened, and a rival tribe had provided false information to Hope. But she suspected something when she could not find her trusted source after the attack. She did track down his family and after doing some research on her own; she concluded that it was a setup.

So Hope moved the man's family away from the region to prevent any retaliation against them and put the terrible events behind her. Her reports on the incident did not include her own informant or his family. She wanted the mess to end there. It obviously did not.

Grace found out some of the details behind her brother's death and used it, and her position within AQNA, to seek revenge on those she believed responsible. She manipulated Janus to attack Vancouver on a day when the French men's hockey team would be easy targets. She knew that one of the hostages would be the brother of the French aviator who killed her own brother.

Yes, several security personnel at the venue were killed in the attack (including Brad Jackson, a louse found at a nearby hotel who provided entry details to Grace when she was his mistress) and members of the French men's hockey team, but it could have been much worse. The hockey rink has a capacity of 18,910 so an attack on a full night would have been catastrophic.

Hope could understand how Grace thought her small, pin-point attack could be minimal yet allow her to gain trust and move higher in the AQNA ranks. Hope also now realized that it had a dual purpose of getting back at the French for their fighter jet's bombing when innocent civilians surrounded the stricken fuel tanker. Hope also noted that the secretaries were not taken or harmed. In fact, eye witness accounts showed that the terrorist Jafer, who wished to do them harm, was shot – not by Canadian police or security personnel – but instead by a Browning 1911. Grace's weapon of choice. She shot him in the back.

Grace also killed Janus. Good riddance, thought Hope. And it got her in the driver's seat.

The $500,000 blackmail money for information she should have given freely to her employer was problematic. But the agency did have a large black-ops budget. Hope could make that problem go away with some creative financial finesse.

Hope noted in her report that information Grace provided did prevent the death of the royal couple, the Duke and Duchess of Cambridge, in the attack in London. Several members of their security team died when the terrorists took their weapons but those men and women gave their lives protecting their charge.

If seeking vengeance while on assignment was not bad enough, the train jumped the tracks with the attack on Lakenheath Air Base. Hope knew Grace planned the entire thing. Grace wanted to get at the two main people she blamed for the death of her brother: the co-commanders of the security group in charge of the sector where her brother and his wife lived.

She wanted those two, who oversaw the protection of those villagers, burned to a crisp by the Western-made bombs.

Of course, the irony was that neither of them was on duty at the time of the attack. Both were on administrative leave due to a fraternization scandal that rocked the 48 SP detachment.

The two individuals lived locally but in separate houses – the investigation and charges of "frat" were still fresh in everyone's minds. One, the female LTC, "accidentally" drowned in her swimming pool around the time of the attack. She was an expert swimmer but apparently took many pills and then a late night swim, which resulted in her death.

The coroner could not nail down the time of death, but Hope suspected it was just after the attack.

The other former SP commander was away. Had been for many months. Some thought he had been promoted not suspended. Others said he was doing a black operation for the government. Hope needed to follow up on him after she returned to the US.

The British firemen were all knocked unconscious but not killed outright. Hope suspected Grace had some part in that, either by substituting knockout pills for ones that killed, or by emphasizing the need to not have British public opinion turned against them. AQNA had many operatives come from the British Isles.

Grace herself spared the Mildenhall Fire Chief and his family.

Hope suspected Grace still had a soft spot for innocent life.

***

Hope should have returned to the U.S. following her report, but Connor had other plans. On the drive back to London he surprised her.

"Hope, I have taken a few days off. I'd like to show you around London. We can take in a show. The south bank is lovely this time of year and…" He smiled mischievously, "I have arranged for spectacular weather for the next week."

Hope was caught off guard by his offer.

"Connor I do have a boyfriend back in the States."

"Oh I know. No evil intentions here. Sure it would just be platonic."

"I just want to show you a good time after all we have been through." He added.

She pondered his invitation. Great looking man offering to take time off just for me and show me London.

What the heck? My boyfriend is away all this week anyway, traipsing across Southwestern Virginia on some campaign. I promise to be a good girl.

She smiled, "Yes."

Connor's boyish grin after her acceptance was priceless.

She extended her hotel stay a few more nights.

Chapter 29

There was an ocean of umbrellas for Tambra's funeral. The colors offset the gray sky like a rainbow. She had many friends.

After her funeral, Sean received a bequest from Tambra's will. Her lawyer gave Sean a key to a safe deposit box at a bank on base. Sean found a single manila envelope inside, ten typed pages of testimony from Tambra, signed and notarized. Her deposition outlined the abuse she received from her husband over the past ten years. She also left him a flash drive.

Sean opened the drive with trepidation. On the device were pictures of Tambra as she documented her own abuse at the hands of Lt. Colonel David Jenkins. The images pained Sean. Tambra included a handwritten note.

Sean,
If you are reading this then I have passed away at the hands of David. I hate to burden you with this, but I don't want to let the bastard get away with it.
Love, Tambra

But David had not killed Tambra. She sacrificed her own life to save innocent people, the very children she worked with at the Bury St. Edmunds School.

Sean did not know what to do. He rationalized that the evidence was only pertinent in case David killed Tambra, so perhaps there was no need to dredge this up now.

He didn't really think it was something he could or should talk over with Emile. Instead he met Kate one Saturday in Cambridge.

They embraced as best they could with Kate's injury but even so Kate could tell his hug was lighter than normal as if Sean did not want to give off any false vibes. They were friends and Sean was making a statement. He did not need to with Kate but did so all the same. A new habit guessed Kate.

"How are you doing Kate?" He did not mention her torture but it was implied.

"My arm is better. My pride is still hurt and the other stuff well it is going to take some time to heal."

"You really went through quite an ordeal. Anything I can do to help? You know I will always be here for you.

"I appreciate that Sean. I am doing all right. I just need time."

Changing the subject quickly she asked, "How about you?"

He debated what she was really asking.

She clarified after a few seconds of silence.

"How do you feel about the two accidents?"

"Oh that. I am over the Libya accident. I have accepted the loss and moved on. It's going to be okay."

"And what about Tambra's loss?" she continued.

"I am in stage four of the grief process: depression. I know Tambra gave her life for a better cause by saving the one thing in life she truly loved: the children in the Bury school. She did what she had to do. I don't know if I could have done it but I like to hope so. I think she may be in a better place."

The conversation eventually moved to Tambra's information file.

They talked it over and in the end, Sean gave it to Kate on the condition she not report the source.

Kate covered up all indications of Sean's involvement with Tambra. Priority number one was not sullying Tambra's name with her infidelity. His reputation could deal with it; he had before. But he wanted her memorial after death to be clean of such blemishes. Kate promised the information Tambra left would make it to the right people. And it did.

***

The Accident Investigation Board for the crash of Strike 02 convened three months after the attack. They revealed their findings after months of interviews, forensics, investigations and detailed evidence analysis.

Sean, Emile and Mark were all present in their Air Force blues. The board found that although Sean and Emile's actions were a little unorthodox (they sited Sean's jet wash maneuver and Emile's delayed AGM-130 lock on), they were justifiable given the extraordinary circumstances of the day.

Sean was exonerated as flight lead and no one doubted his ability to lead men and women into combat. In fact, the board went out of its way to commend Sean for flight discipline. It also noted that Sean's first flight back, after his previous accident, with live weapons proved to be an invaluable badge of courage for his abilities to lead and fight.

An autopsy of the Suburban SUV victims, Missy and Allison Barker, revealed they were dead by the terrorist gunfire before the errant bomb hit them from Strike 01. Furthermore, the AIB revealed that a stuck fin on the GBU-54 made it unable to turn left to follow the commands from Strike 01. Emile was completely exonerated of any wrongdoing.

The board posthumously nominated Major Tambra "Tally" Jenkins the Air Force Medal of Honor for a personal act of valor above and beyond the call of duty. She stayed with her crippled aircraft and single-handedly maneuvered it to a crash zone away from the populated areas of Bury St. Edmunds.

Tambra's husband attended the proceedings. He was the only one who really tried to pin any blame on Sean. He accepted Tambra's medal on her behalf and promised to cherish her memory forever.

It was a touching and completely phony gesture. Emile ended up punching him in the face at the Officer's Club two weeks later, after sweet-talking him into the ladies room. He never reported her for the punch. Sean never could figure out if Lt. Col. David Jenkins was too afraid to admit little Emile had hit him or that he was in the ladies room when it happened.

Mark returned to flight status two weeks after the ejection. His actions that day were exemplary as well, except for his drinking at the pub after the landing. He received a Letter of Reprimand from the Wing Commander, which Bull unofficially ripped up in front of Mark at the squadron roll call immediately after the Accident Investigation Board team left the base.

Twenty days after the Accident Investigation Board, a copy of Tambra's information arrived at the CINC JAG USAFE and CINC JAG ACC offices and to a Stars and Stripes journalist whose reporting was beyond reproach. Tambra's husband was not officially convicted, but he eventually was charged and not promoted. David Jenkins received a dishonorable discharge as part of his plea-bargain deal.

***

All fighter squadrons usually meet after work on Friday to let off a little steam. The 492nd were no exception on the first Friday after the attack. Although somber due to their lost comrade, it was a special occasion in one respect: the Bolar commander, encouraged by Sean, decided to have an impromptu "naming ceremony."

Naming ceremonies meant awarding a call sign to a new aviator. This usually involves some good-natured ribbing and telling of stories about the aviator so that the rest of the squadron can decide what unique name he or she should hold for the assignment. Of course, taking a shot of Jeremiah Weed, the F-15 aviator's whiskey of choice, might erase a particularly bad name if one was so inclined and the aviators allowed it. Alcohol is involved and spouses and other family members are not invited to attend, only to pick the inebriated souls up after the naming.

When the Mayor, the aviator in charge of festivities, announced his plan to rename Emile "Bambi" Bergren, she ran to the stage as if shot out of cannon. She had already consumed three pints of Guiness and that was one too many for her most nights. Emile waved to the crowd, made a short speech and then was hustled away while her fellow pilots and WSOs voted on her new call sign. Sean manipulated the proceedings through his friendship with the Mayor and his negotiations earlier in the day. Democracy though is a strange beast and sometimes even the best-laid plans go awry. Even Sean did not know how the final voting would turn out.

But tonight Sean basked in Emile's glow as she sat weak-legged near the commander as he read out the choices. She sat in the place of honor, the old ejection seat known as the throne. Mark had promised the squadron his ejection seat so there would be two thrones soon.

"Emile shall no longer be known as 'Bambi.' We voted on such illustrious names as 'Pocahontas' and 'Burner' after her command to Rider to burn the civilian aircraft threat. But we have decided on…" he paused for effect as someone in the back cranked up Katy Perry.

"'Roar' will be your call sign from now on," he declared and the entire squadron let out a huge round of applause. Those members seated stood to make it a standing ovation. Emile started to sing her rendition of "Roar" and at some point even Sean made it on the dais to sing with her.

At the end of the night Sean drove Emile home and tucked her into bed, leaving her to sleep off the inevitable hangover.

***

The usual crowd, minus James who was missed and Ralph, who was not, gathered at Sean's place for poker on New Year's Eve. The plan was to play cards until 11 p.m., and then go watch the fireworks in the Abbey Gardens of Bury St. Edmunds. Emile sat on Sean's right; Kate sat on Sean's left across from Emile. Kate never revealed to the poker group that she had only joined to help with her investigation of Ralph. She had fun with the group, and jumped at the chance to become a regular. Mark flanked Emile and Sammy and Brent took their usual seats at the table end.

The deal eventually came around to Emile but instead of choosing a game Sean liked, seven card stud, she went for one of her favorites.

"Five card draw, jacks or better to open," she announced with authority. Sean seemed taken back by her newfound freedom but his smile indicated it was a pleasant surprise.

Emile fired out the five cards like a rotating water sprinkler on a summer's evening.

"Kate, can you start us off? You need to have at least a pair of jacks to bet."

"No."

No. No. No. No. Down the line they went.

"I'll open for twenty-five." Sean sat back after depositing his blue coin, a smug look on his face. Everyone stayed in.

Cards were discarded and then new ones dealt.

"Fifty," bragged Sean, hoping to scare everyone else away. Looking at his cards now, his two jacks had not improved with the draw of three other cards.

"I'll see your fifty," said Emile.

"What, no raise, Em?"

Sean teased Emile incessantly that she had no logic when it came to playing poker. Still, she won more than he did.

"Bump you twenty-five," Kate replied sincerely.

"How many did you take, Kate?" asked Mark, who rarely paid attention to such things until it was too late.

"Four and I had an ace in the hole. I was told this was a friendly game and I did not need to show it."

"Ok, ok. Four cards with an ace. Got it."

Brent and Sammy each folded; Mark dithered for a minute before folding too.

That left Emile, Sean and Kate.

Sean called with 75. Emile raised 50 now that Kate gave her the opening. Kate took the last raise for another 50.

Sean stayed in but regretted it. Sometimes you had to lose and show them you were bluffing so they wouldn't know when you were betting on a good hand. At least that's what Sean believed.

"Cards speak for themselves, ladies. Show me what you got."

Sean plunked down his miserable pair. Emile plopped down two pairs: kings over eights.

"Looks like I'm hot tonight!" exclaimed Kate as she laid down her three aces and scooped in all the chips. The odds of getting a pair of aces with a four-card draw were 3 to 1. Three aces was astronomical. Sean turned to Emile and smiled. "You know what they say..."

"Unlucky at cards, lucky in love," she finished for him with a smile that filled the room.

Sean walked Emile back to her apartment that night after the fireworks display.

***

Emile awoke as the birds outside began their daily serenade. She loved waking up to birds singing. It reminded her to thank God for allowing her one more day on earth. She gave thanks and then rolled over to check the bed beside her.

Her hopes were dashed as she saw the empty space. Sean had left. The covers were pulled back, obviously in his hasty try to beat a retreat from their intimate time last night. Lying on her back she sighed and berated herself for believing that maybe he had changed.

She should have seen the small changes in him after the air base attack as nothing more than a scam to get her into bed. Their friendship could withstand this momentary fling, she knew, but her psyche might not. She loved Sean and it was obvious to her now that he did not love her. He seemed to be up to his old tricks again.

Tears began to form. She felt the floodgates strain against the tide building up as she thought of Sean sneaking out this morning. His naked body would have slowly grabbed clothes and slunk out in the darkness. One by one adding a few critical pieces of his attire before tiptoeing out the door and down the stairs in full flight. Away from her and their relationship before it could even begin.

The tears streamed down her cheeks as she envisioned his escape, just like a thief in the night. That's when she heard the sizzle.

Was she imagining things?

Was that the Hernandez family up this early?

Glancing at her iPhone charging on her bedside table, she frowned; it was far too early for her neighbors to be stirring. They never got up before eight on a Saturday.

Cocking her head to the side just a little, she listened. There it was again: a sizzle, then a pop and now a steady building crescendo of a frying pan. Was that bacon she smelled? Yes! She definitely smelled bacon!

Her tears stopped with the realization that someone was cooking breakfast and that someone was close, very close. Could it be Sean? She still was not 100% sure. It might be some trick. A vendor setting up below her flat on the streets of Bury St. Edmunds, perhaps?

She propped herself up onto one elbow and peaked around the doorframe to see into the kitchen but the door blocked her view. She could see the balcony door was slightly ajar. Had she left that open last night? Maybe.

She glanced around the bedroom.

"Shit!" she muttered, flopping back down on to the bed. In the doorway was her white silk blouse. Just in front of the bed was her brown skirt. On the floor to her left were her blue panties and matching bra. None of Sean's clothes remained. A bad sign. The roller coaster of emotion she had been on the past few months, and equally as topsy-turvy the last few seconds, continued.

Just as she was about to bury her head in the pillow and let it all out with a good old-fashioned cry, Sean popped his head around the door's corner.

"Are you up yet, sleepy head?"

It was him! He stayed the entire night.

Composing herself she pushed the pillow away, turned away from the door to wipe a few stray tears and then faced him sitting up in bed.

"I smelled the bacon and didn't know where it came from."

He slid into view in the doorway with a tray full of breakfast, topped by a flower in a vase front in center. He was half-dressed in his jeans but with just his t-shirt on, no collared shirt, no belt, no shoes. He wasn't a runner this morning; she smiled as she thought to herself.

He read her mind as her eyes roamed his body. He also could sense her relief at seeing him here. It was a big step for him and one that surprised even him, but not as much as he would have thought a few weeks ago.

"It's dangerous to cook in the nude." He grinned as he set the tray on the bed. "Hope you don't mind me slipping on some clothes for the fry up?"

She smiled and shook her head no. She was so happy; words could not do her feelings justice. He slid in beside her and they enjoyed the first of many breakfasts in bed.

Epilogue

Wing Commander Brigadier General Brad "Bull" Cardwell had his disciplinary review board a month after the AIB findings were presented. The board found several deficiencies in the security forces team administration. Major Kate Healy was fired, but not because of her sexual orientation. That never came up during the proceeding and Kate even suspected Agent Rausch went out of her way to protect that information and her attacker.

One of Bull's last official acts was to reassign Major Healy to the Wing Intel office as an Intelligence officer. Her work with the OSI really helped in the investigation and almost prevented the catastrophe. She could no longer remain in the security forces arena, but Bull made sure her career was not damaged.

The board recognized that Brig. Gen. Cardwell's leadership skills were tested on the day of the attack but found his decisions were sound and represented the best solutions with the limited choices he had available.

The board announced they found no evidence of dereliction of duty over the course of events during the attack. But in a strange break with tradition, Bull Cardwell asked to speak after their proclamation.

"Distinguished board members, fellow officers, enlisted personnel and citizens. I wish to put on the record my observations from the attack on Lakenheath Air Base. I believe we faced a calamity that could have been prevented."

Bull paused. Everyone could see he was emotionally drained.

"Every loss of life is tragic, whether it is in Afghanistan, driving to work or defending this base and your loved ones." It was as if every one of those lost lives pulled some life force from him. "Three innocent civilians died. An additional twelve armed forces personnel perished trying to protect RAF Lakenheath from an invading force of fifteen terrorists using subterfuge, light aircraft, machine guns and various weapons of terror.

"People will question my decision to drop bombs on my own airbase for the rest of my life and probably for decades after I pass.

But I am here to tell you we were at war, and you have to take calculated chances to win.

"I put to you that this tragedy occurred due to a series of small, non-random events that formed a chain that led to the horrific attack. Much like an aircraft accident." He looked at Sean and gave him a fatherly smile before continuing. "If one link in that chain had been broken, this disaster may have been prevented. If one person had seen and recognized a terrorist and reported it to the authorities, the chain breaks there. If one more policeman had been on duty at each gate, the chain could have been broken. If the aircraft airborne had one more bomb, the chain may have been broken. If the investigators digging through their clues only had one more pointer towards the terrorist cell's plan, the chain would break. But I am also here to tell you the pendulum of momentum is a fickle thing. The coin can go either way in life or death situations. One more terrorist in the school could have meant the difference between life and death to many of our school children. If the RRT had not been readied when they were, fewer troops would have been available and the BX or commissary civilians may have been savagely attacked. And finally, if not for a brave group of young men and women flying high performance jets under immense physical and physiological pressure, some, if not all of us, may not be here today." Bull nodded thankfully to Sean, Emile and Mark.

Cardwell was done in USAFE. Lt. Col. David Jenkins, former Lakenheath JAG would see to that after Bull pushed for his dismissal. Cardwell did not really care at this point.

But Bull was a fighter and he had friends. He would leave USAFE without his second star promotion. A flag General he knew in PACAF promised him a position in South Korea. He was ready for a cushy job in Asia.

Sam Hendricks

Be sure to look for Sam's next book, *More Than One*...featuring Sean, Emile, Mark, Bull and Hope as a conflict arises on the Korean Peninsula and only the F-15E Strike Eagles can fix it.

Turn the page for the first chapter of *More Than One*...

More Than One

Chapter 1

Why am I here?
Why are these people trying to kill me?
Where the hell is Sean?
All three were good questions and needed answering.

Emile's heart raced. She could literally feel the blood pulsating through her veins as her adrenaline kicked in after the short run past ash and beech trees towards the fallen oak she crouched behind.

Her flight suit hung on her sweaty body like cling wrap. Wet mud completely soaked her right pants leg and a circle of puddle water expanded rapidly across her back. This irritated the hell out of her.

Emile swatted at a mosquito with her right gun hand, the weapon dulled by grease to prevent any sunlight reflecting off the piece.

Fat chance of that. Sunlight.

Emile tried to remember when she last saw sunlight. Yesterday? The day before? They all blurred into one long nightmare.

"Captain Bergren, we know you're out there," echoed a young male voice. Her pursuers knew who she was. Knew she had ejected and knew she was without much help.

Another, older voice joined his chorus.

"Emile, think about it. It is better to surrender to us than to be taken by the local villagers. You know what the village men will do to a female Yankee aviator who just bombed their homeland."

He let the image he had just created hang in the air.

Emile used the time to check her ammo supply and make sure her weapon was ready to go. Judging by the distance of the voices, they were a mile, maybe less, from her position. The hills and valleys made sound travel farther than it should. Then again, the forest absorbed any sound deep inside it.

Off in the distance she heard the barking of dogs. She did not loathe them, not in everyday life that is. But now, on the run, she hated the thought of dogs on her scent. She figured she might be able to lose the men hunting her trail. But not the dogs.

A Bobwhite birdcall punctured the silence. The distinctive loud ringing announced his presence. Emile remembered them from her time at the Blue Ridge Parkway. Her family always picnicked one Sunday in the summer at the Peaks of Otter in the Appalachian Mountains. She fondly reflected on those beautiful and sunny days. Fried chicken, homemade biscuits with ham, potato salad, chips and cookies and a cooler full of soft drinks. The children would splash in the creek down from the cookout site and picnic tables, while the adults played card games and chatted. It was the one Sunday a year that the entire Bergren family played hooky from church.

Her thoughts returned from the idyllic Eastern United States back to the situation at hand. She slowly turned right to see Sean split from his cover behind her and join her quietly at the fallen tree trunk. The Bobwhite was not native to this area but they both knew the call and how to make it. Sean called it, the "don't shoot me stupid, I'm coming to help you" call.

He looked worse than she did, if that was even possible.

His flight suit had a tear along his right arm. Flight suits were tough garments. The 92% Nomex protected aircrew from cockpit fires or fire outside the aircraft upon exit. It provided excellent thermal, chemical and radiation resistance. Unfortunately, none of those threats were after Emile and Sean. Instead they faced armed men who knew them and knew they were somewhere in the woods.

Emile kept searching the area in front of the log. Sean leaned his back against it and scanned their six o'clock.

"How does it look?" she spoke slowly and carefully, without moving her gaze to him. She did not want to see any fear from him nor give any away.

"Not good, Em," he paused, gulping down some much-needed water from the survival kit. "There are way too many of them out there. And the group behind us is slowly making progress too. We have about fifteen minutes, max."

They were officially dating now. Nine months since the attack on Lakenheath and three months since New Year's Eve.

The past three months have been heaven.

She slid her left hand over to touch his left thigh. It was not much in terms of displays of affection but, for that moment in time, it said a mouthful. And yet, something was wrong between them. The first 10 weeks were bliss, but the last two weeks Sean had been different. He had gone back to Charlottesville for a week-long vacation a few weeks ago. Emile did not have the vacation saved up to be able to join him, so he went solo.

She noticed the change in him as soon as he got back.

Bury St. Edmunds-Adonis Health Spa (2 weeks prior)

Sean and Emile walked into the spa arm-in-arm, smiling despite the Monday morning cold rain shower. Pellets of rain tinkled the large blue tinted front windows where a small sign pronounced the establishment closed.

Sean had managed to reserve the place for their private use all day.

The owner always closed on Mondays since business was very light. Sean convinced the owner to allow him and a few friends to use the spa this Monday and arranged privately with two of the staff to provide massages for a couple of hours. The two twenty-something girls were generously compensated for their time and made the cash "off-the-record."

One staff member greeted the first arrivals while the other made sure the temperatures and water for the pool, hot tub, sauna and steam room were good to go. Sean and Emile also brought some lunch in for the group.

Mark and a striking young blond entered a minute later with food, a blender and bottles of rum.

She was much shorter than Mark, but then again, who wasn't next to his lanky 6 foot 2 inch frame. Emile eyed her in a friendly enough way, but her antenna was up. Every instinct she had said "danger" and it was not just because of the girl's natural good looks either. Mark described her as having a down-home country style but Emile did not see her that way. She wore large-framed wine-colored glasses that covered most of her face and hid her eyes.

Why wear those glasses on a rainy day to a spa?

They screamed, "Hear me, see me, look at me!" She looked familiar to Emile. She was enlisted. Mark was fraternizing again.

Mark introduced everyone to his date, Erin Wright.

She wore an aqua thigh-high skirt that hugged her hips quite convincingly. Her white top allowed her ample cleavage to be on display from almost any angle as well.

Erin was a sergeant assigned to the Intel Shop at the 493rd Fighter Squadron at Lakenheath. The 493rd were an F-15C squadron. They flew air-to-air and specialized in preventing enemy aircraft from shooting down or bombing the good guys.

The guys went left to the men's changing room and Emile and Erin went right to their locker room. Erin was no shy wallflower. She quickly slipped out of her clothes and matching purple panty and bra and replaced them with a light blue two-piece bikini that left nothing to the imagination. She let her hair down and the dirty blond tangle came tumbling to her mid-back, just above her behind that was a little larger than perfect but certainly nothing to complain about. Erin's flaw, if you could call it that, was her teeth. They were big and she had a bit of an overbite, but that really almost made her more endearing.

Some women have all of the luck.

Emile modestly slipped out of her jeans, t-shirt and undies and into a one-piece white bathing suit that made her feel bigger than a whale, compared to the skinny Erin.

Erin, to her credit, waited patiently for Emile to finish changing. But the small talk between them was forced, at best. Emile was the queen and Erin was encroaching on her territory. Both knew the score.

Each man seemed to be equally pleased when the ladies entered the pool area. But as the day wore on, Emile had the feeling that Sean was doing just enough, but not much more, to be with her. In fact, Emile thought that if she was not present, perhaps the naughty Erin might just be up for doing both of the guys in a ménage-à-trois, right in the hot tub.

Lunch was a treat. Sean made his world-famous pulled pork barbeque and cole slaw. He brought it in a crockpot and let it simmer for a few hours while they swam and relaxed in the hot tub. Erin provided chocolate chip cookies and brownies for dessert.

She is sickeningly sweet.

Mark kicked in some cold soft drinks and daiquiris, while Emile contributed a delicious Caesar salad. It was a picnic in a spa while the rain continued to beat down the other people of the world working their 9-5 jobs. It was the last good meal Sean and Emile shared before their ordeal.

***

No use thinking about food when you were surviving on energy bars and water. Emile shook the spa memory away and concentrated on the present.

Sean smiled, pushing the water pouch into one of the seven zippered pockets that came on standard issue Air Force flight suits. His left hand slowly touched hers and their pinky fingers entwined gently. Both relaxed just a bit.

But the men who hunted them did not relax. Not even for a moment. They continued to come at them relentlessly. The Bobwhite call, although innocuous in the Eastern United States, was a dead giveaway here. The men stalking Emile knew that bird was not a native of the woods they hunted. Although the strength of the call was weak at their distance, it provided a beacon to their location. They led the dogs in this new direction.

"Well, if I have fifteen minutes I guess I have time for a wee," Sean whispered.

Emile shook her head. Her anatomy and the logistics of a single zippered cloth around her entire torso made bathroom visits in the middle of the woods problematic. She was not ashamed of the fact that she had wet herself intentionally several hours ago in lieu of risking being shot. That was another reason why she limited her water intake as well. All is fair in love and war.

Sean winked at her. "All clear?" he asked.

"All clear my way," came her reply.

Sean began to lift himself from the cover of the downed tree trunk but thought better of it and dropped back to his spot to tell Emile something that had bothered him the past week. It was something that weighed heavily on him and he needed to clear the air. It might be the end of their relationship.

It was a good thing he did not continue to rise, however, as projectiles impacted the tree limbs directly behind them. Emile pivoted and spotted the shooter under a hedge to the left.

She quickly fired off three rounds to discourage the enemy from advancing, but she knew that more were coming.

"We need to get out of here, Sean!"

"I agree. Suddenly I feel like a sitting duck." His hands were shaking slightly after narrowly escaping the burst above them.

"Problem is the group behind us heard that volley of fire and will now be heading our way on the double," he continued.

Fear gripped her.

"You're saying we're trapped?"

"No, I'm saying we're screwed." A devious smile flitted across his lips. "Look Em, I'll cover for you. Go left to the river and, if you need to, jump into it. It's our only way out."

"But Sean…" She started to protest but he silenced her with a glance from where the last shots came.

He knew she was afraid of heights. In an F-15E at 35,000 feet, it was actually not a problem. For some reason, stuffed in a multi-million dollar fighter aircraft gave her the strength to carry on without any problems. It was when she was outside and at the top of something that she melted in fear. They both avoided the overlook of the river as an escape because of her fear. But now they had run out of options.

He mouthed the word "Go!" and turned to pin the shooter under the hedge with his return fire.

Emile crawled behind him and then crouched behind a tree waiting for her chance to escape.

Sean nodded at her and returned to the task at hand.

She leapt from her cover and zigzagged her way behind trees away from their location. As soon as she was sufficiently far enough away, she stood up and dashed towards the river.

She heard the rushing water. She was close.

"Stop!" demanded an enemy force behind her.

She did not stop.

Just a little further. She could see the sunlight as the trees began to open up on the little hillside overlook.

Thump.

Thump.

She felt two sickening thuds as the enemy's bullets found their mark on her back. The flight suit provided no protection from them.

To read more of the exciting sequel to *Just One More...* purchase *More Than One...*at Amazon, BN.com and other online retailers. Also available in eBook format at Amazon, BN, Kobo and Apple.

Sam Hendricks

Additional Books by Sam Hendricks

Fantasy Football Guidebook: Your Comprehensive Guide to Playing Fantasy Football

-Named one of Top 4 Fantasy Football books of All-Time by RotoNation.com
-Award-winning finalist in the Sports category of the National Best Books 2008 Awards, sponsored by USA Book News
-Finalist in the Sports category of the 2009 National Indie Excellence Awards

Fantasy Football Tips: 230 Ways to Win through Player Rankings, Cheat Sheets and Better Drafting (2nd Edition)

Fantasy Football Tips has become an even bigger hit than *Fantasy Football Guidebook*, beating the one-year sales mark in only nine months of availability!

Fantasy Football Basics: The Ultimate "How-to" Guide for Beginners

Fantasy Baseball for Beginners

Financial Planning-The Fighter Pilot Way (Aug 2014)

Media Coverage

Look for Sam's expert advice and rankings in Fantasy Baseball Index, Fantasy Football Index, Fantasy Football Pro Forecast and other fantasy sports magazines.

Sam also participates in a weekly "Ask the Expert" column at www.FantasyIndex.com

Also check out www.FantasyFootballGuidebook.blogspot.com or www.XPPress.com where Sam blogs throughout the year.

About the Author

Sam "Slam" Hendricks grew up in Lynchburg, Virginia and graduated from the University of Virginia. He joined the USAF and flew RF4C fighter jets in Germany during the Cold War. He transitioned into the F-15E Strike Eagle and earned three aerial achievement medals during combat missions in Operation Desert Storm.

Sam left the Air Force in 1993 to work for McDonnell Douglas as an F-15E instructor, a job he has performed for more than 20 years. He and his Danish wife, Birgitte, have spent the last ten years in East Anglia, England.

Sam participates in fantasy sports contests such as the National Fantasy Football Championship (NFFC), National Fantasy Baseball Championship (NFBC) and the Fantasy Football Players Championship (FFPC) where he has finished 7th and 16th overall. He has won numerous league championships in his 20-year fantasy sports career. He is a member of the Fantasy Sports Writers Association (FSWA).

Sam has an MBA in Business and a Masters in Personal Finance. His next book (release date October 2014) will be on personal finance and the day-to-day things we can all do to improve our finances.

CPSIA information can be obtained at www.ICGtesting.com
Printed in the USA
LVOW13s0835040814

397212LV00009B/381/P